Bait and Switch

/A sci-fi Sherlock Holmes/

By Ashley Marie Bergner

Copyright 2012 Ashley Marie Bergner. All rights reserved.

Table of Contents

Case No. 1: Now You See Me...
    Chapter 1: First Impressions

    Chapter 2: Without a Trace

    Chapter 3: The Plot Thickens

    Chapter 4: Only the Beginning

Case No. 2: Suspended Disbelief
    Chapter 1: The Play's the Thing

    Chapter 2: The Interrogation

    Chapter 3: The Drunk Gypsy

    Chapter 4: Caught in the Act

    Chapter 5: All the World's a Stage

Case No. 3: Hide and Seek
    Chapter 1: Double the Trouble

    Chapter 2: The Impossible Theft

    Chapter 3: Trust Me

    Chapter 4: Breaking and Entering

    Chapter 5: Not to Be Trifled With

Case No. 4: Kiss and Tell
    Chapter 1: A Date with Disaster

    Chapter 2: Confessions

    Chapter 3: An Unexpected Visitor

    Chapter 4: Undercover

    Chapter 5: A Dangerous Game

Chapter 6: Collateral Damage

Case No. 5: The Game is Afoot

   Chapter 1: Players and Pawns

   Chapter 2: Hot Clue in a Cold Case

   Chapter 3: Ghost Stories

   Chapter 4: Conflict of Interest

   Chapter 5: The Trap

   Chapter 6: A Bad Feeling

   Chapter 7: Riding to the Rescue

Case No. 6: Double Blind

   Chapter 1: The Conundrum

   Chapter 2: The Cover-Up

   Chapter 3: Loose Ends

   Chapter 4: The Moment of Truth

   Chapter 5: The Gala

   Chapter 6: Calling the Bluff

   Chapter 7: Frankenstein's Monster

   Chapter 8: A New Start

Case No. 1: Now You See Me...

Chapter 1: First Impressions

Jaymie Watson glanced up at the towering, slightly rundown high-rise apartment complex and then back down at her techpad, checking one last time to make sure she was in the right place. She was secretly hoping she'd made a mistake, and that somehow, this wasn't where she was supposed to be. But this wasn't her lucky day.

Quadrant B, building 221. That's where she needed to go, and unfortunately, that's exactly where the navigation app on her techpad told her that she was.

Well, can't blame a girl for hoping, she thought with a sigh. She heard a loud beeping behind her and jumped on the sidewalk just in time to avoid being mowed down by a rusty old hovercraft, its driver scowling as he zipped past her. He shouted something at her in an alien language she didn't understand, and he pointed his finger in the middle of his scaly forehead. She wasn't sure what the gesture meant, but she was pretty sure it wasn't complimentary.

"Welcome to Loudron, I guess," she muttered, then pressed the buzzer on the front door of the apartment complex. Before she had decided to come look at this flat, she should have guessed what the neighborhood would be like—after all, 180 quid a month wasn't bound to get you too much. Still, she had been hoping for a quaint, somewhat quirky older neighborhood like the one she had been living in back when she was working on her undergraduate degree at the university on Scoztan, her home world. But Quadrant B in the city of Loudron had no charm at all. It was grimy, grungy, and decrepit, nothing like the cosmopolitan Quadrant A, where the University of Medical Arts was located.

Still, she knew she shouldn't complain. She was fortunate enough to have been accepted to the university on an academic scholarship that would pay for her seven-year doctorate degree, and if she had to live in a rundown apartment complex in order to attend the school, then so be it. This was the best she could afford, until she met some of her classmates and maybe found a roommate to split the cost of a nicer flat.

The door slid open with a whoosh, and Jaymie took a deep breath and quickly tucked a stray lock of her long red hair behind her ear. A short, purple-skinned humanoid woman appeared at the door, smiling but looking a little frazzled.

"Hello, you must be Jaymie Watson," she said, reaching out her hand in greeting. "I'm Oly Hudson, the proprietor of apartment complex 221. Would you like to come up and see the room you inquired about?"

"Of course," Jaymie replied, trying to smile confidently.

She followed Mrs. Hudson over to the turbolift, casting a glance at the lobby as they went. The room was clean but unadorned, a faded, worn sofa and a slightly scratched table the only pieces of furniture. The paint on the walls was a drab shade of white, and the floors were some kind of cheap, synthetic tile. Jaymie could already picture the look that would be on her mother's face if she ever came to visit. Although that was a *very* big "if."

Mrs. Hudson pressed the "up" button on the turbolift, but nothing seemed to happen. Muttering under her breath, Mrs. Hudson kicked the turbolift doors, and then the lift's repulsors finally began to hum.

"Sometimes it doesn't always respond," Mrs. Hudson explained. "Something wrong with the electrical system, maybe. Just give it a good, swift kick, and it always fires right up, though."

"That's...great," Jaymie said, finding it harder and harder to force a smile. Just what, exactly, had she gotten herself into?

The turbolift car sank slightly as they got in, also not a good sign, and the machine clanked and creaked all the way up the shaft. Jaymie was extremely grateful when they reached the fifty-sixth floor, and Mrs. Hudson stopped the lift.

"You'll be staying in a flat with several other lodgers—that is, if you decide to take the room, of course," Mrs. Hudson said as they walked down the carpeted hallway. "You'll each have your own bedroom and bath, but you'll have to share a commons area and a kitchen/dining room." She stopped in front of a door at the end of the hallway, and swiped an entry card. "Right now there's two other lodgers at this flat. Isin Lestrade works as an inspector at the Civic Security Station—he's a very nice young man, always very polite and pays his rent on time."

"What about the other lodger?" Jaymie asked, and Mrs. Hudson's expression grew a bit nervous.

"Well, dear, he's a little...well...eccentric. He's quite bright really, but some say, well, I've heard, he can be...a bit hard to get on with, on occasion." The door slid open, and Mrs. Hudson ushered her in, adding a little too quickly, "But I'm sure you'll be fine."

"Wait, maybe I should—" But it was too late. The door opened, and a cloud of smoke came billowing out, followed by the sound of someone shouting, "I've done it, Mrs. Hudson, I've done it!"

"Done what?" Mrs. Hudson cried, running into the living room. Against her better judgment, Jaymie followed the landlady, and to her shock found the sofa on fire and a tall, strangely jubilant man standing next to it. He was probably in his late 20s, only a few years older than Jaymie herself was. His dark brown hair was a medium length, sticking out in all directions like he hadn't bothered to brush it after waking up. It was almost kind of cute, but Jaymie wasn't about to communicate that to him. "Eccentric" had been an understatement—he was wearing a trench coat, though why indoors she didn't know, and two different colors of boots. His eyes were also different colors: one was brown, and the other was pale blue.

"Mrs. Hudson, the experiment worked!" he exclaimed, his eyes lighting up just like a child who'd discovered a large jar of candy.

"The experiment? But you've set the sofa on fire—again!" Mrs. Hudson wailed.

The man waved her off. "Inconsequential. What's important is not that the sofa's on fire—it's what *set* the sofa on fire." He held up two glass vials. "Lestrade is convinced the big fire last night in the industrial district was caused by 'jergel,' a relatively harmless but possibly flammable chemical often found at the techpad factories in Quadrant D. But *I* told him that was impossible; a fire of that magnitude and intensity could not have been caused by such a conventional chemical. I found traces of the banned chemical 'zever' at the scene, and procured some of my own to perform an experiment here. The zever looks and smells just like jergel, but burns much hotter and faster, and leaves a slightly greenish-tinted residue. See?" He pointed to the couch, which was still licked by tongues of fire, and sure enough, the burnt fabric had a slightly greenish hue. "The buildings that were burned all had this residue; hence, we can assume the fire was caused by zever." He grinned. "Isn't it magnificent?"

Jaymie knew she should probably be turning around and running out of the room as fast as she could, but even though she was a little of afraid of this man and his crazed sense of genius, she was admittedly impressed by his logic. Not for the first time, and certainly not for the last, curiosity overcame her misgivings. She decided to stay and see how this played out.

"Well, that's bloody wonderful!" Mrs. Hudson cried, quite angry now. "Your experiment worked—now put the fire out before I evict you for destroying my property!"

The man's eyes flashed slightly as well, the first sign of him showing a temper. "I was attempting to put the fire out before you arrived, but I was having a bit of trouble. Which, you should know, also helps to prove my point and show why emergency crews had so much difficulty putting out the fire in Quadrant D. Flames caused by jergel are much easier to extinguish. I think we have a clear case of arson here—and not an accident, like Lestrade wants to believe."

"But who would do something like that?" Jaymie piped up, and the man finally seemed to notice her.

He blinked. "Who knows? A disgruntled employee, a jilted spouse or lover seeking revenge—I'm sure Lestrade will figure it out with a little interrogating. That's not my job, that's his." He sprayed fire suppressant foam on the coach, and the flames at last began to die down. The fire hadn't touched the rest of the room, but one half of the couch was ruined.

Wonderful—now Mrs. Hudson will raise the rent, Jaymie thought.

Mrs. Hudson took in a long, shuddering breath in an attempt to calm herself. "Well, now that you've frightened poor Miss Watson to death, I'm sure she'll be ready to sign the papers for the flat," she said with a not-so-subtle note of sarcasm. "She's certainly seen us at our best."

The man looked Jaymie up and down, examining her somewhat critically. "This is a potential lodger? Mrs. Hudson, why didn't you tell me? I wouldn't have started an experiment if I had known she was coming."

"Yes, you would," Mrs. Hudson grumbled. "You have no concern for my wishes whatsoever."

The man ignored her, turning to Jaymie instead. "And whom do I have the pleasure of meeting?"

"It's Jaymie—Jaymie Watson," she said. "And you are…"

"Sherlock Holmes," he said matter-of-factly. "You look a little familiar, but I'm sure it's just coincidence. You're not from around here, not even from the planet of Eglon, I'd guess. Probably more like Itred, or maybe Scoztan. This is your first time here, and you seem a bit naïve. Congratulations on your acceptance to the medical university, however; quite hard to get in, I hear. I'm guessing you're more into the research side than patient care, though, which makes perfect sense to me. It's best to avoid interacting with people when at all possible."

For a moment, Jaymie was speechless, a confused look on her face. "But Mrs. Hudson—I thought you didn't tell him I was coming. How did he…"

"Elementary," Holmes said, sitting down on the side of the couch that wasn't burnt and leaning back casually. "I just guessed, though it's obvious, really. You have the slightly stunned, baffled look of someone who's gotten in over her head. You have a navigation app open on your techpad, which means you've never been to this area before and needed help to get here. Besides, the very fact you're carrying a techpad makes it obvious you're not a local—anyone from Loudron, or the rest of the planet of Eglon, knows it's pure idiocy to carry around an expensive piece of technology so openly in a neighborhood like this, where it's far too easy to get mugged. You were making yourself the perfect target. However, you don't have an accent that different from the one we have on Eglon, so you must be from the same galactic sector. You do have the unfortunate habit of mispronouncing your 'r's' ever so slightly, which makes it likely you're from Itred or Scoztan.

"As for your educational status, that's quite obvious too. You're wearing a shirt that says 'University of Medical Arts' on it. It's freshly pressed, probably never washed, so you likely just got it. It's the sort they give to all new students, which really just makes you an easier target for upperclassmen, who will try to trick you or play pranks on you, so you might not want to wear it very often. You spend a lot of time in the lab, which is why your fingers are stained by chemicals. Be warned, if Lestrade finds out you know anything at all about science, he may start grilling you for cases. That is unfortunately what happened to me, and I've gone from being a private investigator trying to earn an honest living to a consultant for the Civic Security Station. Hence—" he paused and gestured to the burnt couch "—the need to occasionally set the furniture on fire. I don't make a habit of it, however, and I will warn you before beginning any experiment."

Jaymie couldn't help herself—she stared at Holmes in shock, her mouth gaping open in a very unprofessional manner. Who *was* this man?

Holmes noticed her staring at him, and he raised an eyebrow. "Is something wrong, Miss Watson?"

"Wrong? Of course not!" Jaymie stuttered, throwing up her hands. "There's nothing at all disturbing about the fact that we've only just met, and yet you've managed to tell me everything about myself."

Holmes shrugged. "It's really not that remarkable. I just took little details about your appearance and mannerisms, pieced them together, and made an educated guess about who you are. I could be wrong, but I doubt it." He narrowed his eyes, studying her more closely. "It's much harder to guess at the deeper details, the ones we try so desperately to hide from the rest of the galaxy. Like why you decided to leave your home world, either Itred or—"

"It's Scoztan," she interjected.

Holmes nodded. "Of course. Like why you decided to leave Scoztan when there's a perfectly good medical school there. Or why you're going to a very elite, very expensive university but inquiring about renting a flat in a dump like—"

Mrs. Hudson shot him a murderous glare, and he quickly cleared his throat and corrected himself. "—A far more economical apartment complex in Quadrant B. You're wearing chilz leather boots, so you're certainly not poor. This leaves me to wonder, maybe you were desperate to get away from Scoztan and perhaps...your wealthy but estranged and too-controlling family? They send you gifts, like the boots, but they either won't send you money, or you won't accept it. You probably got a scholarship, so that takes care of your educational expenses, but you've come to look at a flat with the cheapest rent possible. My only question is whether you've been forced to make your own way in the galaxy, or whether you chose this for yourself."

There was a long, awkward moment of silence, and Mrs. Hudson let out a soft, weary sigh. "And...he's scared away another one."

Jaymie's face flushed a bright shade of red, and she felt a mixture of shame and anger. Usually she was pretty good at controlling her temper, even if she was badgered, but this Holmes character had taken it too far. His speech had brought back far too many painful memories she preferred to keep buried in the past, and she didn't like talking about her family, who had spoiled her growing up but failed to give her the two things she really wanted: love and acceptance.

"Listen, Mr. Holmes—you may find it amusing to shock a person by telling her what her profession is, or what planet she's from," she said icily. "But you have no right to pry into a being's private affairs. I don't care how clever you are—my business is my own."

"But I didn't pry, I guessed," Holmes said. "You don't have to tell me if I'm correct, although your reaction makes me wonder—"

"Well, don't wonder," Jaymie shot back. She was partly angry that he wouldn't apologize, but mostly just because she couldn't prove him wrong. He knew he had hit very close to the truth, and the way she had lost her temper had only confirmed his suspicions. Still, she wasn't going to give him the satisfaction of saying that in so many words.

Especially since that's exactly what he wants. She could clearly see the fire in his eyes, that hint of a cocky smile; he got a rush out of this, and he wanted her to confirm she thought he was a genius (he obviously felt that way about himself). Well, she might not be able to match his IQ, but she certainly surpassed him in social graces. Let him be as brilliant and witty as he liked—she just wouldn't be his foil.

She picked up her suitcase and turned towards Mrs. Hudson. "Thank you, Mrs. Hudson. It was very kind of you to show me around today, and to respond to my inquiry so quickly. I think I've seen enough, and I will—"

Jaymie didn't get a chance to finish, and whether that was fortunate or unfortunate, she never really found out. Just as she was about to announce her decision, she was cut off by an altogether extraordinary occurrence.

One minute Mrs. Hudson was standing before her, looking like she was dreading Jaymie's answer, and then the next...she wasn't there at all.

Mrs. Hudson had, quite simply, vanished.

Chapter 2: Without a Trace

For a moment, Holmes was speechless, which Jaymie guessed was a rather infrequent occurrence. He blinked, staring at the spot where Mrs. Hudson had been just seconds before.

"Well, this certainly changes my plans for the day," he remarked.

Jaymie clenched and unclenched her fists, making an effort to take slow, deep breaths and not give in to the hyperventilating panic that threatened to overtake her. Mrs. Hudson had disappeared out of thin air—it was the sort of thing that *just didn't happen*. She wanted to scream, but she couldn't bring herself to do it, not with Holmes here. Though he had to be just as shocked as she was, he was so bloody calm, and Jaymie had a feeling he would only scold her for panicking. She wanted to prove she could be as level-headed as he was.

Holmes walked slowly around the room, and at first Jaymie thought he was merely thinking. However, she noticed his eyes quickly darting about the room like a praxit cat's, taking in every detail. He was looking for any clues that might explain Mrs. Hudson's disappearance, though Jaymie could see nothing out of the ordinary herself. She knew she probably shouldn't press him, but as he kept walking around and around, she grew more and more curious, until finally she couldn't take it any longer and burst out, "So who do you think did this?"

"I haven't the slightest idea," he said frankly. "But at the early stages of an investigation, I think starting with that question is a mistake. It's far better to figure out *how* something happened, and then work from there. If you try to speculate who or why too quickly, it can make you jump to all sorts of wild conclusions, and lead you so far in the wrong direction it may take you hours or days to get back to where you started."

"All right then," Jaymie said, trying to shrug off his rebuke even though she found herself, once again, offended. *How did Holmes manage to push her buttons so easily, and why did she seem to care so much about what he thought of her?* Normally she had thicker skin than this. "Tell me then: *How* do you think this happened?"

"I have my guesses. But I really believe you can answer that question yourself, if you just give it some thought."

"Well, I don't know what to think," Jaymie said, kneeling next to the spot where Mrs. Hudson had been standing. "It's like she disappeared out of thin air, which is impossible." She saw Holmes starting to object, and she quickly added, "And yet it *can't* be impossible, because we just saw it happen. That means hiding somewhere, there must be a logical explanation."

"Good," Holmes said, crouching down beside her. "Keep going."

"It must..." She pushed herself, letting her mind wander back through all she had read and experienced at the university on Scoztan. *Out of thin air...* Something about that phrase seemed to tug at her subconscious, and then suddenly, it came back to her. It was the title of an article she had read once in a scientific journal about a very unusual invention...

"A particle transporter!" Jaymie exclaimed. "One was tested recently at the University of Scoztan, and it successfully dematerialized a scientist at one location and reconstructed him at another location 50 kilometers away. However, this type of transporter isn't always reliable, and I've only ever heard of teleporters that can beam you from one 'pad' to another. I didn't know anyone could use the technology to just beam a person out of a random setting."

"Well, there's a first time for everything, and we might have just witnessed it," Holmes said. "I believe, Miss Watson, we have the beginnings of a theory."

He abruptly jumped to his feet, grabbed a scarf that was hanging on the metal coat rack in the living room, and then punched the release button on the door. "We'd better head down to the Civic Security Station. Lestrade will want to hear about this, and for the sake of Mrs. Hudson's safety, wherever she is, we'd better get started as soon as possible."

"But I don't know if—"

Holmes gave her a puzzled frown. "You're not coming?"

"I...I don't know," Jaymie stammered. "I mean, I barely know you. I don't know what help I'd be, or..."

"Nonsense—you've been a great help already," Holmes said, but Jaymie merely shrugged.

"Well, I did come up with the particle transporter bit, but you probably knew that already. You're the investigator, or 'consultant,' or whatever. Do you really need me?"

Holmes appeared thoughtful. "Yes, I did guess about the particle transporter. But you came up with it more quickly than I thought you would. Not bad for a common citizen. Now come on, we don't have any time to waste."

This is crazy—this is absolutely crazy. Jaymie didn't know if she could trust this Holmes, or even if she particularly liked him, and she had no idea why he wanted her to come along. But he seemed to be taking it for granted that she was coming, and she couldn't really come up with a good excuse *not* to go. Although something told her she'd regret it, she found herself snatching up her knapsack and following Holmes out the door as he jogged down the hallway and over to the turbolift.

#

It was a short walk to Quadrant B's Civic Security Station, although it wasn't really a scenic one. Jaymie found, somewhat to her dismay, that apartment complex 221 was actually one of the nicer buildings in the neighborhood. Many of the metal buildings were rusted, and trash was piled up against the rundown structures and blowing through the streets. Some of the windows in the buildings had been busted out, and most of the glass still lay on the ground, no one having bothered to clean it up. Although there weren't many people in the streets, those who were seemed to keep to themselves, avoiding eye contact with anyone else. It was a much grittier world than the one Jaymie was used to, and she found herself unconsciously sticking closer to Holmes, afraid of what might happen if she lagged too far behind.

Twilight was falling as they reached the Civic Security Station, casting a rather gloomy pallor about the already dreary landscape. The Civic Security office was housed in a worn, rather nondescript building on a street corner, and it was only two stories high, making it appear rather squat compared to the buildings around it. One of its walls seemed to have been recently stripped of paint.

"Graffiti removal," Holmes said, offering an explanation. "It's quite cheeky of vandals to tag the police station. It irritates Lestrade to no end." There was a smile on his face as he added the last bit, and Jaymie wondered if Holmes had ever operated outside the law himself.

They walked through the station's automatic doors and into a lobby illuminated by dull, yellowish lighting. Several inspectors (or at least she assumed they were inspectors, judging by their official-looking uniforms) bustled about, either transporting carts full of what appeared to be evidence, or questioning citizens who had come in to report a crime.

Jaymie was just about to ask Holmes where they would find this "Lestrade" when she heard someone exclaim, "Well, if it isn't Sherlock Holmes!"

She turned around and saw a uniformed young man come walking towards them, a smile spreading across his face. He had closely cropped black hair and was wearing a pair of sun-shielding glasses, which he immediately removed.

"Lestrade," Holmes said, greeting him with a nod. "You know it's absolutely ridiculous to wear those glasses after dark."

Lestrade clapped Holmes on the back, still grinning. "Fashion advice from a man who wears a trench coat everywhere, regardless of the occasion or the weather?" He shrugged. "I like the way the shades make me look, all right? More suave and intimidating, or at least I like to think so. Let me have my vanity—it's a tough quadrant to work in." He glanced over at Jaymie, and his grin widened.

"Wow, Holmes, who's this lovely young lady? This is something new for you—picking up girls instead of picking up criminals."

Holmes wasn't amused. "This is Jaymie Watson, Mrs. Hudson's potential new lodger from Scoztan."

"Yes—I arrived just as he was setting the couch on fire," Jaymie cut in, and Lestrade laughed.

"No one makes first impressions quite like Mr. Sherlock Holmes. I bet Mrs. Hudson was mad as the devil."

Holmes shook his head. "I don't know how Mrs. Hudson is feeling at the moment. She has disappeared."

The grin was instantly wiped from Lestrade's face. "What?"

"She simply vanished—gone without a trace."

Lestrade's brow furrowed, and he studied Holmes, as if trying to discern whether his friend was joking. "Are you sure she didn't slip out while you were distracted, Holmes? She has been known to do that on occasion. Maybe she just got fed up with your company and left."

"No, I was there too," Jaymie said, "and I didn't see her slip out. Holmes and I think she might have been captured by a particle transporter."

"That's crazy! To do that, you need two beaming pads, one at your starting point and one at your destination. And I'm almost positive Mrs. Hudson doesn't have a beaming pad stashed in our flat somewhere."

"But what if someone's figured out a way to transport people without using pads?" Holmes insisted. "Scientists are already researching that. *Your* department would like to have that technology to beam law enforcement officers into and out of dangerous crime scenes."

Lestrade bit his lip, tapping his fingers thoughtfully on the holster for his blaster. "Of course that's true. But I think that tech's years away, and besides, why would someone want to beam up Mrs. Hudson? She may be a landlady in a bad part of town, but she doesn't have any real enemies, and even some of the tenants she's had to kick out who *might* have a grudge against her wouldn't have access to that kind of technology. She's an extremely unlikely target."

"And yet, it can't be impossible, because she was indeed targeted, and she has disappeared," Holmes said. He glanced over at Jaymie, just the slightest hint of a smile on his face. *He had used her phrase*—and somehow, that filled her chest with a strange sort of warmth. She had said something clever enough for him to remember it and use it again.

However, the grim look on Lestrade's face quickly turned the mood solemn once again. "I'll look into it, Holmes, and you know I care about Mrs. Hudson's safety as much as you do. But I can't make any promises. Our department's stretched thin as it is." He looked over at Jaymie, the sparkle that had been in his eyes when they first walked in replaced by a deep and what likely had long been a lingering sadness. "I don't know how much Holmes has told you, or how much you've guessed already, but Quadrant B is pretty much the dump of Loudron. Nobody cares about what goes on here. All the planet's scum seem to congregate here, and as long as Civic Security maintains some semblance of control, the government's happy. Missing person cases aren't all that unusual here, and we don't even investigate cases of vandalism or petty theft anymore. Your hovercar gets stolen? We don't even take down a report, just tell you, hey, tough luck, might as well go drown your sorrows in a pint of ale and start saving for a new hovercar. The government doesn't care how strained our department is; they think we have no problem providing back-up on incidents like that Quadrant D fire fiasco. What an accident that was!"

"But it wasn't an accident!" Holmes insisted. "I sent you a techpad message with evidence—"

"I did get your message," Lestrade interrupted. "And I appreciate your help on the investigation, but there's already been a confession, and the case is closed."

Holmes looked at Lestrade in shock, obviously not expecting that bit of news. "What? Someone came forward?"

"Here's what happened, and I'll start at the beginning, just to get Jaymie up to speed," Lestrade said. "There's these two techpad factories right next to each other in Quadrant D that are owned by rival companies called Future Corp. and Sunset Enterprises. The two buildings caught fire last night and were pretty much completely destroyed. Both had large quantities of stored jergel, which early on was targeted as the fuel that helped the fire to spread so rapidly. We were beginning to investigate how the fire might have started when Sunset Enterprises announced the employee at fault had come forward and confessed. Said he came to work drunk, wasn't being careful about his job, and started the fire accidentally. Future Corp. accepted this explanation and decided they wouldn't be pressing charges in court for the destruction of their factory, and solicitors from both companies are working out some sort of settlement now. The negligent employee was, of course, fired. End of story, case closed."

Holmes paced around the station's small lobby, and a frown slowly spread across his face as he worked through the details in his mind. "Interesting," he murmured. "It all seems to have been quite conveniently explained. The only problem is, that explanation is also entirely ludicrous. I don't care how drunk that employee claims he was—no one 'accidentally' spills an illegal chemical all over two buildings and then just as 'accidentally' sets them on fire. Witnesses can lie, but the evidence never does."

"I'll concede that," Lestrade said, "though I don't want to know how you managed to get inside a closed crime scene in order to find those traces of zever you told me about, or how you managed to get enough of a banned chemical to set Mrs. Hudson's sofa on fire as an experiment. But there's nothing I can do. That employee came forward with a confession, both companies accepted it, and the case has been *closed.*"

"But wrongdoing has occurred here!" Holmes insisted. "Even if we accept that the fire was started by accident—which I don't believe for one bloody minute—someone had to get that zever from somewhere. Illegally."

"Yes, Sunset Enterprise's explanation seems a little too tidy," Jaymie added. "I wonder..." She hesitated. *What did she think she was doing—what did her opinion really matter here?* But Holmes and Lestrade were both listening to her intently now, and so she took the plunge. "Okay, so the accident happens, an employee quickly comes forward, both companies accept the story, and that's the end of it. Doesn't it seem strange Future Corp. isn't even going to attempt to sue Sunset for having poor safety standards and security measures? I mean, they're supposed to be rivals—you think Future Corp. would jump at a chance to take Sunset down. And do they really expect law enforcement to believe no one noticed a drunken employee staggering around? And would the sort of employee who showed up stone drunk to work have the sort of character to immediately come forward and confess? It all seems just a little bit, well, 'off' to me."

"Exactly!" Holmes cried. "You see, Lestrade, at least someone understands what I'm trying to get at. 'Too tidy' is absolutely right, and I don't think we should take anything Future Corp. or Sunset Enterprises is saying at face value. Something's definitely not right about this, and I think we need to take a little trip to Quadrant D to investigate."

"Oh no you don't, Holmes!" Lestrade said, adamantly shaking his head. "I am not taking you down there to poke your head into business you shouldn't! Besides, we can't forget about Mrs. Hudson. Time spent on that Quadrant D case only takes away time we could be using to find her. I mean, it's not like the cases are connected. Let's focus on the one that really—"

A thoughtful look came onto Holmes' face, and he held up a hand, halting the inspector. "Lestrade, shut up."

"Excuse me?" Lestrade looked as if he had just been slapped.

Holmes rolled his eyes and glanced over at Jaymie. "He's always doing that, and it frustrates me to no end. He comes up with a brilliant idea, and then he bypasses it without ever realizing what he's done."

"What? No!" Lestrade's expression was now incredulous. "You've lost it this time, Holmes. You can't possibly believe these cases are connected. That's absurd! They have nothing in common."

"Maybe, maybe not. But you won't find out unless you come with Jaymie and I to Quadrant D."

Lestrade let out a string of curses, but he grabbed his jacket and an access chip for his patrol hovercar. "Fine, let's go. But if we get arrested, Holmes, I'm not bailing you out like I did last time."

"Last time?" Jaymie asked, but the two men were already out the door.

Chapter 3: The Plot Thickens

Jaymie pulled her jacket more tightly around her as she, Holmes, and Lestrade crept through an alleyway in Quadrant D that led up to the Future Corp. and Sunset Enterprises factories. The air had grown chillier since she and Holmes had first arrived at the Civic Security Station, and her breath hung like a faint, frosty cloud on the air. Lestrade had parked his hovercar about a kilometer away and made them walk to the factories, even though Holmes had argued three people in a hovercar at a closed-off crime scene didn't raise that much more suspicion than three people walking around at a closed-off crime scene.

At this hour, the streets were all deserted, no one having a reason to be in the industrial district after dark. The buildings were well kept, sharing the same stark, modern design, as if they had all been created by the same architect. They were efficient and utilitarian, as Jaymie would have expected industrial buildings to look. However, she couldn't help noticing the long rows of almost identical buildings felt a little too precise, maybe even oppressive. She almost preferred Quadrant B to this; though it certainly was grittier, it did have a certain amount of character, and it felt somehow more *real*. Maybe it was just from coming here at dusk when the streets were empty, but still it felt rather bleak.

At least nothing here appeared to be amiss, and the two factories they had come to inspect seemed to be unoccupied. The windows were darkened, and an eerie silence pervaded the air. There were no police officers or security guards patrolling the scene, though the hologram "crime scene" banners hadn't been taken down yet. Jaymie used the light from her techpad screen to examine the side of the Sunset

Enterprises factory and look for the greenish residue the burning zever would have left, but found, to her disappointment, only plain, albeit slightly blackened, metal.

Holmes had noticed it too, and a slight frown crossed his face. "Interesting—someone's cleaned off the green residue since I came here last night. Covering up evidence is yet another sign we're not dealing with an accident."

"So how do we get in?" Jaymie asked, and then was startled by a crash. She looked up and saw a gaping hole in one of the windows above her head, and Lestrade gave Holmes a lethal glare.

"Holmes, this is an investigation!" he hissed. "I thought subtlety was supposed to be the goal here—and throwing a rock at a window is not exactly subtle!"

Holmes dusted off his hands and wiped them on his trench coat. "This place is as deserted as a graveyard. No one would have heard that. However, if there *is* someone inside, they will come running. That way, we can find out their position quickly instead of stumbling around aimlessly inside the factory, just waiting to be ambushed. I suggest we find some corner to conveniently hide behind while we wait and see if my commotion draws anyone out."

"You're crazy," Lestrade muttered. "But you're also crazy brilliant. I don't know whether to love you or hate you for it."

They heard the sound of footsteps, and Lestrade pulled them behind a pile of debris that had crumbled from the building during the fire. Sure enough, two gray-uniformed Sunset employees slipped out of a door on the side of the building. The female employee was clutching what appeared to be a stun blaster, and her partner was talking in hushed tones on his comlink.

Jaymie caught snatches of the conversation: *Yeah, thought we had an intruder...someone just threw a rock...no sign...probably just some kids...everything's secure. Ten-four.*

Jaymie glanced over at Holmes, and he shook his head. The behavior of the two employees was straight out of one of those clichéd crime dramas they were always showing on the galactic entertainment network; from their overly dramatic method of slinking around to their all-too-obvious whispering, it was clear being security guards wasn't exactly their day job. But amateurs or no, Jaymie knew it would be dangerous to be spotted by them, and she didn't know what kind of backup they might have.

"Well, guess we're not getting in that way," Lestrade whispered. "Anyone have any brilliant ideas?"

"Maybe we should just go over and ask them for directions?" Jaymie suggested dryly, and Holmes gave her a withering look. Jaymie's face reddened, and she glanced away, feeling embarrassed. "Sorry. Just trying to be funny."

"Please, don't."

Lestrade rolled his eyes. "Yes—only the great Sherlock Holmes is allowed to be witty at crime scenes."

"Enough," Holmes cut in. "If the two of you are done being juvenile, I suggest we scope out the perimeter. I have an idea where we might *actually* find another point of entry."

#

In the end, however, it was Lestrade who found a way inside. At the back of the factory was a loading dock where freighters could fly up to the building and drop off or pick up goods. There were four separate loading areas, with ramps leading up to openings in the building. Although three of the openings were blocked off, one of the drop-down doors hadn't closed all the way, leaving a crack just large enough to slip through.

"Will we have to worry about setting off any alarms?" Jaymie asked, but Lestrade shook his head.

"The fire took out the security system. We'll just have to make sure we stay out of the way of those would-be security guards patrolling the building."

Lestrade ducked under the drop-down door, followed by Jaymie, and, last of all, Holmes. The inside of the factory was dark and gloomy, lit only by shafts of moonlight shining down through skylights in the ceiling. Jaymie didn't need to see an official investigator's report to know how thorough the destruction had been. They were now in a cavernous room that once had contained dozens of assembly lines; however, the high-tech machinery had now been reduced to a blackened mess that towered above her like some macabre, abstract sculpture. Debris littered the floor, and she coughed, her lungs irritated by particles of soot they'd stirred up while walking across the floor. She couldn't see how any of this could be repaired, and she could only guess at the millions of quid it would take to rebuild the factory and replace the equipment.

Jaymie held up her techpad, once again using the glowing screen to illuminate her surroundings. She was attempting to take a closer look at a piece of machinery when Holmes abruptly snatched the device out of her hands.

"Can I borrow that?" he asked, already typing feverishly on the keypad and accessing the planet's digital information network.

"What are you doing?" she asked, a little miffed, and for a moment, Holmes ignored her. He scrolled through a page of information, and then exclaimed, "Aha!"

"What sort of epic discovery have you made this time?" Lestrade asked with a touch of sarcasm.

Holmes showed them the techpad screen. "I was just musing about the massive amount of zever it would have taken to do this much damage, and wondering where someone could have gotten it. I searched for 'zever' on Eglon's information network, and discovered something quite fascinating."

Jaymie glanced down at the techpad and skimmed through the *Loudron Times* article Holmes had pulled up on the screen, dated three years ago.

Planetary officials today banned the newly discovered chemical "zever," dashing tech industry hopes the chemical would become the wave of the future. Leading corporations in Quadrant D, such as Future Corp., Sunset Enterprises, and Tech-verse, had previously been experimenting with the use of the chemical in the manufacture of techpad devices. In early tests, devices made using zever ran more efficiently and were cheaper to manufacture, leading many companies to prematurely invest in the chemical, only to have the planet's industrial regulatory board deem it "unsafe, volatile, and highly toxic." This comes after two Tech-verse engineers had an accident with the chemical and spent several weeks in the hospital in critical condition. Companies must cease using the chemical in manufacture immediately, and they have three years to safely dispose of the chemical and remove it from their factories. Executives from Sunset Enterprises, the company that originally developed the chemical, declined to comment.

The article was accompanied by a mug shot of the Sunset CEO, Jane Rozine, along with a picture of the Future Corp. CEO, Sade Holbrook, who *had* commented on the banning of the chemical.

"This will be hitting Sunset pretty hard, but I won't deny this will hit us hard, too," he said. "We were planning to purchase sizable quantities of the chemical to further our own research. Now we'll be forced to pursue progress elsewhere."

Jaymie looked up, feeling a sense of disbelief. "Sunset made this chemical? Are you suggesting..."

"At this point, it's just conjecture," Holmes said quickly, "and although normally that's something I hate, I think it's not too wild to assume maybe the fire was fueled by Sunset's own supply of the chemical. Technically speaking, next week is the cutoff date to dispose of the chemical, and although Sunset should have been in the process of getting rid of their supplies of it already, what if they weren't? What if they had it all stored here, and someone used it to start the fire?"

"But surely it would have been secure, at least," Jaymie said. "I can only imagine the fines the government would slap on them if anyone were to have an accident with the chemical."

"Oh, I'm sure it was perfectly secure from outsiders," Holmes said calmly. "I believe they used the chemical to start the fire themselves."

"What?" Jaymie asked, thinking Holmes really had derailed. "Why would a company be daft enough to torch their own factory, damaging several other companies in the process?"

"Holmes may be on to something, though," Lestrade said slowly. "Now that I think about it, it should have struck me as odd that there weren't any injuries during the fire. Both Sunset's and Future Corp.'s factories were completely engulfed in flames within half an hour of the start of the fire, but no one was killed. No smoke inhalation injuries, even. Everyone was outside by the time we got here. I don't think realistically they could have evacuated all those people in time. The fire spread too fast. They had to have some advance warning."

"But why?" Jaymie knew she kept hounding this point, but she was desperate to understand. She felt like Lestrade and Holmes were always ahead of her, and she kept having to fight to keep up with their logic. She had to admit that for her, this was a new experience; she was used to being at the top of the class, always having the right answer. She didn't like being so far behind, and having to ask all these questions made her feel like an idiot.

Lestrade started to answer her, but Holmes stopped him, holding up his hand.

"Yes, Lestrade, I know you have your theories, but we can't keep answering Jaymie's questions for her. She's a smart girl, she can figure this out—she's just been trained, possibly by her controlling and overbearing family, not to do much independent thinking. But she's got this, I know she does. We just have to give her a chance."

"Maybe...well, maybe they thought by burning down the factory, they could collect the insurance money." Jaymie had heard about such scandals attempted by smaller corporations before, but she hadn't thought one as prestigious as Sunset Enterprises would try something like that.

Although Holmes didn't reply, she could tell he was mulling it over. They paused in front of a rather flimsy metal staircase leading up to a walkway hanging high above the factory floor. The walkway appeared to run around the entire perimeter of the building, and it was suspended from the ceiling by thick cables. Holmes grabbed onto the handrail, which was little more than a thin metal bar, and started jogging up the stairs, leaving Jaymie and Lestrade with no choice but to follow him. While Jaymie didn't have a fear of heights, even she had to admit, once they reached the walkway and she looked back down, her stomach started churning. They were about fifteen meters off the ground, and the walkway creaked and shifted underneath their weight. She didn't know how sturdy it had been before the fire, but it certainly didn't look safe now.

They carefully began moving forward, the walkway swaying slightly from side to side. Lestrade gritted his teeth and gripped the railing so tightly his knuckles turned white.

"Holmes, you know how I feel about heights!" he muttered through gritted teeth, and Holmes simply shrugged.

"You could have stayed back at the station, you know. If you're going to complain the whole way—"

"Just shut up, and keep going!"

As they passed from one fire-ravaged room to another, Jaymie began to wonder if there really were any more clues for them to find. In each room they only seemed to find more of the same—blackened, twisted machinery and piles of debris, with everything coated in soot. The moonbeams shining through the skylights didn't give them much light to see by, and the gloom and grimness of their surroundings began to weigh on Jaymie, and she despaired of ever reaching the end of the walkway.

Then she suddenly collided with Holmes, who had stopped without warning on the walkway in front of her. She started to object, but she glanced up and saw he was holding a finger to his lips. He pointed, and up ahead, Jaymie could see a faint, somewhat reddish glow—definitely not moonlight this time.

"I think we've found something!" Lestrade whispered excitedly, and Holmes shot him a glare.

"Must you always state the obvious?"

They crept forward slowly, trying to avoid making the walkway creak beneath them. The reddish light gradually grew more and more distinct, drawing them into a new room. Jaymie picked up on the sound of voices, and the three of them instinctively pressed themselves against the wall, hiding in the shadows. They came around a corner, and Jaymie had to clap a hand over her mouth to prevent herself from gasping.

Down below them, what appeared to be scientists in lab coats were bustling around a large piece of machinery sitting up on a platform. The machine consisted of a large metal archway, about two and a half meters tall, and various cables that were running up to it and around it. Strange-looking tubes were twisted all around the archway, and it was these that were producing the reddish glow. At first Jaymie thought the tubes themselves were luminescent, but then on closer observation, she discovered they were actually filled with a glowing liquid that was being quickly pumped through them.

"What the devil is that?" Lestrade breathed, and Jaymie and Holmes looked at each other. The device was very foreign, very alien looking, but it was enough like the picture Jaymie had seen in that University of Scoztan science journal for her to know exactly what the machine in front of her was.

"I don't believe it," she said, just as the device began to produce a strange, humming sound. The scientists rushed to their stations, and the platform began to vibrate. The low hum filled the air, and the walkway beneath them, the walls of the building—even the very atoms in Jaymie's body—all seemed to vibrate along with it. She could do nothing but stare transfixed at the mysterious device, both fascinated and terrified by what was happening in front of her.

Underneath the arch, the air began to shimmer with a faint, reddish light, and a nebulous form slowly appeared on the pad sitting on the platform. The form gradually began to grow more and more defined, taking on a human-like shape. There was a bright flash, and then suddenly, standing down below them was a man.

Who just happened to be Sade Holbrook, the CEO of Future Corp.

He staggered slightly and shook his head as if trying to clear it, wincing a few times. He leaned against the metal archway for support, still stunned by what he had experienced.

"Well, what do you think?"

Jaymie saw a woman come forward, and recognized her as Jane Rozine, the CEO of Sunset Enterprises. Like the scientists operating the machine, she was attired in a long gray lab coat.

"The technology's progressing nicely," Holbrook said. "Although I really wish we could get away from using that pad."

Rozine frowned slightly. "As I told you before, we're working on it. We can transport any person from any point in the city to the pad in our particle transporter, but we're still working on getting rid of the need for a pad at the destination. Just think of what a great scientific leap it is, though, that we no longer need a pad at the point of origin. Other companies should be willing to pay millions for this technology."

"Not should be, *will be*," Holbrook corrected her. "My scientists assured me your technology was solid, and now that I've seen it for myself, I'm absolutely convinced. Let's pack it up and get moving."

He reached for his metal briefcase, preparing to leave, when suddenly, it happened.

Jaymie knew she shouldn't have risked it. They were already lucky enough to have avoided drawing attention so far, and she should have just stayed put. But she wanted so badly to see what the transporter pad looked like, and curiosity overcame her and she had to inch forward to get a closer look. It was just one step, but it was enough. As she shifted her weight, the walkway swung out ever so slightly from the wall. Although it only moved a few centimeters, the loud, piercing screech that accompanied the walkway's movement was unmistakable.

"Jaymie!" Holmes hissed. He tried to yank her back into the shadows, but it was too late. All the scientists and the two CEOs glanced up at the walkway. At first, they appeared to be just as stunned as the three intruders up on the platform, but it didn't take long for Holbrook's eyes to narrow, flashing with an angry fire.

"Who are you?" he snapped. "What business do you have here? Speak quickly!"

Lestrade didn't have to say it, but he did anyway. "Everybody—run!"

He, Jaymie, and Holmes took off down the walkway just as a heavily armed security team came charging into the room, pulling out their blasters and immediately starting to fire. These thugs were obviously a level above the inept guards they'd run across earlier, and the weapons they were carrying were more than just stunners.

A blaster bolt zinged off the railing right next to Jaymie's hand, and she jerked her hand away just in time, almost losing her balance. Holmes grabbed her and pulled her back towards the center of the walkway, nearly hit by a blaster bolt himself. The six thugs continued to follow them on the ground, firing plenty of shots their way. Jaymie glanced back, only to find that, to her horror, two of the thugs were heading for another staircase, climbing up onto the walkway behind her, Holmes, and Lestrade.

"Fantastic!" Holmes muttered. "It just keeps getting better."

"We've gotten out of worse situations before," Lestrade said, then glanced down at the thugs chasing them, and the thugs coming up behind them. "OK, maybe not."

Jaymie could feel her heart threatening to pound right out of her chest, but she also felt the distinct blossoming of a deep sense of shame. How could she have done this? How could she have been so childish? Taking that one, unnecessary step—a step that was now going to get them all killed. Holmes must have lost all respect he had ever had for her by now. *Just a silly girl, that's what he probably thinks of—*

All of a sudden, another horrible screeching sound filled the air, and everyone instinctively stopped. Jaymie's breath caught as the walkway shuddered beneath them, and the chains holding up the walkway groaned as they slowly began to give way. Apparently, the walkway hadn't been designed to hold this many people at one time. Everyone remained frozen, as if silently willing the walkway to stay together, but it was to no avail. The suspended walkway shifted violently, and Jaymie screamed, scrambling to grab onto the handrail. Holmes turned around just as the chains broke, and the walkway in front of them snapped in two. The two-meter portion Jaymie was clinging to swung down towards the floor, connected to the rest of the walkway behind her by an all-too-thin and now bent piece of pipe that served as a hinge.

"Jaymie!" Lestrade called out. He was stuck on the other side of the walkway, separated from her and Holmes by a chasm of air. Jaymie glanced up and saw Holmes standing above her, a look of—was that...fear in his eyes? The walkway let out another long, low creak, and even the thugs behind Holmes began to look nervous, afraid the whole thing was going to fall apart.

"Get them!" Holbrook screamed at his henchmen, but they were too frightened now to move forward. They began to back away towards a more stable portion of the walkway, from which Jaymie assumed they would resume their fire. She shut her eyes and hung onto the handrail as tightly as she could, willing herself not to give in to panic. She could feel the piece of walkway swaying, and it was still creaking as well. It was going to break off, she knew it, and she doubted she would survive the fall.

"Jaymie!" She heard Holmes yell at her, and he reached out his hand, his eyes strangely desperate. "Grab on, or else you're going to slip off!"

"Always stating the obvious, huh?" she said weakly, but Holmes didn't even seem to hear her joke.

"Hurry!" he exclaimed, as the portion of the walkway she was hanging onto began to slowly peel away.

Jaymie stretched up her hand, straining as hard as she could. Her fingers brushed Holmes', but she wasn't close enough, not yet. Although her arms ached and she longed to simply let go, embracing the brief relief that would bring, she wouldn't let herself give up. With her last bit of strength, she reached up as high as she could, and Holmes grabbed onto her hand and held it fast. Gritting his teeth, he hauled her up onto the walkway, grimacing under the effort. Jaymie grasped the edge of the still-suspended walkway just as the piece she had been clinging to finally broke away, the shift in weight upsetting its delicate balance. It landed on the floor with a sickening clang, and Jaymie gripped Holmes' hand even tighter, her heart thudding.

Holmes pulled her onto more solid ground, his hand locked around her arm in an iron grip. Even after she was safe, it took him a minute to relax his hold on her, as if he were afraid she would somehow slip away again. Then seeming suddenly embarrassed, he let her go, and he stepped back a little awkwardly.

"Thanks," she said, and he nodded curtly, suddenly all business again. He helped her to her feet, and then they looked back at the thugs, who had stepped off the walkway and onto a metal platform welded to the wall. They had clearly had enough of this fiasco, and they looked as though they wanted nothing more than to climb off the walkway and get out of the factory.

However, Holbrook wasn't giving up so easily.

"Stop them!" he yelled at his thugs. "We can't let them escape! This will ruin everything."

"We may already *be* ruined," Rozine tried to cut in, but he turned on her and growled.

"No—I want you to bring this place down." He glanced back up at the thugs on the platform, locking eyes with a tall, dark-haired woman. "Do it—now!!"

The other thugs seemed puzzled, but a grim look came into the woman's eyes. Holbrook had obviously prepared her for this contingency plan, and she knew exactly what he was talking about. She slowly reached into her pocket and pulled out a small, egg-shaped metal object with several blinking lights, clutching it tightly in her hand and seeming to steel herself.

"Oh no—oh no, no, no!" Holmes began to back towards the edge of the walkway. "What is it with corrupt corporations and their insistence on using such dramatic methods to kill me!"

He glanced over at Jaymie, a wild, determined look in his eyes. "On the count of three, we jump."

"What?" she cried. "We can't make the gap! I just narrowly escaped falling to my death. I'm not about to jump, Holmes!"

"Well, we'll have to."

"I don't think I—"

"It's a grenade, Jaymie! Jump—now!"

She saw the thug throw the grenade, the metal device arching through the air towards them.

Without thinking, Jaymie launched herself into the air, not daring to look down at the hard metal floor too far below them. She crashed into Lestrade's waiting arms, and they both slammed onto the walkway. Holmes wasn't far behind, barely managing to grab onto the railing. Then, they were all scrambling to their feet, trying to put as many meters between themselves and the grenade's point of impact as possible.

The thug's aim was slightly off, but with a weapon like a grenade, accuracy wasn't exactly all that important. It smashed into the wall and instantly transformed into a blossom of red-orange fire. The walkway hit the wall, and the cables connecting it to the ceiling snapped, sending the entire section of the walkway Holmes, Lestrade, and Jaymie were on crashing to the floor.

Jaymie covered her head, bracing herself for the collision. She didn't see how they were going to survive this, and a mix of emotions ran through her. What an unbelievable way to die, and yet...what an incredible adventure. If only for a brief, fleeting moment, she had actually felt like a part of Holmes and Lestrade's team, and the way Holmes had looked at her as she was about to slip off the walkway...he had actually seemed worried about her. She wondered if her family would ever learn what had happened to her, or if she would simply join the lengthy list of missing persons last seen in Quadrant B, their fates forever a mystery. She didn't want her life to end here—there was so much she had wanted to do and see, so many more adventures she could have had...

Jaymie closed her eyes, and she waited to hit the floor. Yet instead of slamming into the ground, she began to feel a very different type of sensation, like a sort of tingling all over her body. She looked down and gasped. Her fingers were beginning to dissolve, and all around her was an unearthly reddish glow. There was a bright flash, and suddenly, she was standing on a pad in a cold, darkened room, with Holmes and Lestrade standing beside her, seeming just as stunned.

But even more shocking was the presence of a beaming, purple-skinned woman standing in front of a control panel.

"We did it!" Mrs. Hudson exclaimed, and suddenly, it was just too much for Jaymie. The stress of her near-death experience, and the shock she now felt, finally overcame her, and everything went black.

Chapter 4: Only the Beginning

When Jaymie finally opened her eyes, everything in front of her was a blur, a swirl of indistinct shapes and colors. As she tried to focus, she felt a sharp, shooting pain run through her head, and she grimaced. She felt a hand on her arm, helping her to sit up.

"Sorry—it's an aftereffect of going through a particle transporter," she heard a vaguely familiar voice say. "It'll take a while for you to remember who and where you are, and you may have that killer headache for a few days. Singularly unpleasant, but still better than dying, I'm sure you'll agree."

Grimacing again, Jaymie blinked and struggled to make her eyes focus. There were two men crouched down next to her, looking at her with concern in their eyes.

"Holmes?" she murmured, hazy recollections coming back to her, and she saw one of the men grin.

"See, Lestrade? I told you she'd come out of it quickly."

"No thanks to you," the other man muttered. "What a way to show Mrs. Hudson's new lodger about town."

Mrs. Hudson's new lodger—yes, that was it. Her memories of the last few hours' rather whirlwind and bizarre series of events came rushing back to her, and though she was quite grateful to be alive, she had no idea how they had managed it.

"Where are we?" she asked, looking around and finding they were in a plain, white, and rather sterile-looking room.

"You're at the Civic Security Station in Quadrant D," explained Lestrade, whom she recognized now. "I need to head back down to the Sunset factory, but I wanted to wait around to see if you were OK."

"But the grenade, and then the transporter…what happened?" Jaymie was afraid Holmes might get on her for asking too many questions again, but he seemed willing to indulge her this time.

"Well, it's quite the story," Lestrade said. "Turns out you were right, Jaymie—Sunset *was* after the insurance money. We just got done questioning Jane Rozine, and she confirmed everything we suspected. When the government banned the chemical 'zever,' Sunset Enterprises was hit hard. They had been counting on the use of that chemical to advance their business, and they had nowhere to take the company in terms of techpad manufacture. So, they started looking into other areas of technology research and got into particle beaming. They stumbled upon a design that would let them beam people to different places without using the cumbersome pads required by other devices, but they didn't have enough money to fund the research on their own. They approached Future Corp., who invested some money—under the table, of course, because a partnership between the two companies would have violated the planet's anti-trust laws. They still didn't have enough funding, however.

"That's when Rozine hatched a plan to burn down the companies' two factories with Sunset's remaining zever, collect the insurance money, and take her technology research to another planet. It would have worked great, if Holmes hadn't conducted his little sofa-burning experiment. Somehow, Sunset found out about the zever he purchased, and, knowing Holmes' reputation for being a meddlesome, far-too-nosy busybody—" (Lestrade paused and grinned as he saw Holmes' glare) "—they decided to 'kidnap' him by beaming him out of his flat. However, their technology isn't very precise yet, and they beamed Mrs. Hudson instead."

"And then I figured out how to save you!" Mrs. Hudson interjected, quite proud of herself. "They were holding me captive over in the Future Corp. building, because of course they couldn't afford to let me go. I knew Holmes and Lestrade would come looking for me, so I waited. My captors were watching the experiment over in the Sunset factory on a large monitor, and then I saw the commotion start. I caught a glimpse of Holmes and figured then was as good a time as any to act."

"Apparently she had a small stun blaster hidden in her pocket," Holmes said, sounding somewhat impressed, in spite of himself. "I suppose they never thought to search an 'innocent old lady' for weapons, although anyone who knows Mrs. Hudson would never use the words 'innocent' or 'lady' to—"

"Anyway," Lestrade quickly interrupted, before Holmes could fire up Mrs. Hudson's temper yet again, "Mrs. Hudson managed to convince them she had a more dangerous weapon, and they freed her. She stunned two of her guards and made the remaining one start up the particle transporter, which can be controlled from either factory, since both have destination pads. She transported the three of us just in time. Apparently the process of transporting affects some people more severely than others, which is why Holmes and I woke up before you did. All in all, it was a pretty lucky escape, if you ask me."

"That's...that's unbelievable," Jaymie said, shaking her head and struggling to take it all in. "So what happens now?"

"The CEOs of both companies are now in custody, and the case is being reopened for investigation," Lestrade said. "I think they realize now it was a pretty stupid idea to hang around to test their particle transporter one more time. If they had taken it to Itred right after the fire, like they'd been planning, we might never have caught on to what they were doing."

"But you knew...didn't you, Holmes?" Jaymie asked, gazing at him curiously. "You guessed all the way back at the station. Why didn't you tell us?"

Holmes shrugged, looking thoughtful. "Lestrade suggested it was crazy to think the cases were connected, which immediately made me ponder that very thing. At first, I simply thought maybe someone had used a particle transporter to beam a person into the factory to start the fire. The case somewhat mushroomed beyond that." He grinned. "However, I did manage to come up with the final solution to this puzzle by the time we had reached the factory—though it was only a possible scenario in my mind at that point, of course."

"Holmes, you're unbelievable," Lestrade said, rolling his eyes. "Sometimes, even I can't believe that ego of yours. What am I going to do with you?"

Holmes' reply was simple: "What would you do *without* me?"

#

By the time the officers were done questioning them, it was already midmorning. Lestrade left to go back to the crime scene, and Holmes drove Jaymie and Mrs. Hudson back to apartment complex 221, using a patrol hovercar Lestrade had loaned him. Jaymie passed the time by staring out the window, watching as the sleek, shiny, and very modern surfaces of the buildings in Quadrant D faded to the rusty, tired-looking structures of Quadrant B.

"Welcome back to paradise," Holmes remarked somewhat sarcastically, though Jaymie noticed he seemed to relax a little as they left Quadrant D behind them. Though he probably wouldn't ever say it, on some level he liked it here, or at least felt comfortable. She had a feeling he probably knew this quadrant better than anyone else in Loudron, and it was an inescapable part of who he was. He was a crusader, cleaning up its dirt and grime, and it returned the favor by giving him endless conundrums to solve, providing fuel for his ever-inquisitive mind. Lestrade was right—he was a meddler, but he couldn't help it; without something to stimulate that brilliant, but decidedly peculiar mind of his, the life would slowly be sucked out of his soul.

They finally arrived back at the apartment complex, and they got on the rickety lift, riding in silence as it clanked and screeched its way up the shaft. Jaymie followed Holmes and Mrs. Hudson back to the flat she had been touring when this whole mess had erupted. It seemed strangely quiet and subdued now; everything was exactly as they had left it: the burnt sofa, the empty coat rack, and Jaymie's suitcase lying on the floor, knocked over in her and Holmes' haste to leave the flat.

Mrs. Hudson bent down and slowly picked up the suitcase and handed it to Jaymie, her expression a bit sad.

"Well, I guess that's it, then," she said. "I can't even begin to make amends for the terrible ordeal you've gone through on our account, but please accept my apologies anyway. I'd be happy to show you back down to the lobby, and I'll give you a couple quid to cover your hoverbus fare back to the university. I know a few other landlords who might—"

"Wait—you mean you're not staying?" Holmes interrupted, staring at Jaymie. He was trying to ask it nonchalantly, but in his eyes, Jaymie saw a flicker of disappointment.

"After what we put her through? I imagine she never wants to see us, or this flat, again," Mrs. Hudson said. She patted Jaymie's hand. "I understand perfectly if you'd like to inquire elsewhere about lodging."

Jaymie looked from Holmes, to Mrs. Hudson, then back to Holmes again. She knew what she should do—what was the *logical* thing to do. She should thank Mrs. Hudson politely, take her suitcase, and walk straight out that door, like she had been trying to do before Mrs. Hudson had so mysteriously disappeared.

Or had she really intended to leave then? Jaymie frowned quizzically, knowing that now Holmes and Mrs. Hudson must be staring at *her*. Deep down, had she *really* wanted to stay? Did she *still* want to stay? Although she could always try to convince herself the last day's events were only a fluke, a one-time freak occurrence that would never be repeated, somehow she knew that wouldn't be the case. If she stayed, she sensed that disappearing landlords, exploding factories, and daft experiments might be only the tip of what she'd experience. She could only imagine how her mother would react if she ever happened to meet the rather eccentric and not always socially adept Sherlock Holmes.

And yet...she couldn't deny she was intrigued. In some ways, being around Holmes made her feel inferior, and she knew it would be frustrating to try to keep up with him all the time. But maybe that was good for her; it pushed her, forced her to stretch her mind and take leaps of logic she'd never taken before. Somehow, Holmes seemed to believe she could rise to the challenge.

And though she knew he'd probably never admit it, not even to himself, he *wanted* her to stay.

Jaymie took a deep breath and set her suitcase on the floor. "This is probably the most insane thing I've ever done, but I'm in," she said. "Mrs. Hudson, it looks like you've found another lodger after all."

Mrs. Hudson appeared as if she were about to faint with surprise.

"Welcome to complex 221, Quadrant B, Miss Watson," Holmes said, reaching out and giving her hand a firm shake.

And that was just the beginning.

Case No. 2: Suspended Disbelief

Chapter 1: The Play's the Thing

Jaymie swiped her automatic entry card at the door of her flat, then carefully stepped inside the darkened living room. All the lights appeared to be off in the house, and everything was silent and still. She quietly set down her backpack and let out a long, slow sigh. She had just gotten back from the library at the University of Medical Arts, trying to get in some last-minute studying for her first exam. She massaged her temples, wishing her throbbing headache would go away. Her head was so full of information it was about to burst. How in the galaxy was she going to be able to remember all this for the test tomorrow? She had thought some of the finals she had taken for her undergraduate degree were tough, but they were nothing compared to this. Would she be able to remember that laser biopsy was safe for Andronidans, but not Syfrians, because their skin would react to the laser and vaporize within seconds? Or that humans could receive transplants from any of the humanoid species living on the moon of Udor, but only from the females of those species?

She took out the clip that had been holding up her long red hair and then slipped out of her jacket, trying to will herself to relax. She had studied all she could, and thinking about it now would only make her more anxious. She just needed to take a long, hot shower in the steamer, or maybe even just sit on the couch in the silence and enjoy being alone—the side of the sofa that wasn't burnt, that is. Thank God *he* wasn't—

"Burning the candles at both ends this evening, hmm, Watson?"

Jaymie yelped at the sudden sound, dropping her techpad. She switched on the lights and discovered that unlike she had assumed, she was not really alone. Holmes was sitting leisurely on the living room sofa, holding an unopened book in his lap. He wasn't wearing his signature trench coat, but his hair was sticking out in all sorts of crazy angles, as usual. He blinked and stared at her calmly, his pair of blue and brown eyes just as unnerving as ever.

"Blast it, Holmes!" Jaymie exclaimed, her heart rate finally beginning to return to normal. "What are you doing?"

"Waiting for Lestrade," Holmes stated simply, and Jaymie felt her temper flare.

"What? In the dark? And why did you just sit there for five minutes instead of announcing yourself when I first came in?"

Holmes shrugged. "You weren't Lestrade. I didn't have anything in particular that I needed to say to you. However, you have complained in the past I am not very good at…how do you say it? Ah, yes: making 'small talk.' And so I finally decided that perhaps I should speak up and ask if you'd like to comment on your day. Apparently my attempt wasn't very effective, and you have yet to dissuade me from my belief that the idea of small talk is ridiculous. And as for why I'm in the dark, why should I turn a light on? I don't really need the lights on to just sit and wait, and I thought it was better to conserve power. Our electrical bill will be going back up again now that we have three people in the flat."

Jaymie stared at Holmes, an incredulous look on her face. "I don't even know what to say to that." (She knew it wouldn't be worth the bother to ask him why he had been sitting in the dark with a book he obviously wouldn't have been able to read.) "Look, it's been a long day, and I want to go to bed."

Holmes nodded. "Goodnight then," he remarked as Jaymie headed back to her room. "Oh, and by the way—you may not want to look in the hall closet. One of my experiments exploded prematurely, and I haven't had time to clean it up yet. Pickled Yopilian pomegranates and what not—it's not pretty."

Jaymie stopped. "Pickled what?" She looked at Holmes and then shook her head. "Never mind, I don't want to know."

She had almost reached her room when she heard Holmes' wristband comlink suddenly begin to beep.

"Holmes, are you still up?" she heard Lestrade's urgent voice say. "Something's happened."

Go to bed, Jaymie—just ignore it, a voice inside her warned. *You've got a big test tomorrow, and you need your sleep. Even if Lestrade's calling about a case, you should be worrying about your exam, not...*

Jaymie found herself ignoring her own better sense, and she inched back down the hallway, straining to listen in on the comlink call.

"Yes, I'm waiting for you," Holmes said. "Actually, I'm waiting for the four quid you promised to pay me back today."

"What?" Jaymie exclaimed before she could stop herself, sticking her head back out of the hallway. "That's the only reason you're up at this ungodly hour? For four quid?"

Holmes shot her a glare for interrupting and tried to shoo her away, gesturing at her to go to her room. "However, obviously something has kept you."

"I've got a case, and it looks like a real mind-bender," Lestrade said. "And yes, I'll go ahead and admit it: Civic Security is in over its head."

"And you're calling to confess you need my help," Holmes said matter-of-factly. "Are you going to give me any clues, or will I just have to find out when I get there?"

Lestrade sighed. "It's bad, Holmes. I'm at Madame Zinizi's Theatre in Sector 2, Quadrant B. An actress was murdered in the middle of a play, and she's now suspended, for no apparent reason, in midair. Just floating. It's scaring the devil out of the other actors *and* my team of inspectors, and we have no idea how to get her down or how she got there."

"Interesting." Although Holmes' tone remained the same, Jaymie saw his eyebrows shoot up, accompanied by that familiar gleam in his eyes that always showed up when his curiosity was piqued. "Lestrade, I'm on my way."

He grabbed his trench coat off the coat rack and then grabbed Jaymie's jacket and tossed it to her.

"Well, it appears we're going to the theatre," he said, and Jaymie gave him a look.

"Holmes, I have a test tomorrow! I need to get my rest, and—"

"But you're my assistant, and I'll be needing your input," he said.

"Your assistant? Holmes, wait!"

But he was already out the door, leaving Jaymie with no choice but to follow.

"This is becoming a bad habit," she muttered as she hurriedly slipped on her jacket and ran out the door, jogging to catch up to Holmes.

#

Jaymie wasn't expecting "Madame Zinizi's" to exactly be in the same league as the Loudron Metropolitan Theatre, so she was somewhat surprised when Holmes pulled his hovercar to a halt in front of the playhouse's actually quite tastefully decorated entrance. Quadrant B wasn't really known for its arts or its devotion to culture, but Madame Zinizi's did appear to be making an effort to fight that stereotype. A holo-poster on the front of the building advertised the current play that was running, "Exseloro's Revenge," an older and somewhat outdated play, but one that still had been fairly well regarded in its time. The theatre's façade was a little rundown, like most buildings in Quadrant B, but the black building had no graffiti, and the red carpet leading up to the theatre's golden double doors at least attempted to add a touch of class.

"It was originally funded by a grant from the Eglon government," Holmes explained, as if reading her thoughts. "About twenty years ago, the Ruling Council decided it should do something to try to clean up more rundown communities like Quadrant B, so they built about five of these theatres across the planet and provided funding for their first season of plays. The theatres were quite popular for a while, but then the councilor who'd advocated building them got voted out of office, and the communities couldn't generate enough support to keep them going. Madame Zinizi's is the last one that's still open, and it's actually going to be closing down tomorrow. 'Exseloro's Revenge' will be its last play." Holmes glanced up at the theatre's scrolling marquee and looked strangely wistful. "This whole theatre plan actually wasn't a bad idea, and it's a shame to see it go. But now most of the ordinary citizens don't even come to see plays anymore—the audience is full of crime lords and drug runners. They think coming to the theatre gives them a touch of class and elevates them above normal criminal scum. Not that they'd actually understand any of the complex metaphors in 'Exseloro's Revenge,' however."

They got out of the hovercar, and as Jaymie glanced around, it was hard to believe they were actually at a crime scene. There were no beings standing around the theatre, and the streets were dark and silent. Nothing seemed out of the ordinary, except for the two stern-looking Civic Security inspectors guarding the front doors.

Holmes walked up to the two officers and flashed his identi-card.

"Sherlock Holmes, private investigative consultant," he said. "I believe you called?"

"Lestrade said you'd be showing up soon," the female officer said stiffly, appearing none-too-happy to see Holmes. She looked over at Jaymie a little suspiciously. "He didn't mention you'd be bringing anyone else along, though."

"This is my associate, Jaymie Watson," Holmes said. "She'll be assisting me in investigating the crime scene today."

The other Civic Security inspector's eyes widened. "Since when did you get an assistant?" he asked. "What happened to the great Sherlock Holmes, who always works alone? Back when you worked for Civic Security as an inspector, you'd barely even let Lestrade tag along with you."

"New circumstances arrived, and I adapted," Holmes said. "Now remember, you're paying me by the hour, and I believe this stimulating conversation has already cost the Civic Security Station about 15 quid."

The male officer muttered something under his breath, but he opened the door and waved Holmes and Jaymie into the building.

"I hope you know what you're getting into," the inspector told Jaymie, and she did her best to give him an encouraging, confident smile. Honestly, she still didn't know the answer to that.

"So you actually used to work for Civic Security?" Jaymie whispered to Holmes as they walked into the theatre. "I thought you were always just a private consultant. You don't strike me as someone who would work for, well…"

"The establishment?" Holmes finished. "It was a long time ago, and that's another story for another time. Let's go find Lestrade."

Another story for another time—although that's what he was claiming, his tone left little doubt it was a subject he didn't really want to talk about, and he probably didn't plan on telling her the whole story, either now or later. She'd have to ask Lestrade about it sometime.

The inside of the theatre was dimly lit, with a Tryidian crystal chandelier hanging from the building's arched ceiling and filling the room with a soft glow. Sparkling silver stars were suspended from the black ceiling, giving the illusion that one was looking up into the night sky. The walls were also painted black and were decorated with drawings of exotic constellations from the skies of many different planets. About fifty rows of plush blue chairs stretched out in front of them, and each of these chairs was embroidered with dozens of shiny stars. It was a design that had been used many times by various theatres, but it was still executed well. Or rather, had been executed well about twenty years ago. Now, the décor was starting to show some of its age. The theatre rather reminded Jaymie of an aging actress: it was a little worn, a little faded, but still projected a sense of pride. This theatre had once been a magnificently beautiful place, and it still clung to some of that splendor. That sense of faded grandeur, and also knowing the audience here tonight had witnessed the untimely interruption of the theatre's final show, made Jaymie feel a little sad.

She saw a few Civic Security inspectors combing through the aisles looking for evidence, but most had gathered around the stage. She had purposely avoided looking at the stage itself, keeping her eyes on Holmes as he walked towards it. She had never been to an actual crime scene before (well, unless she counted the Sunset Enterprises factory). Would the murder be grisly? As a medical student, she was used to seeing blood and examining bodies, but never in a context like this. She wasn't sure how she would handle it, and she suddenly regretted letting Holmes talk her into coming along. But it was too late now, and she wasn't going to let herself turn back. Gritting her teeth, she raised her eyes towards the stage, bracing herself for whatever she was going to find there.

Jaymie had heard Lestrade's description of what had happened, but even when she finally worked up the courage to look, she wasn't sure she could believe it. She had thought the disappearance of their landlady, Mrs. Hudson, was the strangest thing she'd ever seen, but this certainly surpassed that. Just as Lestrade had said, there, hanging unbelievably and impossibly in thin air, was the show's murdered lead actress. The woman was suspended parallel to the ground, as if she were lying on an invisible bed. She wore a long purple dress with billowing, sheer sleeves, and a crown sat atop her ebony-colored tresses. Her eyes were closed, and she wasn't breathing, though there were no visible signs of a fatal injury. What was even more bizarre, however, was that she really was just *floating*. Jaymie couldn't see any wires holding her up, or anything else that could possibly be suspending her. She wondered if maybe it was a trick, that the woman was just a hologram being projected onto the stage. But she looked far too real, too defined, and she didn't have that slightly hazy appearance that even the most realistic of holograms always had. Jaymie felt an eerie chill shiver up her spine, and she had to look away, disconcerted by what she had seen.

"That's not right," she mumbled, and then she felt a sudden hand on her shoulder, making her jump.

"Never easy to see your first crime scene," she heard Lestrade's deep voice say. She turned around and saw him staring at the levitating body. "And this is one of the most bizarre ones I've ever seen."

"What happened?" she asked, and Lestrade shook his head.

"That's why we called in Holmes—I have no blooming idea." They walked up a short staircase and onto the stage, and Holmes stepped closer to examine the body. Several Civic Security inspectors were interviewing the crowd of actors clustered on the edge of the stage, the performers' faces a mixture of shock and sorrow. Many of them had red eyes from crying, though several seemed to be just staring off into space, too stunned to start processing their loss emotionally.

"Her name's Oliviana Tryrw, one of the most popular actresses at the theatre," Lestrade explained, gesturing towards the levitating body. "She was playing Queen Clao, who at the end of the first act is supposed to commit suicide by drinking a vial of poison. She collapses onto a bed and dies, and then the curtain goes down for intermission before act two."

"Except, the actors never got to act two, because Oliviana *actually died*," Holmes finished, and Lestrade nodded.

"Apparently yes. She drinks the fake 'poison,' lies down on the bed, then the curtain drops like normal. When it rises again, Oliviana's still there—except the bed is gone, and she's suspended just like this. The crowd clears out in a flash—there's no way an audience of crime lords and drug dealers is going to stick around at the scene of a crime, even if it's a crime they didn't commit. By the time Civic Security gets here, the only ones left are the actors and poor Miss Tryrw."

"And none of you have even attempted to get Miss Tryrw down?" Holmes asked, glancing around at the Civic Security officers standing on the stage. "What sort of investigators are you? Eventually you're going to have to figure out how she died."

"It's not natural," one of the officers muttered, and Holmes sighed.

"Unbelievable. Don't tell me you all have been standing around like a bunch of superstitious school children because you're afraid some unnatural 'dark force' has been keeping Miss Tryrw suspended in the air."

There was a moment of awkward silence, and Holmes shook his head. "Lestrade, the Civic Security Station's hiring standards have dropped drastically over the years. I'm blatantly disappointed by the station's general lack of competency. Apparently I'm going to have to do most of the investigating myself on this case."

He walked over towards the levitating body and stretched out his hand. A sharp crackling sound filled the air, and half the Civic Security inspectors jumped.

Holmes yanked back his hand, but not before Jaymie saw the faint, shimmering outline of an energy orb surrounding Oliviana. Holmes' touch had rendered it visible for the most fleeting of seconds.

"Fascinating," Holmes exclaimed. "It's some sort of invisible force field." He shot the now somewhat sheepish Civic Security officers an admonishing look. "*Not* some sort of dark magic."

"What's generating the shield, though?" Lestrade asked, and Jaymie took a closer look at the body. Now that she knew why it was floating, she found herself feeling less anxious, and she was a little ashamed of herself for panicking. She'd heard the phrase, *There's always a logical explanation for every seemingly illogical phenomenon*, but she was amazed by how easy it was to become spooked or superstitious. She glanced over the body and saw that Oliviana's hands were folded softly on top of her waist, covering up some sort of metal oval.

Holmes spotted it the same time she did.

"Clever," he said. "It's a tiny energy shield generator. Miss Tryrw is holding it, and it's creating a protective orb around her. It'll keep her suspended till it runs out of power, and the force field prevents us from grabbing her before then." He rubbed his chin in thought, pacing around the body. "Yes, very clever indeed; far more clever—and dramatic— than your average Quadrant B criminal is capable of. Someone obviously had a flair for the sensational, and wanted to make a statement with Miss Tryrw's death."

He spun around on his heels and headed back off the stage. "Lestrade, I would like to question each one of the actors individually. While I am gone, please station some of your officers around the body and have them guard it—I want to know the second that shield gives out. It's a job I am sure they can do competently, since they did nothing *but* stare at the body until I arrived." He motioned for Jaymie to follow him. "Watson, come with me. We're going to get to the bottom of this."

Chapter 2: The Interrogation

"So, Mr. Hawkes—tell me about what happened."

Jaymie blinked and struggled to focus as the final actor left to question took a seat in front of her, Holmes, and Lestrade. She had never sat in on an official interrogation before, but it proceeded far more slowly and methodically than the ones she'd seen in crime dramas on the entertainment network. Holmes had questioned each of the actors in turn, and all the interviews were the exactly the same: The actors all seemed to be shocked, saddened, and completely clueless as to why this had occurred. Their stories contained the same set of details, and nothing suspicious or incriminating was brought forward. Jaymie was sure Holmes was a better judge of people than she was, but at least to her, the actors all appeared to be telling the truth. No one seemed to have any idea why someone would want to murder a well-loved actress.

Jaymie was growing frustrated by their apparent lack of progress, but Holmes seemed as cool and patient as ever. He paid just as much attention to every interview, even though the stories were mind-numbingly similar.

He got right to the point with Eben Hawkes, who had played the lead male role opposite Oliviana: "Prince Karsac," Queen Clao's oldest son. Hawkes had bloodshot eyes, and he appeared to be exhausted and in a foul mood. He was still wearing all of his stage makeup, and his bright red lips and powdered skin made him appear somewhat garish under standard lighting. He had dark, curly hair, similar to Oliviana's, which made him look like he really could have been related to her.

"Listen, Mr. Holmes, I'm sure all the other actors have already told you what happened," Hawkes said in a tone that hinted at his sense of irritation. He shifted in his chair, as if trying to find a more comfortable position, but his body remained tense. "Six hours ago, we all showed up at the theatre for tonight's performance in good spirits. Of course we were a little sad this was our last show, but we've known it was coming for a while, and most of us have other jobs lined up by now. The first act of the play was going great—probably the best performance we've ever done. Oliviana was on fire—she's always good, but she seemed even more passionate tonight, all smiles behind the stage during scene breaks and just killing her lines on the stage. She loves this job, and she was the one who was most upset about this theatre being shut down. She's a favorite with the audience and the theatre owners."

"Did you know her well—I mean, personally?" Lestrade cut in. "And do you have any idea how she died or why someone may have wanted to murder her?"

Hawkes shrugged. "We've been acting together for 10 years—of course I know her well. And no, I don't have any idea why someone would want to kill her. I was behind the stage when the murder must have happened, but I didn't hear any sounds of a struggle. It doesn't make any sense to me, and I'm as clueless as anyone else who was here."

Well, Hawkes was right. That was exactly the same story all the other actors had told Holmes, nothing out of the ordinary. However, Holmes had reacted differently this time. His change in posture was subtle, but he had leaned forward slightly, and there was that curious light in his eyes. Something about Hawkes had aroused his interest in a way none of the other actors had.

Holmes studied Hawkes, his eyes narrowing ever so slightly. "Mr. Hawkes, humor me for a moment," he said in a tone that made "humor me" pretty much an order. "Tell me, what is 'Exseloro's Revenge' about?"

Hawkes frowned, looking at Holmes as though he thought he was crazy. "Everybody in this star system already knows the plot to this play. Don't tell me you've never heard of it."

"Oh, I know the story," Holmes said. "I just want to hear you tell it to me."

"What? The lead actress in our play just died, and you want me to take a break and tell you a story?"

"Just do it, please, Mr. Hawkes," Lestrade said, though he shot Holmes a quick look that said, *Do you really know what you're doing?*

Hawkes' face reddened in annoyance, but he sat back and obliged Holmes. "Fine. 'Exseloro's Revenge' is the most famous work by Edvart Piurtewl, a playwright from Itred. It's about Queen Clao, the ruling monarch of a failing empire. A band of marauders from the moon of Yuxilipi are about to invade, and they make her an offer: surrender willingly, and they will spare her life and the lives of her family. However, her family line must commit to being slaves to the ruling clan of the Yuxilipi forever. Queen Clao doesn't want to surrender, but her son, Prince Karsac, her heir, disagrees. He disobeys her orders and contacts the Yuxilipi, agreeing to surrender. Queen Clao is outraged, and feeling trapped, she commits suicide at the end of act one. The Yuxilipi arrive, hear about the story of her death, and are impressed by her bravery. Disgusted by her son's betrayal of her, they slaughter the entire royal family line, forcing Karsac to drink the same type of poison that killed his mother."

"Yes—it's a fascinating story," Holmes said. "Queen Clao really is a magnificent character, though it's been said that her story should have been told by a better writer than Piurtewl. She chose death rather than slavery, refusing to sell her soul for the sake of her mortal life. Tell me, Mr. Hawkes, was Oliviana Tryrw anything like her?"

Hawkes blinked. "I don't understand."

"Miss Tryrw—was she anything like the character she played?" Holmes repeated. "Please try to keep up with the interrogation, Mr. Hawkes. I would have thought someone who makes his living in live theatre would be a little more quick-witted."

Hawkes scowled, Holmes' insult clearly striking a chord. "Yes. That's why she was cast. Oliviana was a very confident and self-assured woman. She ruled that stage like a queen. Yuli Undar, one of the owners of Madame Zinizi's theatre, said it was the part she was born to play."

"Is she the sort of woman who could make the same sort of choice Queen Clao did?" Holmes asked, and Hawkes lurched, a look of disgust on his face.

"No! She wouldn't take her own life, if that's what you're implying. She seemed so happy and energized before the play started, just like a normal day at the theatre. She wanted her last performance to be her best. She was supposed to leave for Itred tomorrow to join an acting troupe there."

"I just have to consider every option," Holmes said. "I don't think suicide is likely here, considering the circumstances of her death.

Judging from the details provided by your fellow actors and the stage hands, she died on the bed right after she said her last lines. No one who works for this theatre moved the furniture, and Oliviana certainly couldn't have done it herself; therefore, it had to be the murderer who removed it and levitated her. But I do think that like Queen Clao, she was killed by poison. There's no blaster wounds on her body, no signs of trauma. It was the easiest option, and makes the most sense. She has to drink a 'vial of poison' as part of the play already—how simple for the killer to substitute actual poison. Anyone in the theatre, including one of her co-stars, could have easily done it."

Hawkes' eyes filled with horror, and his powdered face grew even paler. "No! I know what you're getting at, but I swear, I swear I didn't kill her!" His previously blunt, somewhat antagonistic manner gave way to genuine panic. "You have to believe me—I'm not a murderer!"

"But it *is* your character who gives Queen Clao the glass of wine she later slips her own poison into," Lestrade said. "You were the last known person to handle the chalice before Oliviana drank out of it."

"How can you say that!" Hawkes exclaimed. "Like I said before, Oliviana and I have worked together for years. I would never dream of murdering her. I—" He paused, suddenly seeming vulnerable. "If you had any idea how I felt about…about…" He shook his head, quickly raising his guard again. "Look, it's been a long day, and one of the worst days of my life. Just know that I would never kill one of my co-stars, especially not Oliviana. Please believe me."

Holmes stared at him for a moment longer, that steely pair of eyes—one blue, one brown—trying to delve deep into the actor's soul. Hawkes was attempting to sit still and meet Holmes' piercing gaze, but

Jaymie could see him starting to squirm, and his hands were shaking. Hawkes' breathing became more shallow, more desperate, as if he were afraid this man was going to rip apart his soul with nothing more than a look.

At last, Holmes released him from that terrible gaze, and Hawkes let out an involuntary sigh, sinking back into his chair.

"I believe you," Holmes finally said, rising to his feet. "But I just needed to be sure. All the other actors seemed confused and scared when I questioned them, but you're the first one who's reacted in a hostile manner. Why is that, Mr. Hawkes? I don't think you're the murderer, but you've played a part in this drama besides simply being Miss Tryrw's co-star. What is it?"

"I have nothing to do with this," Hawkes insisted. "I—"

He was interrupted by the sound of heavy footsteps, and one of Lestrade's Civic Security officers came dashing into the room.

"Lestrade—the force field failed!" he exclaimed. "You'd better come see this."

"Mr. Hawkes, wait here for a moment," Lestrade ordered as he and the others rushed out to the stage. "And Inspector Croff, watch him and make sure he doesn't leave until we're done with the investigation."

As they ran into the grand hall, they discovered Oliviana lying on the stage, no longer suspended by the orb of energy. Her arms had fallen limply at her sides, and the tiny energy shield generator had rolled out of her hands and had come to a stop at the edge of the stage. The woman's skin was a ghostly pale color, but she had a peaceful look on her face. At least she didn't appear to have died in pain.

Holmes walked over to the body, kneeling beside the murdered actress and waving at Jaymie to come over and join him.

"Come here, Watson," he said. "I'd like your medical opinion on what you think happened here."

"Um, I don't know," Jaymie said a little hesitantly. *I'm a doctor, not a coroner*—and those were two very different things. She didn't even know what she was supposed to be looking for.

"Well, she's dead," Jaymie said at last, and Holmes rolled his eyes.

"It took five years of undergraduate study for you to be able to tell me that?" He sighed. "And to think there are still some who extol the virtues of public education."

"This isn't really my line of work," Jaymie said tersely. She was tempted to explain in great detail exactly what she *was* studying and how she probably knew a few things that even he, with all his genius, didn't know, but she wasn't going to play that game with him. Even if she was a little miffed by his sarcasm, she was determined to remain professional. "But I do think you're right about the poison."

She knelt next to the body and gave it a quick examination, finding no bruises or anything out of the ordinary. "The autopsy will reveal more, of course."

"True—but I think the body reveals plenty of details about the crime right now." He leaned in closer to the body and carefully pried open the woman's mouth, sniffing inside it—much to Jaymie's amazement and disgust. Then, he brushed his finger across Oliviana's lips, picking up a thin white powder.

"Just as I suspected," Holmes said. "It's cavlrun, a byproduct of the illicit drug tampor, a popular choice for murder by poison. Tasteless when consumed, it leaves a metallic tang in the mouth after death and this white film on the lips and tongue. Frankly, I'm a little disappointed. Cavlrun is such an obvious choice for a seemingly unconventional killer. I had hoped for something a little more clever."

He glanced up and saw Jaymie giving him a disturbed look. "What?"

"Holmes, this is a murder!" she said. "Don't you think you're being a little too blasé?"

Lestrade shook his head. "Sorry, Jaymie, but you'll have to get used to this. Holmes isn't exactly the poster child for compassion, and after spending some time with him, you'll learn he unfortunately lacks some features shared by most normal, decent beings—namely, a soul."

One of the Civic Security officers snickered, then quickly straightened and snapped to attention once again as soon as he saw Holmes' glare.

"Why am I always the one who is chided for being blasé at crimes scenes, when everyone else seems to find great amusement in insulting me?" Holmes asked, but Lestrade merely grinned.

"We're trying to keep you humble—and trust me, it's not an easy job."

"Commoners," Holmes muttered. He continued searching the body, gently lifting Miss Tryrw and examining her clothes for any details they may have missed. As he lifted her, Jaymie saw something small and sparkling fall out of the woman's pocket.

"Look at this!" She picked up the object, and Holmes and Lestrade leaned over her shoulder as she examined it. It was a platinum pendant of some sort, suspended from a chain that appeared to have been recently broken. There was a slit in its side, and Jaymie guessed the pendant probably opened up, like a locket. The pendant had a lovely scrollwork design on the front: a black rose etched into the dark gray metal.

"I think it's a hologram locket," she exclaimed. She pressed a button on the back, and the locket popped open. In the air above the locket a tiny picture materialized of a man with dark skin and brilliant violet eyes. He was handsome, with chiseled features and high cheekbones, and his long hair was gathered in a ponytail at the nape of his neck. Jaymie didn't recognize the face, and it was clear Holmes and Lestrade didn't either.

"Anyone know who this is?" Lestrade asked, but the actors who were still standing around the stage shook their heads, seemingly equally puzzled.

"Now the plot thickens," Holmes muttered, taking the hologram locket from Jaymie and staring at the tiny projection. "Whoever this is likely was very important to Miss Tryrw, significant enough for her to carry around an expensive piece of jewelry with his picture in it. And yet not one of her co-stars here seems to know who this man is. The chain is snapped, and she didn't bother to fix it—or didn't have time to before she died." He frowned slightly. "I'd very much like to see if—"

"Um...sir?"

They heard a hesitant voice behind them, and they all turned around.

Inspector Croff, the Civic Security officer who was supposed to have been guarding Eben Hawkes, was standing rather sheepishly behind them with what was shaping up to be a rather ghastly black eye.

"Mr. Holmes? We sort of…have a problem. Mr. Hawkes has, well, escaped."

Chapter 3: The Drunk Gypsy

Hours later, Jaymie found herself trudging through the muck in a back alley in Quadrant B, struggling, yet again, to keep up with Holmes. It was sprinkling now, and the chill dampness in the air seemed to seep right through her thin jacket, making her shiver.

Although Holmes and Lestrade had rushed outside as soon as Inspector Croff brought them the news, it was too late to catch Eben Hawkes. Apparently he had been sitting in the interrogation room quite calmly, until one of the Civic Security officers had called Croff's comlink and mentioned a hologram locket had been found. Hawkes had suddenly attacked Croff, giving him a black eye and then fleeing from the room. Holmes and Lestrade had searched the streets outside Madame Zinizi's Theatre, but Hawkes had gotten too good of a head start and was nowhere to be found.

Holmes had taken this setback in a surprisingly serene manner, and he now seemed very preoccupied with the hologram locket. Lestrade and his team finished processing the crime scene and obtained a warrant for Eben Hawkes' arrest, although his recapture was unlikely. In Quadrant B, it was far too easy to lose track of beings who didn't want to be found. Holmes had requested he be allowed to hang on to just one piece of evidence—the locket—and had announced he was going on a walk and asked Jaymie to come with him.

And so now the two of them were walking through a seemingly endless series of dank, dark alleys long past midnight, and Holmes had yet to fill her in on any of his thoughts, despite her repeated attempts to get him to tell her where they were going.

"Do you still really believe Hawkes is innocent?" she asked, trying to jump over a puddle of gooey sludge but not really succeeding, splashing mud on her chilz leather boots. Her mother would kill her if she knew the abuse these shoes had gone through after she had given them to Jaymie as a yuletide present a year ago. These boots were designed for rich girls who wanted to go on "high society" outings in the countryside (the sort where there was as little contact with dirt and nature as possible)—not amateur investigators crawling through alleyways.

"Absolutely," Holmes said. "Or at least, of the murder itself."

"But you have to admit, his behavior was very suspicious this evening," Jaymie insisted. "I mean, he wasn't exactly cooperative during your interrogation, and then he punched poor Inspector Croff and fled the crime scene. Those don't really sound like things an innocent person would do. How do you actually know he's not guilty?"

"It's…difficult to explain," Holmes said slowly. "I'm just sure about this one. Oh, I know he's not completely innocent—he wouldn't have run if he was. But I'm very sure he didn't commit murder, and he had no desire to harm Miss Tryrw. Acting suspicious is merely one sign of a guilty conscience—it's by no means a clincher. Just think about it—what motive, really, does Hawkes have to kill Oliviana? None of the other actors noticed any bad blood between them, and he has no reason to get rid of her. If they were both divas of the stage, competing for the same roles, then I'd be more willing to suspect him of murder. And as I said, I…I've just got an inkling about this one. Now, the picture of a man no one seems to know hidden inside a locket found on the dead woman's body—*that's* a far more telling clue. I'm hoping if we can catch

Hawkes, and put his *real* version of the story together with the story of the man whose picture is in the locket, we can find out what really happened."

"But you told Lestrade you didn't know who the man in the locket was," Jaymie said, and Holmes nodded.

"No. But I know someone who will."

They exited the alleyway, and there in front of them was a little hole-in-the-wall pub called the "Drunk Gypsy." Or at least, that's what Jaymie assumed the pub's name was. The holo-sign hanging above the doorway was damaged, and not all of the letters were properly displayed on the screen. The pub didn't have much of a door, either: it still had an old-fashioned, non-automatic metal door with broken hinges that didn't even allow it to close all the way.

"Um, Holmes, are you sure about this?" Jaymie asked, and Holmes looked at her, puzzled.

"Of course. I would never bring you to a place I didn't believe we could get out of safely. It's been at least three years since someone tried to assault me here, and there is another exit at the back, in case we need to make a hasty escape."

"That's very comforting," Jaymie said sarcastically. "I'm guessing whoever your source is doesn't frequently rub shoulders with Civic Security."

"Padric O'Vax has been a bartender in Quadrant B for more than 30 years," Holmes explained. "He knows everybody who's anybody in Quadrant B, a group which admittedly consists mostly of criminals. Since Lestrade and his team had no idea who the man in the locket was, it probably means he's not an upstanding citizen, or an incompetent criminal, which is the only sort of criminal Civic Security seems capable of apprehending."

Holmes started to enter the club, but Jaymie grabbed his arm and pulled him back.

"Look, Holmes, as much as I don't want you to go in there alone, I'm not sure I should be here."

"Why?" Holmes asked. "Don't you want to get to the bottom of this?"

"Of course I do. I want justice for Oliviana Tryrw, but I don't know if I can keep tagging along on cases like this. I'm not a professional, and I have to focus on my schooling. I've got this big test tomorrow, and it's already past midnight. I don't want to flunk my first test because I'm exhausted."

"But you can't go yet," Holmes said. "I may still have need of you."

"Of me? But why?" Jaymie couldn't help asking. "You're a professional investigator, and I'm just a graduate student. If you need an assistant, fine, I understand that. But why draft me? I'm nothing special." She had wanted to state it calmly, but a slight hint of bitterness slipped through. She could hear her mother's lectures all over again, telling her how disappointed she was in Jaymie's decision to pursue an education as a medical doctor, instead of joining the family's highly profitable law firm or marrying some rich, mindless businessman and spending the rest of her days as a trophy wife.

"Because you're perfect for the job," Holmes replied. "You're capable, have shown an ability to not give into insane panic in tense situations, and you have, I believe, the potential to someday exceed the level of average intelligence shared by most beings in this universe."

"Wow, thanks," Jaymie said, and Holmes nodded.

"You're welcome."

Jaymie sighed. "Holmes, that was sarcasm. Telling me I'm pretty much an idiot now but do have the potential to one day actually become intelligent is not the best way to recruit me."

Holmes appeared thoughtful, letting his gaze wander past Jaymie and down the length of the alley. "If you want to go back to the flat to study for your test, I will not stop you," he said finally. "And if you want to spend your time on Eglon as an ordinary student, I promise—for the most part—that I won't interfere. But what I'm trying to do is offer you a chance to go beyond that: to become something extraordinary."

He turned and strode into the pub, probably not even caring he was putting his personal safety at risk.

Jaymie paused, her emotions at war within her. She didn't know why she found trailing Holmes so bloody intriguing, but she couldn't let her academics suffer. She should just head back to the flat now and let Holmes pursue this on his own. But something he had said had truly resonated with her. *The chance to become something extraordinary.* What did he mean—really? That somehow her destiny should be tied up with his, that something better was waiting for her down the same path he was following? Was that path truly better than the path she had chosen for herself through the University of Medical Arts?

Go back, Jaymie, the voice of reason told her, and she knew she should listen. But somehow, she didn't want to. Even though at the time she had tried to brush off her mother's bitter words, they still lingered inside her like a poison, causing her to doubt her every move. She knew her mother would not approve of her hanging around Holmes any more than she had approved of Jaymie wanting to become a doctor, but Jaymie wanted so badly to believe that what Holmes had said about her destiny was true. Not once in her life had she ever felt extraordinary—until she had met Sherlock Holmes, and she experienced a spark inside her that just might be the beginnings of something special.

All right, Holmes, I'll take you up on that offer, she thought. She squared her shoulders and marched into the pub after him. *I'll make a gamble.*

She glanced one more time at the alleyway behind her, but she no longer feared it, or the darkness of Quadrant B.

And it was the last time she ever looked back.

#

Jaymie coughed slightly as she stepped into the bar, clouds of smoke from exotic pipes billowing around her and creating swirling patterns in the air. She waved her hand, trying to dispel some of the hazy mist in front of her. She finally spotted Holmes leaning up against the bar, where a tall, fair-haired man was just slinging him a pint full of dark ale. The bartender looked almost human, except for the fact that he had four arms and large, dark-colored spots on his skin. He appeared to be in his late 30s, although for many humanoids, looks could be deceiving. The Gerfrians aged backwards, appearing younger as they grew older, and the Odon never looked older than teenagers, even though they lived for hundreds of years. Jaymie had a feeling this particular bartender was a lot older than he appeared; his eyes were deep, having the look of someone who had experienced a great deal in his lifetime. She assumed this had to be Padric O'Vax.

"So what brings you to my pub after midnight, Mr. Holmes?" she heard the bartender ask, and Holmes shrugged.

"The same thing as always, Padric—information. Surely you don't think I keep coming back for a pint of the worst beer in the galaxy."

Padric laughed, wiping his four hands on his apron. "Such a charming one you are, Mr. Holmes." He glanced up and saw Jaymie watching them, and he raised an eyebrow. "Ah—don't tell me you've got another lady friend, Mr. Holmes? I would have thought after—"

"This is Jaymie Watson, my assistant," Holmes said, quickly cutting him off. For the slightest second, he looked almost uncomfortable, but he breezed through the moment so fast, Jaymie wasn't sure if she had just imagined it. "She's helping me on the Oliviana Tryrw case."

"Yes—a sad story, it is," Padric said, grabbing a bottle of blue Yopilian liquor and starting to mix up a drink for another customer. "Never saw her perform myself, but heard only the highest praise about her from my customers."

"You mean...you've heard about it already?" Jaymie asked in surprise. "But the murder happened just a few hours ago!"

"I have very reliable networks of information," Padric said, flashing her a knowing grin. "News has a way of getting to me very fast."

Holmes took out the platinum locket and handed it to Padric, who examined it curiously.

"Seen anything like this before?" Holmes asked, and Padric nodded.

"Yes, but not in years." He held the locket closer to one of the softly glowing lamps hanging above his head. "See this black rose? It was the symbol for a group of pirates from Itred who used to be the scourge of this sector. Then infighting broke up the gang, and they haven't been heard from in at least ten years." He pressed the button on the back, and as the locket popped open and the picture appeared, his eyes widened in shock.

"What the bloody devil?" He snapped the locket shut and shot a fierce glance at Holmes. "Where did you get this?"

"It was inside Oliviana's pocket," Holmes said. "None of the actors, or any of the Civic Security inspectors, knew who the man in the picture was. I'm guessing you do?"

Padric set down the drink he was mixing and waved one of the other bartenders over, a purple-skinned Udorian female. "Finish this for me, would you?" he asked her, then motioned for Holmes and Jaymie to follow him to the back of the pub. "This isn't the sort of conversation we should be having in public."

Padric led them through the pub to a tiny room in the back, presumably his office. Like the rest of the pub, it was dimly lit; the overhead light had burned out some time ago, and Padric had apparently never bothered to replace it. An antiquated computer sat on the desk, along with stacks of yellowing papers and a beat-up lumi-lamp that shed dingy-colored lighting on the desk.

Padric sank back into a lounge chair with a sigh. "Of course none of the actors or Lestrade's yes-men recognized the man in that picture. I'm not even supposed to know who he is, and I'd be a dead man if they ever found out that I did. His name is Jok Urdi, and you may soon wish you didn't know it either." He pointed to the black rose symbol on the front of the locket, then opened the pendant back up, revealing the picture. "Remember that group of pirates from Itred I was telling you about? Well, Urdi used to be the first mate on the pirate gang's flagship, *The Prydion Skye*. He staged an unsuccessful mutiny which eventually led to the collapse of the organization. Supposedly the captain killed him, and for ten years nothing was heard about him. Then recently, I've been hearing rumors—and mind you, they're rumors *only*. But there's supposedly a new tampor-smuggling ring that's started up in Quadrant B, super-secret, the type where beings only know the person behind them and the person in front of them in the smuggling chain, and if you do anything to compromise the organization, you're dead before you can even begin to reflect on how stupid you were. And the man in the hologram—Jok Urdi—is supposedly the head of this new smuggling ring."

"So you think Jok Urdi is connected to Oliviana Tryrw?" Jaymie asked. "That seems impossible. Why would a talented actress get involved with a pirate and drug runner?"

"I just pass along information, I don't speculate," Padric said, handing the locket back to Holmes. "But you can bet a million quid Miss Tryrw wouldn't be carrying around this pendant unless she had some kind of significant understanding—probably romantic in nature—with Urdi. And by the way, you might want to find a convenient way to lose this pendant, considering the last person who had it wound up dead."

Jaymie felt an icy chill grip her heart, but Holmes seemed unperturbed. He slipped the locket back into his pocket and then stood up, tossing Padric a handful of quid.

"Thank you, Padric. You've been most illuminating, as always."

Padric shook his head. "And let me guess, now you're going to stick your nose into business you have no business sticking it into."

Holmes grinned. "I'm a private investigator—the business of criminals *is* my business. And you know me—I'm very good at ignoring words of warning."

Oh, how true that *is,* Jaymie thought.

She and Holmes quietly made their way back out of the Drunk Gypsy, for the most part ignored by the other patrons. Jaymie's mind, however, was spinning. *An actress the lover of a high-profile drug runner?* It seemed a crazy leap of logic, but the more time she spent with Holmes, the less things seemed to shock her.

"So what do we do now?" Jaymie asked as they stepped back into the gloomy alley outside the pub. "Find Jok Urdi?"

"Eventually, yes," Holmes said. "But honestly, something's still bothering me, and I bloody wish Hawkes hadn't dashed off. I still think he's—"

It happened so fast Jaymie barely even had time to react. A man in a black trench coat suddenly darted out from behind the building and jumped at Holmes. Jaymie screamed, and Holmes glanced around just in time to see the mysterious attacker and dodge out of the way. The man stumbled but quickly regained his footing, coming at Holmes again with his fists swinging. His first punch landed on Holmes' jaw, but Holmes ducked the next one and delivered a solid punch of his own, hitting the attacker squarely in the gut and knocking the wind out of him. The man pulled out a blaster and aimed it at Holmes, and Jaymie's heart leapt. She picked up a heavy piece of debris from a pile of trash and threw it at Holmes' attacker, knocking him over.

Holmes quickly pinned the man to the ground and wrested the gun out of his grip, tossing it to Jaymie. The man continued to struggle, but

Holmes' grip was too tight, and he was helpless to resist as Holmes pulled back the hood obscuring the man's face.

"Eben Hawkes?" Jaymie asked, stunned as she recognized the dark-haired actor.

"You know, for a man who keeps claiming to be innocent, you are making it increasingly difficult for people to believe you," Holmes said. His chest was heaving, a sign he was quite out of breath from his efforts. "Care to explain why you tried to kill me, or would you prefer I simply call Lestrade and have him give you a ride back to some lovely and most likely permanent accommodations in the Civic Security Station prison block?"

Hawkes coughed, reaching up to brush away the trickle of blood that was running down his face from a cut he had received when he hit his head on the ground. "I wasn't trying to kill you—that's only a stun blaster. I just wanted to scare you off. You don't know what you're getting into, and I was actually attempting to help you."

Jaymie examined the blaster Holmes had tossed her, and sure enough, it was only a stun weapon. Hawkes was telling the truth, though this situation was making progressively less and less sense.

Holmes released Hawkes from his grip, and the man sat up, moaning.

"Well, since most people don't attempt to save me by *shooting* me, care to explain what your reasoning is?" Holmes said.

Hawkes' eyes darted around, and Jaymie feared he was going to bolt, and she put her finger around the trigger of the stun blaster. Hawkes noticed what she was doing, and the panicked look in his eyes turned to one of resignation.

"Fine. I don't want you to investigate this case," he said. "But obviously, you're not going to listen to me, so I might as well tell you everything. And maybe ultimately you'll get me a little less jail time if I cooperate—"

"That's a conversation you'll have to have with Inspector Lestrade," Holmes said. "But I believe you will tell me everything you know anyway, because I'm sensing that despite whatever you've done that's going to earn you jail time—in addition to trying to assault me, of course—what you really want is justice for Miss Tryrw. And maybe revenge on Jok Urdi?"

Hawkes blinked in surprise. "You know him? But how…" He shook his head. "Never mind. I don't care how you know. I don't know how much digging you've done, but I'll confirm that Urdi is back. He faked his death ten years ago and has slowly been building a drug empire back on Itred, and recently expanded it here to Eglon." He let out a heavy sigh. "You'll tell me I'm stupid, and yes, I already know: I got involved as a drug runner. At first it was just to earn a little extra money, to survive. We found out Madame Zinizi's Theatre was closing, and I panicked. Everybody else seemed to be finding other jobs, but I couldn't. Drug running pays good money—really good money—and I got caught up in the system. Unfortunately, Oliviana did too. I guess we were both really good at it, and we began working our way up through the ranks of the organization. Oliviana was even better than me, and she even caught Urdi's attention. As you've probably guessed after discovering the locket, she ultimately became his lover. But it never sat right with her, or me either. I began dumping all my drugs in the river and paying for them myself instead of selling them, because I felt guilty. I encouraged her to get out—to leave Urdi. I...I fell in love with her, though I don't think she ever noticed, or would have returned my love even if she did. Finally, I was offered a job with an acting company on Itred, but I offered to give it to her instead if she got out. She agreed, and told Urdi she was leaving. He was livid, threatening that she'd be sorry if she left. She left anyway, and told me the whole story about what had happened." Hawkes glanced away, his hardened expression breaking down and tears glistening in his eyes. "I begged her to get out of Quadrant B right away, to skip the last performance of 'Exseloro's Revenge,' but she couldn't do it. She wanted to give one last performance."

"And unfortunately, it became the last performance of her life," Holmes said. "Is it your belief Urdi had her poisoned?"

Hawkes nodded. "He wanted to keep her quiet, and probably scare me into keeping quiet too. That's the reason for the dramatic murder—if he hadn't wanted to intimidate me, he would have probably just killed her in some alley and hidden the body. " He shuddered, glancing away from Holmes. "It's a terrible business, and I know I've already ruined my career. I don't have the right to care about it anymore, I understand that. I just hope something I've told you helps bring Urdi down."

"You've been marginally helpful," Holmes conceded. "Although really, I could have deduced most of what you said from the evidence we already observed back at the theatre."

Hawkes looked perplexed. "Really?"

"Of course. Some kind of drug involvement seemed inevitable as soon as I spotted the tiny force field generator. Those are a favorite tool of drug runners—very useful for lifting large quantities of drugs and protecting them during that process. The force fields are maneuvered using these convenient little remote controllers; you just switch on the force field, use it to levitate the objects, then steer those suspended objects and load them onto a ship. If anyone tries to steal the drugs, they will be zapped by the field. Also, another clue drugs were involved was the fact Miss Tryrw was poisoned by cavlrun. Although other criminals have access to the chemical, it makes sense it would be a tampor dealer. It's logical Oliviana's killer was involved in the drug trade, and therefore, not too big a leap to assume she also was dealing drugs, and something most likely went wrong. However, I do appreciate you confirming all these facts for me. It's always nice to know I'm on track."

Hawkes gaped at Holmes, his expression a mixture of wonder and disgust. "I don't get it—how...how do you do that?" He turned to Jaymie. "Is he always like this?"

"Oh, this is tame by his standards," Jaymie said. "His arrogance truly knows no bounds."

Holmes gave her an admonishing glare. "I'm not arrogant—I'm simply always right."

Hawkes started to protest, and Jaymie—desperately wanting to avoid allowing him to get involved in what would likely be a lengthy and pointless argument with Holmes—quickly changed the subject.

"So why did you try to attack us, Mr. Hawkes?" she asked. "Why didn't you just tell Holmes the truth in the first place?"

"Because I didn't want the fact Oliviana was a drug runner coming to light," Hawkes said bitterly. "Do you have any idea what this will do to her reputation? I wanted her to be remembered as the brilliant artist that she is—not a criminal."

Jaymie sensed he was starting to become hostile once again, and she was afraid he was going to lock down. Holmes seemed to think he had figured out all the important details in the case by now, but Jaymie just wanted to make sure. Hawkes might be holding onto some final, important detail, and if they badgered him too much, he might take it with him—stubborn and silent—to jail.

"I can understand what you're going through, and I'm sorry for your loss," Jaymie said, kneeling down beside him and putting her hand on his shoulder. "We're not going to be able to keep the truth about Oliviana from coming out, but I think society will be more forgiving of her than you think. After all, even though she spent some time in the drug business, she left willingly, and that has to count for something."

Hawkes bit his lip, and she saw him blink several times in succession, embarrassed by the fact he was fighting back tears and couldn't conceal it. "We'll see," he said, but Jaymie could tell her words had touched him and given him a flicker of hope.

"Did Urdi attend the performance this evening?" Holmes asked. "Did you see any of his operatives back stage before the show, where they might have had access to the vial Oliviana later drank from?"

Hawkes shook his head, but Holmes didn't seem too discouraged.

"That's probably to be expected. If Urdi's as good as he's supposed to be, he wouldn't have had trouble slipping an agent into a low-security theatre and making sure that agent remained undetected. Do you know where Urdi is now?"

Hawkes' face paled slightly. "Oh no. I'm not going to take you to his secret compound."

"Well, it's now less of a secret because you just told me a compound does, in fact, exist," Holmes said. "And I'm going to try to find it whether you help me or not, and your assistance might increase the chances of me making it out alive, which I would very much prefer."

"You know what, Mr. Holmes," Hawkes said, "you're crazy enough that I'm starting to believe you really could figure out a way to march into that compound, arrest Urdi, and come back out completely unscathed. Look, I can't take you there personally—Urdi's thugs would just pump me full of blaster bolts the second they caught a glimpse of my face. But I can tell you how to get there. I'm just warning you: You'd better plan on bringing a lot more back-up than just an insane, narcissistic private investigator and his assistant."

Chapter 4: Caught in the Act

Jaymie sat hunched against the side of a warehouse on the far northern edge of Quadrant B, trying not to think about how uncomfortable she was. Her pants were soaking wet from a puddle she had accidently sat in, and she had burning eyes and a splitting headache, yet another reminder of how sleep-deprived she was. Holmes and Lestrade crouched near her, arguing quietly about whether or not they should have trusted Hawkes' instructions. The whole situation reminded her a little too much of slinking around the dark alleys near the Sunset Enterprises factory, and it wasn't exactly a pleasant memory. The only difference here was that in addition to her, Lestrade, and Holmes, there were also at least a dozen Civic Security inspectors waiting around a corner. And none of them were too thrilled with Holmes' suggestion that he and Jaymie be allowed to enter Urdi's secret compound alone and unarmed. Personally, Jaymie wasn't too fond of that idea herself.

"Holmes, this is insane!" Lestrade hissed for at least the third time, and once again, Holmes disregarded him.

"Is that your only objection?" Holmes asked. "Because you know as well as I do that we've faced worse odds before, and 'insane' is not the worst thing I've ever been called."

Lestrade ran a hand through his hair and drew in a long, slow breath, an indication he was hovering on the edge of losing his temper. "One of these days, I'm just going to wash my hands of you, Holmes. What guarantee do you have you're not going to get inside that compound and then have Urdi's thugs vaporize you with blasters?"

"I don't have one," Holmes said. "At least not concrete enough to please you. I simply believe Urdi won't allow his men to do that."

Lestrade sucked in a sharp breath. "You have no idea how much I've gambled on your hunches, Holmes."

"Your job, your life, your hovercar—trust me, you've reminded me on *multiple* occasions how much you've—"

"Holmes!"

"All right, all right, think about this logically: Urdi will be shocked when Jaymie and I show up. He won't shoot us right away, because he'll want to know how the security leak in his organization came about. If he just kills us, he'll never know, and trust me, he'll *want* to know."

Jaymie breathed a quiet sigh of relief. That did make sense, and it did make her feel better about the plan.

"Now granted, as soon as he knows who we are and why we've come, then he'll have no problem vaporizing us," Holmes added, which quickly deflated the very meager positive feelings Jaymie was starting to have about this mission.

"He's barking mad," she heard one of the Civic Security officers mumble, and neither Jaymie nor Lestrade rushed to stand up for Holmes.

"Thanks for the support," Holmes commented dryly, glancing at his "friends." "Now come on, we're wasting time. Lestrade, you know about the rest of the plan: don't raid the building until my signal. If I press the panic button on my comlink once, that means I want a stealth raid, and you should come in slowly and carefully, catching Urdi off guard. If, however, things go very badly very quickly, I will press the panic button twice, in which case I don't care how stealthy you are: just come in, and come in NOW. Understood?"

Lestrade cursed under his breath, but he nodded. Holmes started towards the building, and Jaymie found herself following him, falling right into his crazy plan. However, Lestrade grabbed her arm and made her stop for a moment, a look of deep concern in his eyes.

"Look, I know the fact we share rent for Mrs. Hudson's flat doesn't give me the right to give you advice or tell you how to live your life," he said. "I've only know you for a couple of weeks, but I've known Holmes a lot longer. Odds are, he's going to go in and come back out just fine; I don't know how he does it, but somehow that man seems to have nothing but amazing luck. You'll probably be fine too, but I want you to take in the meaning of that word: *probably*. Holmes seems to have latched onto the idea of having you as an assistant, and he'll have your back inside that compound. But you *will* be in danger, and no one will think you're a coward if you wait back here with us."

Jaymie nodded. "I know, and I appreciate what you're saying. But for some crazy reason, I trust him."

Lestrade sighed. "I had a feeling you'd say that." He pulled one of the blasters out of his double holster and slipped it to her. "Well, if you're going to go, at least take this. I know Holmes doesn't want you to take any weapons inside, but trust me, all of us out here will feel better if you have something."

Jaymie's hand trembled a little as she took the cold, metal weapon, but she forced herself to keep up a brave face. "Thanks, Lestrade," she said, and desperately hoped she wouldn't have to use it.

Tucking the blaster into her jacket, she hurried to catch up to Holmes as he sneaked up to the front of the building. He took a quick glance around the corner and then darted back, pressing himself up against the side of the warehouse.

"There are two guards standing at the entrance," he said with a sigh. "How predictable. Nothing says, 'This abandoned warehouse isn't *really* an abandoned warehouse, it's actually a crime lord's secret hideout' quite like two solemn-faced thugs with blaster rifles guarding the front. Honestly, these crime lords would remain undetected far longer if they put some effort into being subtle."

"So how are we going to sneak in?" Jaymie asked, and Holmes gave her a puzzled look.

"Sneak in? I planned to just walk up to the guards and let them capture us. They'll slap electro-binders on us, and then take us to see Urdi."

"What?" Jaymie exclaimed. "You know, Holmes, it would be really nice if you clued me in on some of your plans ahead of time. Then I might not actually volunteer for them."

"Nonsense," Holmes said. "You'd come anyway. Besides, I think deep down you enjoy the suspense."

"Holmes!"

But it was too late. He was already marching towards the entrance, immediately alerting the guards to his presence. One of the guards leveled his blaster rifle at Holmes and ordered him to stop.

"What are you doing here?" the guard said. "I've never seen you before—you're not authorized to be in this area."

"I have a deal to make with Jok Urdi," Holmes said. "I think he'll be most eager to talk to me."

The guard frowned. "I doubt that. Why don't you get out of here and stop wasting our time? And I'd make it fast, or else you'll be leaving with a few blaster burns as souvenirs."

"I can see why you're a henchman," Holmes remarked. "Wit is not your specialty."

The guard's eyes flashed angrily, and he wrapped his finger around the trigger of his gun.

"You're a real comedian, aren't you?" he told Holmes. "Too bad this will be your last performance—"

"Wait—we've come to talk to Urdi about Oliviana Tryrw!" Jaymie burst out suddenly, and the guard blinked, lowering his gun in surprise. He hurriedly whispered something to the other guard, who in turn pressed several buttons on his comlink, obviously some kind of code. Seconds later, a reply of several beeps came back.

"You're supposed to come inside," the other guard said gruffly, though Jaymie thought she could now see a slightly uneasy look in the man's eyes. He pulled out two pairs of electro-binders. "But unfortunately, you'll have to wear these."

Chapter 5: All the World's a Stage

Surprisingly, the warehouse was, for the most part, empty. It was a purely utilitarian building, consisting of one wide, open room with a scuffed metal floor and a few crates sitting around. It was lit by blistering white overhead lights, and at the far end of the room was a desk and a small, open-cockpit hovercraft. It didn't look like Urdi kept many illegal drugs in stock, but that was somewhat expected. Drug runners tended to move product in and out rather quickly, so in case there was ever a raid on a hideout, there wouldn't be anything for Civic Security to find.

Jaymie must have been dawdling and glancing around for too long, because one of the thugs grabbed her arm and yanked her forward. The electro-binders shifted, slightly burning her skin, and she gritted her teeth. The guard smiled when he saw her in pain, but she fought to keep her face expressionless and appear calmer than she felt. Inside, she could feel her heart pounding madly, and she had to keep reminding herself of Holmes' assurance that they would be fine, and that he had everything under control. She could still feel the hard metal point of her blaster pressing up against her ribs from where it rested in the pocket of her jacket. She had no idea why the thugs hadn't bothered to search her and Holmes, but she supposed the blaster wouldn't really do her any good anyway, since both her hands were now bound.

She saw a man emerge from a back room, and instantly she recognized him as Jok Urdi. He was wearing a suit of chilz leather, the same expensive fabric as Jaymie's boots but in far better condition. He was also wearing diamond cufflinks, and a platinum wristband comlink that probably cost more than most middle-class citizens made in a year. Jaymie herself came from an affluent family, but she had never liked people who so shamelessly and condescendingly flaunted their wealth. Urdi was obviously one of those people. Although in the picture inside Oliviana's holo-locket his features had appeared noble, in person those same features were more rigid and harsh. His hair was pulled up in a tight topknot, a style popular in the Yopilian culture he had come from. His eyebrows were bunched together, and a dark cloud of irritation billowed in his eyes.

"So…these are our spies?" he asked, glancing at Jaymie and Holmes with a look of disgust. "Who are you, and why have you come here asking after this woman named…what was it? 'Olivia' or something like that?"

"I'm sorry, but it's too late to play innocent," Holmes replied. "If you hadn't known her, you wouldn't have called us in so quickly. You may decide to kill us, but please, don't insult our intelligence."

Urdi stared at them for a moment, and then unexpectedly, a hint of a smile flickered across his face. "Cheeky. You're not an average sort of Civic Security officer, are you?"

"I'm a private investigator," Holmes corrected him. "Assigned to the case of poor Miss Oliviana Tryrw, whom you had murdered this evening."

Urdi's eyes flashed. "And what makes you think you have proof of this?" He looked over at his thugs. "You know, I take back what I said. I don't want to know how this man knows what he *thinks* he knows. Just shoot him."

"So you'll not be wanting your locket back, then," Holmes said, and Urdi's eye twitched. It was only the slightest of movements, but Jaymie had a feeling that, at least for him, it was very telling. As a drug lord, he had probably learned to be much like a gambler: it was all a game of bluffing, lying, and never letting your opposition doubt you had the upper hand. It was deadly to reveal a sense of surprise or even the slightest indication you were losing control of the situation. And that's exactly what that little twitch had done.

"My what?" Urdi asked, feigning ignorance.

"We found a platinum locket engraved with a black rose on Miss Tryrw's body," Holmes said. "And in case you're wondering, no, I wasn't stupid enough to bring it with me. I left it with my good friend Inspector Lestrade, who coincidentally enough is now waiting outside with a squad of about twenty Civic Security officers, ready to raid this facility at any moment. It looks like you've overplayed this hand, Mr. Urdi, and the game, I'm afraid, is over."

Urdi swore and whipped out his blaster, pressing the point of the gun to Holmes' forehead. Jaymie stifled back a scream at Urdi's rather sudden and violent reaction, but Holmes flinched only slightly as the drug lord waved his blaster in front of his face.

"Call off your goons, or I'll shoot you," Urdi snapped, and Holmes merely shrugged.

"Trust me—that isn't the best threat. Most of the officers in Civic Security hate me, so using me as a hostage will be highly ineffective. They'll just let you shoot me, then come in here and shoot you and your men. I'll just be collateral damage."

"You're bluffing," Urdi said, and Jaymie desperately hoped that, at least in this instance, the crime lord was right.

"You can't know for sure," Holmes said. "That's the irritating thing about life—so many of our actions are based on assumptions we're forced to make. You have no proof I have back-up outside, just as I have no solid proof you killed Miss Tryrw. We have to take—or not take—each other at our word. However, I know enough about you now and the details surrounding this case that I feel very comfortable making the accusation you are indeed guilty."

Jaymie watched Urdi's face for any tell-tale expressions, but his face remained as hard as a stone statue's, with the exception of his very alert and very piercing eyes. He seemed to be making an extra effort to keep his emotions hidden.

"Granted, you must be very good at what you do, because I'd never heard of you before, and I make it my business to be in the know about all of the high-profile slime slinking around Quadrant B," Holmes went on. "You've managed to stay under my radar, which isn't easy. But you made a mistake, as all criminals eventually do. I don't care whether you're a petty thief or a powerful crime lord—eventually, you all slip up. And too often, it's because of a woman: in your case, Oliviana Tryrw. I don't know how you met her—maybe you attended one of her plays and were transfixed by her performance, or something like that, and then you recruited her to join your organization when you learned she was worried about her financial future. Or maybe you didn't fall in love with her until after she came to work for your organization. She was a beautiful woman, probably intrigued by the prospect of romancing a 'dashing rogue,' but she just wasn't cut from the same cloth as you. She didn't like where the relationship was taking her, so she tried to leave you. You were angry and tried to take back the necklace you gave her, but it broke and she got away. So, you did what you likely do to all your agents that go rogue: you got rid of her. And now that makes you a pirate, a drug runner, *and* a murderer."

Urdi's jaw tightened slightly. "If you're looking for a confession, you won't get one."

"I don't need one," Holmes said matter-of-factly. "At least not to have you arrested."

A wry smile played at Urdi's lips, and he fingered the shining comlink on his wrist. "But you want one, I can see. I know who you are now: you're Sherlock Holmes, that great meddler they warned me about."

"They?" Holmes asked, but Urdi simply kept smiling.

"You'd like to know that, wouldn't you? Because you like to know everything. But what does it really matter? As you just told me, you already have enough information to arrest me." He held out his wrists as if preparing for electro-binders to be slapped on them. "Go ahead—call in your friends, arrest me. And yet, I can see you hesitating, and we both know you could have called in back-up ages ago. You haven't done it because your curiosity hasn't been completely satisfied—that's your weakness, and that will be your undoing."

Now it was Holmes' turn to blink in surprise. Although he was just as good at bluffing as Urdi was, he had just made a slip, much like Urdi had done earlier. Holmes didn't like being made to feel self-aware, and he especially didn't like someone implying he had a weakness. And he had just let all of that show.

Jaymie saw him reach into his pocket to press the panic button on his comlink, then his eyes widened.

Urdi grinned and brandished Holmes' comlink. "You're right—I'm a pirate and a drug runner. But before that, I was a good old-fashioned pick-pocket." He once again leveled his blaster at Holmes' head. "I'm a hard man, not a cruel one, so I'll give you what you want before I dispatch you. Yes, I killed Oliviana Tryrw, but if you think it gave me any pleasure, you're a fool. I loved her, but she crossed me, and she knew what the consequences would be. I was hoping her death would send a strong enough message to Eben Hawkes, who's obviously the one who told you about this. After I silence you and your friend who was unfortunate enough to tag along, I'll deal with him."

A lump rose in Jaymie's throat. *Holmes, do something!* she pleaded silently. She could tell by the look in his eyes he was brainstorming furiously, trying to recalculate his plan. She just hoped he would be fast enough.

One of the guards shoved Jaymie forward, and she saw Urdi lower his pistol at her.

"Don't hurt her, she doesn't know anything about this," Holmes said. "The only score you have to settle is with me."

"Really, someone as brilliant as you are should be a better liar," Urdi said. "She's heard the same information you have, and she'll have to die as well. Like I said, I'm a hard man."

"And also the ill-gotten son of a Syfrian swamp beast," Holmes replied. "With all the honor of a Dorgan. The game is still over for you, Urdi. If it's not me that stops you, it'll be someone else down the line."

"Oh, Holmes..." Jaymie moaned. If they weren't doomed before, they were certainly doomed now. Urdi obviously wasn't used to being insulted so casually, and she saw his eyes narrow. Holmes' taunt was rather like sticking a hot poker in an already raw and open wound.

Yes, they were most certainly dead...

She glanced over at Holmes in what were surely her final moments before death, and she saw him mouth the words "trust me." Although she didn't really like placing all her confidence in a man who waltzed so, well, eagerly into trouble, she realized at this point, she didn't have a choice. If Holmes had a plan, it was pretty much her only ticket out of this situation. She saw Urdi start to squeeze the trigger of his blaster, and she took a deep breath, praying it wouldn't be her last.

Urdi fired, and at the same moment Holmes lunged and crashed into Jaymie, the blaster bolt whizzing above their heads as they both hit the floor. His hands still bound, Holmes rolled over and swung out his foot, tripping one of the guards. Caught off balance, the guard fell over, and the device controlling their electro-binders skidded across the floor.

Holmes scrambled to grab it, dodging another blaster bolt from Urdi. He pressed the "release" button on the device, and with a painful shock, Jaymie felt her electro-binders deactivate and slip off. She grabbed the blaster from inside her jacket and switched it to stun. She fired at Urdi, and although her aim was off and she missed him by about half a meter, she did force him to take cover.

"Why didn't you search them for weapons, you idiots?" Urdi shouted at his guards.

Jaymie saw one of Urdi's thugs aiming her weapon at Holmes, but Jaymie fired first, felling the woman with a stun bolt. She heard banging on the door, and then suddenly there was a loud crash as the door burst open and Lestrade and his team of officers came charging in, laying down a steady stream of stun bolts.

Most of Urdi's thugs were hit by the first round of fire, but for the benefit of those still standing, Lestrade shouted, "This is a Civic Security raid! Put down your weapons, you are officially under arrest! You'll be taken in for questioning and all the contents of this facility will be seized under Eglon statute 6X42-L, and—"

"I know!" Urdi said, throwing down his weapon in disgust as a trio of Civic Security inspectors surrounded him with high-powered blaster rifles. Jaymie was surprised he had given up so easily but figured he didn't really have a choice. With only three of his guards conscious, he was sorely outnumbered, and he had no way of knowing how many of Lestrade's officers were still outside.

Lestrade brought out his own pair of electro-binders and slapped them onto Urdi's wrists, then several of the Civic Security officers escorted the drug lord outside. Holmes followed them out to the street, where the officers shoved Urdi into the back of a patrol hovercar.

"You can tell Hawkes he got lucky," Urdi said, scowling at Holmes. "But warn him that he'd better be watching his back."

"Revenge is awfully hard to accomplish when you're locked away in prison," Lestrade said, and Urdi shrugged.

"Didn't say it would be me who wanted to get revenge."

And with that, Lestrade slammed the door to the vehicle, and the hovercar went zipping away into the night.

"Well, Holmes, you've done it again," Lestrade said, shaking his head. "Although I wish you wouldn't always cut it this close. You know next time, you *might* want to consider pressing the panic button before I hear the sounds of a firefight."

"Actually, there was a slight issue with the panic button," Jaymie said. "Urdi pick-pocketed Holmes' comlink."

"What?" Lestrade sighed and rolled his eyes. "Very nice, Holmes. You do know how pathetic that is?"

"So I made one little mistake," Holmes shot back. "I guess this proves I am indeed human, even if I do supposedly lack a soul. But I did manage to ultimately salvage the situation, with the help of Miss Watson. She responded just as I hoped she would."

Jaymie's face reddened slightly. "Actually, my aim was terrible—I'm pretty sure downing that female guard was only a lucky shot."

"That's not the point," Holmes said. "What matters is that you *did* something. You don't know how many people simply freeze up in tense situations like that. At least you attempted to respond in a constructive manner."

He gazed at her thoughtfully for a moment, as if evaluating her. He did that to her occasionally, but this time a slight smile spread across his face. "See, I knew she'd be perfect, Lestrade." He gave Jaymie a pat on the back. "I told you, Watson: you're capable of far more than you think you are."

Jaymie's face turned even redder, and she glanced away, trying to hide her embarrassment. But Holmes was already off again, headed back to the crime scene.

Lestrade lingered behind for a moment with Jaymie, and he shook his head again as he watched Holmes march off.

"Well, who would have thought," he remarked. "I think the man who always works alone has finally found an assistant—that is, if you want the job."

"You know, I really just wanted a flat to rent," Jaymie said, and Lestrade laughed softly.

"I should have warned you that you'd be getting far more than that if you took the room," he said. "Still want somebody to try to talk you out of it?"

Jaymie grinned. "I doubt I'll find another flat with this much entertainment for so cheap."

She looked up and saw the sun just beginning to creep above the horizon, and she stifled a sudden groan. *Her test!* By the time she got back to apartment complex 221, it would be time to turn around and leave again. And she hadn't gotten a single wink of sleep.

But it was worth it, she thought as she saw Lestrade walk over to join Holmes, and the two started discussing some piece of evidence Holmes had pulled from the crime scene. She saw Lestrade throw up his hands and knew an argument was coming.

And somehow, in the middle of this mess, she felt—for the first time in her life—like she belonged.

It was a pretty good feeling, even better than the feeling she got a week later when she learned she'd also aced that test. Apparently she *was* capable of more than she thought.

Case No. 3: Hide and Seek

Chapter 1: Double the Trouble

Jaymie's breath caught as she stepped outside the library at the University of Medical Arts and into the biting winter air. There was a light dusting of snow on the ground beneath her feet, and a chill wind seeped in through her jacket, raising goose bumps on her skin.

"Blast!" she cursed, struggling to slip on the pair of gloves she had recently purchased, her trembling fingers making the task difficult. As a native of Scoztan, she wasn't quite used to the bitter Eglon winter yet, and she found herself longing for the more mild temperatures of her home world. At this time of year, she would be still riding hyverns through the fields on her family's estate. She closed her eyes and briefly transported herself back there. She could feel a warm breeze sweeping past her face as her hyvern, "Fleet," galloped through fields full of ryzies, delicate white flowers that were sprinkled throughout the gently waving grasses. Mountains rose up in the background to pierce the brilliant turquoise sky, their snowy peaks reaching towards the glowing, green-tinted sun.

She had loved those long rides during Scoztan's seemingly endless summer, really the only time she had ever felt relaxed and at peace on her family's giant estate. The acres and acres of land, and the large mansion with its holo-entertainment center, indoor garden full of exotic plants, and zero-g workout room, were filled with luxuries most beings only dreamed about—luxuries her mother loved to flaunt. But to Jaymie that was all so oppressive, and the finery seemed far too empty to her.

Somehow apartment complex 221 in Quadrant B felt more like home than the grand "Watson Meadows" estate ever had. Maybe that's because she was earning money to pay for her own rent through her job as a student worker at the university, making the flat one of the few things in her life that hadn't been handed to her on a silver platter. Or maybe it was because, in a strange way, Holmes and Lestrade were starting to feel like family...

Jaymie's foot slipped on a patch of ice, jerking her out of her thoughts. She threw her hands out in front of her in an attempt to balance herself, and she skidded around and grabbed onto a glowlamp pole for support.

"Oh, that was close!" she exclaimed, grateful she hadn't tripped and injured herself. She took a moment to regain her composure and was about ready to head back down the street when someone slammed into her from behind.

At first, Jaymie assumed the person behind her had slipped, as she had done, and she grabbed onto the pole again to steady herself, then reached out to help the other person. However, she felt her knapsack being yanked from her shoulder, and to her shock, she saw the person who had "bumped" into her running away with her knapsack in hand.

I've just been mugged—it took a second for the shock to sink it, but as soon as it did, Jaymie felt a flash of both fear and anger.

"Hey! Hey, you! Stop!" She started after the thief, desperately searching around for anyone who could help her. "Stop, that's my bag!"

Several students strolling down the pathway looked over as she ran past them, but no one moved to help her. Their blank, clueless expressions revealed they either didn't know what was going on or were too busy to care.

"Stop!" Jaymie cried after the thief, who of course was wearing a hooded jacket that made it impossible for her to identify him. *Why couldn't anyone be put upon to help her?*

Her lungs burned with effort as she ran, and she tried shouting one more time, as loud as she could, "Give me back my bag!"

But the thief obviously had no intention of doing so. He arrived at the street corner just as a hoverbus came drifting down the road, and he darted behind it. Although Jaymie sprinted towards him, by the time she reached the corner, the hoverbus had passed, and the thief was now lost in the crowd.

Dumbfounded for a moment, Jaymie stared down the street with her mouth hanging open, unable to believe what had just happened to her. She hadn't had any money stored in the bag (which would make it a disappointing theft), but she had at least 200 quid's worth of academic books in there, plus her techpad with an entire semester of notes on it.

"This can't be happening," she moaned as she searched the crowd one last time, in vain. There was no way she could afford to replace those books right now, and she would be forced to call her mother and ask to borrow some money. Her mother would give it to her, but she would recite that same lecture about how silly it was of Jaymie to have insisted on trying to support herself and live alone on another planet. The thought of having to listen to that speech (which she'd heard many times before) galled her, but there was no way around it.

She supposed there was nothing to do now but find the Civic Security Station in Quadrant A and report the crime. If this had happened in Quadrant B, she would have already given up all hope of recovering her bag, but theft was a little less common in the more upscale Quadrant A, and she wondered if there was a slight chance the thief might eventually be caught. That at least might save her from having to call her mother and beg. She'd also have to call Holmes and have him pick her up in that rattle-trap hovercar of his, since the thief had also stolen her pass for the hoverbus.

"Just great," Jaymie muttered. "And why does it have to be so bloody cold?"

#

"So tell us—what details did you notice about the thief's appearance?"

Jaymie took a deep breath and tried not to let it out as a heavy sigh. The Civic Security officer had already asked her this question about five times, in various forms, and she was forced to repeat, yet again, that she hadn't really *seen* any details.

"It happened so fast—I was slipping on the ice, then I was bumped from behind, and I saw someone running off with my bag," she explained. "I'm pretty sure the thief was humanoid and male, but that's about all I know."

"I see," the Civic Security inspector said, typing some notes on her techpad. She was nodding sympathetically, but Jaymie could tell by her tone that what she was really thinking was probably something like, *You've given us basically nothing to go on—your bag is pretty much as good as gone.*

Jaymie heard an automatic door swish open, and she glanced over her shoulder and saw Holmes come striding into the lobby, dressed as always in his favorite trench coat. It wasn't wrinkled today, which meant it must be his once-a-week time to wash and press it. He also seemed to have remembered to run a comb through his hair before coming to the Civic Security Station, an even more infrequent occurrence. He ignored the receptionist who tried to make him check in and walked straight over to Jaymie.

"So is this the boyfriend who's supposed to come and pick you up?" the officer interviewing Jaymie asked, and Jaymie's face flushed.

"Um, no. It's not like that—we're not together. We're more like friends...well, sort of. It's complicated."

The officer nodded again, obviously not believing a word of it.

"Watson, there you are," Holmes remarked. "Terribly unfortunate, hmm? You know, this really is somewhat ironic: you live in the most crime-infested quadrant on the planet, and yet it's in the most upper-class quadrant that you actually end up getting mugged."

"I guess I'm just lucky," Jaymie muttered. "Anyway, thanks for coming to get me—I hope it wasn't too much of an inconvenience."

"Actually, it was," Holmes replied. "I was in the middle of something, but I suppose that couldn't be helped. I don't know who else you could have called. That's why I don't have many friends—the more you have, the more inconveniences like this seem to crop up. People are so needy, I've found."

The officer raised her eyebrow and glanced over at Jaymie. "'Complicated,' eh? I see what you mean now."

"What?" Holmes asked, looking confused.

"Never mind," Jaymie said, rolling her eyes. "Let's just go, Holmes."

"We'll be in touch, and we'll let you know as soon as we locate your bag," the officer told Jaymie. "Don't worry, I'm sure—"

She was interrupted by a loud squawk over the PA system. "Attention, Civic Security personnel: robbery reported in progress at the Quadrant A Bank of Eglon branch, repeat, robbery in progress. All available units requested to respond immediately."

Everyone in the station seemed to freeze in shock. Jaymie guessed it had been some time since a major incident had occurred in the famously crime-free quadrant, and for a minute, no one seemed to know how to react, as if the call was just something they had collectively imagined.

And then, everyone seemed to erupt into panic. Officers began scrambling to action, shoving blasters into their holsters and heading for patrol hovercars. Jaymie could hear someone barking orders, attempting to organize the chaos, and she felt her own adrenalin level start to spike.

She glanced over and saw that tell-tale spark in Holmes' eyes.

"Come on, Jaymie," he said, grabbing her by the hand and leading her outside.

"What are you doing?" she asked.

"Going to the crime scene," Holmes said, opening the door to his hovercar and jumping inside.

Now it was Jaymie's turn to be confused. "But you're only a consultant with Quadrant B...aren't you?"

Holmes shrugged. "Something interesting is happening, and I don't have anything else to do. I figured I might as well attempt to be of service."

"Didn't you say earlier that I interrupted you while you were doing something important, and…" Jaymie let her voice trail off, and she shook her head. "Oh, never mind. It's like trying to reason with a brick wall. Let's head over there and find out what's going on."

Chapter 2: The Impossible Theft

Crime might not have been a frequent occurrence in Quadrant A, but that didn't mean the Civic Security inspectors in that quadrant were inept amateurs (despite what Holmes might have to say). By the time Jaymie and Holmes arrived at the scene, there was already a team of armed officers surrounding the perimeter, and as she listened to the officers' comlink chatter, she overheard that another group had already entered the building.

Holmes hopped out of his hovercar, rubbing his hands together gleefully. He started walking towards the building but was stopped by one of the inspectors standing guard outside the bank.

"Sorry, Sir, but you're not authorized to be here," the officer said, and Holmes flashed his identi-card.

"Sherlock Holmes, private investigator. I've done a considerable amount of investigative work with Quadrant B Civic Security, and even a few cases in Quadrant A. I was in the area, heard about the commotion, and thought I might be of service."

The officer stared at them for a moment, and then a light of recognition slowly began to dawn in his eyes. "Wait a minute, I think I've heard about you. 'Insufferable meddler,' I think the chief called you. Well, I'm sorry, Sir, but I don't think you're needed here. The thief's already gone."

"Ah, so you *do* need me," Holmes said, with a hint of a wry grin.

"What's this all about?"

Jaymie heard a sharp voice break over the wail of the sirens, catching everyone's attention in the same way a person might be startled by an unexpected clap of thunder. She looked over and saw a tall woman marching towards them, surprisingly sure-footed on the icy streets despite her fancy shoes with ridiculously thin heels. She was wearing a Civic Security uniform, and judging by the way officers scurried to get out of her way, she was the one in charge. Her hair was brilliant red, even redder than Jaymie's (although unlike Jaymie's, it wasn't natural).

"Chief Athelney!" the officer next to Holmes and Jaymie exclaimed, instantly snapping to attention. "What did you find inside the building?"

The woman ignored his question. "Inspector Bryde, perhaps you'd like to inform me who let this man into the crime scene," she said, her voice icier than the freezing winter air. "Because whoever it is can consider themselves immediately fired."

"Chief Athelney," Holmes said, sticking out his hand in greeting. "Always a pleasure to see you."

Athelney refused to shake his hand, and instead she gave him a deadly glare. "When I told you if I never saw you again, it would be too soon, I wasn't joking. This is a crime scene, not some sideshow for your amusement. You have no legitimate reason to be here."

"Heard you have a spot of trouble," Holmes said, sidestepping her insult and making it clear he had no intentions of leaving. "Lost a burglar, have you?"

Athelney's face reddened, and Jaymie could tell the woman's temper was flaring. "'Lost' isn't the word I would have selected. Seems we had a little miscommunication from the bank. The robbery wasn't in progress when they called; it happened last night and somehow triggered none of their alarms. They didn't even realize what had happened until the president arrived this morning and found something missing. But tell me—what are you doing here, Inspector Holmes? Aren't you roaming a little far outside your territory?"

"Oh, I'm not an inspector anymore, just a private consultant," Holmes said, and Athelney's lips curled into a sneer.

"Ah, so they finally fired you? Apparently they were tired of putting up with your incompetence."

"No—I had to quit," Holmes said, enjoying this interchange entirely too much. "Incompetence is apparently no longer a cause for dismissal in Civic Security, which is evidenced by the fact you've been promoted."

Inspector Bryde's mouth fell open in shock, but Athelney merely blinked, as if unwilling to process Holmes' verbal barb. This was a woman who wasn't used to being trifled with, and Jaymie felt a flicker of nervousness. Holmes clearly had no qualms about goading the chief, but Jaymie was afraid of what might happen if he pushed her too far.

"I've had no regrets about leaving Quadrant B," Athelney said. "I transferred with the highest recommendation, and yes, I've been promoted to chief. I suspect my career has already far eclipsed yours."

"On paper, yes," Holmes said. "But titles never much interested me. What I love is a good puzzle, which appears to be what your station has stumbled into. I'm just here to help."

"No, 'to meddle' is far more likely," Athelney corrected him. "Some things apparently never change." She glanced over at Jaymie, turning up her nose slightly. "Ah, so now you have a minion, too? How much do you have to pay her to tolerate your company?"

"Actually, I volunteered," Jaymie cut in. "I'm his assistant. We, um, solve cases together."

"Well, you're not needed on this one," Athelney said. "You both need to leave immediately, or I will be forced to…"

Her voice trailed off as she saw a somewhat pudgy but very well-dressed man come jogging over to them, his chest heaving with effort. His face was red, though he looked more panicked than angry, and he was waving a techpad in the air. As Jaymie looked closer, she noticed he was humanoid rather than human, with two layers of gills blending into the side of his face. She guessed on his home world he had probably been amphibious, though that sort of lifestyle was difficult to maintain on a more metropolitan planet like Eglon.

"Have you caught the thief yet?" he asked in between rapid gulps of air, and Athelney let out a terse sigh.

"We've only just arrived here, Mr. Yigiol. It will take us a while to comb your bank for clues."

Realizing Athelney had no intentions of introducing them, Jaymie stuck out her hand. "Hi—my name's Jaymie Watson, and I'm the assistant of Sherlock Holmes, a private investigator from Quadrant B. We heard the commotion and thought you might be needing—"

"I'm so sorry, Mr. Yigiol," Athelney interrupted, stepping rudely in front of Jaymie. "I did not authorize these two to enter the crime scene, and they were just in the process of leaving." She shot Jaymie and Holmes a fierce glare, and Jaymie felt her courage crumple inside her, crushed by the woman's overbearing gaze.

However, Mr. Yigiol's eyes lit up as he looked at them. "Holmes—the famous Sherlock Holmes? Didn't you just solve the mystery behind the Sunset Enterprises fire in Quadrant D?"

Holmes nodded. "One and the same. However, the recent Quadrant D fire is not the best example of my work. I prefer to reference—"

"That's brilliant!" Yigiol said. He reached out and shook Holmes' hand vigorously. "I'm Kyol Yigiol, manager of the Quadrant A Bank of Eglon branch, and I'd like to let you know your deft solving of that Quadrant D case saved the Bank of Eglon a great deal of money. You see, Sunset Enterprises asked for a loan after the fire to start 'a new business venture,' and we were all set to approve it, having no idea illegal activity had been going on. When you revealed that the fire was no accident, we denied their request quite quickly. You have my most sincere thanks, Mr. Holmes. Perhaps you can help us investigate last night's theft. If you solve the crime, I'll pay you and your assistant 10,000 quid apiece."

Jaymie felt as though she had just been hit by a hoverbus, and her eyes widened in surprise. "What? 10,000 quid?"

Athelney was stunned as well. "Pardon me, Mr. Yigiol, but my team and I are perfectly capable of handling this case. We've only just arrived here, and I promise, we'll solve this crime in a timely manner. There's no need to hire a...*consultant*." She made "consultant" sound like a dirty word.

"No offense intended," Yigiol said, "but I've had plenty of dealings with the government, and unfortunately the response has not always been, well, efficient. I'd like to bring Mr. Holmes on board as well. If Civic Security solves the case, fine—you'll save my bank 20,000 quid. But I have a great deal of confidence in Mr. Holmes' abilities, and it can't hurt to have as many hands working on this case as possible."

"Of course," Athelney said, smiling politely but her voice dripping poison. "Why don't we take a look at the recordings from the security cams?"

Mr. Yigiol nodded. "I'll have our security staff prepare them, and we can view the recordings in our conference room."

"Fine," Athelney said. "All right, then, come along Inspector Bryde. And I suppose you too, Mr. Holmes and Miss Watson."

"With pleasure," Holmes said, and Jaymie could tell he absolutely meant it.

#

Minutes later, they were all sitting around a conference table on the fifth floor of the bank, and Eva Ty'upe, one of the security guards on duty the previous night, caught everyone up to speed.

"We're guessing the break-in occurred about 0200 hours this morning," Ty'upe explained. She was a Gerfrian, with a slightly orange hue to her skin and iridescent highlights in her jet black hair. "As you already know, no alarms went off and there were no signs of a forced entry. Whoever the thief was, he or she was very good. We didn't even realize the bank had been broken into until Mr. Yigiol checked the vault this morning and saw the Gvidi diamond was missing."

"That's all that was stolen?" Holmes asked. "No money missing, nothing else?"

"Everything else appeared to be in order," Ty'upe said. "Large jewels, a statue from the 211th century, and several priceless historical artifacts were left behind; literally the only thing missing was the diamond. It belongs to the House of Gvidi, an estate managed by Fradik Gvidi, one of the current members of the Eglon Ruling Council."

"Has he been informed yet that the diamond is missing?" Athelney asked, and Yigiol blushed.

"Well, no. We were rather hoping you could help us find it, and recover it before Gvidi ever found out. You see, he never really wanted to store the diamond here in the first place. He wanted to keep it at his house, but his wife persuaded him to store it here, believing it would be, um, safer."

"Well, it's been quite the day for irony, hasn't it?" Holmes remarked. "And I'm sure you don't want to hear this, Mr. Yigiol, but secrecy may not be an option at this point. People will have noticed the swarm of Civic Security inspectors in front of the bank and guessed that *something* has happened."

"Well, we're telling the media it's just a drill," Yigiol confessed, and Holmes frowned.

"It's your business, so you can tell the media whatever you want. But I've found covering up the facts only tends to lead to a worse quagmire in the long run. And when—not if, *when*—the media learns the truth, they *will* crucify you."

Yigiol's face paled, and he swallowed painfully. "Um, that's part of why I hired you, Mr. Holmes. We need this case solved—very fast."

Holmes nodded. "Then I'll do my best. Why don't we look through the security recordings?"

Ty'upe pressed the "play" button, and images from the security recordings flashed up on the view screen in front of them.

"I'll go through these rather quickly, as there isn't much to see," the security guard said as she zipped through the footage. "This first view is of the bank lobby from closing time to opening this morning. As you can see, the only beings visible are me and the other security guard—Yorvil Box—making our rounds. Nothing out of the ordinary."

She switched to another view, and they went through the same process, with Ty'upe fast-forwarding through the recording and explaining what they were watching. All Jaymie saw was more and more of nothing. All the hallways and rooms on all of the floors seemed as still as a crypt. Even inside the vault, there was nothing.

Ty'upe paused when they came to a recording of the actual Gvidi diamond. A murmur went through the crowd as those who had never seen the diamond before first caught sight of it, and though Holmes rolled his eyes at what he likely thought was their rather clichéd response, Jaymie couldn't blame them. The diamond *was* impressive. Though it was dwarfed in size by some of the other jewels stored next to it inside a case made of security glass, it outshone all of them. It was perfectly clear, like glass, and an artist had fashioned it into an exotic, asymmetrical shape, with seemingly thousands of facets to catch the light. It glimmered under the low lighting in the vault, sparkling like a tiny star.

Yet as Jaymie kept staring at it, something strange seemed to happen. The diamond began to pulse with light, and deep in the heart of the jewel, she saw a swirling vortex, like a black hole except with burning white light instead of endless darkness. The vortex slowly began to expand, sucking in all the light and matter around it. It came closer and closer until it seemed to stretch beyond the view screen itself, as if it were going swallow up Jaymie and everything else in the conference room...

She gasped and jerked backwards, and the moment she blinked, the vortex disappeared.

She glanced around the room, and saw that everyone else had the same look of wonder and shock on their faces that she did. Even Holmes appeared a little stunned.

"And that's why that diamond is so valuable," Ty'upe said softly, clearly guessing what had happened. "It's a rare vortex diamond, the only one in existence in this sector. That 'black hole' effect you experienced is one of the diamond's features: If you stare into the jewel for long enough, you'll see that swirling pattern. One of the strangest things about that phenomenon is that it works even if you're just looking at a recording, or even a picture of the diamond. Scientists can't explain why that occurs."

"Well, it does help to explain why the thief would take only that diamond, and leave all the other valuables behind," Holmes said. "How much is it worth?"

"It's priceless," Yigiol said, staring once again into the diamond on the screen. "I was so honored to have it here, to have been entrusted with safeguarding it. To think of the shame that will come on me, on the Bank of Eglon, if this gets out…"

"Focus, please, Mr. Yigiol," Chief Athelney said brusquely. "There's no use lamenting the fact the robbery occurred; helping us solve it will be a far better use of your energies. Now, Ty'upe, continue with the recording."

Ty'upe obediently pressed "play" again, and they all returned to watching the screen. Jaymie avoided looking directly at the diamond this time; although the vortex effect was admittedly impressive, it was also more than a little disconcerting, and she didn't want to experience that feeling of vertigo again.

After watching the vortex appear inside the diamond, Jaymie found that when they actually reached the footage of the theft itself, it was almost anticlimactic. All of a sudden, the diamond simply disappeared. Jaymie blinked, at first wondering if this was yet another example of the jewel's strange "powers," but that didn't appear to be the case. The diamond had now simply vanished.

Holmes darted forward. "Rewind," he said, but Ty'upe shook her head.

"It wouldn't do any good, I'm afraid. There's nothing to see, other than the fact it just disappears."

"Is it possible the thief switched off the security cam, just for a second?"

Ty'upe shook her head again. "No. The computer shows no break in the recording, and no one—not even the security guards—can turn those security cams off. The only one with that kind of control is Mr. Yigiol, who can override any system in the bank."

Holmes rubbed his chin in thought, staring hard at the view screen. "Well, you've obviously got a very well-informed thief on your hands. Have there been any reports lately of employees exhibiting suspicious behavior, or do you have any other reason to believe this might be an inside job?"

Yigiol appeared offended. "No, I would never suspect any of my employees of trying to rob this bank. I interviewed every one of my employees personally before they were hired, and they all underwent thorough background checks. I can assure you, Mr. Holmes, there are no criminals amongst our ranks."

Holmes smiled ironically. "I'm sorry, Mr. Yigiol, but your simply vouching for their character won't automatically clear their names. Nobody hires someone thinking he or she is a crook, and yet many crooks still get hired, because they're good at pretending. Heaven knows we've elected enough of them to the Ruling Council over the years. If this is an inside job, it's a good one, and the identity of the thief wouldn't be immediately obvious to you. The best criminals are always the subtlest ones, the ones you'd never suspect at all."

"Are there any more security recordings then?" Chief Athelney asked, irritated that Holmes kept butting in and probably even more irritated that he was almost always right.

"No—at least, nothing of note, Chief," Ty'upe said. "This is the only one which comes close to revealing anything."

"No offense intended, but I'd like to see all of the recordings for myself, just to be sure," Holmes said. "Best to leave no stone unturned, as they say."

Ty'upe shrugged and then played several more recordings, showing them various views inside and outside the main safe. Once again, they saw nothing, nothing, and more of nothing. Jaymie could tell Athelney was growing impatient, but then suddenly Holmes lurched forward in his chair. "Stop!"

Ty'upe immediately hit the "pause" button. They were watching the recording from a cam directly outside the safe, and at first Jaymie saw nothing but patterns created by shadows on the marble floor.

"Can you enhance that image?" Holmes asked, and Ty'upe quickly typed a series of commands into her techpad. The image lightened, and Jaymie, along with everyone else in the room, let out a gasp. She could see the outline of a figure clutching the Gvidi diamond. The figure was short in stature, slightly overweight. And though the image was a little blurry, there was no mistaking the thin rows of gills on the side of the burglar's face. It was Kyol Yigiol.

Yigiol's face turned a sudden and very stark shade of white.

"Mr. Yigiol," Ty'upe stammered in disbelief, and everyone turned to stare at the president of the Bank of Eglon Quadrant A branch.

Dumfounded, Yigiol gazed at the view screen and at the unmistakable image of himself.

"What in the galaxy..." he breathed. "Heavens of mercy, I don't know what this is, but I swear, it isn't me."

"Well, it bloody *looks* like you," Athelney exclaimed, quickly motioning for Inspector Bryde to move beside the door, in case Yigiol tried to make an escape. She pulled out a blaster, as did the rest of her officers.

Yigiol began to tremble at the sight of the officers' weapons. "I'm...I...I don't know what is happening. This is impossible. I did not rob my own bank. I was not even here last night. This must be a trick somehow, some sort of deception..."

"Is there any sign the recordings have been tampered with?" Athelney asked.

"No, Sir...I mean, Ma'am," Ty'upe replied. "I downloaded them directly off the main computer this morning. I...I didn't even see Mr.

Yigiol…I mean, the being who looks like Mr. Yigiol, when I went through the recordings. I…frankly, I can't really believe it."

"Please tell them, Eva, I wouldn't do this!" Yigiol begged. "I'm not a thief, you know that."

Ty'upe hesitated, seeming torn. "Sir, the thief is wearing the same clothes you were wearing yesterday—including that expensive, custom-made jacket from Odon you just bragged about purchasing. I'm sorry, Sir, I don't want to believe it, but it really does appear to be you."

As Inspector Bryde called for back-up, Yigiol laid his head in his hands.

"I don't know what to say to make you believe me, but I swear, this isn't me!"

Jaymie watched him, and she felt her heart go out to him. The image on the screen was unquestionably Yigiol—even with the blurriness, there was no doubt it was him. He was also the only one who could control the security recordings; he could have easily turned them off while swiping the diamond, and then manipulated them to make it appear as if there were no breaks in the footage. And yet…the look of distress on his face right now was so genuine, and he appeared truly horrified at what he was being accused of. Jaymie wanted to believe he was innocent, but she had also heard what Holmes said about the best criminals being the subtlest, the ones you'd never suspect. What was she supposed to believe?

"We'll be bringing you in for questioning, and you'll likely be spending some time in my Civic Security Station's prison block," Athelney told Yigiol as one of her inspectors slapped a pair of electro-binders on his wrists and escorted him towards the door. "Bryde, you'll accompany me back to the station; other inspectors, keep looking for evidence."

Yigiol turned back to look at Holmes, his eyes full of pleading. "Please, Mr. Holmes! Don't you at least believe me? Is there any doubt at all in your mind about the recordings?"

Holmes' face was stern, though Jaymie sensed that sternness was not necessarily directed at Yigiol himself. "I see no reason to believe that image is not of you. You do appear to be, at least for the moment, the prime suspect. I'm sorry. Just remember—you hired me to solve this case, and that means I have to uncover the truth, regardless of where it might lead or who it might point to."

A very dejected Mr. Yigiol was ushered from the room, his employees watching him with a look of stunned betrayal on their faces. Jaymie cast a quick glance out the window and saw that despite Mr. Yigiol's wish to keep the public from learning about the crime, a large crowd had already gathered and were pressed around the perimeter of holo crime scene tape Athelney's staff had set up. She could also see several reporters typing furiously on techpads and holding up portable cams, interviewing bystanders and Bank of Eglon employees. So much for keeping this case under wraps.

As soon as Athelney and her team left, Ty'upe stepped towards them uncertainly. "I can escort you out, if you'd like, Mr. Holmes. I'm guessing you won't have any further business here."

"What do you mean?" Holmes asked. "I was offered a case, and I don't walk out on cases until they're solved."

"But the recording, and what you said to Mr. Yigiol..." Ty'upe let her voice trail off, obviously feeling confused.

"I didn't want to do anything to delay Chief Athelney's hasty departure," Holmes explained. "Honestly, all the hot air that woman creates makes it bloody difficult to think, much less breathe, sometimes. But now that she's gone, I fully intend to stay and start searching for evidence before her team bungles matters completely. I can't promise you I'll clear Mr. Yigiol's name, but I don't believe the evidence we've seen here today is absolutely irrefutable." He clapped Jaymie on the back. "Come on, Watson, we have work to do."

Chapter 3: Trust Me

Jaymie was sure Ty'upe would never have admitted it, but she could tell the security guard was a little sweet on Holmes. Ty'upe shouldn't have let him wander all around the bank during the middle of a Quadrant A Civic Security investigation, and she had a feeling Athelney would have been livid if she knew how freely Holmes was being allowed to "meddle." But Ty'upe had been more than cooperative, and she had agreed to escort Holmes wherever he wanted to go inside the building and help him gather evidence. Holmes seemed to take it all in stride, but Jaymie found herself feeling slightly vexed that Ty'upe was *so* cooperative. And the fact she was feeling slightly vexed made her even more frustrated.

"So you're certain there was no sign of a forced entry?" Holmes asked as the three of them walked down a hallway, their shoes clacking on the cold marble.

Ty'upe nodded, brushing a strand of shimmering hair behind her ear. "No sign at all. No alarms went off, no one tried to hack into the security system. After you noticed the image of Mr. Yigiol on that one recording, I went back and watched each of the recordings from the different security cams again, enhancing all the footage. I caught sight of him one more time, but otherwise, nothing."

Holmes nodded thoughtfully. "Interesting. Well, have you checked your computer for any signs of *authorized* entry last night, then?"

Ty'upe gave him a strange look. "Um, no. Why would I have done that?"

Holmes sighed. "Why does no one ever think of these things? If Mr. Yigiol entered the building, it wouldn't have been a break-in. He would have simply entered his pass codes, and he would have been allowed inside. Checking the computer system will let us know when he came in."

Ty'upe's face flushed. "Oh, right." She punched in some numbers on her techpad, and then drew in a sharp breath. "Yes—at 0200 hours, Mr. Yigiol typed in his security codes and entered the building." Her face creased with anxiety. "It's not looking very good for him, is it?"

"Innocent until proven guilty," Holmes murmured. "Don't jump to conclusions just yet."

Ty'upe smiled and nodded again, but Jaymie could tell she wasn't quite buying it.

"So how exactly do you know Chief Athelney, and why does she seem to hate you so much?" Ty'upe asked, changing the subject as they turned into a different corridor.

"We used to work together at the Quadrant B Civic Security Station," Holmes said. "We got along well enough in those days; she was fairly straight-laced, a very 'let's-do-this-by-the-book' sort of officer, which was perfectly fine. Personally, I prefer to be given a little creative license, but I respected her methods. Then, she got promoted to sergeant, and suddenly it wasn't just do things by the book, it was do things by *her* version of the book—and if you didn't fall in line, she liked to make things very difficult for you. Needless to say, she wasn't fond of my occasional 'unconventional' methods of solving crimes, and she transferred out of the Quadrant B station the first chance she got. Apparently she hasn't grown any fonder of me since."

They came to a halt in front of the safe that had housed the diamond.

"Um, this is probably about as far as I can take you," Ty'upe said. "Chief Athelney doesn't want us to let anyone inside the vault. She—"

"Actually, I'm sorry Mr. Holmes and Miss Watson, but you really shouldn't be here at all. I'm going to have to ask you to leave the building immediately."

Jaymie turned and saw Inspector Bryde standing behind them. He was trying to make himself appear as stern and authoritative as possible, but the look in his eyes betrayed his real feelings. He was more than a little intimidated by Holmes, and he seemed to know Chief Athelney was simply treating him as an errand boy.

Holmes glanced back at the vault. "Ten minutes, Inspector Bryde—that's all I need."

Bryde's eyes darted around uneasily. "I'm sorry, Mr. Holmes, but the chief's orders were to escort you out right now. The, well, the bank theft has put her in a bad mood, if you know what I mean, and she was very insistent you be made to leave the building."

"Mr. Yigiol was also quite insistent earlier on Holmes being allowed to help," Ty'upe tried to advocate for them, but Bryde was too afraid of Athelney to be dissuaded from his orders.

"Please, I'd really rather not have to call for back-up. Everyone's a little on edge these days, especially after the other break-in and all."

Holmes' eyebrows spiked up. "The *other* break-in?"

"Yeah, nothing major really. Had one of our secretaries attempt to steal a techpad from the Civic Security Station. She was caught, but by then she'd already gotten rid of the device. It was a little strange, though, she kept saying it wasn't her, that she didn't do it. But we saw her on the security cams, pocketing the device and—"

"Blast!" Holmes exclaimed, throwing up his hands. "Why did no one mention that detail sooner?"

Bryde looked terribly confused. "Um, I didn't think it was relevant. What does employee theft have to do with this case?"

"If it was an ordinary employee theft? Nothing. But *this* employee theft—everything." Holmes scrambled to take out his techpad, and Bryde quickly held up a hand.

"Mr. Holmes, really, you need to leave."

"No, I really need to look around inside that vault." Although Holmes didn't lay a finger on the inspector, the look he gave him was the equivalent of grabbing Bryde by the collar and shoving him up against the wall.

Bryde gulped nervously and appeared as if he was almost ready to relent, but then Jaymie heard the sound of footsteps coming down the hallway. Her heart sinking, she looked up and saw Chief Athelney striding towards them, anger flashing in her eyes and her lips pursed tightly together.

"I thought I gave you an order, Inspector Bryde," she said. "I was hoping *not* to see Holmes and his little minion still here."

Jaymie's face flushed bright red at the derogatory term, and she saw Holmes stiffen.

"Her name is Miss Watson—and I thought you would have at least had the professional courtesy to call her that."

"Out, Holmes!" Athelney ordered. "Before I have you dragged out in electro-binders."

"I haven't gathered enough evidence yet," Holmes said. "If you can spare me—"

"We don't really need any more evidence at this point," Athelney snapped. "Anything else you could gather would be inconsequential. Mr. Yigiol hasn't exactly been cooperative during the interrogation, but I'm sure we already have enough evidence to convict him in a court of law. I don't care if that greedy banker promised to pay you 10,000 quid to clear his name—this is my crime scene, and I want you to get out. Now."

Ty'upe and Bryde both looked extremely uncomfortable, but Holmes' face remained expressionless. Jaymie was sure he was frustrated, but he was doing a very good job of keeping his emotions in check. He slowly slipped his techpad back into the pocket of his trench coat, his eyes never leaving Athelney's fuming gaze.

"Very well then. Good luck with the case, Athelney. It's a pity we couldn't have cooperated."

"Yes, a pity," Athelney said, in a tone that left no doubt she didn't find it to be a pity at all.

#

Holmes wouldn't admit he was angry. He walked silently back to his rusty hovercar, pushing his way through the crowds that were still gathered outside the bank. It was a quiet, rather awkward ride home, and an equally awkward ride up the rickety turbolift to the flat in apartment complex 221.

"I'm sorry, Holmes—she shouldn't have treated you like that," Jaymie finally said as Holmes swiped his entry card and opened the door to the flat.

"It's nothing," Holmes said, yanking off his coat and slinging it at the coat rack. Although it missed the rack by several centimeters and fell instead in a heap on the floor, he didn't even seem to notice.

"Of course it's nothing," Jaymie said. "That's why you're on the verge of throwing a massive temper tantrum."

"I'm not angry!" Holmes exclaimed as he walked into the kitchen. Seconds later, Jaymie heard the door to the flash-freezer slam, and the sound of pots banging. "I'm just very put out!"

Jaymie tried to hold back a sigh. "Well, for someone who claims not to be angry, you're doing a very good job of acting like you are. Look, I know you're frustrated that Athelney made us leave, but maybe we can still puzzle this case out, using the facts we already have."

Holmes came back into the living room, carrying a plate of food in one hand and a glass of aqua-spritzer in the other. The aqua-spritzer was just plain, carbonated water, and most beings used it as a mixer in other, more exotic drinks, since it tasted terrible on its own. Jaymie had no idea why Holmes insisted on drinking it straight, and he always made a horrible face after each gulp.

Holmes sat down, took a big swig from his glass, and then grimaced. "Blast, I always forget how awful this tastes." He coughed and set the glass down on the table next to the couch, quickly eating a bit of his pastry to lessen the drink's aftertaste. Jaymie wanted to ask why he always drank aqua-spritzers if they were so awful, but she was pretty sure she wouldn't get a logical answer. She'd become accustomed to many of Holmes' quirks by now, even if they didn't make sense. Some things he simply did because he was Sherlock Holmes.

He took out his techpad and began skimming through the notes he had taken at the crime scene earlier, his brow furrowed in thought. Jaymie knew he was trying to work through all the details they had observed, trying to line them up in a way that would clear Mr. Yigiol. She didn't think it was going to be an easy task.

"So what really happened at the Bank of Eglon Quadrant A branch last night?" Holmes mused, tapping his fingers thoughtfully on the armrest of the couch. "This case seems far too cut and dried for my liking, but we have precious little reason to believe that—"

Holmes' comlink suddenly beeped, and he scrambled to answer it. He received very few comlink calls (he rarely gave out his contact code), and the ones he received tended to be quite important.

"Hello, Mr. Holmes," came the shaky and very weary voice of Mr. Yigiol.

Jaymie sat up in surprise.

"Listen, Mr. Holmes, I don't have much time," Yigiol continued. "I've only been allowed to make one comlink call, and I chose to call you. Please, Mr. Holmes, you have to help me. Even my wife doesn't believe me, and I'm told I'll likely be convicted based on the evidence that's been found. I will level with you—I have no idea how to refute the evidence, except to tell you, once again, that when I said I did not steal the diamond, I was telling the truth." The agony in the man's voice was heart-wrenching. "I'm at my wit's end, Mr. Holmes—can you help me?"

Jaymie heard someone yelling at Mr. Yigiol in the background, probably one of the Civic Security inspectors letting him know he was running out of time.

"I'll give you and your assistant 20,000 quid each, if you can restore my good name," Yigiol offered in desperation. "Please, Mr. Holmes, please don't give up on—"

The link suddenly went dead as Mr. Yigiol's allotted call time ended.

Jaymie stared glumly out the window and watched as twilight fell across Quadrant B, making the slums of Eglon appear even drearier than they did in daylight. Holmes set down his comlink and laid his head in his hands, running his hands through his already tousled brown hair.

"All right, Watson, this is what we know. We have proof someone used Mr. Yigiol's code to enter the building at 0200 hours this morning. We have an image of Mr. Yigiol that shows up on the security recordings. That is enough proof for Chief Athelney, and Yigiol will no doubt be pegged with this crime."

"Could that recording have been faked?" Jaymie asked, but Holmes shook his head.

"Unlikely. I don't see any way it could have *not* been Mr. Yigiol." He sighed. "What do *you* think, Watson?"

Jaymie glanced down at the floor and bit her lip. She already knew what she wanted to say, but she kept hesitating, because she knew Holmes would scold her for it. "Look, I know you're all about quantifiable evidence," she began slowly. "And you don't like operating on just feelings. But I...I just don't *feel* like Mr. Yigiol did it. I don't really have any logical reason why. It just seems like he didn't take that diamond."

"Blast it, I feel the same way." Holmes darted to his feet and began pacing restlessly around the flat. "I'm just sensing...I...oh, I don't know what I'm saying. I honestly don't think Mr. Yigiol did it either, though I have no way of backing that up. We'll need proof to get him out of jail, not a hunch, but I don't know what else to do."

"Can you call the Quadrant A Civic Security Station and see if someone will fill you in on the rest of the clues they've collected?"

"No, I tried that before on a previous case," Holmes said. "Quadrant B Civic Security will usually cooperate with me, but Chief Athelney probably won't even let the secretary at her station tell me 'hello.'"

"Well, I guess our only option then is to break into the Bank of Eglon and gather our own evidence."

Jaymie had meant her comment to be an exaggeration, and she expected Holmes to tell her she was being ridiculous and come back with one of those brilliant breakthroughs of his. What she wasn't anticipating was for him to fully agree with her.

"Yes, Watson, I'm afraid you're right. We'll have to break into the bank."

Jaymie nearly lurched out of her chair. "What? No, Holmes—I wasn't being serious! We can't break into a bank, especially not one in Quadrant A. Chief Athelney will have you arrested and lock you in a cell in her prison block for the rest of your life."

"Believe me, she's tried to do far worse. Now come on, the bank will be closed by now."

"But...but we'll be breaking the law!" Jaymie stammered.

"It's no different than what we did when we searched for evidence in the Sunset Enterprises factory after the fire," Holmes remarked.

"Except here, the security system will be functioning. That will complicate matters slightly."

"Yes, only slightly," Jaymie said sarcastically. "Let's please just find a different way to do this. Can we at least check with that security guard, Eva Ty'upe? Maybe she could get us in?"

"She's not on duty tonight—I asked her before we left. She works two jobs apparently, and tonight she's working a shift at another business."

"But…but…"

Holmes glanced over at her, a serious look in his eyes. "Jaymie, do you truly believe Mr. Yigiol is innocent?"

"Well, yes," she said.

"Then we have to find a way to prove it." He looked her in the eyes and put a hand on her shoulder. "And this is the only way. Trust me."

Jaymie found herself nodding slowly, even though inside she could feel her stomach churning. "Ok," she said, dreading what they were about to do but also knowing they didn't have a choice. She was surprised by how easy it was to give in, but she figured by this point, she'd learned to just trust Holmes.

And she'd soon find out if that was the best thing—or the worst thing—she'd ever done.

Chapter 4: Breaking and Entering

Just once, Jaymie wished Holmes would exhibit some other emotion besides either calmness or manic brilliance. He never seemed anxious during any of these wild adventures, and breaking into a bank appeared to be no more nerve-wracking for him than simply strolling down the sidewalk. Jaymie, on the other hand, was so nervous she could barely breathe; her stomach was still churning, and she could feel her hands trembling as she clutched Holmes' techpad, which he had given her to look after.

Holmes had parked his hovercar in a public parking garage nearby, after arguing with the robot attendant for at least 10 minutes about why the rate had increased since the last time he parked there. They were now making their way to the bank's back entrance, which was, of course, protected by a pass code.

Having never been an accomplice to a burglary before, Jaymie had no idea how Holmes intended to get inside the building. She certainly wasn't expecting it to be simple, and so she was shocked when Holmes simply walked up to the control box, punched in a code on the keypad, and the door slid open.

"How…how did you do that?" Jaymie asked in amazement, but Holmes merely shrugged.

"I watched Miss Ty'upe punching in her security code on her techpad earlier today. I was really hoping it would be the same one she uses to get inside the building, although I must admit, having the same pass code for multiple functions really isn't the best practice in terms of security."

Jaymie had to admit it—she was impressed. "Holmes, I know I'm only going to contribute to your already inflated ego by saying this," she said, "but you're brilliant. I should have guessed you'd be one of those beings with a photographic memory."

"Only when it's important. Now let's hurry up and get inside, we're wasting time."

Jaymie and Holmes moved quickly through the empty, darkened halls of the bank, riding the turbolift up to the fifth floor, where the safe was. Holmes informed her there would be two security guards on duty, and as they came in, Holmes had spotted both guards patrolling through the first floor lobby together. Patrolling each floor took about ten minutes (another tidbit of information Ty'upe had provided), which meant they'd only have about 40 minutes until the guards reached the fifth floor, or possibly even less, if the guards split up.

"I'm going to check for fingerprints around the safe," Holmes said, taking back his techpad. "There's a fingerprint scanner left on here from my Civic Security days. I'm hoping we can use Ty'upe's code to—"

"Use my code to what?"

Jaymie jumped at the sudden noise, and her heart sank as she turned around and saw Ty'upe standing next to the turbolift, her hand resting on her stun blaster.

"Um, I think we're in trouble," Jaymie said.

Holmes stared at Ty'upe curiously. "This may not be the best question to ask at this time, but aren't you supposed to be somewhere else this evening?"

"The bank wanted extra security guards on duty, and I got called in," she said. "I wish I could say I was surprised to find you here, but I was kind of expecting it. You two are a piece of work."

"I assume we'll shortly be taking a little drive to our overnight accommodations at the Civic Security Station then," Holmes said, but there was a little smile tugging at the corners of Ty'upe's mouth. Jaymie found it odd, and a little out of character for the usually quite formal and professional security guard, but she was relieved Ty'upe didn't seem to be angry.

"I'm sure you didn't come to steal anything," Ty'upe said teasingly, and then her face grew serious once again. "Look, I want to clear Mr. Yigiol's name as much as you do. And I don't think Chief Athelney is as eager to do that as we are."

"Has she already scanned for fingerprints?" Holmes asked, and Ty'upe nodded, concern in her eyes.

"Yes, and she found a match. I'm afraid it's not looking very good for Mr. Yigiol."

Holmes waved his techpad over the door to the safe, then seconds later, results popped up on the screen. Holmes accessed the bank's security network using Ty'upe's password, which caused the security guard to raise her eyebrow.

"How did you do that?" she asked, and Holmes shrugged.

"I watched you typing it in earlier."

"And you wrote it down." There was a definite note of displeasure in Ty'upe's voice.

"No. I just remembered."

He compared the data from the fingerprint scan to the bank's files, which contained personal information on every employee, including Mr. Yigiol.

"Yes, it's definitely a match," Holmes confirmed. "Any chance these fingerprints could have been left over from Mr. Yigiol checking the safe on the day before the robbery?"

"Not likely," Ty'upe said. "The entire building is cleaned by robots every day after closing time. This surface would have been spotless at the time Mr. Yigiol broke in—I mean, *allegedly* broke in. The Quadrant A officers asked us to shut off the robots so they wouldn't clean the area today and cover up any evidence."

"Should we check for DNA then?" Jaymie said, and Ty'upe gave her a withering look that made her wince.

"Isn't that a little redundant?" Ty'upe said in a tone that seemed uncharacteristically condescending.

Jaymie blushed, wishing she could take back her comment. Of course, that made sense. She was still trying to get the whole feel of this investigative process, and she was a little unsure of how to go about gathering evidence.

However, Holmes was having an entirely different reaction to Jaymie's comment. He had gotten that faraway look in his eyes, a sign his brain was processing facts at a million kilometers an hour.

"Ty'upe—no offense intended, but please, shut up. As for you, Jaymie, you're a bloody genius."

"What?" both women asked at the same time, looks of disbelief and confusion on their faces.

Holmes ignored them, now too wrapped up in thought. He switched settings on his techpad scanner, waving it slowly over the front of the safe. Ty'upe shifted uncomfortably, and Jaymie glanced over at her. She didn't think it was just her imagination anymore; the security guard *was* behaving strangely.

Holmes waited until the data had finished processing, and then his eyes widened.

"Unbelievable," he said. He looked over at Jaymie. "It's not a match."

"But…but how can that be?" Jaymie asked. She wasn't entirely sure what had just happened.

"This DNA sample was collected from the same area as the fingerprint, but the DNA is not Mr. Yigiol's," Holmes said. "It also doesn't match up with any of the other bank employees."

Holmes stared hard at his techpad, on the cusp of an epiphany.

"Think, Sherlock, think!" he mumbled to himself. "How can the impossible be possible? How can the fingerprints, the recording, the security log all point to Mr. Yigiol, but then the DNA clearly turns out not to be his? I don't bloody—" He stopped, and then a look of realization dawned in his eyes.

He slowly turned to Ty'upe. "There's only one way this is possible. Mr. Yigiol did not rob the bank, but a version of him did. The burglar we're looking for is actually a shape-shifter."

"What? There's no such thing!" Ty'upe exclaimed. "That's absolutely ridiculous!"

"Then you haven't read your history," Holmes replied. "All beings from the world of Tweryt can shift forms. That world was destroyed in an ill-fated nuclear weapons experiment, but not all Tweryts were on planet at the time the accident occurred. Thus, there are still a limited number of shape-shifters in the galaxy. It's a fascinating ability, being able to make yourself look like any sentient being in the universe. You can sound like them, even leave their fingerprints. But what Tweryts can't do is change their actual DNA. That's the only hitch that prevents them from being the perfect criminals."

"That's crazy," Ty'upe said, and Jaymie almost believed she wasn't bluffing. But suddenly, far too many things made sense.

"Not really," Jaymie replied. "And you can't really be Ty'upe either."

The security guard's eyes narrowed, and Jaymie saw a small smile of pride spread across Holmes' lips. She had drawn exactly the conclusion he wanted her to.

"You've been acting strangely all evening," Jaymie went on. "Not overtly so, but there's definitely something off, and your mannerisms aren't exactly like Ty'upe's. Also, you told Holmes earlier today that you wouldn't be working tonight, and then you show up and oh-so-conveniently tell us a completely different story. It's looking an awful lot like you're a shape-shifter impersonating Ty'upe—and an awful lot like you're the thief who stole the diamond."

Ty'upe smiled, though it was not a very "Ty'upe" sort of smile. "You think you're pretty clever, don't you?" she sneered. Jaymie could see her body tensing, like a cat ready to spring, but she kept waiting, studying them carefully. She blinked, seeming perfectly calm, and then suddenly, she exploded into action.

She threw out a quick punch at Holmes, forcing him to duck. Jaymie reached for her stun blaster, a cheap model she'd started carrying since teaming up with Holmes, but the burglar kicked her in the leg, causing her to lose her balance and the gun to go skittering across the floor. Landing hard on her knee, Jaymie gasped for breath, praying nothing had been broken.

Holmes saw her hit the ground, and his eyes flashed angrily at "Ty'upe." He swung out a carefully executed punch, hitting the burglar square in the jaw.

The burglar stumbled back, rubbing her jaw and shaking her head as if trying to clear it. "Sensitive, aren't we, Mr. Holmes? You must not like me bullying your helpless little assistant. It's not like you to take interest in a girl who isn't up to your speed."

Jaymie struggled to get back to her feet, the thief's insult sticking her like a barb. She didn't need to be reminded yet again of how far she was falling behind. Just once it would be nice to feel like she was actually contributing to something, instead of always feeling like a "tagalong."

No, I do matter, she told herself, thinking back to the arrest of Jok Urdi and how Holmes had thanked her for her help. Holmes had told her then that she mattered—now she just had to convince herself.

The burglar performed a flying, martial-arts style kick, obviously very nimble on her feet, but Holmes was just as fast. Even though he fought with far less flair, his movements were more precise: quick, accurate, and always on target. He dodged the shape-shifter's kick and then threw out another punch of his own, and suddenly, next to him, the burglar appeared less accomplished, and her fighting style seemed overly dramatic. Dropping to a crouched position, the shape-shifter kicked at Holmes' knees, hoping to bring him down in a manner similar to the way she had dropped Jaymie. Holmes saw what was happening and tried to react, but as he twisted around, his foot caught on a crack in the marble floor. He went down, hard, and the burglar was instantly on him. Whipping out a cord, she wrapped it around his neck, and Jaymie's eyes widened in horror as the burglar quickly tightened the thin strip of plastic.

Holmes kicked and struggled, but the burglar kept her grip firm.

"Watson, a little help here would be nice!" he wheezed, struggling to loosen the cord but having little luck.

Her heart pounding, Jaymie's eyes darted around the room, searching for something she could use as a weapon. The burglar was between her and her stun gun, and she knew she had no hope of overcoming the lethal woman, even if she charged at her. She could see Holmes' face beginning to turn blue, and she saw the first look of genuine panic in his eyes.

Think, Watson, think!

The burglar was no longer paying attention to her, having obviously written her off as useless. *Not up to his speed*—again, Jaymie's pride burned at the insult.

"I'm not useless—I do matter," she repeated to herself, gathering her courage. She would show this overconfident shape-shifter a thing or two.

Just then, her eyes alighted on a decorative vase sitting on a pedestal. It was probably worth several hundred quid, and she breathed a quick apology to the bank management for what she was about to do.

She could now hear Holmes choking on every strangled breath, and she saw the burglar reaching back for Jaymie's gun. *Come what may, this was absolutely worth it...*

Jaymie suddenly dived towards the vase, grabbing it off the pedestal and flinging it at the burglar's head. This same sort of ploy had worked with the fleeing actor, Eben Hawkes; she only hoped it would work with the shape-shifter too.

The woman saw it coming, but in order to dodge out of the way, she had to loosen her grip on the cord around Holmes' neck. Holmes gulped in air, almost choking on the sudden influx of oxygen, and although he had to be disoriented, it didn't take him long to recover his wits. He grabbed the hand the burglar was using to grip her gun and twisted it around, snapping her wrist.

The burglar screeched and cried out in pain as she dropped the gun, clutching her now-broken wrist. Holmes scrambled to his feet and pointed the gun at the shape-shifter, and Jaymie darted up beside him.

"Well, I could have handled that a lot better," Holmes remarked to Jaymie, massaging his neck. Jaymie could see a bright red line where the cord had dug into his skin, and she shuddered. She glanced down at the floor where the burglar sat, still holding her wrist and giving them an icy glare.

"So, Quadrant A Civic Security should soon be on their way," Holmes said. "I may not have much faith in their investigative abilities, but I know they will respond to the alarm generated by the panic button near the safe, which I happened to press right before you knocked me over."

The burglar cursed.

"I'm guessing that means you didn't notice the button was there," Holmes continued, unfazed. "You should always look around for details like that. It's disappointing a thief as clever as you isn't more observant."

"Everyone makes mistakes," the burglar spat, and Holmes shook his head.

"Perhaps, but not everyone makes the right ones. Now..." He paused, looking at his wristband comlink and timekeeper. "If my timing is correct, we only have about a minute and a half left before Civic Security officers storm the building."

Jaymie listened, and sure enough, in the distance she could hear the wailing sirens of patrol hovercraft.

"Do you care to reveal to us your true identity?" Holmes asked. "Because I know there are ways to force a shape-shifter to reveal his or her true form, but that borders on torture, and I don't approve of shameless cruelty."

"Yeah, which is why you kindly decided to break my wrist," the burglar said sarcastically, then grimaced, struck by another wave of pain.

"I did the absolute minimum required to regain control of the situation," Holmes said. "You're the one who instigated the violence, not Watson or I."

Although the burglar continued to glare at them, Jamie began to notice a subtle but strange rippling on the burglar's skin. She had never seen a shape-shifter actually "shift" before, and she watched with horror and fascination as the burglar slowly began to switch forms. Her skin lightened a few shades, then stretched and contracted erratically for a few seconds. The skin grew rougher, and the burglar's shoulders slowly widened, and she increased a few inches in height. The shape of her face began to change, her jaw growing squarer and her eyes turning from black to a dark shade of blue. Stubble popped up on the burglar's chin, and Jaymie realized the woman wasn't just changing forms, she was changing gender.

"Interesting," Holmes remarked, studying him thoughtfully. "I still have absolutely no idea who you are."

Downstairs, Jaymie heard the sound of a door being busted open, and moments later, the clomping of boots as Civic Security officers charged up the marble staircase. A squad of Civic Security officers soon came bursting into the room, blasters aimed and ready to fire.

"Hands up!" Chief Athelney cried, shoving her way through the cluster of officers. She brandished her blaster, but then she seemed to stop in shock as she saw Holmes and Jaymie standing above the still-kneeling burglar.

"Chief Athelney—pleasure seeing you again," Holmes remarked, straightening his trench coat. "But we've been through that before, haven't we?"

Athelney cursed, uttering an obscenity that made even her staff flinch. "Holmes, your shenanigans are going to drive me to insanity. If you hadn't so obviously apprehended the thief, I would arrest *you* right now for burglary and not even care you were probably innocent."

"I'm glad to see you've held true to your commitment to uphold justice," Holmes said dryly. "I'd be happy to explain in great detail the reason for my presence here, but I'm sure you have a much better use for your time. You should probably arrest the thief before he gets any ideas about escaping. He may also need some medical attention."

Athelney gazed at the man on the ground and shook her head, though whether the reaction was one of exasperation or grudging admiration of Holmes' handiwork, Jaymie couldn't tell.

"Miles Zawker—I honestly never expected to see you again," Athelney said, and the man simply grunted. "One of the best cat burglars of his day, known particularly for jewel theft from the wealthy."

Holmes sighed. "How typical. Don't thieves try to steal anything unexpected or original anymore?"

Athelney ignored him. "Last time I saw Zawker, he was serving three life sentences on the prison moon of Iurtyn for kidnapping some politician's wife and stealing a royal tiara or something to that effect. How did you escape?"

"He's a shape-shifter," Jaymie answered for the burglar, and Athelney blinked in surprise.

"Come now—that's a little far-fetched, even for you, Holmes."

Holmes handed the chief his techpad. "You're welcome to examine the analysis for yourself. Watson here was the one who finally connected the dots: we checked fingerprints and DNA, and found they didn't match. Our conclusion? Shape-shifter."

The Civic Security inspectors studied the burglar with a newfound sense of wonder, most of them having never witnessed something quite that fantastical before.

"Are you sure this is his final identity?" Inspector Bryde asked. "No disrespect, Mr. Holmes, but if he shifted once, to make himself look like Mr. Yigiol, couldn't he pretend to be Zawker?"

"Unlikely," Athelney said. "Can't you see his wrist is broken? Shape-shifting is a difficult, uncomfortable process, and when shape-shifters are in extreme pain, it's more difficult for them to maintain a form that's not their own. It says that right here in Holmes' notes. But just to make sure this *is* the burglar's true form…"

Her hand darted forward, and she jabbed her finger into the soft area directly behind Zawker's left ear. The man suddenly shrieked in pain, making Jaymie and all the Civic Security inspectors cringe. Zawker continued to moan, but he did not change forms.

Athelney stepped back, seeming satisfied. "Happy, Bryde? Apparently all shape-shifters have a pressure point, a fact also mentioned in Holmes' oh-so-helpful notes. Press down hard enough on that spot, and it makes them return to their original form. It really is Zawker we've captured, though I never would have guessed he was a shape-shifter."

She waved her officers over. "Come on, let's secure him and get him back to the station. He has a long night of questioning ahead of him."

"Is there anything else you—" Jaymie started, but Athelney cut her off.

"I'll call you if I need any more information. Now, I told you once before to stay clear of this crime scene, and I really meant it. I have the authority to arrest you, so you'd better get out of here while I'm feeling generous."

Holmes didn't respond for a moment, staring at Zawker as the man's body continued to twitch from the pain of Athelney's "test."

Curled up in a fetal position and whimpering, the burglar no longer looked very intimidating.

"I don't like Civic Security officers who play dirty," Holmes remarked quietly, and Athelney merely shrugged.

"Yes—well, you don't like Civic Security officers in general, do you? I suspect Zawker will cooperate far more readily now. The diamond's likely already out of his possession and on the black market at this point, but he'll help us track it down. You can judge my methods all you like, but you can't deny they work."

"But at what cost, Athelney? Perhaps that's something you should consider."

With that, Holmes turned and strode towards the turbolift, and Jaymie quickly followed him. Neither of them said a word as they made their way back to his hovercar, though they were both undoubtedly thinking the same thing.

The image of Athelney stabbing her finger into Zawker's pressure point—it bothered her, and she couldn't seem to get it out of her mind. She supposed it had been necessary to prove Zawker really *was* Zawker, but there had been a certain harshness to the chief's action, just as there seemed to be a harshness to everything the woman did. Then again, Holmes himself had broken the man's wrist, though he claimed he hadn't used more force than necessary. Did that really make him any better than Athelney? And how much was Holmes really willing to do in pursuit of a case? What cost was *he* willing to pay?

Jaymie massaged her aching temples, deciding she wasn't ready to think about that now. Her head hurt, and she just wanted to go home and collapse into bed.

"Thank you for your help tonight—you did a fine job," Holmes told her as they walked out onto the street, hit by an icy blast of winter air.

"Oh, no problem," Jaymie fumbled, never really sure how to respond to Holmes' compliments, especially since they came so rarely. "I probably could have thought of something better than breaking the vase."

Holmes smiled. "Well, it worked. Though Mr. Yigiol may be taking it out of the 20,000 quid he promised to pay you."

The money—Jaymie had almost forgotten about it. Had she really just earned 20,000 quid? She had never had that much money before—well, that much money she had actually earned herself. It filled her with a sudden sense of pride; she had actually done something all on her own, something that hadn't been granted to her just because of her family's position in society.

"I think I can spare them a few hundred quid so they can buy a new vase," she said, and Holmes laughed.

"Glad to have you on board, Jaymie," he said, and she realized it was the first time he had actually called her by her first name.

Chapter 5: Not to Be Trifled With

When Jaymie woke up the next morning, she was surprised to find she had a message from the Civic Security Station in Quadrant A on her comlink. Thinking some of the inspectors must have come up with some more questions for her regarding the bank heist, she was even more surprised when she saw it was a notice from Inspector Bryde, informing her that her knapsack had been recovered.

"Bloody good luck," was Holmes' response when she told him about it over breakfast. He didn't have much else to say, apparently lost in his own thoughts. He'd seemed in such good spirits the night before, but something must have come up, and now he was working through some new puzzle. Still, he didn't object or seem overly inconvenienced when she asked him to drive her to the station to pick up her bag.

Jaymie allowed him to sit in silence for the first 10 minutes of the ride, and then she couldn't stand it any longer and finally had to speak up.

"All right, Holmes—something is bothering you. Admit it."

"Nothing's bothering me," Holmes said, letting out a sharp breath. "I just wish I felt more confident this case really was wrapped up. The more I think about it, the less certain I am that we drew the right conclusion."

Jaymie studied him for a moment, trying to guess what he was angling at. "You're not convinced Zawker did it, just like you weren't convinced Mr. Yigiol did it." She mentioned this not because she personally had any doubts about Zawker's guilt; it just seemed like the most likely place where Holmes would get hung up.

Holmes sighed. "Yes—and I know you're going to tell me I'm crazy. Athelney used the pressure point, and he didn't change forms, which leads us to believe 'Miles Zawker' really is the shape-shifter's true form."

"But…" Jaymie prompted.

"I didn't really expect him to change so quickly when I asked him to," Holmes confessed. "I wasn't threatening him, and he knew I wasn't intending to use the pressure point. Why would he give up his greatest asset—his ability to hide his identity—before he was forced to?"

"But we have to keep coming back to the fact that Athelney *did* use the pressure point," Jaymie said. "How could Zawker have resisted that? If he was faking it when he changed into Zawker, Athelney's test would have revealed that, right?"

"Supposedly yes," Holmes said. "It takes a great deal of concentration to maintain a 'shift' even under the best of circumstances, and especially when the shifter is in pain. But perhaps it is possible a shape-shifter could, if he or she had enough willpower, maintain a false form even through the excruciating pain of someone hitting their pressure point.

"You see, Jaymie, I'm just not one hundred percent convinced the shape-shifter we've captured really and truly is Zawker. He seemed, well…so…good at pretending to be a woman. Male shape-shifters always have a difficult time copying female mannerisms, though female shifters seem to have no problem copying males. Why that occurs probably says something fundamental about men and women in general, which I'd really rather not waste time getting into at the moment. However, Zawker was quite good at operating in his female form, which makes me wonder if he is indeed female.

"*Then* there's the added issue of the Quadrant A Civic Security Station break-in. From Inspector Bryde's description of the crime, it seems likely this was also committed by a shape-shifter. But was it also 'Zawker'? Why would he break into a Civic Security Station to steal a secretary's techpad? What does that have to do with the Gvidi diamond? Are they connected? If so, *why* are they connected? What am I missing?"

Holmes' barrage of mind-bending questions made Jaymie's head spin. She tried to block out his continued muttering, and she thought back over their interactions with the shape-shifter the night before, considering Holmes' theories. She searched for this mysterious 'connection' or missing puzzle piece he seemed to believe was hiding out there somewhere, but then she finally had to shake her head.

"Holmes, I'm sorry, but you're going to drive the both of us mad. I think sometimes you really do over-think things. You analyze everything so deeply; maybe this time you're making something out of nothing?"

Obviously frustrated, Holmes bit his lip, for once incapable of explaining himself. "I just...I just feel something's not right."

Feel—there was that word again. She could tell he hated using it, because a "feeling" wasn't the same as real evidence, but there seemed to be no other way he could put it. Well, he had felt Mr. Yigiol had been innocent, and that hunch had turned out to be right. Though the theory Zawker wasn't actually Zawker didn't seem to be all that plausible, Jaymie was willing to take a chance and trust him on this too. But there was no doubt that even though Holmes felt strongly about these sorts of hunches, and they usually happened to be correct, he didn't necessarily *like* having them. He wanted to prove them, to find hard evidence to back them up, and he grew upset when he couldn't do that. He was a man at war with himself, second-guessing everything he sensed instinctively, and yet also relying on that instinct to guide him. He wanted to be right more than anything else, and that driving need bordered on obsession. Maybe sometimes, his brilliance was less of a blessing and more of a curse.

Although Jaymie suspected Holmes hadn't given up on his theories, he said nothing else about the case, and soon they arrived at the Quadrant A Civic Security Station. Jaymie had wondered why Holmes hadn't really complained about the "inconvenience" of driving her to the station, but she soon guessed the reason why: as she stopped at the front desk to check in and pick up her bag, she saw him subtly start poking around and questioning some of the Civic Security inspectors wandering about, attempting to gather more evidence.

"Here's your bag, Miss Watson," the administrative assistant told Jaymie, handing her the knapsack.

Jaymie took it back and quickly looked it over, almost afraid of what she'd find. It was a little dirtier than the way she'd left it, but nothing a good run through the steam cleaner wouldn't fix. And, best of all, her textbooks and techpad were all still inside, looking as though they hadn't even been touched. The only thing missing was her hoverbus pass, which only had a few quid's worth of credit on it anyway.

"Almost everything's still here," she remarked in amazement. "I can't believe it. I mean, I'm not complaining, don't get me wrong. But why is my techpad still here? I thought the thief would have taken it."

The administrative assistant shrugged. "Don't know. The officer who found it and filled out the report said it was just sitting in some alley. Maybe the thief was looking through it and got scared off, who knows? Perhaps—"

Jaymie never got a chance to hear the secretary's theory. One second she was staring at the secretary sitting behind the front desk, clutching her recovered knapsack, and then the next, there was a brilliant flash of light, and the world seemed to turn upside down as a powerful shockwave of energy knocked her to the ground. The walls were rocked by the force of an explosion originating somewhere in the back of the station, and she heard a sharp, pealing scream. She instinctively covered her head with her hands, trying to protect herself from flying debris. There was a loud "boom" from a secondary, less powerful explosion, and a ceiling tile broke free and slammed into the floor right next to her, almost hitting her.

Jaymie felt herself trembling, and she wasn't sure at this point if it was safer to stay where she was or run. However, as several minutes passed, she figured they had experienced the last of the explosions. Her heart pounding, she tried to scramble to her feet, only to feel Holmes' hand on her arm, pulling her up.

Warning klaxons were now blaring overhead, and Civic Security officers went running towards the back of the station. She saw billows of smoke rolling out of the hallway, and she noticed officers were beginning to round up the few citizens who were in the lobby, escorting them to a safe area where they would probably be inspected to see if they had any devices or materials that would connect them to the explosion before they were ushered outside to safety.

Determined not to be rounded up before he could figure out what was going on, Holmes ducked into an alcove and pulled Jaymie inside with him. He waited until he spotted Inspector Bryde heading back to the point of the explosion, then he slipped in behind the young inspector, following him to the prison block. Jaymie coughed as the acrid smoke filled her lungs, but she kept trailing Holmes.

Still unaware he was being followed, Bryde came to a door protected by a pass code, separating the prison block from the area of the station that was accessible to the public. He punched in a number, then dashed into the hallway. The door closed again quickly, but not before Holmes and Jaymie slipped in after him.

Jaymie looked down the long row of cells, and she couldn't help letting out a gasp as she surveyed the destruction the blasts had caused. The door to one of the cells had been blown open, and it was now a pile of crumbled stone and twisted metal bars. On the ground next to the cell lay a prone figure who was grimacing and clutching her side, her fingers covered with blood from the wound.

Chief Athelney.

Athelney glanced up and saw Holmes, but either his presence didn't register, or she was too overcome by pain to order him to go away. Although her staff was trying to provide medical aid, she kept pushing them aside, attempting to stand up but not having the strength to do so.

"Holmes, come here!" she barked wearily after she finally seemed to notice him. She sat up slightly, and even though her eyes watered as she fought the pain, she wasn't willing to shed even a single tear, or display any sign of weakness in front of her staff. "You can't..."

She collapsed again, and one of her employees slipped an emergency breathing mask on her, giving her more oxygen.

"What happened here?" Holmes asked Inspector Bryde, who looked about as stunned as Jaymie now felt.

Bryde shook his head, not even bothering to reprimand Holmes for sneaking into an area someone who was not a Civic Security inspector had no business being in. "It's Zawker—somehow, he's managed an escape, though I don't know *how* he bloody did it. Blew the door clean off his cell, right after the chief was finished interrogating him. She wasn't very far down the hallway when it happened, so it's a miracle she wasn't killed."

Holmes' eyes darted around the smoke-filled hallway. "Any idea where he is now?"

"No. He swiped Athelney's security chip, which he could have used to bypass any of the codes needed to get out of the building. No doubt he's already out on the streets by now."

Holmes' expression grew troubled. "This is serious, Bryde. I was suspicious of this earlier, but I'm certain now: I don't think 'Zawker' is the shape-shifter's true form."

"Sir!" A young Civic Security officer interrupted their conversation, dashing over to them and carrying a blackened envelope in her hands.

"It's addressed to you, Mr. Holmes," she said urgently. "It was just lying in the cell, in the middle of the floor. Chief Athelney's on her way to the med center right now for treatment, but before she left, she told us to give this to you and have you open it right away. She said Zawker must have left it for you."

Holmes slowly took the envelope and turned it over, and, sure enough, his name was scrawled in beautiful, flowing cursive on the front. It had been a long, long time since Jaymie had actually seen a handwritten letter; everyone communicated by comlink or techpad messages now, and the type of postal service she had read about in her history books wasn't even in existence anymore. Why would Zawker use this form of communication, and why did he want to communicate with Holmes in the first place?

Holmes opened the letter, and Jaymie couldn't keep herself from looking over his shoulder and reading along with him, burning with curiosity.

"Dearest Sherlock Holmes," the letter began, "by the time you get this, I'll be long gone, laughing as I imagine the look on your face. Leaving a note for you may seem overly maudlin, but I couldn't resist. I'm disappointed in you, Holmes. I expected the bumbling fools at Civic Security to buy the disguise, but I thought you'd know better. True, I never told you I was a shape-shifter, but you fancy yourself such a genius, I thought you'd guess.

"You'll be tempted to try to track me down, but do yourself a favor and don't. Be careful, Sherlock: you may not know it yet, but you've stumbled into something deeper now, something of a vastly larger scope than you've ever dabbled in before. The missing diamond should be the least of your worries. I was told not to warn you, but you know how well I take orders. You've always fascinated me, and a world without you would be a frightfully dull place. So let me go, and keep watching your back. You have enemies with more power and influence than you can possibly imagine. Your dearly devoted 'femme fatale,' Irene Adler."

"What the devil is that all about?" Bryde asked in astonishment (he had apparently been peeking over Holmes' shoulder as well).

For a moment, Holmes said nothing, staring blankly ahead. "Impossible," he breathed, and Bryde gave him a look of concern.

"You know this woman?" he said. "Who is she?"

His face grim, Holmes crumpled up the letter, and he tossed it onto a piece of still smoldering debris. The paper immediately burst into flames, bright tongues of fire quickly reducing the letter to a pile of ash. "Someone not to be trifled with."

Case No. 4: Kiss and Tell

Chapter 1: A Date with Disaster

Lestrade sat back in the plush, high-backed chair inside the Matrié d'Poll, a restaurant currently regarded as the most elegant place in Quadrant A to start off "a night on the town." With low lighting, gold candelabra on every table, and waiters dressed in fancy uniforms that were probably more expensive than all the suits Lestrade owned combined, the restaurant was very romantic and decidedly upper-class.

And expensive, Lestrade thought to himself as he glanced over the menu and winced. The cheapest item on the menu was three times his hourly wage at the Civic Security Station.

He let out a sigh and readjusted his necktie, resisting the urge to look at the timekeeper on his comlink once again. *Why was it taking his date so bloody long to get here?* Was traffic really that bad? Had something come up that was keeping her at the office later than normal? Or, mostly likely (though Lestrade desperately hoped this wasn't the case), she had stood him up.

He saw a waitress casually walk by his table, observing him but trying (unsuccessfully) to appear as though she *wasn't* observing him. Lestrade had been sitting here alone for an hour and still hadn't ordered any food, and the waitress was likely getting a little antsy. There was a crowd of people in the lobby waiting to get a table, and although a waiter at a restaurant as fancy as this one would *never* consider rushing a guest, a customer who lingered without ordering was not a welcome occurrence, and he or she was gently urged to either make a purchase or let another customer use the table.

The waitress walked back and forth a few more times, then she finally decided to move in.

"Can I get you another glass of wine, Sir, or perhaps an appetizer while you wait?" she asked, her smile almost appearing as if it wasn't forced.

It was a good ploy, but it didn't work. Lestrade wasn't ready for "another" glass of wine (he hadn't even ordered a "first" glass yet, which the waitress was obviously aware of), and she'd already tried the appetizer bit—twice.

"No thank you," he said, and though the waitress smiled again and nodded, he noticed her façade of politeness had become the slightest bit more strained.

As soon as she left, Lestrade finally couldn't resist any longer, and he looked at his timekeeper. *2000 hours*—he had officially been waiting here for more than an hour, and he had to admit to himself that his date was probably a no-show. He supposed he should have figured as much. He'd met this girl only once—by accident, really. He and another Civic Security inspector had been feeling brave one night and decided to try their luck socializing at an upper-class Quadrant A nightclub. This girl had walked in, mistaking it for another club, and had come over to ask Lestrade for directions. It had taken quite a bit of finagling on his part, but he had finally gotten her comlink contact code, and after several unreturned calls, he had finally convinced her to meet him here tonight.

Only now, he could see she had probably just been leading him on. She was quite out of his league, he should have known that, but he'd been stupid enough to try anyway. Now he was forced to spend an evening alone with only his wounded ego for company.

"That's it," he muttered, standing to his feet as the waitress passed by, yet again. He threw a few quid on the table as a tip for the waitress, just to thank her for her trouble, even though he hadn't ordered anything. He grabbed his suit jacket and was just about to walk out, when he saw the hostess walking towards his table, smiling.

Lestrade's heart skipped slightly, and he allowed himself to hope, for a fraction of a second, that maybe his date had arrived after all, and the hostess had come to escort her to the table. However, he wasn't that lucky. The hostess *was* bringing someone to his table, but it certainly wasn't Ilsa Dvorr.

It was Sherlock Holmes and Jaymie Watson.

"What in the galaxy—"

"Please, Lestrade, we have no time for paltry questions," Holmes said, holding up a hand. Although he had a fiery, slightly possessed look in his eyes, which meant he'd uncovered something big, what was noticeably missing was that cocky grin of his, what Lestrade called his "thrill of the chase" look. Holmes had had a breakthrough on a case, but it appeared to have left him strangely unsettled. The great Sherlock Holmes looked almost...afraid.

Lestrade felt a sudden surge of concern for his friend, and it was powerful enough that he forgot to be irritated that Holmes had barged in on his personal life once again.

"Holmes, what is it?" he asked. "You look uneasy—and you *never* look uneasy."

"She's back," was all Holmes said, and for a moment Lestrade was clueless.

"She?" he said, then jokingly added, "come on, Holmes, you don't know any women. Well, except for—" He paused, and a look of horror dawned in his eyes. "God save us. This had better not be about Irene Adler."

Holmes slowly nodded. "I don't know how she escaped Traxil."

"And what exactly is 'Traxil'?" Jaymie asked. "A person? A place?"

"It's supposedly the highest security prison in the known galaxy," Holmes explained. "It's surrounded by five different force fields, the last of which is designed to vaporize all unauthorized ships entering or exiting the perimeter. There hasn't been a single successful escape attempt in the prison's entire thousand-year history—but somehow, she did it. And now she's here."

"Well, that's just bloody fantastic," Lestrade said, collapsing back into his chair. "Any other good news you'd like to share, just in case my day wasn't ruined already?"

"Oh, it gets worse," Holmes continued. "We discovered she's not just a thief, assassin and person of general poor moral character: she's also a shape-shifter."

Lestrade sucked in a sharp breath. It took all of his self-control not to let out one of the alien curses he'd learned during his days in Civic Security, knowing that was an excellent way of getting himself kicked out of the restaurant and barred from ever returning.

"Holmes, why does the only woman you've ever glanced twice at have to be one of the most dangerous women in the galaxy?"

Holmes started to offer a retort, but Lestrade shook his head.

"Never mind, I think I just answered my own question. Holmes, you always have been, and always will be, attracted to anything that pushes you to your limit or would cause most normal, rational beings to run away in fear. But I really think you've done it this time. I told you that woman would be the death of you, and you probably should have listened when—"

"Excuse me, can someone please explain what is going on?" Jaymie interrupted, finally seeming to run out of patience. "Because I'd really like to understand what you're bloody talking about."

She was trying to ask it as calmly as possible, but Lestrade could hear the strain and frustration in her voice, and he suddenly realized he and Holmes had been babbling on about a very serious subject she probably knew nothing about. Or, more accurately, a subject she knew nothing about because Holmes had once again neglected to keep her in the loop. And that had to stop. *Now.*

Holmes started shaking his head. "I'm sorry, Watson, but we don't have time for that right—"

"No, we do," Lestrade said curtly. "Sherlock, I think it's past time for you to start explaining some things to poor Jaymie. She needs to know what kind of danger you've landed her in before you continue dragging her from quadrant to quadrant on this mad quest of yours."

"But—"

Usually Holmes could talk his way out of anything, and usually he was successful at manipulating Lestrade. But not today. Lestrade was already irritated about his no-show date, and now this bit of news about Adler. He was not in a charitable mood, especially not towards Holmes. The detective had been running around, letting Jaymie play the role of his assistant for far too long. It wasn't a game anymore—and Jaymie needed to know that.

"Let's go," Lestrade commanded, grabbing Holmes by the arm and pulling him through the restaurant. Holmes tried to protest, but Lestrade would have none of it.

"Did you drive or take the hoverbus?" Lestrade asked.

"Lestrade, it's utterly ridiculous for you to be dragging me along like a—"

"We took the hoverbus," Jaymie piped up over Holmes' continued protesting, and Lestrade nodded.

"Good. Then we can just ride back together in my hovercar."

He barged through the automatic door of the restaurant, not even noticing the hostess's rather puzzled expression and offer of "Come again soon!"

He marched Holmes to the hovercar and rather unceremoniously shoved him into the front seat. It wasn't until he had whipped around the front of the restaurant, preparing to head back to apartment complex 221 in Quadrant B that he noticed a tall brunette, dressed in a sparkling purple dress, walking up the short flight of steps to the Matrié d'Poll entrance. Lestrade stared in shock. It was Ilsa Dvorr! She had shown up after all. His hand hovered briefly over the break, and he was tempted to stop the hovercar, rush in after her, and leave Holmes to clean up his own mess. But as he glanced back at Jaymie, who was looking confused but stubbornly unafraid, he knew he had a responsibility to her—if not to Holmes—to clear this up. He watched Ilsa disappear into the restaurant, and then cursing softly to himself, he pushed the throttle forward and headed back to Quadrant B.

"Are we going back home, then?" Holmes asked, and Lestrade shook his head.

"No. I just decided that I need a drink. And you're buying."

Chapter 2: Confessions

Jaymie stared into the pint of ale sitting in front of her, trying to force her mind to focus. What had started earlier today as a slight headache had mushroomed into a full-blown migraine, and she knew she wasn't likely to get any relief soon. She, Lestrade, and Holmes were sitting in a booth at the back of a pub called the Drunk Gypsy, where she and Holmes had come several months ago to question a bartender named Padric O'Vax about a clue in a drug-running case. Lestrade made Holmes buy all three of them a pint of ale, and now Jaymie presumed she was going to hear the background of a story she wasn't entirely sure she wanted to understand.

"So, Holmes," Lestrade said after finishing his pint, "are you going to tell this story, or shall I?"

Holmes was silent for a moment, trying very much not to look like he was sulking but in the process only managing to look very much like he was sulking.

"I still don't see why—" he started somewhat moodily, only to have Lestrade cut him off.

"All right, it appears as though I'll have to tell it," he remarked, clearly not in the mood to put up with any nonsense from Holmes. "To start with, Jaymie, you should know Irene Adler is the first and only criminal who has ever duped the almighty Sherlock Holmes."

"Perhaps 'duped' is not the best word," Holmes cut it, and Lestrade gave him an incredulous look.

"Holmes, 'duped' is a *nice* way of putting it. She played you like an Andronidan lute. She came to Eglon, pretending to be a poor 'damsel in distress' whose inheritance had been stolen from her. And this inheritance happened to include a collection of thousand-year-old scrolls of ancient philosophy. Holmes was ensnared by his own curiosity and followed her about for several days, investigating. How she managed to charm him into believing her rather maudlin 'tale of woe,' I have no idea, and I don't really *want* to know."

Jaymie glanced over at Holmes, an unpleasant knot in her stomach. "So you fancied her, then?" There was a slight edge in her voice as she asked the question, and it surprised her a bit to find it there. Under the surface was a simmering feeling that just might be jealousy, though she couldn't quite quantify it.

"Of course not," Holmes said, perhaps a bit too quickly. "She is a thief, a liar, and not to be trusted. That would, understandably, be a turn-off for most."

"Is it a turn-off for you?" Jaymie shot back, surprised to find herself so uncharacteristically ill-tempered. Despite what Holmes said, she could think of only one thing that could muddle his normally razor-sharp wits: a certain emotion he himself probably wouldn't even admit to having. *"Femme fatale" indeed*—Adler intrigued him in a way Jaymie hadn't thought he could be intrigued. And somehow, the fact it was Adler who had stimulated those feelings made her angry at Adler *and* Holmes.

"Yes, it's a 'turn-off'!" Holmes insisted. "She may call me her 'dear Sherlock Holmes,' but trust me, she would slit my throat had she the chance. The only feelings I have for her are of extreme annoyance and a deep desire to see her brought to justice."

"I'm sure," Jaymie said, in a tone that indicated she wasn't sure at all. "And I'm positive that's all you were feeling when she told you her 'poor, distressed heiress' story."

"No!" Holmes replied, then thought about what he'd said and added, "I mean, yes. Wait—blast, this is a trap, isn't it? Why so many accusations, Watson?"

"Well, why are you so defensive?"

"Please!" Lestrade said, giving both Jaymie and Holmes a stern glare. "It's bad enough I have to play 'storyteller'—don't make me be a referee as well."

Jaymie bit her lip, and she instantly felt ashamed of herself. Lestrade's reprimand had diffused the heat of her anger (though it didn't quite get rid of the feeling itself), and she realized she was being petty. It still bothered her quite deeply, but to continue going on about it would be juvenile. *You're overreacting, Watson*, she rebuked herself. *The ale's gone straight to your head—you have to look at the bigger picture here.* However much she might hate it.

"I'm sorry, please go on," she told Lestrade, and Holmes nodded in agreement, probably the closest they would get to an apology from him.

"Well, whatever you might say, Holmes, Jaymie does have a point," Lestrade said. "You were intrigued by Adler, don't deny it. And it was too late when you finally came to your bloody senses and figured out she was not an heiress at all and was actually trying to steal the scrolls from their rightful owners. It was the one humble moment of your career—you sneak into this mansion with Adler, supposedly going to take the scrolls back from the being who had 'stolen' them. You waltz on out of the mansion, carrying a stack of scrolls under your arm, only to find a squad of Quadrant C Civic Security inspectors standing there waiting to arrest the burglars." Lestrade's face broke into a grin. "Oh, the look on your face must have been priceless."

"They actually believed he'd stolen the scrolls?" Jaymie said, and Lestrade's grin only widened.

"Oh, of course not. But they couldn't resist a chance to 'arrest' him after all the grief he'd given Civic Security over the years. I couldn't believe it when he called me and asked me to come bail him out of prison. I don't think I've ever laughed so hard as when I walked into the Civic Security Station in Quadrant C and saw Holmes sitting in a corner cell, pouting, his arms folded across his chest. He knew he'd been had, and so did everyone else. It made him quite cross and—"

"Yes, Lestrade, I'm sure she gets the idea," Holmes said grumpily. "And no matter how much you and all the rest of Civic Security seem to find it amusing, I'd really appreciate it if people stopped bringing up this story."

"Well, we probably would if that was the *end* of the story," Lestrade said. "But Irene Adler wasn't done with Sherlock Holmes. Although she escaped from getting arrested, she was livid Holmes had failed her. She only made off with a few scrolls before Civic Security showed up, and the rest were moved to an undisclosed and more secure location. And of course, Holmes wasn't done with her either. He was quite put out she'd tricked him, and he made it his mission to bring her to justice."

"And it wasn't easy," Holmes said, finally seeming to accept the whole story was coming out and figuring if he was doomed, he might as well tell it in his own words. "Ms. Adler is a woman of many guises, conjured up to keep Civic Security off her tail. However, most of the time on Eglon she was posing as a nightclub magician called the 'Black Addler.'" He rolled his eyes. "I personally think it's an utterly ridiculous stage name, and I told her so, many times. I hate puns in general, but bad puns are even—"

"Holmes, focus!" Lestrade ordered. "Whatever you think of her stage name, she was an amazing magician. Some of her tricks bordered on the downright magical. She even managed to stump Holmes, which is not an easy feat. I can't tell you how many magic shows Holmes and I have been to, where afterwards he sat down and told me exactly how every single trick in the show was done, regardless of how often I told him I didn't want to know because it would spoil the fun. But he couldn't figure out Adler's tricks, no matter how much he puzzled over them, and he could never quite seem to keep up with her. She was always a step ahead of him, always eluding capture, until one night. Holmes disguised himself as one of her assistants, switched places with a real assistant, and arrested Adler at the climax of her show. I guess it was fitting, since it was also the climax of his career as a Civic Security inspector. He quit the department the next day."

"But why?" Jaymie couldn't help asking. "Surely capturing Adler would have at least been good for a promotion. What made you leave?"

"I was tired," Holmes said simply. "Tired of trying to fit my sometimes...'creative' investigative methods into the inflexible straightjacket of Civic Security regulations. The Quadrant B chief at that time, Nattip Bradstreet, ordered me not to go undercover as part of the magic act, said it was too risky. I told him he couldn't catch Adler any other way. Turns out, I was right, he was wrong, but he was still upset

I'd ignored his orders. He gave me a choice: said I could quit, or he'd publicly fire me. And of course you know what I chose."

"You always did have to have the last word," Lestrade said. "Or at least appear that you did. Trouble is, Irene Adler is the same way. She's as stubborn and clever as you are, Holmes, and apparently even the most secure prison in the galaxy isn't enough to contain her. Any idea why she's back?"

"To torment me? Kill me? Wreck havoc on the galaxy? Who knows," Holmes said with a sigh. "She's obviously back in the business of petty theft; she stole the Gvidi diamond, though I doubt that's the only reason she's here. She tried to warn me there's a...what was it? Ah, yes: there's a greater force at work here, or something like that. But what she meant by that I haven't a bloody idea."

"Well, we'd better catch her this time, and think of a better place to hold her than the prison on Traxil," Lestrade said. "And preferably, let's do it soon. I don't want to have to keep watching my back for several months or, heaven forbid, several years like last time."

"We trapped her once before, and I can do it again," Holmes replied matter-of-factly. "She's not infallible."

"Yes, but neither are you," Lestrade said sternly. "Holmes, we can't afford to be overconfident about this case. Adler is a deadly opponent, especially since she's a shape-shifter. She can go anywhere, be anyone—she could pretend to be me or Jaymie, walk up to you, and then whip out a blaster and blow you away before you even had a chance to blink. Holmes, there's a reason that woman's stage name is a play on the name of one of the most deadly serpents known to mankind. And as your assistant, Jaymie's now caught in the crossfire as well. What happens if Adler decides to come after her?"

Holmes was silent for a moment, glancing over at Jaymie and studying her carefully. "Perhaps I *have* underestimated Adler, but I think you underestimate Watson," he remarked quietly. "I believe she's fully capable of handling herself. Watson, what do you think?"

Jaymie looked down at the pint of ale in her hands, the mug now completely empty and her head buzzing slightly. "I think...I think I need another drink," she said. "Something stronger this time—please."

"Of course," Lestrade said, quickly waving the bartender over. "We'll add it to Holmes' tab, which he is not to make a single complaint about. In fact, he probably owes you several rounds of drinks for the next confession he's about to make to you."

"What?"

Holmes and Jaymie voiced the question at the same moment. The bartender slid a tall, clear glass filled with a greenish-colored liquid over towards them, and Lestrade handed it to Jaymie.

"Yes. Holmes, you've come clean about Adler, you might as well tell the entire story. She deserves to know this too."

"Lestrade, I—" For the first time in the six months Jaymie had known him, Holmes' voice faltered. He couldn't seem to make himself continue, but the strange, almost vulnerable look in his blue and brown eyes said everything that needed to be said. He was begging (something that had to be absolutely humiliating for him), silently pleading with Lestrade not to go on. There was genuine pain in that look, and Jaymie wondered what could be so dreadful he didn't want Lestrade to force him to say it.

Yet even though she knew Lestrade would never want to hurt his friend, apparently he had decided this was important enough he had to tell it.

"Jaymie, you probably assumed from the way Holmes talks about Loudron that he's native to this city," Lestrade began. "And that is true, at least in part. Yet while Holmes was born in Loudron and has lived here all his life, his parents were both from the moon of Ionia. Now, you've probably never heard of it, but that's understandable because almost no one has. It was destroyed in the same nuclear accident that destroyed Tweryt, the planet it orbits. This is, of course, the planet of the shape-shifters, which might have come up in you and Holmes' discussions. The Tweryts are a little more well-known than the moon dwellers, who purposelessly kept their culture isolated from the rest of the galaxy. Still, none of the beings in the Kraxis star system are exactly known for being social, which is due in part to their, well, 'unique' abilities.

"You see, the star system is a bit of an anomaly. All the worlds in that system are slightly radioactive, and if normal beings ever visited them, they would develop radiation sickness and eventually die. However, the slightly radioactive state of the planets and moons didn't harm the native inhabitants; in fact, it enhanced them, and they developed unusual powers. Some beings could shape-shift, others had the ability to turn invisible, and some could reportedly even teleport without a teleporter, though that's just a rumor. They tried to keep these abilities a secret, because of course, if the rest of the galaxy were to find out about them, these creatures would be exploited.

"Sadly, that's exactly what happened to the people of Tweryt and Ionia. Beings from another planet came in, used some of the radioactive elements found in the natural environments, and tried to develop a nuclear weapon to end all nuclear weapons. Unfortunately, something went wrong, and Tweryt blew up, and took the moon of Ionia with it."

"Oh, Holmes," Jaymie breathed. "What a terrible thing to happen. To lose your entire culture..."

"You don't have to feel sorry for me," Holmes said stiffly, adjusting the collar of his trench coat. "I wasn't born there, so I have no memory of what it was like. Just stories my parents told me. I've been able to think of Loudron as my home."

That was probably true, but reading between the lines, Jaymie could tell the loss still registered for Holmes, somewhere deep down below that unyielding determination of his to keep a stiff "Eglon upper lip," as she'd heard it called. Maybe he didn't even realize he felt the loss, but you couldn't lose your entire culture and not feel *something*.

"But if you're from Ionia, then you must have some sort of special ability," Jaymie said. "Maybe I, well, I probably shouldn't ask, but...what is it? Would you tell me?"

Holmes glanced over at Lestrade, who gave him a nod. "I think she needs to know."

Holmes let out a long, slow sigh, pushing his mug of ale away from him. "All right. Watson, I'm a telepath."

It was a good thing Jaymie had already finished her drink, or else she probably would have dropped the glass on the floor and shattered it.

"What?" she sputtered. She had guessed at several possibilities, but that certainly hadn't been one of them. Surely it wasn't possible—beings just couldn't read other beings' minds! The concepts of shape-shifting and turning invisible were hard enough to grasp as it was; the thought of Holmes having some sort of psychic power was almost more than she could take. If he could read people's minds, could he also control them? Would he do it to criminals? Would he do it to...

Jaymie's face turned a brilliant red. "Oh, blast, have you done it to me before? Are you in my head right now?"

"No! Absolutely not!" Holmes snapped so harshly that it made her and Lestrade flinch. Noticing their reaction, he immediately appeared sheepish and continued in a softer tone, "I just want to make sure you understand I have never once even *considered* reading your mind, nor do I intend to do so in the future."

"But you could," Jaymie said, still struggling to come to grips with this revelation and what it meant for their "partnership." She believed him when he said he'd never read her mind, but the thought that he had the power to do so was more than a little eerie. There were some thoughts she'd had in the past she desperately didn't want Holmes to know about.

"I may have the ability, but I'm not a practicing telepath," Holmes said. "Believe me, it's a 'talent' I would give anything to be rid of."

"Did you ever use those abilities when you were a Civic Security inspector?" Jaymie asked, but Holmes adamantly shook his head.

"No. When I joined Civic Security in Quadrant B, I vowed to never use my telepathic abilities to solve a case. Quite frankly, I never found using those abilities to be very fair. It felt like cheating somehow."

"Yet what if reading a criminal's mind meant saving a life further down the line?" Jaymie persisted. "Believe me, I don't like the idea of telepathic powers anymore than you seem to, but that appears like the one situation where it might be ethical."

"Yet at what cost?" Holmes said sadly, a twinge of regret in his voice. "The mind is a sacred, secret thing—no one deserves to have theirs penetrated. I did it only once, but I will never do it again because of the agony it inflicted. I'm supposed to have mild powers of mind manipulation also, which I despise even more. Reading or controlling someone's mind is something I will absolutely never do. Not for any reason. If I started, it could be like opening the proverbial 'Pandora's Box'—when would I stop? Where would I draw the line, and eventually, would I draw one at all?"

Jaymie felt an icy chill shivering down her spine as she thought of one person possessing all that power. She had never heard Holmes speak about something in such a deadly serious tone before. He was a man she thought feared nothing, but he was clearly afraid of his own power.

"Now, the one thing I can't control is my ability to instantly size up a being's character," Holmes said. "It's tied into my ability to read minds, but unlike the mind reading, I can't stop myself from evaluating another person like that. It just happens."

"That's how you were sure the Bank of Eglon president, Mr. Yigiol, and that actor, Eben Hawkes, were innocent," Jaymie said, some of the pieces about Holmes that had always puzzled her now falling into place. "You couldn't prove it by reading their minds, but you sensed the innocence in them."

"I suppose that's the best way to put it," Holmes said. "Still, I only use those feelings as a guide—I have to find the facts to back them up."

"Well then." Jaymie didn't know what else to say. Her head was spinning madly now, and this time, it had nothing to do with alcohol. She felt like she desperately needed yet another drink, though she knew she had had enough already.

"Look, I know this is a lot to spring on you all at once," Lestrade said. "And Holmes will be cross with me for quite some time for forcing him to talk about his past. But you're into this mess deep enough by now that you have a right to know what's going on. You might be upset with Holmes for keeping this from you, and frankly, I was too when he first told me the truth about himself several years ago. It's not that he doesn't trust you; in fact, you're one of the few people he *does* trust. Even though I sort of forced his hand, I couldn't have made him stay here to tell this to you if he really hadn't wanted to. Probably part of him has wanted to tell you for a long time, but you know how that goes. He's just...well, he's just Sherlock Holmes."

Jaymie nodded, still at a loss for words. *He's just Sherlock Holmes—* yes, somehow that really did explain everything, however frustrating that might be.

Holmes cleared his throat. "Well, thank you, Lestrade, but now I'd appreciate it if you'd stop speaking about me as if I weren't here. Since you have laid bare all of my life's secrets, am I free to return to actually attempting to solve this case?" He looked over at Jaymie, his vulnerable moment now lost once again amidst that devil-may-care bluster of his. "Watson, are you ready?"

Truthfully? She wasn't—she'd just learned her eccentric, slightly sociopathic roommate was a telepathic alien being followed by a dangerous, shape-shifting woman who was also possibly an ex-love interest of his. But she'd have to once again let go and just trust Holmes, and hang on for the ride.

"Let's go," she said, picking up her empty glass as Holmes and Lestrade started for the door. She started to slide the glass back towards the bartender, but then she glanced at it more carefully and realized she'd missed something earlier.

Spying what appeared to be a piece of paper stuck to the bottom of the glass, she peeled it off and unfolded it. It was a short message scrawled in rather uneven penmanship: *"Looking for snakes? Best place to search is under a rock."*

Jaymie's heart thudded. *Snakes*—obviously referencing the "Black Addler," Irene Adler's stage name. She glanced over at the bar and saw Padric O'Vax wiping off glasses and putting them back on the shelf. She caught his eye, and he gave her a slight nod, then immediately turned back to his work. He had given them a tip, and though she longed to ask him more about it, to see if she could get him to tell her what he meant, she sensed this was all he felt safe sharing.

"Jaymie, are you coming?" she heard Holmes call to her, and she quickly slipped the piece of paper in her pocket and set down the glass. She might not be an expert at playing this detective game yet, but she was learning. Padric had trusted her enough to leave the note with her; she would make the most of it.

Chapter 3: An Unexpected Visitor

Jaymie meant to share the note with Holmes and Lestrade the minute they arrived back at the flat, but a rather shocking surprise waiting for them quickly put all thoughts of the note from Jaymie's mind.

A number of overhead lights in the hallway leading up to their flat had run out of power and de-luminated, so the corridor was only dimly lit. As they stepped out of the turbolift, Lestrade stumbled over a basket of laundry someone had left outside their door, the inspector unable to see the obstacle in the low lighting.

"Blast!" he cursed, slamming into the wall in a failed attempt to catch his balance. "Why does no one bother to report to Mrs. Hudson when the lights go out?"

"Because they always assume someone else will do it," Holmes said matter-of-factly. "It's an all-too-common trait of human nature, and I believe that—"

He stopped and suddenly stuck out his hand in front of Jaymie and Lestrade, bringing them to an abrupt halt and nearly causing Lestrade to trip again. A figure was standing in front of the door to their flat, her profile silhouetted against the dingy gray wall. She was wearing a long coat similar to Holmes', and she had short, brilliant red hair. She almost looked like a certain Quadrant A Civic Security chief, but Jaymie couldn't quite believe it. The woman had been gravely wounded in an explosion less than 24 hours ago—surely she must still be in the hospital!

"Chief...Athelney?" Lestrade asked in amazement.

"Yes—now please open the bloody door so we can go inside the flat and talk. I don't think I was followed, but I don't wish to take any chances." She glanced at Lestrade. "I came to speak with just Holmes and Watson, but if you're one of their associates, I suppose there's no harm in letting you listen in, unless…" She narrowed her eyes slightly and looked at him more closely, as if scrutinizing him. "Wait a moment—are you that hot-shot inspector who used to work for Quadrant B who once had the impertinence to ask me out on a date?"

Lestrade remained absolutely expressionless, though his face might possibly have turned just a shade paler. "I'm, um, positive that couldn't possibly have been me."

Athelney's eyes seemed to bore straight into his soul. "Good answer. Now stop gaping and let us in, please?

"Yes, ma'am." Lestrade scrambled to pull out his entry card and quickly swiped it. The moment the door slid open, Athelney marched into the flat, switching on a light and then gesturing for them all to have a seat.

"All right, I'm going to get straight to the point," she said. "My doctor would kill me if she knew I were here. I made the nurses give me a double shot of healing serum, which will keep me on my feet for another hour or so, but then I'll crash again. I need the three of you to shut up and listen, so I can get through this as quickly as possible."

"It is slightly irregular to have one's guest direct you what to do in your own flat," Holmes started to protest. "I—"

"Shut it, Holmes," Athelney said. "I do not have time for your drama now. I…" She hesitated, her next words seeming to come with great difficulty. "I…I never imagined I would say this, and part of me still can't believe I'm going through with this, but I have to ask: Holmes, I need your help."

That stopped Holmes dead in his tracks. He turned to look at Athelney and blinked. "What?"

"You heard me," Athelney said. "And I'm not going to repeat it. This Irene Adler is becoming a real problem, and I...well, I'm no longer convinced I have the resources to catch her."

If Jaymie hadn't been standing there in the room as Athelney said it, she never would have believed those words had come out of the chief's mouth. Not only had the woman admitted she needed assistance from Holmes, she actually looked worried. She hadn't lost that determined, proud look, but she was perilously close to a woman being broken.

Jaymie could tell Holmes desperately wanted to make some sarcastic comment, but even he seemed to realize now was definitely not the time to be rubbing Athelney's sudden vulnerability in.

"I completely agree: Adler *is* dangerous," Holmes replied. "We need to capture her as soon as possible, and of course Watson, Lestrade, and I will help. But why, pray tell, the sudden change of heart? You didn't seem to want my help back at the station earlier today."

"Things have changed," Athelney said curtly. "Two explosions went off in the prison block, as I'm sure you're aware. But what you probably don't know is that while the first freed Adler and knocked me out of commission, the second killed Jok Urdi."

Holmes' eyebrow spiked up in shock. "That's not possible. He's not even supposed to be in the Quadrant A prison—that was a Quadrant B case."

He glanced over at Lestrade, searching for affirmation, but Lestrade could only shrug awkwardly. "I tried to stop it, but they decided to transfer him to the Quadrant A station. They thought it was, well, more secure."

"I see," Holmes said. "That appears to have worked out about as well as most Civic Security plans—namely, they don't work at all."

Athelney scowled. "Well, we can sit here arguing about what went wrong in the past that landed us in this mess, or we can put all that behind us and focus on dealing with the problem we have now. The point is, I don't think that letter Adler left you was just a bluff—and yes, I did read it before I gave it to you. I knew you'd never let me see it once you had it, so I took the liberty of reading it myself before passing it on. Apparently Adler is part of something big, and that appears to have involved Jok Urdi."

"I guess that does explain why Adler broke into the Quadrant A Civic Security Station before stealing the diamond," Jaymie said. "She probably took that secretary's techpad so she could find out more about the station's security system, and its layout."

Holmes nodded. "Good work, Jaymie—I'd forgotten about that. We got so caught up in the theft of the Gvidi diamond, and why that particular object was stolen from the Bank of Eglon, but I'm now starting to wonder if it's irrelevant to this case. Adler had to commit some crime and get caught so she'd end up in prison, where she could assassinate Urdi. Perhaps the diamond just happened to be an easy target."

"But why did she see the need to take out Urdi?" Athelney said. "It doesn't make much sense to go to all that trouble to kill someone who's almost certainly going to be convicted in court and given a death sentence."

"She had to prevent him from slipping up, of course," Holmes said. "Someone must have thought there was a danger of him talking to Civic Security, so Adler had to silence him." His gaze darkened. "But if that's true, then we also have to accept Urdi isn't the real one pulling the strings. He answered to a higher authority, who no doubt sent Adler after him when he became more of a liability than an asset."

"Well, what if that 'higher authority' *is* Adler?" Athelney suggested. "She could be the head of some sort of organized planetary crime ring."

"No—'organized' and 'Adler' are most definitely NOT two words that go together," Holmes said. "She's just an assassin for hire, and she's fiercely independent. She does contracts, not camaraderie. There's someone else out there—and Adler and Urdi were both just pawns."

Jaymie shuddered, and she was sure she was thinking the same thing everyone else was: *What could be worse than the most notorious, drug-dealing, murder-committing crime lord in Quadrant B?*

"Well, I'm guessing if we want to have a crack at this supposed 'super criminal' orchestrating everything behind the scenes, we've got to catch Adler," Athelney said. "And that's probably easier said than done."

"Well, it would be nice to have an actual place to start searching," Lestrade said. "Adler could be anywhere."

"Blast, I can't believe I almost forgot—we actually do have a clue!" Jaymie quickly took out the slip of paper the bartender had given her earlier. "Padric O'Vax slipped this under my glass at the pub—it says: '*Looking for snakes? Best place to search is under a rock.*'"

Holmes skimmed the slip of paper, then he glanced over at Jaymie with a newfound sense of respect. "Padric left a clue for you? Good girl, Jaymie—you must have impressed him the first time I took you to the Drunk Gypsy. He doesn't leave clues like that very often."

"Well, that's wonderful, but it would have been nice to have something a little less cryptic," Athelney said. "What is this, some sort of metaphor only you are supposed to understand?"

Holmes shook his head. "Padric isn't a poet—he doesn't do metaphors. He's more literal than that."

"Oh, so we should go outside and start overturning every rock we come across to see if Adler's hiding underneath it?" Athelney asked sarcastically. "Or are you meaning slightly less literal than that?"

Holmes ignored the sarcasm, puzzling over Padric's clue in his mind. "We can't go thinking of it like a riddle, because he hates riddles. He wants it to be subtle enough that not just any bloke can read it and figure it out, but obvious enough that it won't take us hours to—"

"Wait!" Lestrade exclaimed, his eyes lighting up. "What if instead of 'under a rock,' we change it to 'on the rocks'? As in 'On the Rocks,' the hot new nightclub in Quadrant D?"

"And what makes you an expert in Quadrant D nightlife?" Athelney said, raising an eyebrow. "Isn't that a little out of your territory?"

"He makes it his mission to learn these sorts of things," Holmes said. "It's part of his endless and generally unsuccessful quest to meet women."

"Thanks, Holmes," Lestrade said, shooting him a deadly look. "Anyway, the club just opened, and it's quickly becoming one of the most popular clubs on Eglon. Maybe Padric is telling us to go there to look for Adler."

"Well, it's as good a guess as any," Athelney said, standing to her feet and moving towards the door. "I'll call in the Quadrant A squad and—"

"No," Holmes cut in. "I'll handle this. I'm taking Lestrade and Watson in with me, but that's all. Anything more will draw too much attention and scare Adler off. She's going to be skittish enough already, and she'll bolt the second she starts feeling suspicious."

"Fine then—but what's to prevent her from bolting right when you show up?" Athelney fired back.

"She won't recognize us," Holmes said calmly. "We'll be in disguise."

Lestrade's eyes widened. "What? Oh no, Holmes, absolutely not. I'm not doing the disguise thing with you again. The last time we tried dressing up as Jvorian smugglers, we ended up getting caught, hung upside down above a slime pit, and almost fed to a tyrillean eel."

"We didn't get caught because the disguises I picked out were bad," Holmes said. "We got caught because *you* forgot that reaching out your hand for a handshake is the greatest insult that can be offered by a Jvorian. And we were never in danger from that tyrillean eel—I had everything under control."

"Yeah, no danger at all—we were just nearly digested," Lestrade said. "But Adler is going to know us way better than those smugglers did. Are you sure she won't see through our disguises? She is a shape-shifter, the master disguise to end all disguises. And what if she's not even appearing as Adler right now? How will we find her in the club, especially since we know she can resist her pressure point?"

"Adler has many faults, and one of them is vanity," Holmes said. "Her 'Irene Adler' body is her most attractive form, and I doubt she'll be able to resist showing it off in front of a crowd of such willing admirers. She's arrogant, overconfident, and has no reason to believe Civic Security will find her there."

"So how did Padric know?" Athelney said, and Holmes shrugged.

"I never ask where Padric gets his information, and he wouldn't tell me if I did. I suspect we wouldn't want to know anyway."

"Well, that doesn't sound like the most trustworthy type of source," Athelney said.

"Exactly—but that's the only type that has real, useful information," Holmes replied. "Now, Ms. Athelney, you need to get yourself back to the hospital, and I need to conjure up some disguises. Lestrade, where did I stick that cape?"

Chapter 4: Undercover

Jaymie had no idea where Holmes had come up with such an eclectic collection of materials for disguises, but once he was finished working his magic, she had to admit he had done a masterful job. He might not have been an actual shape-shifter, but he was bloody close. As they walked up to the entrance to the nightclub On the Rocks, she caught a glimpse of their reflections in a windowpane and guessed that even their own mothers probably would have had trouble recognizing them.

Jaymie was dressed as a Drydion, with a high black ponytail (courtesy of temporary hair dye, which Holmes used to cover up her red hair), bright gold eyes (contacts), and yellow-tinted skin. Lestrade was dressed as a Tryidian smuggler and wore a brown velvet vest, raggedy shirt, baggy pants, and a multi-colored head scarf, in keeping with the Tryidian's "gypsy" style. Holmes' costume, however, was the most impressive (probably not by coincidence, Jaymie thought somewhat sardonically). He had applied various plastic pieces to his face to alter its shape, and then covered it all with a generous, very realistic coat of face paint, giving his skin the bluish, mottled appearance of a Syfrian. Contacts had turned his pair of blue and brown eyes into black eyes without irises, and instead of a nose, he had two thin slits above his mouth. Jaymie was pretty sure it would throw Irene Adler off, no matter how well she claimed to know Sherlock Holmes.

Pausing a few meters in front of the nightclub, they stopped to review their plan one last time before going in.

"So, are we ready?" Holmes asked. He had already given them a brief lesson on the accents of the species they were supposed to be portraying. Since the lesson hadn't gone very well, he had eventually instructed them to speak as little as possible.

"I think so," Lestrade said, then grimaced. "I just wish my eyes weren't so itchy." He reached up to rub his eyes, but Holmes grabbed his hand and stopped him.

"Lestrade, don't, you'll smear your eyeliner."

"I don't care," Lestrade hissed. "I'm a man—I shouldn't even be wearing this stuff! I think it makes me look ridiculous."

"It makes you look like a Tryidian," Holmes corrected. "Now, whether or not Tryidians' penchant for exotic clothes and makeup makes them look ridiculous is another matter entirely, but not one which is of consequence to us at this—"

"All right, all right, I get it," Lestrade muttered. "Let's just get this over with."

He tapped his side, making sure his blaster was still securely hidden in its holster beneath his vest. Jaymie also had a gun tucked into her jacket, though Holmes, as always, refused to carry a weapon.

"Very well, I think we're prepared," Holmes said. "This will be a success—we all have to believe that."

"Yes, how could it not go well?" Lestrade said, still slightly grumpy. "Especially since we're dressed to kill—or dressed to *be* killed."

Jaymie almost laughed, but Holmes' frown stopped her short. She had noticed he never seemed to find it amusing when others made jokes during investigations, though his own sarcasm always seemed to be fair game. She could see Lestrade rolling his eyes behind Holmes' back, and she almost laughed again.

As they walked towards the club, she was struck by the fact she was even in the mood to laugh; if she had been thrown into this same situation six months ago, her stomach probably would have been tangled in a knot by now. Yet though she still felt a surge of adrenalin, she was surprised she wasn't really experiencing a sense of crippling panic like she used to. She had a healthy respect for the danger they were about to walk into, but her fear wasn't paralyzing.

You've come a long way, Jaymie, she thought, though she wondered if she'd really gotten braver or just seen so much by now that nothing that came up in these crazy adventures with Holmes could really shock her anymore.

They waited until a crowd of Yopilians arrived and walked into the club, then Holmes, Jaymie, and Lestrade casually slipped in behind them, wanting to make as low-key an entrance as possible.

Jaymie was immediately hit by a blast of sound as they entered the club, the pulsating, exotic beats of the Cvxion rave band almost overpowering. The nightclub was dimly lit, even more so than the Drunk Gypsy, and the flashing lights that winked on and off in a mix of gaudy colors made her feel dizzy. She stumbled slightly, and Lestrade grabbed her elbow to steady her.

"You'll get used to it," he whispered. "It's the latest fad in nightclubs—they call it flash-lighting. It's a little off-putting at first, but it'll help us in the end. Makes it easier to slip around without being noticed."

Jaymie nodded, and as she took a quick look around, she could tell he was right. She couldn't see all that far in front of her, and it was difficult to notice details in the chaotic lighting. The club was packed tonight, with a wide variety of species represented, including a few from the cultures the three of them were portraying. Although Jaymie guessed few of the club's visitors could actually understand the lyrics of the pounding music, which were in the native Cvxion language, that didn't seem to stop them from grooving to the beat. Most of the beings in the club were out on the dance floor, showing off the latest dance moves popular in their respective cultures, though some sat off to the side in booths, sipping drinks or sampling hors d'oeuvres.

"How exactly are we supposed to find Adler in here?" Jaymie asked, but Holmes didn't respond, his mind caught up in the sudden influx of sensory input. He was slowly surveying the inside of the club, looking for anything suspicious that could point them to Adler.

Thinking maybe he hadn't heard her, Jaymie was about to ask her question again when he leaned towards her and quietly replied, "The key to finding Adler is to look for trouble—and she'll be at the center of it."

He motioned for them to follow him, and they carefully made their way around the dance floor, trying not to run into any of the other beings. So far, they didn't seem to be drawing any undue attention, and their disguises must have been realistic enough to fool the beings around them.

They were headed towards a line of booths at the back of the club when suddenly Holmes motioned for a quick halt and abruptly turned around.

"Don't look back—just listen," he hissed, and Jaymie's breath caught, wondering what had attracted his interest. She shut her eyes, and took in the cacophony around her and tried to sort it all out, looking for the one thread of conversation Holmes seemed to believe was so important. Finally, she found it—at a table directly behind them.

"I don't know...it's a funny business all around, this magician, I think," a woman's voice said, with what was possibly a faint Itredian accent. "Seemed a little peeved when my boss didn't want to hire her."

"Yeah, having live performers in nightclubs was a big trend several years ago, but so much anymore, it is not," replied a much deeper voice, likely male and alien. "Too expensive now, and not demand enough."

Knowing she was risking Holmes' censure but too curious not to do it, Jaymie cast a quick glance at the two speakers behind her. They were sitting across from each other in a booth: one a female human with dark hair and dark skin, and the other a heavy-set Drydion male. The woman was wearing the same uniform as the bartenders in the club, so Jaymie guessed she was an On the Rocks employee, possibly on her break or just getting off her shift.

"I know, that's what my boss tried to tell her," the woman replied, rolling her eyes. "Said she was a day late and a quid short, as it were. She kept insisting, though, saying she really needed to perform at this particular club. Of course, she wouldn't say why, and my boss finally had to tell her to leave and ask her not to come back. It's really strange, I think. My boss is wondering if she might be some sort of contact for a crime ring. That happens a lot in Quadrant B, I hear; some beings use their job as a nightclub singer or performer as a cover, while their real purpose is passing on secret messages to members of crime rings or dropping off small shipments of smuggled goods, drugs, or stolen valuables. It's actually a pretty ingenious idea, but my boss doesn't want an organized crime ring using his club as a base. They can take their business to…"

The woman's voice trailed off, and her eyes darted over towards Jaymie and her friends, as if she had suddenly noticed someone was watching her. Jaymie tried to look away as nonchalantly as possible, but she knew it was too late.

"Hey, keep your ears to yourself," the woman said, scowling at Jaymie. "What's so interesting about our conversation?"

"Um, I, listen, um, not," Jaymie said, trying to replicate the Drydion speech pattern and doing a thoroughly miserable job.

The look in the woman's eyes grew more suspicious. "You're not what?" She started to rise up in her chair, but Lestrade quickly intervened, stepping between Jaymie and the woman.

"Sorry, m'lady, our friend's a little drunk—she means no disrespect," he said.

Drunk? Jaymie shot him a glare, but she realized she was now doomed to play along.

"Perhaps…too many…not thinking." Jaymie did her best to do a convincing "drunken stagger," and the woman sighed.

"Just keep an eye on her, OK?" she told Lestrade. "This is a club, not a second-class Quadrant B pub. People come here to drink and have a good time, but not get so drunk they can't stand up. If my boss sees her, he'll kick her out."

"Understood," Lestrade said, bowing respectfully and then pulling Jaymie away from the table.

Jaymie braced herself for the lecture she knew would be coming from Sherlock Holmes, but she was surprised to find he had nothing to say. In fact, as she glanced around, she realized he wasn't even with them.

Holmes had disappeared.

#

Lestrade's first reaction was one of irritation. Holmes was always doing this sort of thing: running about and having the habit of not telling people (namely, his friends) where he was going. Yet that sense of irritation quickly turned to concern as he realized even Holmes, as eccentric as he was, wasn't likely to have run off at a time like this. He would have wanted to hear the club employee's entire conversation with the Drydion, and he would have tried to help cover for Jaymie's slip-up (though he would have scolded her thoroughly for it afterwards). Yes, something seemed to be not quite right about this particular disappearance.

"Come on," he whispered to Jaymie, guiding her towards the back of the club and hurriedly glancing around, hoping to catch a glimpse of Holmes or at least a clue as to where he might have gone. The pulsating lights and the crowd of beings in the club were both a blessing and a curse. As he had pointed out to Jaymie earlier, they made it easier to sneak around without being noticed, but they also made it bloody impossible to find one specific being in the chaos—especially a being who *didn't* want to be found. If he were here on duty as a Civic Security inspector, he would have blocked off all the entrances and exits, marched in with a squad, switched on all the lights, and ordered everyone to freeze while he searched the room. Yet he had to admit, and Holmes certainly would have agreed, that wasn't always the best way to catch a criminal like Adler. It just would have made it a lot easier to find Holmes, especially if there was something shifty going on.

"Something's not right—isn't it?" Jaymie asked, and Lestrade nodded, knowing there was no point in keeping the truth from her.

"I don't like this. It's not completely out of character for Holmes, but I don't think he chose to leave us, not this time."

He caught a sudden flash of movement somewhere across the club, and his head jerked around. On past the dance floor, he saw a blond woman in a dingy gray uniform swing around a tall Syfrian, who was stumbling slightly. Lestrade might have assumed the pair was dancing, if he hadn't noticed the Syfrian was wearing the exact same clothing Holmes had been wearing when they walked in...

He began shoving his way through the throng of dancers, no longer caring that he was attracting far too much attention. Jaymie scurried behind him, doing a good job of keeping up with him. Despite her earlier mishap, he realized what a good asset she was to Holmes. She learned quickly, and was capable of filling in a lot of the details herself. She might actually make a good inspector someday, if she could be pried away from Holmes or—

Someone suddenly slammed into Lestrade, knocking both him and Jaymie to the ground. He heard some angry shouts as dancers had to dash out of the way to avoid tripping over them.

"Watch it, pirate scum!" growled a Cvxion, the being who had accidently run into him.

Lestrade's temper flared, but he bit back a retort, knowing that was the quickest way to start a fight. He had bigger problems to worry about now.

Unfortunately, though the altercation had been brief, it had delayed them just a second too long. Lestrade and Jaymie burst through the door of the club into the brisk night air, the stars sparkling vividly in the sky above. A few clusters of beings were gathered near the front of the club, talking, but there was no sign of Holmes or the woman who must have been Irene Adler.

Chapter 5: A Dangerous Game

"Blast, we're too late!" Lestrade cursed, ripping off his head scarf in frustration and not caring that it spoiled his costume. "Oh, this is bad. Adler's always enjoyed toying with Holmes, but this time she might really kill him, especially if she's receiving orders from some crime lord. If only I knew where she was taking Holmes!"

Jaymie pulled the little scrap of paper back out of her pocket, the one on which Padric O'Vax had scribbled his clue. Should they go back to Padric? If he had known Adler was fishing around at On the Rocks for a job, would he perhaps know what other places she might frequent?

"She could be anywhere on this bloody, God-forsaken planet," Lestrade muttered as he paced in front of the club. "She could be heading back to Quadrant B to some hive of criminal activity, or to Quadrant A to rob some poor, unsuspecting fool, using Holmes as a hostage or—"

"Lestrade, shut up."

Jaymie hadn't realized the words had come out of her mouth until the inspector whirled around to face her, blinking in surprise.

"Sorry—that was a very 'Holmes' sort of thing to do, wasn't it?" she asked, a little surprised herself. "I shouldn't have interrupted you so rudely, I...I just had a thought. Adler can morph into any form she chooses, but that includes her body only; if she wants to change her outfit, she actually has to put on new clothes, right?"

"Right," Lestrade said slowly, not quite catching on yet.

"Well, if that blond woman really was Adler, I noticed she wasn't wearing an evening gown or anything fancy inside the club. It was more like an industrial suit, and it was dirty, like the sort of uniform worn by the workers at the Quadrant D docks. Maybe she came into On the Rocks wearing a fancy dress to ask for a job, and then changed into a different disguise. I bet she spotted Holmes and kidnapped him, and will take him along with her to wherever she's headed next."

"That's a pretty speculative shot in the dark," Lestrade said. "However, it is the best thing we've got. We'd better get over to the docks as quickly as we can."

#

The Quadrant D docks were busy at all times of the day and night, so no one seemed to look too askance at Jaymie and Lestrade as they wandered through the streets after midnight. They had changed out of their "alien" costumes and were wearing plain, grungy clothes from Holmes' costume closet, the closest things Lestrade could find to industrial uniforms.

Jaymie had never visited this section of Quadrant D before, and she couldn't help marveling at the massive structures stretched out before her in a seemingly endless parade of commerce. The "docks," as they were called in slang, were hundreds of landing pads grouped together at the edge of Quadrant D. Incoming freighters touched down on the kilometers-long metal slabs, where they could dump their cargo and pick up new goods to transport to other worlds. Some of the freighters were more than a kilometer high, large enough to hold hundreds of hovercars, while others were little more than modified skiffs designed for transporting small loads of goods short distances. Beyond the docks you could also find a series of large shipyards, where new freighters were being built from the ground up, their half-finished metal skeletons gleaming dully in the moonlight.

"Any idea where to start looking?" Lestrade asked as they darted out of the way of an open skiff delivering several metal crates to one of the freighters. "Did Adler have any insignias on her uniform?"

Jaymie shook her head in frustration. "I didn't catch that many details." Now she was wondering if she had even guessed correctly about the dock worker's uniform in the first place. She was so used to Holmes latching onto small details and using them to solve a major puzzle, and she had thought she could replicate that. But maybe she was just making something out of nothing.

"Hey, I'm not doubting you, if that's what you're thinking," Lestrade said. "Your guess was better than anything I could have come up with. In fact, I still believe you're right. We just need a little extra help with some clues." He sighed. "I know Holmes would kill me for this, but I'm going to use the badge."

Jaymie raised an eyebrow. "You mean you're going to pull rank on some poor dock worker?"

"Don't look at me like that. Holmes likes to be more subtle, but I don't think we have time for that now."

They started for a nearby dock, which was surrounded by a protective electro-fence designed to keep out trespassers. A sign above the entrance read "Horizon Shipping," a name Jaymie recognized as one of the largest shipping companies on Eglon. Boasting the "fastest interplanetary shipping service in the galaxy," the company had charted a highly efficient series of hyperspace routes, a closely-guarded secret many other shipping companies would have paid dearly to learn.

Gazing past the shimmering blue force field that served as the dock's protective fence, Jaymie saw a giant freighter sitting on the

Horizon Shipping landing pad, lights shining from the thousands of windows on the ship's twenty-four decks. According to a schedule projected on a view screen near the entrance, the ship was supposed to complete its loading cycle in about thirty minutes and take off for Yopilia within the hour.

Apparently well aware of that deadline, a woman wearing a hat and a name badge with the title "dock supervisor" on it rushed past the entrance, waving her techpad and ordering the workers loading goods onto the ship to hurry.

"You'd better speed up that loading process or the freighter's going to take off without you!" she hollered at an employee piloting a skiff. "We don't have all night!"

She turned around and saw Lestrade and Jaymie standing near the gate, and she jumped back, startled by their unexpected appearance.

"Oh, I'm sorry," she said quickly, looking slightly embarrassed. "I didn't realize we had some new employees coming in. I promise, I'm not normally such a slave driver. We're just running a little behind this evening, and sometimes it takes a good scolding to get something through Decker's thick skull…" Her voice trailed off as she gave them a closer look. "Wait—you two aren't Horizon employees, are you?"

Lestrade shook his head and pulled out his Civic Security inspector badge. "I'm Isin Lestrade, technically off duty. And technically this isn't my quadrant either, but it's a bit of an emergency, and I don't have a lot of time to explain. I just need to know: have you seen anything suspicious going on in the Quadrant D dock area during the past couple of days? Any strange activities, unusual characters, or the like?"

Jaymie could tell the woman was thinking it over carefully, but she finally shook her head. "Sorry, but no. I stick mostly to the Horizon Shipping dock, and I run a very tight ship. I haven't seen anything strange lately or—"

"Pardon me, ma'am, but I think I may be able to help them."

Jaymie turned and saw a young man, apparently the "Decker" the supervisor had been yelling at earlier, hopping off a skiff. He was wearing a gray uniform similar to the one Irene Adler had on when she left the club, and his unkempt, reddish hair stuck out from underneath his hat.

"A couple guys were talking about it the other day," he said. "They said they saw some activity at the Sunset Enterprises dock, you know, that company that got busted for trying to burn down their own factory so they could collect the insurance money. Anyway, that property's supposed to have been foreclosed, but my buddies were pretty sure they saw someone wandering around that area that didn't look like a government official. It might be worth checking out."

Sunset Enterprises—what a coincidence, Jaymie thought. She didn't like the sound of this.

Lestrade glanced over at her, obviously thinking the same thing. "Thanks, we'll try it," he said, waving to Decker and the dock supervisor as he and Jaymie took off towards the abandoned Sunset Enterprises lot.

"Want me to call Quadrant D Civic Security and send them over to help you?" the supervisor asked, now looking more than a little concerned.

"Maybe you'd better," Lestrade called back over his shoulder. "I've got a feeling we're going to need it."

#

The power to the massive warehouse sitting on the abandoned Sunset Enterprises dock appeared to have been shut off, but there was enough lighting from the docks around it that Lestrade didn't have to switch on his portable glowstick.

They sneaked up to the side of the building, and Lestrade pulled out his blaster, his finger poised over the trigger. He was in full "inspector mode" now, preparing for the worst. They found an entrance to the warehouse that wasn't locked, and after scoping out the perimeter, Lestrade motioned for Jaymie to follow him inside the building.

Faint streams of light filtered in through windows caked with dirt and grime, and Jaymie could see thousands of tiny motes of dust drifting through the air. Although the warehouse had probably only been vacant for a few months, it was amazing how quickly things could fall into a state of disrepair. All the materials that had been stored in the warehouse had long since been removed, leaving nothing but an empty, cavernous space in which their footsteps echoed eerily as they walked.

"I don't like this," Lestrade muttered, taking cover inside what likely had been an office. "If Adler's here, we'd be fools to just go wandering about. She'll shoot us before we even know she's behind us."

"It's too bad the power's probably off," Jaymie said. "Otherwise we could switch on all the lights, and try to flush her out."

Lestrade nodded. "That's what I was thinking. I doubt we've still got power, but it's worth a—"

Unfortunately, Adler was already one step ahead of them. The entire warehouse floor suddenly flooded with light, and Lestrade whipped around, sticking out his blaster and dashing in front of Jaymie to shield her.

"Hello, Lestrade. You're here sooner than I expected."

Adler had sneaked in behind them, holding a gun of her own and smiling cattily. She had traded her dingy gray dock worker's uniform for a utilitarian leather jumpsuit, the kind often worn by pilots. She had pulled her long blond hair into a tight bun at the back of her neck, and she had a knife and another blaster tucked into a holster slung over her hip. Even though her attire was plain, she was still stunning, and she obviously knew how gorgeous she was and wasn't afraid to work that to her advantage.

"Let's not do this, please," she said. "Why don't you drop your weapon, and we can discuss this like civilized beings."

"The bloody devil I will," Lestrade said. "The minute I drop my weapon, you'll shoot me."

Adler laughed lightly, though that laugh also had a sour undertone. "Well, then, what if I told you that if you didn't drop your weapon, I'd shoot your friend, little Miss Jaymie Watson?"

"If you hurt Jaymie or Holmes, then shooting you will be the kindest thing I'll do to you," Lestrade said coldly. "We're at a stand-off, Adler, admit it. And since Jaymie has a blaster as well, that makes you outnumbered. Now, where's Holmes?"

"Safe, though a little drugged at the moment," Adler said. "It's called 'ybine,' a little paralyzing compound I picked up on my intergalactic travels. It works instantly, and it renders the subject incapable of disobeying your orders. Holmes followed me out of the club like a baby, no struggle, no mess. I was hoping you wouldn't notice he was gone for at least several minutes."

"Too bad," Jaymie said, disliking this woman even more than she had before, if that was possible. "And you really should have changed into your dock worker disguise *after* you left the club. It was far too easy to find you."

Adler's eyes narrowed. "Well, look who's so proud of herself—Holmes has trained you well, hasn't he? Perhaps it was a slip-up on my part, but there was really nowhere else to go between there and here. Besides, dock workers go to that club all the time during their breaks. It wasn't likely to arouse suspicion."

"Yeah—that's why we ended up here on a lucky whim," Lestrade said sarcastically. "Listen, Adler, Holmes may have the patience for this kind of banter, but I'm not playing your game. Just give us back Holmes—preferably, *now*."

"What, so you can arrest me and throw me back in the prison block? Hardly my preference. In fact, Civic Security is probably already on their way, aren't they?"

Lestrade said nothing, and Adler sneered.

"You're so predictable. Look, I know I haven't got much time to get out of here, and you're wasting it. Walk out of the building now, and I'll let you go alive."

"We're not leaving without Holmes," Jaymie said stubbornly, but Adler shook her head.

"Then we are again at an impasse. Holmes is too much of a meddler, and I can't just let him go wandering about, sticking his nose into other beings' business."

Jaymie's stomach twisted. "So you're going to kill him?"

For a moment, Adler hesitated uneasily, the first time she had shown anything but ruthless confidence. Jaymie's accusation had bothered her, which was a little unexpected from a woman who had been trained as an assassin and had likely killed more beings than she could remember.

"That's not my intention," she finally said. "But I can't have him following me around either. They...they wouldn't like it."

"The leaders of the crime ring you're involved in?" Jaymie asked, quite certain she knew what Adler was talking about. "It's the big conspiracy you were trying to warn Holmes about, though he probably didn't listen as well as he should have. It's the person who had you snatch the Gvidi diamond, and then assassinate Urdi."

Adler sighed. "I really wish you hadn't told me that. You and Lestrade know more than I thought you did, and far more than you're supposed to."

"We're not idiots," Lestrade said. "We may not be Holmes, but we can keep up with him."

"Oh, neither of you could possibly hope to reach the level of genius he has," Adler said, her lips curving into an acrid smile. "He needs a partner more on his level."

Jaymie's fists clenched, and she fought to control her temper. She could easily guess the unspoken ending of Adler's statement—that *she*, not Jaymie or Lestrade, was the associate Holmes needed. She simply had to convince him to operate on the other side of the law, the domain where she was queen.

Although Jaymie knew Adler was deliberately trying to provoke them, and that lashing out at her was exactly what she wanted them to do, Jaymie was rapidly losing patience with the woman's arrogant taunting, and the way she spoke about Holmes with such familiarity. Jaymie wanted nothing more than to walk up to her and punch her solidly in the nose, almost not even caring the woman had a blaster pointed at them.

Adler's taunting apparently wasn't sitting very well with Lestrade either. "Is that so, Adler? Well, if Holmes was really such a genius, he would have noticed you sneaking up behind him in the club and wouldn't have gotten himself drugged."

"Touché."

They all jumped at the sudden noise, and Adler glanced around, only to find Holmes pointing a blaster at *her*.

"What....how?" she stammered, and Holmes merely shrugged. He had already cleaned off most of his alien face paint, though touches of it were still smeared on his skin. He'd also removed his special contacts, and while his pupils appeared a little dilated, he seemed to be more alert than he should have been with ybine in his system.

"I do make mistakes, as Lestrade was correct to point out. However, you've made more than your fair share over the past several days, Ms. Adler, and I really think you're beginning to lose your touch. That drug you injected me with was bloody uncomfortable, and would have kept a human lethargic for hours. However, as you should have known, I am *not* human and have a much higher rate of metabolism. My body burns through alcohol and other drugs much faster than a human body does. That's why it's nearly impossible to get me drunk, and why your little paralyzing potion wore off so quickly. And as for how I got this blaster, well, you had a spare gun hidden in your jacket, which you forgot to take with you. You also left the controller for my electro-binders in that jacket, making it far too easy for me to free myself." He brandished the gun at Adler. "Now, I believe this is the part where Lestrade says, 'You are now under arrest.' I'd say it, but it would really peeve him, because he loves saying that line, and besides, I'm not a Civic Security inspector anymore and—"

"Oh, shut it," Adler spat. "Why do you always have to talk so much?"

"I'll gladly shut up, but that means, my dear, you must start doing some talking yourself," Holmes said, grabbing a chair from one of the abandoned office's cleared-out desks and sitting down in front of Adler, still holding his blaster. "And to start you off, here's a question I believe we'd all very much love to hear the answer to: who's pulling the strings behind this operation?"

Adler fumed, her green eyes sparkling with an angry fire burning straight up from her soul. "You don't get it, do you? I tried to tell you in that blasted note, but you wouldn't listen. This is huge—it eclipses me, and even Urdi. Got that? What do I have to tell you to make you as afraid as you should be, Holmes? Urdi is one of the most notorious pirates in the galaxy, one of the most ruthless, conniving men in the drug running business, so bad even the government was too afraid to take him on in his glory days. Well, he was only a *pawn* in the organization I'm working for. A pawn, Holmes! And if my employer wasn't afraid to have him killed, what do you think he'll do to you when he finds you?"

"So you were trying to protect me?" Holmes said. "Still not sure if I believe that, as there's been an awful lot of blaster waving going on this evening, quite a bit of it in my face and in the faces of my friends, which is never advisable. Adler, you are a master con artist, but—" He paused, and a light of realization slowly dawned in his eyes. "Unless...you want to save me because you believe I might be the only one who can save *you*. You're afraid whoever came after Urdi will soon come after you too."

"I'm not expendable," Adler snapped. "They know that."

"But for crime lords, there is such a thing as collateral damage," Holmes said. "Adler, I don't have to tell you organized crime is a dirty game, and even the best sometimes find themselves on the wrong end of a blaster. You're smart enough to elude them if you want to. Why not just leave now, and slip under the radar like you're so good at doing?"

"You mean we're just going to let her go?" Jaymie interrupted in disbelief, the thought making her bristle.

Holmes continued staring at Adler, ignoring Jaymie's comment. "You were supposed to kill me, I wager," he said quietly. "But you didn't want to do it, so you cooked up this elaborate scheme to kidnap me and hide me somewhere. I appreciate the thought—as dying is not something I'm particularly keen to do—but your employer isn't going to like it. You don't have much of a choice, Adler; you've either got to shoot me, or get out of whatever organization you're in and go into hiding."

Adler shook her head. "I don't know what I'm doing. I'm a bloody fool, that's what. I should have shot you. I know you don't believe this, but there's no running from what I'm involved in. If you knew how big it was, what it was working towards... So much of the crime that goes on in Quadrant B is just petty crime, little people stealing and cheating to get ahead in their own miserable lives. But not all of it. There's a hand that's moving so many of the pieces, sometimes without the pawns even realizing they're pawns."

"You're still being too cryptic," Lestrade said. "What pawns? Who's moving the pieces?"

"I...I can't say," Adler said. "Just...I shouldn't be helping you. Just think about it, you'll figure it out." She nodded towards Jaymie. "That day she showed up at apartment complex 221, Quadrant B—that was a momentous day in more ways than one. It didn't start there, but that's where this all took an important turn. You've got to watch—"

And all of a sudden, without any warning, the lights winked out.

Chapter 6: Collateral Damage

"Jaymie!"

She felt Lestrade grab her and yank her towards the floor as the sound of a blaster shot zinged through the air. Jaymie's heart leapt into her throat, and she scrambled in her coat for the small blaster she had hidden there. She heard a soft thump, like the sound of a body hitting the floor, and then the sound of a rusty automatic door sliding shut. Holmes cursed somewhere in the darkness, followed by a loud crash. The lights came flooding back on, and she saw Holmes standing next to a power switch, staring at the body of Irene Adler, which now lay crumpled on the floor.

Adler had been hit in the head with a blaster shot that had burned straight through her temple. She had obviously been felled by a master sniper; despite the pitch blackness of the room, the sniper had nailed his or her target, and taken only one swift, clean shot to do it. Adler had died almost instantly, probably before she even hit the floor.

Jaymie heard the sound of banging on the door, and Lestrade swung around towards the building's entryway, leveling his gun. There was a crash as the door busted open, and a squad of Quadrant D Civic Security inspectors burst into the room. They had apparently heard the blaster fire and decided to forgo a stealth entrance.

Lestrade's shoulders seemed to sag with relief at the arrival of the reinforcements, and he quickly waved them over. "Lestrade, Civic Security, Quadrant B," he said, flashing his badge. "And I'm bloody glad you're here."

"We've got some officers scattered around the perimeter, just in case any hostiles try to escape," one of the inspectors said. She glanced down at the body, whom several other officers were already examining. "Did you have to shoot her?"

Lestrade shook his head. "No. We think the crime lord she was working for put out a hit on her. Whoever shot her didn't attempt to harm any of us, and he or she's probably already on the run. You need to have your squad fan out right away, and see if you can catch the shooter before they clear the dock area. In fact, it may already be too late for—"

"We can speculate later—shouldn't someone be calling a med crew?" Holmes interrupted, but as the inspector who was examining Adler glanced up, his face was grim.

"There's no need to call an ambulance," he said. "She's already gone. It'd just be a waste of time and resources."

Holmes stiffened, but he said nothing, only acknowledging the officer with a blank stare.

"Listen, you're welcome to stay and help us cover the crime scene, but your two friends are going to have to go," the head inspector told Lestrade, nodding towards Jaymie and Holmes. "No offense to them, but they're not authorized to be here."

"Yeah, they know the drill," Lestrade said. "Come on, Watson, Holmes, let's go."

However, neither Jaymie nor Holmes seemed quite ready to move. Jaymie couldn't take her eyes off Holmes, who in turn couldn't take his eyes off Adler. He hadn't said anything to the officers, hadn't rebuked Lestrade for calling in the sort of back-up he always seemed to think was unnecessary, and hadn't even objected when the lead Quadrant D inspector asked to have them escorted away from the crime scene. He just kept staring at Adler, his face an unreadable mask. It was only his eyes that gave him away: a look of somewhat stunned disbelief, and...something that was harder to place. Was it sadness in the blue eye, regret in the brown eye? Jaymie wasn't sure. But Adler's loss had done something to him, and she could only begin to guess at what it was.

Two of the officers brought over a body bag and carefully slid Adler's body into it.

"Great, just what we need—Quadrant B scum skulking their way over here now," one of the inspectors looking on muttered, and Holmes' head snapped around.

"It's not charitable to speak ill of the dead," he said, and the officer appeared a bit taken aback.

"Sorry, I—"

"Let's try to behave in a professional manner, please," the head inspector chided the officer, then glanced over at Lestrade. "I'm sorry, but I'm really going to need you to get your friends out of here."

"Yes, ma'am." Lestrade took Holmes by the arm and guided him out of the warehouse, leaving Jaymie to follow, lonely and trailing, behind.

"Is that assassin going to come after us too?" she asked as they walked to the hovercar.

"I don't know," Lestrade admitted. "They didn't take a shot at us when they could have. Or maybe that shot that hit Adler was meant for Holmes. I doubt it, but of course I could be wrong. The only beings who could tell us are Adler and the being who fired that shot—and that means it's probably an answer we'll never know."

"Oh, we'll know," Holmes said quietly. "Because if it was meant for me, they'll try coming after me again. But I think for whatever reason, that shot *was* meant for Adler." He shook his head. "It's a pity—such promise." He didn't have to explain what that meant.

No one spoke on the ride back to the flat, and Jaymie spent most of the time staring blankly out the window. The shock of what had happened hadn't fully hit her yet, and she knew it would take time to process it. Even though as a medical student she had witnessed death before, this experience was particularly jarring, and it didn't quite seem just. She hadn't liked Irene Adler, but that didn't mean the woman deserved to die in that way.

She couldn't forget the look on Holmes' face, the way he had stared at Adler. Her death had wounded him, in a very deep part of his soul Jaymie had only been able to catch the briefest glimpses of in the past. He had to know he never would have succeeded in recruiting Adler to his side of the law, just as Adler had probably known she never could have recruited him to hers. But there was still a certain dynamic between them, and Adler *had* intrigued him, probably in a way Jaymie never would. And somehow, that made her sad.

They pulled to a stop in front of apartment complex 221, and Lestrade turned around, glancing in the back seat.

"Hey, are you OK?" he asked, and Jaymie quickly brushed the tears from her eyes.

"Yeah, I'm fine," she said. "Just struggling to keep up with all this."

Lestrade watched her for a second longer, and she was afraid for a moment he could sense the real reason for her sadness. But whether he missed it, or whether he just decided to let it go, he simply nodded and got out of the car.

"Well, come get me if you need anything," he said. "I mean that."

"I know," Jaymie said, not having the heart to tell him the one thing she needed was probably the one thing he couldn't help her with.

Holmes remained silent, lost as usual in his own thoughts. He stepped out of the hovercar, but instead of going up to the flat, he turned and headed back down the street.

"Holmes, are you mad?" Lestrade exclaimed. "It's after 2 a.m.—where do you think you're going?"

Holmes merely waved him off. "To think, Lestrade, to think. I have a feeling that tonight we've set something terrible in motion, and I won't be able to rest until we've stopped it. I've just been handed the biggest case of my career, but I have no blasted idea how to start unraveling it." He threw up his hands in frustration. "I have *nothing*, Lestrade—and for the first time in my life, I feel bloody helpless."

With that, he shoved his hands into the pockets of his trench coat and strode on down the street, fading into the shadows beyond the dingy light shining down from the glowlamps.

This time, Lestrade didn't even try to stop him.

Case No. 5: The Game is Afoot

Chapter 1: Players and Pawns

"And...checkmate."

Lestrade tapped the white square on the virtual chess board, moving his holographic playing piece right in front of Holmes' king. He leaned back in his chair and grinned, watching as Holmes stared intently at the game board. Although Holmes was desperately searching for a way to escape from Lestrade's trap, there appeared to be none. He had lost, and somehow, Jaymie doubted he was going to be a good loser.

"Ready to give up?" Lestrade said.

"Shut up—I'm thinking," Holmes said, his eyes remaining fixed on the game board. "There *is* a way out of this, I know it."

Lestrade sighed. "Oh, stop it, Holmes, you're done. Be a gracious loser and admit I finally beat you. Heaven knows how many times you've beaten me in the past—let me enjoy my small victory."

"You mean, 'let me gloat as much as I please,'" Holmes muttered.

Lestrade's grin grew even wider (if that was possible). "So, you're conceding?"

"No!" Holmes snapped. "I just need a little more time..."

Lestrade pushed back his chair and stood up, reaching for his coat. "Sorry, Holmes, but I have to leave for work. The game is over."

"Wait—why not the best two rounds out of three?"

Lestrade laughed. "Oh no—I can't be late for work. Besides, if we play again, you might beat me. I want to bask in this moment of glory." He slipped on his coat and waved to Jaymie. "Good luck with your classes today, Jaymie, and don't let Holmes con you into playing a game with him. I want this feeling of defeat to linger with him for a while."

"Miserable vodog," Holmes muttered, referring to his friend as a Yopilian rodent, a favorite insult on that particular planet.

"You know what, you've been in a terrible mood the past few days—I think you need a case," Lestrade said. "It's been two weeks since you took on something, and meddling always improves your mood."

Holmes took out his techpad, scrolling half-heartedly through his messages. "But all these inquiries are so dull," he remarked with a sigh. "A missing bracelet obviously stolen by someone's ex-boyfriend—boring. An ordinary pub break-in—not worth my time." He tossed his techpad on the couch. "What I really want is another clue about this supposed crime ring Adler was involved in! I hate waiting around for the other side to make a move. All the cases I've solved recently are apparently somehow connected, if Adler is to be believed. The Sunset Enterprises fraud, Jok Urdi's drug-running scheme and assassination, the stolen Gvidi diamond, and the death of Irene Adler—they're all connected, but how? And why? And what is this building towards?"

"I don't have any answers for you, Holmes," Lestrade said. "It scares me, and it should scare you, too. But you're not going to solve this case by just sitting here holed up with your thoughts. You've got to get out and dig up some clues. And that will probably happen while you're working on another case. You always seem to stumble upon the solution when you're least expecting it."

Holmes sighed again. "Yes, you're right. I need some kind of stimulation. But not any of these cases—they're a little below my level."

Lestrade grabbed Holmes' techpad from the couch, despite his friend's protests, and began searching through his messages. "See, here's a perfectly good case. Some professor at the University of Medical Arts—you might even know him, Jaymie—says he thinks someone may be trying to hack into his computer and tamper with some of his files regarding a research project. He's offering to pay you 1,000 quid to catch the offender."

Holmes rolled his eyes. "Cybercrime—how dull."

"But it's 1,000 quid," Lestrade countered, handing the techpad back to Holmes. "Which will go a long way towards helping you pay your portion of the rent this month. It's either that or you can come with me to the Quadrant B Civic Security Station and sort through some cold cases. Chief Bevill was going to go through some today and offered to pay you if you had any theories that led to an arrest."

Holmes was silent for a moment in thought, a slight spark finally entering his eyes. Jaymie knew it wasn't the pay for the cold cases that was intriguing him: it was the idea of an unsolved puzzle, one that presumably couldn't be cracked by anyone but him.

"Fine—Lestrade, I'll look through the cold cases. Jaymie, why don't you stop by that professor's office on your way to class and get some more details. I doubt it's anything worth checking into, probably just another professor trying to hone in on his research. Happens all the time."

"Um, sure, I guess I could do that," Jaymie said, and Holmes clapped her on the back.

"Splendid, Watson. See you tonight."

"But wait—"

However, he'd already grabbed his trench coat and was out the door, whistling one of the songs they'd heard several weeks ago at On the Rocks, the new nightclub in Quadrant D.

Lestrade shot her an apologetic look as he scrambled to gather the rest of his effects and catch up with Holmes. "Sorry, Jaymie—you know, you don't really have to take orders from him if you don't want to. And don't you give him a bloody penny of that 1,000 quid if he doesn't help you with the case."

He'd made it halfway out the door when he suddenly paused and looked at her more carefully, a slight hint of concern in his eyes. "Are you sure you're OK, Jaymie? You've been a little quiet lately. Anything bothering you?"

"No, I'm fine," Jaymie insisted. "Just sometimes..." Her voice trailed off, and she shook her head. "No, really, I'm fine. Just a little preoccupied with school. And money—which is still a little tight."

"Hey, if you need a ride, I can swing you by the university on my way to work," Lestrade offered, and Jaymie glanced at him, looking puzzled.

"It's not exactly on your way. I thought you told Holmes you needed to get to work right away, or you'd be late."

Lestrade grinned. "Nah, just told him that so he'd give up sooner on that ridiculous game of chess."

Jaymie smiled slightly, but her heart wasn't really in it. "It's fine, I'll take the hoverbus. Got to get my money's worth out of my pass, right?" Although she could tell Lestrade didn't really believe she was fine, he didn't press her, and he slipped out the door, leaving her alone with her thoughts.

#

Several hours later, Jaymie stood in the turbolift at the main research center on the University of Medical Arts campus, tapping her foot as she waited for the lift to reach the thirty-fourth floor. She glanced down at her techpad, skimming the message Holmes had forwarded her: "Watson, please inquire about the case regarding the file tampering. We can speak about it during dinner this evening."

He hadn't even forwarded her the professor's name—just an office number, and a note indicating this was a new professor in the medical research division at Caridvinial Hall, a building named for the scientist who accomplished the first successful brain transplant on Eglon.

She knew what Holmes had done: he had brushed off this case and given it to her almost as an afterthought. She knew she probably should be mad at him, but she wasn't, not really. Holmes hadn't meant to insult her or make her feel like an errand girl; he just needed something more mentally stimulating, and this wasn't it. He thought sending her to investigate would pacify Lestrade yet confirm what he thought—that this case was too "dull" to interest him, as he had put it. However, what he probably hadn't realized was that in doing so, he was also implying this case was just right for Jaymie, who operated at a lower intellectual level than he did. *He was serving her leftovers.* And no matter how she looked at it, that hurt.

She pictured him sitting at one of the computers in the Quadrant B Civic Security Station data lab, poring over old files and looking for any clues that sparked his interest. She knew he was also searching, at least subconsciously, for anything that might be connected to the crime ring puzzle Adler had left him when she died, a project that had consumed him the past few weeks. He'd likely forgotten all about Jaymie by now, and might not even remember he'd sent her on this case, till she reminded him at dinner.

Holmes—what was she to do about him? She'd never met anybody who so fascinated her—and frustrated her—at the same time. Still, regardless of how she felt about what Holmes had done, this was her first solo case, an important milestone, and she would make the most of it. Maybe she'd impress him enough that next time, he wouldn't just give her the scraps.

The turbolift glided to a halt, and she stepped out into a long, sterile hallway, seemingly identical to all the other hallways in all the other buildings on the university campus. She walked past a row of offices, stopping in front of room No. 1893, the office of the professor she had come to help. She pressed a button, and the door to the office slid open for her. Shouldering her pack and taking a deep breath, she paused for just a second to collect her thoughts, and then she stepped inside.

Unlike many of the offices in the building, which had smooth, synthetic tile floors, this office was carpeted, and some attention had been given to décor. There was a comfortable-looking couch, presumably for students to sit on while waiting to see the professor, along with a view screen tuned into Eglon's 24-hour news digi-channel. Yet what drew her attention most was a shelf of books standing up against a wall, containing a mixture of classic literary works and historical medical volumes. Such a collection was a rarity in universities these days; most professors and students had long since switched to electronic books that could be downloaded to one's techpad, though a few kept antique books for nostalgic reasons.

Jaymie may have been born into a world of digital information, but she still loved sitting in her family's library of antique books and cracking open one of the old tomes. There was just something special about the way an actual book felt in her hands, and she'd always thought keeping old books was a sign of a person who appreciated culture and who recognized care should be taken not to lose history in the endless forward march of technology.

"Excuse me?"

Jaymie's head snapped around, and she suddenly realized she'd been staring at the bookshelf for several minutes, drawn in by her sense of curiosity, and she'd completely lost track of time. A secretary sitting on a hoverchair behind an elegantly styled metal desk was now staring at *her*, and the look in her eyes was more than slightly disapproving.

"I'm sorry, the professor isn't scheduled to meet with any students today," the secretary said, her tone clipped. "You'll have to come back tomorrow, during his open office hours."

"I'm not a student—well, actually I am, but I'm not here as a student," Jaymie said, then shut her eyes and tried to keep herself from wincing. *This was not going well.* "The professor contacted Sherlock Holmes about a case, and I'm here to get some more details on that."

The secretary's skeptical look hadn't changed. "The professor is very busy, and I'm not sure if he can meet with you today. You might have to send him a techpad message and have him schedule an appoint—"

"No, it's fine—go ahead and send her in."

The voice came from the office behind the secretary's desk, and although it didn't sound unpleasant or harsh, the secretary didn't exactly seem pleased to hear it. She made an effort to smile at Jaymie, though it came across as very strained.

"Well. It appears the professor's schedule has an opening after all."

"Thank you," Jaymie said, scurrying to get out of the secretary's stern gaze. "I won't keep him long."

She stepped into the office just as the professor spun his hoverchair around, and her first reaction was one of shock.

He was young—very young—probably no older than thirty. Most professors in the research division at the University of Medical Arts were at least ten years older than that, as it had taken them several decades to gain enough notoriety to be deemed worthy of a teaching position in such a prestigious department at a very elite school. Many professors worked their whole careers without even getting a shot at a post like that, while this professor couldn't be that far out of medical school himself.

He must have had one impressive dissertation, Jaymie thought. *Or know a lot of very influential people.*

He had brown hair, green eyes, and a very nice smile—professional, but with a slight hint of mischief, which was also very unlike most of the stern professors in this division. He was wearing a finely tailored suit but had discarded the jacket and rolled up his sleeves so he could work more easily. In other words, he was gorgeous, and Jaymie suddenly felt like she was 13, trying not to gape and desperately hoping her face wasn't as red as it felt.

"Um, hi," she said. "I'm, uh, here to talk about the case."

It wasn't exactly the way she had planned to make this introduction, but it was the best she could manage under the circumstances. Oh, Holmes would have killed her if he were here...

The professor stood up, reaching out to shake her hand. "You can call me James." He smiled at her again, the type of smile Jaymie's friend Maio always used to refer to as the infamous "devastating smile." It wiped every single thought from Jaymie's head, and she might have stood there speechless for several minutes if the professor hadn't broken the silence.

"I'm guessing you're not Sherlock Holmes."

Jaymie's face turned even redder. "Sorry, no. I'm Jaymie Watson. Holmes, was, um, otherwise occupied today. I'm his assistant, or apprentice, or well, something like that. He sent me in his place."

Holmes is blowing you off—Jaymie knew this professor "James" had to be reading between the lines, but if he was offended, he didn't show it. He gestured for her to sit down, and she slid somewhat awkwardly into the leather hoverchair in front of his desk. All the furniture in his office was very sleek and minimalist, but it wasn't sterile like the rest of the building. She could see hints here of a man who probably loved art almost as much as he loved medicine, judging by the view screen behind him displaying a digital work of art and the tall, abstract sculpture made of smooth black volcanic rock sitting in a corner.

"Very good then," James said, leaning back in his chair. "So, do you work for Holmes full time, or is this more of a freelance business for you?"

"It's more like a hobby. I'm a graduate student—well, here actually," she said. "I'm studying to be a doctor—" She paused, mentally kicking herself. Wasn't *everyone* here studying to be a doctor? "I'm going to be specializing in medical research, so I know this division well. I'm surprised I haven't had any classes with you yet."

"I'm fairly new here—this is my first term, actually, and I'm not teaching any graduate classes yet," James said. "I recently completed a research project on Itred regarding a new type of synthetic nerve material."

"'The Pulsator Project?'" Jaymie asked in surprise, her admiration for him increasing still further. "That was a major news event last year, and I did a report on it as part of my undergraduate work. I'm sorry I didn't realize you'd been a part of it." She could have gone on about the project, but she didn't want to gush. "Major news event" had been a definite understatement: some leading scientists had called the project's creation of synthetic nerve material, which could help reverse paralysis, the most important advancement in medical science of the century.

"Don't apologize," James said, waving it off. "Not a lot of people know I was involved. My name, well, got left off the list of research team members who were supposed to receive credit for the work. The head scientist and I had a bit of a falling out a month before we published the research, and he 'accidentally' forgot to credit me."

"I'm so sorry," Jaymie said, horrified. She'd heard of stunts like this happening before, and it was more common than members of the research community wanted the public to realize. Research scientists often had massive egos, and when those egos clashed, the more powerful or well-known scientist sometimes retaliated by diminishing his or her rival's apparent involvement in the project. The scientists who'd been snubbed rarely made a fuss about it, however, knowing controversy could be as bad for their own careers as it was for the career of the more well-known scientist. They often just had to grit their teeth and go on, and find another project to work on. Still, Jaymie knew that couldn't be easy.

"It must be terrible to work so hard on something, and not get any credit for it," she said, but James shrugged sadly.

"I was fairly put out at first, but as I'm sure you're aware, there wasn't really much I could do. As the rookie on the project, it was doubtful someone would believe my word over the word of the head scientist. I learned a lot working on that project, and I'm grateful I was given a chance to contribute to it, credited or no. Besides, it might have ultimately worked out in my favor. One of the other scientists who worked on the project is actually a tenured professor here at the University of Medical Arts, and when he heard what had happened to me, he told me he didn't think it was fair. He invited me to come here, tour the school, meet the other faculty, then he blew me away when he announced there was an open position here on staff, and it was mine if I wanted it."

"That's quite an honor," Jaymie said. "I mean, you can't be more than thirty!"

"Actually, I'm still twenty-nine—won't be thirty till next month," he replied teasingly. "And really, it's not as prestigious as it sounds. My own mother told me she didn't care if I was already a professor at a university; she would rather I be married with children now."

I know the feeling, Jaymie thought, but she laughed. She suddenly realized ten minutes had gone by, and they hadn't even started talking about the case yet. She was more and more impressed with this professor; she'd never met an instructor quite like him. So often, accomplished people either gloated about their skills or seemed ashamed of them, but James fit neither extreme. He was comfortable with who he was, but he didn't behave as if he were superior to her. He didn't speak to her as if she was just another lowly medical student using up his valuable time; he talked to her as if she *mattered*. And that felt quite good.

"Well, I suppose this brings us to the reason why I contacted you and Holmes," James said. " I've been working on a research project for the past several months, a somewhat secret project, I must confess. It's based on some of the results from the synthetic nerve study, though it will take the technology in an entirely new direction. I wish I could tell you more about it, but it's a joint project with another professor, and we're not allowed to share any details about it until the work is ready for publication. This kind of research hasn't ever been done before, and I'm a little nervous about others getting too curious and trying to steal my ideas. All my files are secured on a private, portable hard drive that I own but keep at the university. Several nights ago, my security program reported two attempts at unauthorized access. Now, I know something about computers, but wasn't able to trace the hacking attempt back to its source. I'm concerned if the person knows the files are there, he or she may try again."

"Any suspicions of who it might be?" Jaymie asked, not wanting to admit she hadn't understood half of what he said. She'd already done enough to make herself look like an idiot today; she didn't want to make it worse.

James shrugged. "I have some guesses of who might want to steal my research, but nothing solid. Just shots in the dark, really. That's where I was hoping you and Holmes could come in. I can log you into my computer, and you can start taking a look through my files, to see if you can pick up any clues."

Jaymie stared into those green eyes of his, wanting to impress him but having the sinking feeling she was going to have to be honest. So far, he'd given no indication he wasn't seeing her as an equal, but the fact was, she simply *wasn't.* She was a medical student, not a technology expert, and while Holmes wasn't either, he out of anyone could probably figure out who the hacker was just by talking to the professor and piecing together the clues. But Jaymie knew she probably wouldn't be able to do that. She was going to have to commit what Holmes would probably consider to be a cardinal sin: admitting to a client you were clueless.

"Listen, I'm really sorry," she began, "but I have to confess, I'm out of my depth. Holmes calls me his assistant, but what that really translates to is this: I mostly just tag along on cases, and he's the one who actually solves them. I...I don't want to offend you, but you've probably guessed this already. Holmes is just—"

"Blowing me off?" James finished, with an ironic smile. "Tell me— was it the money? Because I can pay more, if you think I wasn't being fair."

Jaymie shook her head. "It's not that. Money doesn't actually mean anything to him. He just, well..."

James laughed softly. "It's OK, you can say it: 'He didn't find my case intriguing enough.' I suppose after catching the Gvidi diamond thief and bringing in Jok Urdi, a little case of cybercrime isn't all that exciting."

Jaymie stood up and prepared to go, picking up her satchel and feeling absolutely worthless. "Look, I'm really sorry to have wasted your time. I'm sure there's someone else who—"

James gave her a puzzled look. "You don't have to leave. If Holmes won't take the case, perhaps you'd like to take a crack at it."

"That's just it—I'm not a detective," Jaymie insisted, wishing he would stop prolonging the embarrassment and just let her go. "If Holmes had really wanted to solve this case, he would have come. Instead, he just sent me."

James studied her for a moment, though it wasn't quite in the same way Holmes normally studied her. There was more of a curious look in his eyes as he evaluated her, as if he were trying to see what she was made of.

"You know, Miss Watson," he said slowly, "I've only known you for about fifteen minutes. But I think I can safely make the assumption that you, my dear, are far underestimating yourself. The moment you walked in, I knew exactly what Holmes had done. Believe me—his reputation does precede him. I could also tell what that's done to you: you felt guilty, though you had no need to, and I could see that hollow look of disappointment in your eyes. I probably haven't earned the right to be blunt with you, but I often speak my mind more boldly than I should, one of my many faults. Holmes has treated you like an errand girl, but you are capable of so much more than that. I could see you tuning out when I was talking about my case, but not because you didn't understand. It was because you didn't *think* you could understand, so you didn't try. You don't know your own power, Jaymie Watson, and I don't think Sherlock Holmes does either. It's a shame."

Jaymie couldn't help herself—she gaped at the professor, though this time for an entirely different reason. She wasn't one to wear her heart on her sleeve, but apparently James had seen through her anyway. He'd exposed a very tender part of her soul she liked to pretend didn't exist, because then it didn't hurt. Yet, she didn't feel scrutinized or belittled by his very candid assessment of her. He'd been blunter than what was likely proper, but he hadn't done it to hurt her.

"I don't know what to say," she said finally. "I...wasn't quite expecting that."

"I'm sorry, I've said too much," James said, his tone apologetic. "You'll have to forgive me. I'm just intrigued by you—the girl who impressed Holmes enough to make her his assistant, but who is wounded by the fact he's too blind to realize fully what she's capable of."

Jaymie glanced away, embarrassed, absently running her finger up and down the back of the hoverchair. "I appreciate your compliment, but I'm afraid I still can't help you on your case. I really don't know anything about computers, and I can't promise you Holmes will take up your case either."

James nodded, not quite seeming to agree but willing to concede the point. "Very well then." He took out his business card and scribbled a note on the back. "But if you change your mind, call me. My work comlink code and my personal comlink code are on there. In fact, why don't you call me anyway, regardless. I'd like to take you to dinner sometime."

Jaymie almost dropped his business card. She had thought the professor was out of surprises, but apparently, she was wrong.

"Is this...a date?" she asked in shock, knowing she had to sound utterly ridiculous but unable to come up with anything else.

James grinned. "You can call it whatever you like. As I said, you intrigue me, Jaymie Watson, and I'd like to find out more about you."

"Um, yes," Jaymie said. "I mean, thanks. I'm free anytime. I mean, not that I—" She finally just stopped, her words sputtering out and leaving her speechless. She clutched her bag, both desperate to get out of the office so she could breathe again, yet afraid to leave in case she had only imagined all this, and she didn't want it to end.

"I'll call you tonight," she said, pausing at the door and ignoring the shocked look on the secretary's face, knowing the woman must have been eavesdropping and most certainly did not approve of what she'd heard.

"That sounds perfect," James said, and Jaymie almost melted on the floor. He reached to press a button that would shut the door behind her, but she stopped him, stepping back into his office for a moment.

"Wait—I just realized I don't even have your full name."

"Oh, of course," he said, smiling. "It's Moriarty...James Moriarty."

Chapter 2: Hot Clue in a Cold Case

Chief Inspector Bevill watched as Sherlock Holmes zipped through the files in the Quadrant B Civic Security Station's cold case database. Holmes was sitting at a hoverchair in a tiny cubicle at the back of the station, surrounded by bleak, pale-gray walls that gave the room a gloomy aura. Not that any of the other "décor" at the station was likely to be featured on one of those design shows on the planet's digi-entertainment network, but this room seemed more depressing than most.

Bevill hated having to transfer a file over into the cold case database, because to him it was basically like giving up. Files that were sent there did nothing but metaphorically collect dust, and they all represented families, companies, and other victims that might never get to see justice for the crime that had been committed against them. If the Eglon government would give him more funding, he would divert more inspectors to clearing out those cold cases, but right now he could barely seem to keep up with all the current crime on the streets of Quadrant B.

That's why he had no problem with bringing in Holmes as a freelance detective every once in a while. Although many of the Quadrant B officers couldn't stand the man, Bevill had never really had an issue with him. Sure, Holmes was difficult to work with on occasion (well, more like all the time), and it was hard for anyone else to fit in a room with Holmes and his sizable ego. However, the man was a genius—and Bevill was more than willing to admit that. Holmes could look at a handful of seemingly insignificant clues that meant nothing to everybody else, and then solve the case in five minutes. His brain just seemed to operate on a higher plane than those around him, and his quick thinking had saved countless lives. Too many inspectors—as well as Nattip Bradstreet, the Quadrant B chief who had preceded Bevill—had focused on their dislike for him as a person, and they weren't willing to recognize his brilliant work.

Yet as Bevill watched Holmes work this afternoon, he noticed the detective seemed to be a little off his game. He was uncharacteristically quiet, and so far, he hadn't insulted anyone (usually by now he would have had half the staff on duty utterly furious at him). He kept scrolling through the files, but had taken precious few notes on his techpad.

"Everything going OK in here?" Lestrade asked, strolling into the room. He glanced over at Bevill and nodded in greeting. "Good to see you, Chief, though I'm a little surprised to find you here. Thought you were out working a case."

"I finished up early," Bevill said. "I just came back here to check up on Holmes, but I was about ready to leave."

Holmes sat back and finally seemed to acknowledge their presence. He ran a hand through his hair, leaving it even more tousled, and let out a frustrated sigh.

"Can't seem to make anything of these cases today," he said. "Hasn't anyone taught Civic Security inspectors how to keep better records?"

"Yeah, well maybe you're just not looking hard enough," Lestrade said. "How about we take a break for lunch?"

"Not hungry," Holmes said moodily, returning to staring at the screen.

Lestrade rolled his eyes. "He's in one of those moods," he told the chief. "He's not going to leave until he's solved *something*. He's sat there for days before, the stubborn rogue. Sometimes I've considered hiring a professional sitter for him, just to make sure he takes care of himself."

Bevill laughed. "Don't let him hear you say that too loudly. But really, it's fine. He can sit there as long as he likes. Those are all cases that have puzzled us, and Holmes is pretty much our last shot. If he can't solve them, then there's probably—"

"That's it!"

Holmes shot up out of the hoverchair, looking like he'd been struck by lightning. He grabbed his techpad and began typing furiously. "Lestrade, I've finally found something—I think we've got a lead."

"What is it?" Lestrade exclaimed, glancing at the screen and trying to determine what had so caught Holmes' interest. His friend had transferred one of the cold case files onto his techpad and already had begun making annotations.

"I breezed past it the first time I was going through the records," Holmes said, pointing to the file onscreen. "Quite honestly, I thought it was ridiculous at first. It's a report from a housekeeper who claims to have witnessed supernatural activity in her employer's home. Now ordinarily, I'd pass this off as the rant of an obviously crazy woman. She claims she kept seeing a ghostly figure who'd just appear and then disappear right before her eyes. She was relieved of her post and filed several complaints with Civic Security, but no one really investigated, assuming she was barking mad. Yet here's where it gets interesting—

this isn't just any housekeeper...it's the housekeeper of Jane Rozine. Does that name ring a bell?"

Lestrade gave Holmes a puzzled look at first, but then the light of recognition slowly dawned in his eyes. "Rozine—that's the Sunset Enterprises CEO! But how did this case end up in the Quadrant B files? I thought Rozine lived in Quadrant D."

"She did," Holmes said. "But the housekeeper resides in Quadrant B, so maybe Quadrant D Civic Security forwarded us a copy of the case. Anyhow, I'm not really concerned with how it got here; I'm just fascinated by the contents of the report itself." His eyes shone with excitement. "It can't just be coincidental when a housekeeper claims to be seeing ghosts in the home of a woman who's the head of a company doing research on teleporters, which can make people mysteriously appear and disappear."

"So Rozine was testing her own device, possibly at home," Lestrade said, not quite understanding where Holmes was going with this. "I'm not seeing why you're so excited."

Holmes shook his head in exasperation, pushing the techpad into Lestrade's hands. "Read further, Lestrade, because you're missing the whole point. After the housekeeper is fired, Rozine has an encounter with this apparent ghost. Scares her out of her wits, actually. The officer who arrives on scene said she was pale as a sheet. She originally called it in as a burglary, but was forced to admit her experience matched that of her housekeeper, whom she'd just fired for being crazy."

Lestrade wasn't quite sure why, but he felt a slight chill slither up his spine. *If it wasn't Rozine testing her own device, then what* was *it?*

"I'm guessing you must think this is somehow connected to Adler's puzzle."

"Well, this is undoubtedly connected to the Sunset Enterprises case, which *is* connected to Adler's puzzle. I can't pass this up, especially since it's the most promising clue I've gotten so far." He hurriedly began gathering all his things and shoving them into his leather satchel. "Chief Bevill, any chance you have current contact information for that housekeeper?"

Bevill pulled out his techpad and searched through his case files. "I've got an address here, should be current. I'm forwarding it to you right now."

Holmes grinned, the first sign of cheer he'd shown in days. He had finally found something worth pursuing, and he seemed to know he was back in business again. "Fantastic. Lestrade, it looks like we're about to take a little tour of a haunted house."

Chapter 3: Ghost Stories

Lestrade wasn't usually a superstitious man, and he didn't put much stock in ghost stories. Yet like most children born on Itred, he had grown up hearing tales of various sprites, fairies, goblins, and other supernatural tricksters, some of which were just mischievous and others that were downright malevolent. He always told his grandmother he had never believed those stories she told him, but the truth was, he had spent many a night shivering in his bed, too afraid to look out the window for fear he'd see a specter drifting there, come to snatch away his soul to "the dark place," the space between the worlds of the natural and the supernatural that allowed nothing to escape once it had entered that realm of nightmares.

As he stood with Holmes outside Jane Rozine's mansion, he had the unpleasant realization many of those stories were coming back to him, haunting the edges of his thoughts. Rozine's house was now abandoned, having been foreclosed by the Bank of Eglon after the details about her fraud attempt had surfaced. It was a grand house in one of the wealthiest parts of town, and it had five floors and an iron fence running all the way around the property. Lestrade was sure the fence was just for decoration; when someone lived here, the house doubtless had been protected by some kind of invisible force field fence that would have zapped any intruders with an unpleasant jolt, stunning them until law enforcement could arrive. The mansion was shaped like a giant egg, an architectural style that had become popular several years ago. It had a façade of marble and a garden full of exotic plants growing in the front yard, with a Tryidian stone path winding its way through them. There was even a fountain, though it no longer had any water in it. All the lights were turned off in the house, and someone had placed electro-bars across the windows, presumably to halt looters, and there was some mud splattered against the side of the house due to a recent rain. The grass was at least a foot high, months having passed since its last trim, and the house overall had an aura of neglect. It was more than a little spooky, although Lestrade wasn't about to admit it.

The poor housekeeper, Yyssa Gdo, looked even more nervous than he was. She had very reluctantly agreed to come back to the house and describe to Holmes what she had seen during the "ghostly visitations," as she called them. Probably the only reason she had agreed to talk to them was that Holmes was the first person who didn't seem to think she was crazy.

"Shall we go in?" Holmes asked, unsurprisingly nonplussed by the house's eeriness.

Lestrade sighed, peering into the dark void looming inside the house's oval windows. Something still felt a little off about this misadventure, but he knew he wouldn't be able to stop Holmes from entering the house. Holmes' curiosity, once piqued, was insatiable, and he was determined to drag Lestrade and the housekeeper along with him...

"Sorry to interrupt whatever fascinating thoughts must be going through your head, but any time you'd like to return to reality, that would be splendid."

Lestrade snapped out of his daydream and glanced over at Holmes, who was giving him a disapproving glance.

"Mrs. Gdo is quite anxious to get inside and start the investigation," Holmes added.

She's anxious all right, but not to get inside, Lestrade thought, but he didn't say it. If he'd seen what she claimed to have observed inside the house, he would have been reluctant to return as well.

"All right then," Lestrade said, taking out his blaster, just in case. "Let's go."

Their hastily obtained search warrant had come with an access code that allowed them to bypass the security deterrents set up by the bank to protect the house from burglars. Holmes punched in the code on the keypad next to the door, then he gestured for them to enter the house as the door slid open.

Lestrade sneezed as a swirling cloud of dust blew towards them, stirred up by the opening of the door. Their footsteps echoed as they all walked down the marble floor of the short entryway. Two large mirrors hung on either side of the hall, covered by a thin veneer of dust that distorted their reflections into ghostly caricatures of their true selves. Although this was probably the fanciest house Lestrade had ever been in, its grandeur was lost in the gloomy pallor that had settled over all the rooms. Maybe it just came from knowing the story of Jane Rozine and her once promising company's downfall, but the house left one with a sad, lonely feeling that detracted from the richness of the furnishings.

"All right, Mrs. Gdo," Holmes said, halting in what appeared to be a large drawing room. He sank back into one of the plush velvet couches, a sunbeam shining on him and casting his shadow across the floor. "I want you to describe these ghost encounters to me one by one. I know you've already told your story to the inspectors at Civic Security, but I want you to go into even more detail. Where were you when these incidents happened? What did the specter look like? What did he do?"

Lestrade sat on a chaise lounge across from Holmes, but Mrs. Gdo looked as if she wasn't about to touch the furniture. "Well, it happened three times," she said, and though her voice trembled slightly, she was making an effort to maintain a brave face. "Twice at night and once in the afternoon. The first time I was just standing in the kitchen, putting the dishes in the sanitizer, when I saw this...this shimmering curtain. I know it's not the best way to describe it, but—"

"That's perfectly adequate," Holmes said. "In fact, it's exactly what I expected. Continue."

Mrs. Gdo appeared a little surprised, but she went on as instructed. "I saw the transparent profile of a man, for about five seconds or so, and then he was gone again. Gave me such a fright, it did, and I ran from the room. I didn't want to say anything the first time it happened, for fear Mrs. Rozine would think I was crazy." Mrs. Gdo slowly wrung her hands together and glanced nervously around the room. Lestrade could tell coming back to this house was doing nothing for her nerves, and he wondered how long she would consent to be interrogated here. Holmes, however, seemed oblivious to her anxiety, and he was staring intently at her, very intrigued by her story.

"So I tried to forget what I'd seen, and I finally managed to convince myself I was imagining it," Mrs. Gdo said. "About two weeks later, I was dusting in the library when it happened again. This time, the specter appeared and disappeared in less than a second, but I'm sure it was the same one. I knew I wasn't imagining things now, and though I tried to tell Mrs. Rozine, she wouldn't believe me. Was very stern, she was, and said there weren't no such things as ghosts, and accused me of being drunk. I should have quit and found a new post, but the pay was too good, and the Rozines were such a distinguished family, and I didn't think I'd find anything better. A whole month went by, and I hoped maybe the ghost had gone away for good and had found peace so he didn't have to keep returning to haunt me. But then, one day in broad daylight, in the front entryway, he appeared again. And I saw his eyes this time—and they were brilliant, piercing green. I screamed bloody murder, and Mrs. Rozine came running. Of course, the ghost was gone by the time she got there, and she fired me on the spot." Mrs. Gdo shook her head bitterly. "Of course, the ironic thing is, one week after I left, Mrs. Rozine saw the ghost for herself, and then several days later her factory burned down. A bad omen, it was. She should have listened to my warning about the ghost."

"Yes, she should have," Holmes said thoughtfully, glancing back down at his techpad, which had a copy of Jane Rozine's report on it. "You know, Mrs. Gdo, I bet you've had a lot of people tell you that you're crazy, but I want you to know I believe every word you've said. However, I completely disagree with the conclusion you've drawn."

Mrs. Gdo blinked and stared at the detective, as though not quite sure what to make of his statement. "I don't understand."

Holmes popped up from the couch and began pacing around the room as he worked through his thoughts. "Obviously, you saw someone appear miraculously, but I do not believe it was *supernaturally*. Mrs. Gdo, the shimmering you saw during the ghost's appearance is consistent with the type of phenomenon that occurs when a being teleports. Someone was obviously 'beaming' into this house, and they had the misfortune of running into you and had to quickly disappear again."

There was a look of cautiously hopeful relief in Mrs. Gdo's eyes, though the expression on her face was still a little skeptical. "So it wasn't a ghost—it was someone using technology to spy on Mrs. Rozine?"

Holmes nodded. "That's what I believe. But why? Now, there's the puzzle."

He fell silent but continued pacing, retracing his steps again and again around the drawing room, his feet stirring up little clouds of dust from the carpets, which hadn't been cleaned in half a year.

Mrs. Gdo looked over at Lestrade, the look in her eyes quietly pleading. "Am I free to go now?" she asked.

"Mrs. Gdo, there's no reason to be afraid," Holmes said. "I've already explained to you the impossibility of this being an actual ghost, and..."

"Holmes, you've bothered the poor woman long enough," Lestrade cut in. "Of course you can go, Mrs. Gdo. And Holmes *will* get you that payment he promised you in exchange for your time. He'll be contacting you about when you can come to pick it up."

"Thank you," Mrs. Gdo said with a quick nod, and then she turned and was out the door.

Holmes sighed the moment she was out of earshot and gave Lestrade a withering glare. "Lestrade, you shouldn't have let her give in to those childish fears. I could have explained the science of teleporting to her if need be, though I don't see why. Any thinking person can see—"

"Yes, Holmes, but sometimes superstition is more powerful than reason," Lestrade said. "And don't be too hard on her. If you were alone in some dark room and something materialized in front of you, you'd be a little spooked, wouldn't you?"

Holmes stared at him blankly.

"Never mind," Lestrade said, rolling his eyes. "That's how almost anyone *except* you would react. Even though it's not a ghost, it's still more than a little disconcerting to have someone break into your house for an unknown reason."

A cloud passed over the sun, cutting off the sunbeam that had been shining across Holmes and for a moment veiling the room in shadow. The darkness gave the room an even more uncanny atmosphere than it had before, and Lestrade was suddenly aware of the deep, oppressive silence of the house. There was no hum of an atmospheric recycling system, a sound beings took for granted in modern buildings, or even the sound of hovercars passing by outside. It was like the house had become a vacuum, devoid of noise and light and movement. It was starting to get more and more spooky, and even Lestrade found himself not wanting to linger.

"So, what's your theory on how this 'ghost sighting' is connected to Adler's puzzle?" Lestrade said, and Holmes shrugged.

"Well, we know the phenomenon—whatever it was—couldn't have been Rozine testing her own device because Rozine *herself* reported a strange encounter. Now, Rozine has to know this isn't a ghost, so why does it intimidate her? *Because it's not one of her own people*. What if it's a representative from this crime lord's organization, trying to spy on her and steal her technology?" He paused and shook his head. "No, he wouldn't be stealing it, because he's already one-upped her—he can beam into *and* out of places without a telepad. Why would he care so much about Rozine's technology, which was obviously inferior?"

Holmes stopped in front of a large portrait of Jane Rozine and a man, likely her husband, that was hanging above the fireplace, and he slowly traced his finger around the gilded frame, studying the portrait. "What am I missing?" he said softly. "Rozine, you landed yourself in something very dark and dangerous, something you weren't willing to tell Civic Security about even though it may have gotten you out of some time in prison."

"Listen, I know you're not going to like this, but I'm going to speculate," Lestrade said, walking over towards Holmes and joining him in studying the portrait. "What if this crime lord was originally working with Rozine, or at least said he was, but was siphoning off her technology for his own profit? He managed to steal Sunset Enterprise's initial research and develop the technology faster than Rozine did. When he teleported into her house, she figured out he was ahead of her, and she panicked, fearing he'd get the technology to market ahead of her. So, she torched her whole factory so she could collect more money and speed up the research process."

"Actually...that's not bad," Holmes said. "As far as the completely unreliable practice of speculation goes. But you still haven't explained why this crime lord would send someone to spy on Rozine in the first place and inevitably tip her off. Was there some piece of the research he still needed? Did she hide something here he wanted to discover or—"

Lestrade's comlink suddenly beeped, and as he glanced down at the time, he cursed. "Blast, I've got to get back to the station to clock in for my regular shift. Holmes, I'm sorry if you're not done poking around, but I'm going to have to head back." He saw the hopeful look Holmes was giving him, but he didn't back down. "Oh no, I'm not leaving you here unsupervised. We can come back tomorrow if we have to."

"Good," Holmes said. "Because I think this house has more secrets left to share with us. It'll probably work out for the best to come back tomorrow anyhow. It just, well, it just doesn't feel right without Watson here."

Lestrade, who was getting ready to open the door, stopped and glanced back, raising an eyebrow. "Wait a minute—is it just me, or did the great Sherlock Holmes just admit he might possibly be in need of another being's help?"

"Don't be so boorish," Holmes said. "I suppose I've simply come to rely on Watson's input more than I realized. I seem to work faster when she comes with me on a case."

"Well, you might want to try telling her that, then," Lestrade said, giving Holmes a reprimanding look. "I think her sense of self-esteem took quite a hit after you assigned her your cast-off case this morning."

From the vacant, slightly incredulous expression on Holmes' face, Lestrade deduced his friend had no idea what he was talking about. And therein lay the problem.

"Holmes, you all but said, 'This case is a waste of my time—here, why don't you take it?' She probably felt you were giving her the leftovers."

"But that's not what I meant at all," Holmes said, only the slightest hint of defensiveness in his tone. "I thought it would be more convenient for Watson to go, since she attends the university. I thought she might already know this professor and be able to get the facts more quickly than I could. You know I don't have, well, how is it you put it? Ah yes—the best 'bedside manner' when meeting new clients. Besides, that job will pay fairly well, and I know Watson could use the extra money. I merely have to pay rent, while she has to pay for rent *and* schooling."

Lestrade fought to keep his mouth from dropping open, because he knew Holmes hated it when people "gaped." Yet he couldn't have been more surprised at what was possibly the most selfless thing the famously narcissistic Holmes had ever said.

"Holmes, that was actually...thoughtful of you," Lestrade said, marveling at his own words. "But it might have been beneficial if you had communicated all of that to Jaymie."

"I assumed she understood my reasoning," Holmes said, and Lestrade sighed.

"You are unbelievable," he muttered. "Holmes, no one understands you as well as you think they do. Sometimes it's nice to actually hear the words 'you matter to me' from another being. You can't expect Jaymie to constantly read your mind; after all, *you're* the supposed telepath. And you'd better appreciate her while she's still around. I know you think about nothing but the present, but someday she'll graduate and move on to her own research. And maybe, well, *maybe* she'll find a boyfriend, and she won't have time to go running around with you anymore."

Holmes blinked, as if the concept was so foreign he couldn't even process it. "But why would she want to do a thing like that?"

"Stuff like that happens all the time to normal people," Lestrade said dryly. "She seems pretty happy where she's at right now, but maybe someday she'll be ready to move on. I'm just saying you might want to let her know you appreciate her now, or she might be gone even sooner."

Holmes responded by striding out the open door, clearly not pleased with this topic of conversation. Lestrade didn't push it, but he truly did hope Holmes would think about what he'd said. Jaymie was an asset he knew Holmes was taking for granted, and he was afraid Holmes wouldn't realize just how much it would hurt to lose her until it was too late.

Don't ruin the best thing that ever happened to you, Holmes, Lestrade thought as he secured the door behind them. *Because that's one mistake you just might not be able to fix.*

Chapter 4: Conflict of Interest

Jaymie readjusted her lab coat and tried to shift to a better position on the very hard and very uncomfortable metal stool. She was endeavoring to pay attention to Professor Cvobroden's lecture on Drydion anatomy, but her mind just couldn't seem to focus today. The professor had been lecturing for about an hour, and Jaymie had only written two notes on her techpad. Normally this file would already be several screen-lengths long.

When Professor Cvobroden finally wrapped up the lecture and they came to the experiment portion of the lab, Jaymie's friend and lab partner, Tria, elbowed her and grinned.

"Having a wee bit of trouble focusing this afternoon?" Tria asked, and Jaymie's face reddened.

"Sorry, just, um, my mind's just wandering a little today."

"Out a little late on one of your detective adventures with the mysterious and dashing Sherlock Holmes?" Tria teased, and Jaymie rolled her eyes.

"'Dashing' is not the adjective I'd use for Holmes," she said. "And no, I'm not working on a case with him. He gave me my first solo case today. It's with Professor Moriarty—have you heard of him?"

Tria set down the beaker she had been holding and stared at Jaymie incredulously. "Have *I* heard of him? Who *hasn't* heard of him! His classes for next term are already completely booked, and it's no wonder. He's blooming gorgeous!"

Jaymie's face turned even redder. "Well, I might have noticed that."

"Oh, if I was still an underclassman, I'd have signed up for one of his classes myself," Tria said. "It's too bad he doesn't teach any classes for graduate students. All the female staff members in the building keep making excuses to go up to his office. He's quite the campus celebrity—and quite wealthy too, I heard." She grinned. "And you've got a case with him? Lucky girl."

"Actually, well, um, he sort of invited me to go on a date with him."

"What?" Tria squealed, then quickly lowered her voice as Professor Cvobroden shot them a disapproving glance. "Jaymie Watson, are you serious?"

Jaymie shrugged. "I know, I wasn't really expecting it, and I didn't know what to say."

"Shut it!" Tria said. "Jaymie, that's amazing! You told him yes, didn't you?"

"Well, I was so surprised, I'm not actually sure what I said," Jaymie confessed. "I...I don't know, I'm kind of having second thoughts. I mean, I'm a student, and he's a professor, so I don't know if it would be proper and all that."

"But you're a graduate student, and he's barely that much older than you," Tria said. "You have to take it, Jaymie—do you realize how many women in this building would kill to have a shot at Moriarty?"

Jaymie glanced down at her beaker, slowly swirling the blue-colored liquid around in the glass. "Well, I'm not sure what Holmes would say. He sent me here to solve the case, not schedule a date."

"But you want to say yes, admit it," Tria said. "You can't turn down this opportunity! This is quite possibly the best thing that's ever happened to you."

There was something about that last statement that bothered Jaymie, but she supposed Tria was right. Professor Moriarty was quite out of her league, but it wasn't as though she'd forced him into this. He had made the first move. *Besides,* she realized as an afterthought, *this might be the first thing I've ever done that would actually impress my mother.*

"You're right, I will call him and accept," Jaymie said.

"I can always call him for you, if you're too nervous," Tria offered jokingly, and Jaymie gave her a mock glare.

"How thoughtful of you. How about passing me that vial of rdyon instead?"

#

"Holmes, how long did you say this had been in the flash-freezer again?" Lestrade stabbed the green lump with his fork and gazed at it uneasily, not daring to put it into his mouth.

"I told you—I last cleaned out the freezer five years ago, so it is definitely newer than that," Holmes said, already on his second helping of the dish that appeared as though at one time, it had been some sort of vegetable matter.

"Five years!" Lestrade cursed and dumped the remains of his dinner in the kitchen trash compactor. "Holmes, when I asked you if we had something in the flash-freezer for dinner, I meant something that could actually still pass as food. You know, it's not a sin to take some initiative and go grocery shopping once in a while instead of waiting for me to do it."

"Lestrade, you are being overly sensitive," Holmes said. "This food is perfectly acceptable, isn't it, Watson?"

Jaymie stared at the green blob on her plate and swallowed—hard—and tried not to think about getting sick to her stomach. "I'm sorry, Holmes, but I'm with Lestrade this time. I really don't think that's edible."

Holmes let out a heavy, rather long-suffering sigh. "But research has shown food can remain in a modern flash-freezer for up to seven years without any ill effects. Granted, it may lose some flavor and consistency while being frozen for so long, but there is absolutely no danger of food poisoning from consuming such products."

"'Some flavor and consistency'—that's all, huh?" Lestrade said sarcastically. "You're a piece of work. I think Jaymie and I are going to run to Gfxo's Café for some take-out."

Holmes took another bite of the green paste, followed by a long sip of aqua-spritzer, either unbothered by the food's terrible taste or unwilling to back down now that he had taken such a strong stance. "If you must. But hurry back, because I'd like to compare notes from our various investigations today. We'll need to get Jaymie up to speed before she accompanies us on our trip back to the Rozine mansion tomorrow."

Jaymie awkwardly set down her fork, forcing herself to look Holmes in the eyes. She knew it would have to come out sooner or later (and considering who her flatmates were, probably sooner), but she wasn't sure how to go about starting the conversation.

"I'm sorry, Holmes, but I won't be able to come with you tomorrow," she said.

"Yes, of course," Holmes said absent-mindedly. "Lestrade and I uncovered a major clue today, and I think we all need to return to the mansion as soon as poss—" He paused, finally processing what he'd heard. "I'm sorry, what did you say?"

"I'm really sorry, but tomorrow just won't work," Jaymie said. She took a deep breath, then decided she might as well say it. "I've got a date."

"A what?"

Holmes stared at her in shock, as if she'd just told him she had contracted some strange, alien disease and she would soon be sprouting an extra set of arms and her skin would start turning orange with bright purple spots.

"Well, you know that professor—James Moriarty—you sent me to interview today?" Jaymie said. "Turns out I couldn't help him on the case, but he asked me to dinner."

Jaymie had rarely seen Holmes speechless, but apparently her announcement had done the trick. His expression was one of incomprehension slowly turning to displeasure, and she braced herself for the volcano she knew would soon be erupting.

"Watson, I sent you to interview this Moriarty, not take him to dinner," Holmes said sternly, but Jaymie shook her head.

"He asked *me* to dinner—I didn't encourage any of this," she said. "He seemed nice, so I, well, I said yes."

"Yes, but first impressions can be deceptive," Holmes said. "Just think of Jane Rozine, fooling all those people all that time. What if he's just invented this whole 'case' as a means to deflect attention off himself, and he's the one who's actually trying to steal some other professor's research?"

"Holmes, that's ridiculous," Jaymie said, "and you know it. I'd really like to help you on your case, but I've already made a commitment for tomorrow."

Holmes pushed away his plate of green "goo," quite obviously brooding now. "I forbid you to go," he said, and Lestrade finally rose to Jaymie's defense.

"Holmes, she's an adult, you can't do that. If she already has plans, we can go by ourselves, then clue her in when we all get home."

"Yes, I suppose that's what I'll have to do," Holmes said, then paused. "Wait, Watson, what restaurant are you going to?"

"No, don't tell him!" Lestrade cut in as Jaymie started to answer. "I've had more than one of my dates sabotaged by him. Don't breathe a word about it."

"I wasn't intending to do any such thing!" Holmes insisted. "I just thought it might be a wise idea for us to know where she's going, in case she ran into any trouble, or needed help or—"

"Holmes, she'll be fine! Don't be a stalker."

There was a long, uncomfortable moment of silence, and no one quite seemed certain what to say. Holmes was staring very intently—and very unhappily—at his plate, purposefully avoiding eye contact with the rest of them, and Lestrade looked as though he wanted to escape as badly as Jaymie did.

"Um, well, do you still want to get some take-out?" Jaymie finally asked, turning to Lestrade and praying he'd say yes. She was desperately hoping to change the conversation to another subject—any subject, in fact.

"That'd be great," Lestrade said, grabbing his coat. "We'd better let Holmes stew here for a while by himself—and believe me, it may be a while."

"I'm not stewing!" Holmes snapped, his tone completely disproving his statement. "And I'm not hungry anymore, so I'd prefer you not bring me anything from the café."

"I didn't offer to," Lestrade fired back, then started for the door.

Well, that could have gone a lot *better,* Jaymie thought as they stepped outside the flat and headed to the turbolift. She knew she didn't need to feel guilty, but that didn't change the fact she still did. She felt as if she'd just let down a friend, and while what she'd done wasn't quite wrong, it didn't feel quite right, either. If Holmes had come running back out of the flat, she probably would have relented and canceled her date, if he'd just told her he needed her to solve the case and couldn't do it without her.

But he didn't, and so she and Lestrade continued on down to the café, and by the time they returned, Holmes had already retired to his room and shut the door.

Chapter 5: The Trap

By the time Lestrade finished his shift the next day and picked up Holmes to take him back to the Rozine mansion, it was already nightfall. A light, misting rain dusted them as they parked and stepped out of the patrol hovercar onto the street in front of the mansion, and Lestrade wiped the moisture off his face, cursing himself for forgetting to bring an umbrella.

He already knew he wasn't at his best this evening. He hadn't slept at all the night before, and now his eyes were red and burning. He'd been in a bad mood all day, even snapping at the Civic Security Station's secretary and temporarily earning the nickname "Inspector Holmes" as repayment for his ill humor.

Holmes had been the one to react first to Jaymie's "announcement," and the storm cloud that had descended over his mood had yet to lift. And what Lestrade had discovered, as he thought about it more and more, was that he didn't really like it, either.

She won't have time to go running around with us anymore—he remembered telling Holmes that yesterday, but he hadn't realized how quickly that prediction would come true. Although he'd lectured Holmes, he supposed he'd been taking Jaymie for granted, as well. He'd thought of her as Holmes' friend/sidekick/assistant (it had always been complicated), but now he was slowly coming to realize how much the dauntless, redheaded Scoztan girl had come to mean to him too. This was the first time in the six months since they'd met her that she wasn't helping them on a case, and now everything felt, well, "off" without her. Watson had become a buffer between him and Holmes, balancing out their strong personalities and preventing them from arguing too much.

He missed that smile of hers, and that take-no-nonsense attitude towards the two of them. She wasn't fazed by any of the strange conundrums Holmes had thrown her way, and she'd put up with far more grief from him than even Lestrade would.

And now they'd lost her, and as Lestrade punched in the access code that would open the door, he was left with a terrible, empty feeling. In reality, he supposed he was overreacting; this was just one date, and maybe it wouldn't go well, and life would return to normal. Yet there was just as much chance it wouldn't. After all, why *wouldn't* the professor be enthralled with Jaymie? He knew she didn't have a great sense of self-confidence, but if she could only see what the rest of them saw in her... There was a determined, adventurous sparkle in those gray eyes of hers, and she was so smart—so smart she didn't even realize it. She wasn't movie-star beautiful, but she was cute in a way that perfectly suited her. Then again, what she looked like wasn't even the point, really. It was that spirit of hers that Lestrade—

He stopped, surprised by where that train of thought was taking him and what its consequences might be. It might have gone further, had not Holmes pulled to an abrupt halt, causing Lestrade to run into him.

"Please, try to watch where you're going," Holmes said, and Lestrade bit back a snarky retort.

"Sorry," he muttered, switching on his portable glowstick. "You know, maybe night wasn't the best time to come here."

"We could have left earlier, if you hadn't been late," Holmes said.

Lestrade hadn't been late—he'd had to work—but there was no point in arguing about that. They were both in a bad mood, and the last thing they needed right now was a major fight.

"So tell me again, what exactly are we looking for?" Lestrade asked, and Holmes shrugged.

"Anything out of the ordinary. Perhaps Jane Rozine's 'ghostly visitor' was just coming to spy on her, but I doubt it. He risked discovery multiple times, and even had the audacity to show up in broad daylight. I think he was looking for something, and if he didn't find it, it could still be here. Now, let's stop wasting time talking and start searching. It'll go slower, because we only have two people instead of three, but I suppose that can't be helped."

No, it can't, Lestrade thought moodily, though unlike Holmes, he knew who was to blame for that. And it wasn't poor Watson.

An unsettling silence fell across the darkened house as Lestrade and Holmes wordlessly explored the hallways, looking for anything suspicious that might pop out amongst the faded grandeur of the once stately rooms. They explored the upper floors first, combing through all the bedrooms, and then the living quarters on the ground floor, the kitchen, and what used to be Mrs. Gdo's room. Yet all they found was nothing, nothing, and more nothing. It wasn't until they veered into the library, their last stop before heading to the basement, that Holmes caught a whiff of something promising.

"Lestrade, stop."

Holmes paused in front of a high-backed velvet chair sitting by a fireplace that was now only full of blackened cinders. Lestrade glanced around the room at the shelves of old-fashioned books, but saw nothing unusual. Then again, this was how it always went; Holmes usually spotted things everybody else seemed to miss.

"There," Holmes said simply, shining his glowstick over towards a particular book sitting on the shelf. At first glance it didn't look any different from the books around it, but Lestrade dutifully followed as Holmes took a closer look. It appeared very much like the antique books around it, and Lestrade still had no idea why this one had caught Holmes' eye.

"'Solar Songs,'" Lestrade murmured, reading the title aloud. "Holmes, it's a book of poetry. You hate poetry."

"Yes, of course I do, but even I can appreciate the value of a book this ancient. Lestrade, this is easily the oldest book in this library, and it was very important to Jane Rozine. In fact, it was sitting off to the side of the teleporter control panel in the Sunset Enterprises factory the day we broke in."

Lestrade didn't ask how Holmes had managed to remember that, or even notice it in the first place.

"I thought it odd then that she would carry around such an ancient and fragile book," Holmes went on. "It must have been very, very special to her, but why?"

Holmes picked up the book and slowly cracked it open, thumbing very gently through the yellowed and brittle pages. Lestrade found himself holding his breath as Holmes skimmed the volume, turning through page after page, and then suddenly—stopping.

He pointed to one paragraph of poetry, which had been underlined with a pen. Unlike the rest of the book, this ink was not faded, and appeared to have been added long after the book had been contemporary.

"Now, what kind of person makes a mark in an antique book?" Holmes mused. "Either an idiot who has no regard for preserving cultural history, or someone who is desperate to remember something or communicate something to a future reader."

It had to be the latter, but Lestrade didn't know what kind of message Jane Rozine might have been trying to leave. There was nothing special about the wording in the paragraph; in fact, it wasn't even the best poem in the book.

"I sail the solar wind on a ship with metal wings," Lestrade read. "I am master of day, night, and impossible things…"

All of a sudden, there was a horrible screech, and both Lestrade and Holmes jumped, nearly dropping the book. Lestrade whipped out his gun and whirled around just as the bookcase behind them rose up into the ceiling, revealing a secret compartment the size of a small closet.

"What the bloody devil…"

"A secret room, Lestrade," Holmes said calmly, as if he had expected this. "With an opening device activated by reading a certain line of poetry. Clever, if not a little overdramatic. I wouldn't have underlined that passage, personally, because I think it makes it too obvious, but I suspect Rozine guarded the book much more closely than this before she was arrested. She probably rather hastily stuffed it in here before her inevitable capture."

He handed the book to Lestrade and shined his light into the hidden room. It too was lined with shelves, though they all appeared to be empty. Well, almost empty, except for an outdated techpad sitting on the bottom shelf.

"Holmes, wait!" Lestrade said as his friend reached for the object, fearing it might be booby-trapped, but Holmes ignored him, as usual.

Holmes picked up the device and attempted to switch it on, but nothing happened.

"Blast, it's out of power," Holmes said. "We'll have to take it back to the flat and charge it. But first we're going to comb through this hidden room and make sure Rozine didn't leave any other clues."

"You know, maybe we should check in with Jaymie, like we promised," Lestrade said. Despite Holmes' protests, Jaymie had made him promise he would check in with her every hour during his investigation, just to verify he was all right.

"Lestrade, she is not even thinking about us, no doubt, and would consider a call an untimely interruption," Holmes said, sounding suspiciously like he was pouting. Again.

"Come on now, you've got to have a better opinion of Jaymie than that," Lestrade said. "You know she'll worry if you don't check in. But I guess we might as well finish searching the room first before we call her. Then we can just tell her we're on our way home and—"

Lestrade paused, getting a sudden sense that something wasn't right. He could have imagined it, but he thought he heard a faint whoosh, like the sound of a door opening. Holmes apparently hadn't heard anything, and was still poking around inside the secret room. Yet Lestrade couldn't shake this distinct feeling of unease. He switched his own glowstick back on and slowly inched towards the door, his blaster drawn. Something just didn't feel right.

"Lestrade, why are you sneaking about?" Holmes called from the hidden room. "Sometimes, I think you are overly suspicious."

Lestrade ignored him. His eyes could be playing tricks on him, but he thought he just might have seen a shadow fall across the hallway that hadn't been there a few seconds before. What if—

The stun bolt hit him before he even had a chance to raise his own gun. He saw a dark flash of movement outside the room as he slumped down to the floor, and then unconsciousness overtook him.

#

Jaymie sat alone in the lobby of the Matrié d'Poll restaurant, clutching her handbag and trying unsuccessfully to convince herself she wasn't nervous. James Moriarty wasn't late, she was just really early, and now she was forced to kill time in the lobby while she waited for him. He'd offered to drive all the way out to Quadrant B to pick her up, but she'd told him it would probably be better if she just took the hoverbus and met him here. Truth be told, she was a little afraid of what Holmes might do to him if he ever showed up at the flat. By now Holmes and Lestrade should already have arrived at the Rozine mansion, but Jaymie was pretty sure if Moriarty had come to pick her up, Holmes would have found an excuse to wait around and perform a not-so-subtle interrogation.

She tapped her foot on the floor, her feet aching from the ridiculously high heels she'd squeezed them into. She hated dressing up, and she hadn't worn a dress this fancy—made from a shimmering red material manufactured on Scoztan—since her graduation from secondary school.

"These bloody shoes are killing me," she muttered and started to slip them off, just to get some relief, but a waiter happened to pass by and glanced down somewhat disapprovingly at what she was doing. Jaymie quickly straightened up and tried to smile politely, although inwardly she was groaning. She had a feeling this restaurant was probably too fancy for her, and she had to keep fighting to silence her doubts about this date. Moriarty was out of her league, and this was just more proof of that. Did she really and truly belong here?

Why am I sitting here in this absurd dress, in a restaurant my mother would feel more than at home in but somehow isn't, well, me? she wondered. Was this all just a joke or—

"Jaymie, it's so good to see you!"

She looked over and saw that Moriarty had just walked in. He took off his black trench coat and handed it to the hostess, who had offered to hang it up for him.

"Hello," she said, standing up to greet him and mercifully not tripping on her high heels. She stood there awkwardly for just a moment, but Moriarty smoothly took control of the situation.

"You look incredible," he said with that devastating smile of his, and Jaymie's head buzzed.

"So do you. I mean…" She stopped. *Here she went again, making herself sound like an idiot.* "This seems like a really nice restaurant. I've never eaten here before." She winced, wondering if maybe she shouldn't have admitted that. Oh, how did she always manage to thoroughly bungle things like this in such a short amount of time? "I'm so glad you suggested this place. It seems really…nice."

Moriarty stared at her for a moment, then finally his lips broke into a teasing smile. "You know, you really shouldn't lie, Miss Watson. It doesn't suit you."

Jaymie's face flushed a brilliant red, and she struggled to cover for herself. "I'm serious. I think this is a lovely place to spend an evening."

"But you'd rather not be here, wouldn't you?" he countered. "It's all right, Jaymie, you don't have to pretend. You looked thoroughly miserable when I walked in, and I was afraid it was at the thought of having to meet me."

"Oh no, it's not that," Jaymie said quickly, wishing she could sink into the floor and disappear forever. "I really wanted to...to...talk to you, it's just that... Well, this restaurant really isn't my style. I'm really sorry. I didn't want to seem rude and tell you I didn't want to eat here. I'm just..."

Not that kind of girl. She couldn't say it, but that was just the truth. Although she had been raised by a wealthy family and should have been used to—maybe even expected—this type of environment by now, it just wasn't her. She felt more at home in the rundown, unassuming apartment complex 221 than the glitzy, glamorous world of the upper class. She didn't want to disappoint Moriarty, but she couldn't deceive him, either.

Moriarty let out a long, slow sigh, but it sounded more like one of relief than of frustration. "You're not being rude—I've actually never eaten here myself," he said, and Jaymie blinked in surprise.

"I'll confess—I wanted to impress you, but shouldn't have let my ego get so carried away," he continued. "I know your family's wealthy; one of the other professors was talking about you the other day, and he mentioned you were the best student in his class and that the school was lucky to have you. He said you came from a very well-off family and could have picked from a number of elite schools. I felt like I should, well, come up with something amazing for a first date. I assumed you were used to restaurants a lot more elegant than this, and I was afraid you wouldn't think this was good enough. I should have been a gentleman and asked you where *you* wanted to go."

So maybe Moriarty isn't entirely at peace with his wealthy background, either, Jaymie surmised. She shouldn't have been surprised; he hadn't put on any airs when she first met him, and she had to admit, although he looked extremely dashing in that finely tailored black suit, perhaps he wasn't any more comfortable in this fancy environment than she was.

Jaymie glanced over and saw the hostess watching them in an increasingly less discreet manner, probably wanting them to hurry so she could seat them and help her next customer.

"Really, it's fine—don't you already have a reservation here?" she asked Moriarty. "Maybe we shouldn't just cancel—"

"Too late, we already are." He turned and waved the hostess over. "I'm sorry, we won't be needing a table after all," he told her. "You can cancel the reservation for James Moriarty."

The hostess took a step back, as if shocked someone would actually make a cancelation at a restaurant as renowned and hard to book as this one. "Excuse me, sir? Are you certain you'd like to do that? You'll lose the 50 quid deposit you've already made."

Moriarty shook his head. "That's fine—just use that deposit for another customer. We have somewhere else to be."

Grabbing his coat, he took Jaymie by the arm and guided her out of the restaurant, and she numbly followed him, feeling just as stunned as the hostess looked.

Twilight had fallen over Quadrant A, and as the sun sank beneath the horizon, colorful lights were popping up all over the quadrant's nightlife district. As one part of the quadrant was falling asleep, another was coming to life, and the air felt alive with possibility.

"Where are we going?" she asked Moriarty, and he simply grinned.

"You tell me. What do you feel like?"

Jaymie thought for a moment, a gentle night breeze blowing back a few wispy bangs from her face. She closed her eyes and inhaled the crisp, cool air, finally able to breathe freely. She suddenly didn't feel the need to impress Moriarty at all, because she had come to the realization she didn't have to.

She opened her eyes and at last returned his smile. She was going to take a risk, but she felt like she could do anything tonight.

"Let's go…somewhere magical," she said.

Chapter 6: A Bad Feeling

And magical it was.

Moriarty pulled his sleek but not extravagant hovercar to a halt in front of Dizzy Blues, a popular pub featuring live jazz music that had just opened up not far from the university. Jaymie had heard other students talking about it, but hadn't had anyone to go with until now. Holmes was not a fan of jazz; he claimed it was "too disorderly" for him.

Though the pub had some tables indoors, no one was sitting inside tonight. Everyone had gathered on the pub's open patio, whose only ceiling was a sky full of stars. The fenced-in patio was crawling with exotic blue gbrolinin vines, which attracted "sprytes," a type of bio-luminescent insect. Hundreds of the tiny bugs flitted around the vines and added to the area's general ambiance. Each table had been hand-crafted from intertwined metal chords, and no two were alike, giving the patio a touch of whimsy. Although most restaurants had switched to artificial illumi-candles, Dizzy Blues used old-fashioned candles, the warm flames beckoning with a friendly light. A group of musicians played off in a corner, the rich, sonorous tones of the vifron blending with the breathy cadence of the flot. A drummer kept a steady but not overpowering beat, and several couples were dancing out in an empty space between the tables in the center of the patio. The overall effect was absolutely enchanting, and Jaymie felt herself relax as soon as she stepped under the vine-covered archway leading to the tables. Now *this* was atmosphere.

She and Moriarty found a table close to the band, and soon were sipping glasses of Itredian wine.

"This is amazing—I'm sorry I didn't come here sooner," Moriarty remarked, lightly tapping his finger in time to the music and watching the sprytes fluttering around their table.

"I've passed by it so many times on my way home from class but just never went in," Jaymie said thoughtfully. "I don't know why—I guess it's easy to get so busy you don't think you have time to stop and just enjoy something."

"Is Holmes quite the taskmaster?" Moriarty asked, a smile playing at his lips, and Jaymie shrugged.

"It's not that. It's just...his projects tend to be all-consuming, and it's hard not to get swept up in his enthusiasm."

"So is this what you want to do when you grow up then?" Moriarty asked teasingly. "I mean, is the University of Medical Arts going to have to worry about you dropping out to become a private investigator?"

Jaymie didn't answer right away, and her hesitation surprised her. Of course she wouldn't drop out; she didn't like the thought of quitting, and she was committed to earning her medical degree. But as for where she would go when she graduated, she suddenly realized she wasn't sure. In the past she'd always thought she would work at some university, doing teaching and research, but she hadn't given much thought to her career lately. She'd always been one to set goals and plan for the future, but spending time with Holmes had caused her to live more in the moment.

"I don't know what I want to do, I guess," she confessed. "I don't think I could actually be a private investigator; I just enjoy helping Holmes once in a while. But after I graduate, I...I guess probably won't be following him around anymore." It was the first time she'd actually allowed herself to give voice to that thought, and she found it filled her with a sudden sadness. She'd gotten so used to him being a part of her life, but of course it wouldn't be that way forever. She supposed she'd have to move on, and he'd find something (or someone) else to intrigue him.

And does that make me just a brief diversion for him along the way? she thought, the words having a bitter tang.

"It'll be his loss, then, not yours," Moriarty said, and Jaymie shifted, feeling slightly uncomfortable.

"I'm not sure about that," she said, but Moriarty was already shaking his head.

"You idolize him, Jaymie—you don't have to apologize for it, but it's true. And he may be brilliant, but I don't think he deserves such blind admiration."

Blind admiration—that phrase vexed her, and she didn't want to think about whether or not it was a correct assessment. "I'm not obsessed, if that's what you're implying. I do have other interests besides running about with Sherlock Holmes."

"Then what are they?" Moriarty countered, his deep green eyes suddenly very intent. His tone wasn't accusatory, but his expression had grown serious, and he wasn't teasing her anymore.

Jaymie struggled for a moment to think, and then she realized she'd just given her answer.

"There's so much more to you," Moriarty finally said after an uncomfortably long moment of silence. His tone was softer now, and he placed his hand on hers. "And the fact is, I don't want to see this Holmes eclipse everything that's wonderful about *you*. I told you this the first time I met you, and I'll say it again: I don't think he appreciates you like he should. Would it be as hard for him to let go of you as it would be for you to let go of him? Because it *should* be." He glanced at her, his eyes sad. "I don't want to watch you let your entire life slip away, waiting for him to be enthralled with you. There's so much more that you could be."

Jaymie looked away, her heart torn. Deep down, she had the sneaking suspicion Moriarty's evaluation of her was dead-on, however much she might not want to acknowledge it. Holmes did take her for granted, and she shouldn't idolize him, because she had a feeling he really didn't need her as much as she seemed to need him. But some part of her still believed he thought of her as more than just an expendable assistant—she was his friend, and though he might not be good at expressing it, he'd miss her if she walked out of his life. Or maybe that was just wishful thinking...

"Let's not talk about Holmes anymore," Moriarty said with a sigh, sitting back in his chair. "I apologize—it was my fault for bringing it up, and it's upset you. I shouldn't make you dwell on Holmes if you'd rather—"

Holmes...

And that's when Jaymie suddenly remembered: he should have checked in with her long before now! She glanced at her comlink, to see if she had any messages waiting for her, but there was nothing.

Moriarty must have seen the change in her expression, and he looked at her in concern. "What's wrong, Jaymie?"

"Oh, it's nothing," she said. "It's just...well, Holmes is doing some investigating tonight, and I made him promise to check in with me, just to make sure he hadn't run into any trouble. Except, he's missed his deadline, and I'm wondering why."

"I'm sure it's nothing," Moriarty said reassuringly. "You know how he is."

Yes, she did know how he was—all too well, in fact. Jaymie stared at her comlink, knowing she should probably let it go. Holmes likely hadn't missed the check-in time for any serious reason; no doubt he and Lestrade were caught up in the investigation, or maybe he was still angry with her for not coming with them. And yet...there was that small shadow of doubt lingering at the back of her mind, that stubborn inkling that just wouldn't go away. The chances might be slim, but what if he *had* missed the check-in because he was in danger? If she ignored it, and made the wrong call, she might never get a chance to undo her mistake.

Jaymie tried contacting both Holmes' and Lestrade's comlinks, but she received no answer from either of them. Her sense of unease growing, she pushed back her chair and stood up, reaching for her handbag.

"I'm sorry, but I have to go and check on them," she said. "Everything's probably fine, but it's a risk I just can't take."

"No, no, I understand," Moriarty said, though Jaymie wondered achingly if he really did. "You can take my hovercar. I'm certain there's nothing to worry about, but if you need to, go ahead and go."

"Thank you," Jaymie said, taking the control chip for his hovercar and feeling absolutely awful. "I'll be back soon."

But will you be here waiting for me? she wondered sadly as she made her way through the maze of tables. They hadn't exactly parted on the best terms; they'd quarreled about her supposed obsession with Holmes, and now here she was, dashing off in the middle of their date to "rescue" the detective, even though there was more than likely nothing wrong. She knew exactly what Tria would say: Jaymie was making this a horrible first date, and if she walked out now, she'd probably not get a second one. Moriarty would view this as her choosing Holmes over him, even though it wasn't really like that. However, none of that could be helped now; she'd already decided, and she could only pray she'd made the right choice.

This had better be worth it, Sherlock Holmes, she muttered as she revved the repulsors of Moriarty's hovercar. *This had better be worth it...*

#

When he finally regained consciousness, Lestrade's first sensation was that of a throbbing pain pulsating inside his skull. He struggled to open his eyes, and found he couldn't see anything but a vague blur. He blinked once, twice, and then again, grimacing at the pain the movement caused. Slowly, the objects in front of him came into focus, and, as they did, so did the recollection of what had happened to him before he passed out.

He was now sitting in an uncomfortable, stiff-backed chair inside the library in Jane Rozine's mansion, his wrists strapped to the chair's armrests with electro-binders. Holmes was seated next to him, similarly restrained. Though his friend's eyes were closed, Lestrade didn't think he was unconscious. He had a barely perceptible frown, an indication he was scheming about how to get out of the bloody mess they'd landed themselves in.

Lestrade looked around slowly, attempting to move his head as little as possible so the pain wouldn't spike again. He saw no sign of their attacker, and everything in the room appeared exactly as it had before Lestrade was shot. Well, almost exactly. The bookcase that had risen up to reveal the secret room was now back in place, and the book "Solar Songs" had been placed on the shelf once again, as if it had never been disturbed.

"Holmes!" Lestrade hissed, and his friend's eyes flew open.

"You're finally awake," Holmes said abruptly, but Lestrade could see a certain flicker of concern in his eyes. Holmes had been worried about him, and he was obviously more than a little worried about their situation now.

"So, what exactly is going on?" Lestrade asked, but Holmes shook his head.

"Well, clearly I was a fool. I was so intrigued by the secret room I didn't realize we had a spy until he hit you with a stun bolt. I tried, of course, to resist, but that was unsuccessful, and so now, as you are well aware, we find ourselves strapped to these two chairs awaiting what is likely to be an unpleasant fate."

"Do you think the attacker is the same 'ghost' who was spying on Rozine?" Lestrade said.

"No, not likely. Mrs. Gdo was quite adamant about that specter's brilliant green eyes, and the man who attacked us had dull, brown ones. He also doesn't seem to have the level of intelligence I was hoping Rozine's adversary would have, and my guess is, he's just a no-account minion."

Unfortunately, the "no-account minion" picked that exact moment to walk back into the room, and his eyes snapped at the insult.

"You're not in a position to be speaking so flippantly," the thug said. "And I'm not a 'no-account minion.' The name's Jinxx—and before you ask, no, that's not my real name. No one goes by their real name in this business, and I know you know what I'm talking about. Besides, knowing my name's not going to matter much to you two in a few minutes anyway."

Lestrade felt that familiar rush of adrenalin as his sense of danger increased, but Holmes appeared as calm as ever.

"I wasn't being flippant—for I am never flippant," Holmes said. "I was serious. I sincerely doubt you are the crime lord who scared Adler so badly, although perhaps you are the one who sniped her."

The man gave an unpleasant, snorting laugh and continued pacing about the room, as if searching the bookshelves for something. That's when Lestrade wondered if maybe, Holmes still had the techpad. The henchman was certainly acting as if he hadn't gotten what he'd come for. Had Holmes had time to stash the device, or maybe even close the secret door, before this thug barged in? It gave Lestrade a faint glimmer of hope, though it was a meager one indeed. Keeping that secret probably wouldn't save them, and they had few options for escape. His wristband comlink was also gone, which meant there would be no chance of contacting Jaymie.

"Well, if you don't feel inclined to respond to that, then perhaps you'd be so kind as to inform us what our fate is going to be," Holmes continued, addressing Jinxx. "I know you're probably obligated to kill us, but personally, I find the prospect bloody frustrating. I don't know nearly as much about this case as I'd like, and if I'm going to die, I'd at least like to know the name of the person who ordered you to kill me."

"Nice try," Jinxx said, sliding his blaster out of its holster and slamming a new energy cartridge into the gun. "And if this is part of some clever attempt to bargain for your freedom, it's not going to work."

"Oh believe me, I know better than to try something clever with a man for whom operating an automatic door is probably something of an intellectual challenge."

Lestrade closed his eyes and winced, half expecting the searing pain of a blaster bolt to come burning through him right now. Holmes was in rare form today. Lestrade was pretty sure he knew what Holmes was doing; he was trying to get Jinxx riled up, so he'd slip and give away something important. However, it could also just as easily get them shot.

Thankfully, all Holmes' smart-mouthed retort earned him was a solid back-handed slap across the mouth.

"You know, Adler died trying to help you, though I don't know why," Jinxx said. "You should have listened to her warning. Nobody messes with Apex."

It was almost invisible, but there was a slight spark in Holmes' eyes at the mention of the word "Apex." It was a new clue, whether the thug had meant to give it away or not.

"And what, pray tell, is Apex?" Holmes asked, and Jinxx grinned. It wasn't just a cocky, "I've got all the good cards in my hand and you have nothing" kind of smile; there was a touch of pure evil, and Lestrade felt a cold fist of fear suddenly clutch at his heart.

"This crime lord, is that the title he goes by?" Holmes continued, undaunted. "How trite. Or is it the name of his pet project, which seems to be engineering all the criminal activity on this planet? It's a big task, mind you, one that's just as likely to backfire as to succeed."

"You know, I might answer that, if you tell me what you found in this library," Jinxx said.

"Nothing," Holmes said with a face so straight as he lied that even Lestrade would have believed him, if he hadn't known any different. Holmes was a master bluffer, and had cleaned out many a card table while gambling at the Drunk Gypsy. But in order to be a successful bluffer, sometimes you actually had to be holding the right cards, and right now Holmes just had an empty hand.

"You know I don't believe that," the thug said. "Want to try again?"

"Even if I was lying—which I'm not—why would I tell you?" Holmes asked. "You'd kill me the minute I told you. If talking and not talking both lead to death, I'd prefer to take my secret with me."

"You know, most beings would risk taking the option that at least gives them a shot at surviving." Jinxx studied them thoughtfully for a second, drumming his fingers on the barrel of his gun. "But then again, you're not 'most beings,' are you, Mr. Holmes? I was told you'd be like this, but I'll admit, I don't really understand it. What kind of being would rather go to their grave knowing their secret is safe than gamble on the chance that telling the truth might spare their life? You're a hard man, Holmes."

"Not hard, just stubborn."

Lestrade looked over and saw Holmes subtlety fiddling with the electro-binders holding him to the chair. He was still trying to work out a way to escape, but Lestrade had the sinking feeling it was going to be futile.

Lestrade had never felt truly helpless before. Naturally, he'd been in some pretty rough spots during his career at Civic Security, including some grim moments where the danger had been very tangible indeed, and he'd honestly wondered if he'd make it out alive. Yet he'd always had his blaster, or some sort of weapon, in his hand, and that had given him some measure of control, no matter how small, over the situation. At least then he could fight back. But now, he had no options. He was an unarmed prisoner, kept alive at the whim of some powerful crime lord's hit man, all the while knowing the chasm separating him and eternity could be bridged with one shot from a blaster. And there was nothing he could do about it. He didn't think he could even play his "I'm a Civic Security inspector, and if you kill me, you'll be in big trouble" card. Most Quadrant B crooks were smart enough not to kill inspectors; as they put it, "kill one copper, and they all take it personally." But if this organization Jinxx was involved in really was as serious as Lestrade thought it was, they probably wouldn't have cared if he were a member of the Ruling Council. He'd gotten in the way, and now he had to be gotten rid of. It was as simple as that.

Holmes finally gave up on the electro-binders, and he apparently sensed Lestrade's despair.

"Don't give up," he mouthed, but Jinxx caught the interchange and laughed.

"The game's over, Holmes. You should have quit while you were ahead. Final chance: tell me what you found in this room, or I'll tear this mansion apart after you're dead."

Holmes said nothing, and Lestrade knew the game really *was* over. Blast, if only he had his comlink, they could at least tell Jaymie goodbye. He had the fleeting thought they were long past their scheduled check-in time by now, but even if she did eventually show up to check on them, it would probably be too late. He would die without ever being able to tell her he was sorry, that he wished...

"Well, the boss will be pleased to hear you died bravely," Jinxx said. "Although he told me you would. He's impressed by your work, Holmes, he really is. I suggested he try to recruit you, but he said he wouldn't insult you by making you an offer you'd certainly refuse."

Holmes' eyes narrowed slightly, the look on his face both suspicious and hesitantly flattered. "Who is 'he,' exactly? What sort of man dabbles in teleportation technology, drug running, diamond theft and assassination? What is he? A twisted man of science? A mafia lord?"

The thug kept smiling, and he slowly lowered the blaster towards Holmes' head. "Yes," was all he said. "And that's the last thing you'll ever—"

The next second—the tiny space of time between the moment Jinxx pressed down on the trigger and the moment the bolt of energy shot out of his blaster—was the longest moment of Lestrade's life. For years afterwards, he would remember every single detail about this second, the closest he had ever come to staring down death, and each fragment of time was captured perfectly in his memory. It all happened instantly, but in his mind it was like watching a slow-motion replay.

Jinxx squeezed the trigger, and Holmes ducked, the bolt of energy burning the side of his head but his dodging motion saving him from a killing blow. And then, Jinxx didn't even have a chance to blink before a bolt of energy burned through his chest, and he crashed to the floor, a look of shock frozen on his face.

Lestrade himself couldn't help gaping in shock as his eyes traced a line from the body lying on the floor to the end of a blaster being held by a slender, redheaded young woman in an evening gown.

Jaymie Watson.

Chapter 7: Riding to the Rescue

It took several seconds for Lestrade's brain to start working again and process what he had seen, because what had just occurred was so miraculous it didn't even seem possible. Jaymie stood in a beam of moonlight in the hallway, looking very much like one of the avenging faeries found in Scoztan lore. The cool blue light fell across her glittering red evening gown and caused the dress's tiny sequins to sparkle in the darkness. She had pulled her long red hair into an elegant bun at the top of her head, and she was barefoot, her dress shoes perhaps discarded in her haste to get here. Lestrade had never seen her like this before, and he couldn't help staring at her, completely dumbfounded. How she'd managed to get here, he had no idea, and he supposed it didn't matter. She'd just saved their lives, pulling off what basically amounted to a one-being undercover raid, and taken a shot with the coolness of a Civic Security veteran. And she looked amazing.

"Watson, that is a stunning dress."

Holmes was the first one to break the silence, though even he seemed to be having trouble wiping the astonished look off his face. Lestrade had the fleeting thought this was the first time he'd heard Holmes make a compliment like that—ever. And the fact it was the first thing out of his mouth was just another indication of how rattled he must be.

Jaymie lowered her blaster, the look of disbelief on her own face making Lestrade wonder if she was as surprised by her actions as he and Holmes were. Although her hands were trembling slightly, if she was feeling any fear deep down, it didn't show in her eyes.

"Thanks," she said, slightly breathless, and Lestrade suspected she had run at least part of the way here. He glanced back down at Jinxx's body, now lying prone on the floor, and realized Jaymie hadn't used a stun bolt. She'd shot to kill, the exact same call he would have made, but he was still surprised she'd made that choice on her own.

She picked up the control for their electro-binders, which Jinxx had dropped on the floor when he collapsed, and she released Holmes and then Lestrade.

"I guess, uh, maybe we should call Civic Security," Lestrade said, rubbing his wrists from where they had been burned by the electro-binders. He felt like he should say something else, but his thoughts still weren't collected enough to enable him to say anything profound.

Jaymie shook her head. "They should already be on their way—I called them as soon as I got here. I went ahead and came in because, well, I wasn't sure how much time we had."

"Good call," Holmes said, glancing around the room. He was apparently still somewhat stunned as well, because he was *never* that succinct.

Lestrade could now hear the wail of sirens in the distance, and he felt a lump in his stomach as he thought about what would have happened if Jaymie *hadn't* decided to come in.

"However, it was somewhat foolhardy of you to run in here without back-up," Holmes finally told Jaymie. "You had no idea how many hostiles—pardon the military term—might be in here, and you could have been walking into a trap or—" He suddenly stopped and threw up his hands. "You know, I should just shut up. What you did might have been crazy, but I'm bloody glad you did it."

"Yeah," Jaymie said. "Me too."

They slowly made their way out of the mansion, finding a squad of Civic Security patrol hovercars from both Quadrant B and Quadrant D waiting for them. Officers were jumping out of their cars with blasters drawn, preparing to secure the scene and not yet realizing their services weren't really needed anymore.

"You guys all right?" Chief Bevill yelled, running towards them as his officers surrounded the perimeter.

Holmes didn't even offer a smart retort about Civic Security arriving—once again—too late to do anything useful.

"I'm fine," he said distantly, and Bevill gave him a curious look.

"You sure about that?" he asked. "It looks like you've seen a ghost."

"Yes—something like that."

Holmes still hadn't bothered to meet Bevill's gaze, and perplexed, the chief followed his line of sight to Jaymie, who was now being questioned by one of the officers. Lestrade realized for once, Holmes wasn't the center of attention at a crime scene. Jaymie was the one who'd called Civic Security in, and the only one of their investigative trio who was holding a weapon, so the officers had apparently decided she was the one in charge. This time, he and Holmes were just the victims who'd been rescued.

"Ah, it must be the famous Miss Watson," said Dr. Ethan Dric, walking over towards them. He was Quadrant B's medical examiner, and Holmes found him to be extremely irritating. Of course, Dric took endless delight in rubbing this in. "I'm guessing she's the one who saved you space scouts' sorry bums when you got in over your heads. Pretty impressive for a graduate student, huh?"

"She's not just a medical student—she's a private investigator," Holmes said, and Lestrade realized this was the first time he'd heard Holmes refer to her as more than just his "investigative assistant." Apparently, there were a lot of "firsts" this evening.

Dric clapped Holmes on the back. "Well, how does it feel not to be the knight in shining armor, galloping in to save the day like you normally do?" He grinned. "You know, this just might be the most subdued I've ever seen you. Jaymie Watson must be pretty remarkable to evoke this kind of reaction—maybe you even fancy her a bit, eh? This is the only time I remember finding both you and Lestrade speechless and staring like idiots."

"Well, pardon us for being a little stunned at the moment," Holmes said brusquely, finally regaining some of his wits. "We've just survived almost getting murdered—again."

Dric's grin hadn't diminished a bit. "Oh, I'm sure that's all of it."

"Dr. Dric—it sounds like there might be some work for you to do inside the mansion," Chief Bevill cut in, his tone slightly disapproving. He didn't tolerate a lot of banter at crime scenes, especially the sort of juvenile banter Dric was so fond of. "Just got a message from Lieutenant Yariop about the body her team just found. There won't be any charges filed here, but I still need you to do your investigation."

Dric straightened instantly. "Yes, sir. I'll head in there now."

They watched Dric hurry over to the mansion, and then Bevill cleared his throat. "Well, gentlemen, I'll be asking you to file a report as well, but I'm sure you know the drill." He glanced over at Jaymie, who was still being questioned by an officer. "You know, you are two very lucky young men," he said quietly. "Not everybody has a friend who would do what she did for you."

"Yes," Lestrade said, watching her wistfully as the officer questioning her finally nodded and waved her on, clearing her to leave the scene. "Believe me, I know."

#

Jaymie wasn't sure what she *should* be feeling right now, but the only thing she *was* feeling was a sense of numbness. On her way back to Moriarty's car, she had to pass by groups of Civic Security officers, journalists, and bystanders gathered at the scene, and she tried to keep her head held high and appear as calm as possible. She was attempting to put on a brave face, and judging by the looks of shocked admiration from the Civic Security inspectors as she walked by, it was working, at least somewhat. But if they could have peered inside her head and read her thoughts, they'd know how close she was to collapsing and curling into a helpless, fetal position.

She still couldn't believe she'd done it. She hadn't initially planned to go inside the mansion, but when she'd arrived, she just had this sense she couldn't afford to wait for Civic Security. Although she hadn't meant to shoot the thug either, she had reached the room as he took that first shot at Holmes, and she hadn't had time to switch her own gun (which she'd recently upgraded) to "stun." Firing at the thug had been a gut reaction, an instinctive decision she'd simply known was right. And even though directly before and directly after, her stomach had been an impossible knot of fear, at that one moment, she'd never thought more clearly or calmly in her life. Things had suddenly become so simple—it was either Jinxx or Holmes and Lestrade—and she'd done what she had to in order to save her friends.

However, she wasn't sure what to do now. Holmes and Lestrade were still being questioned and would likely be tied up for some time, since they actually knew more about the situation than she did and could give Civic Security more details. She knew she should probably stick around and listen to what they were telling the officers, but truthfully, she wanted nothing more than to just go back to apartment 221 in Quadrant B and bury herself under the covers of her bed.

Then again, she supposed what she *really* needed to do was take the hovercar back to Moriarty, but she wasn't quite sure she was ready to face him. Their date was obviously over for this evening, and maybe their relationship (or whatever potential there had been *for* a relationship) was over as well. Although he had seemed very sympathetic when she had to rush off and had even offered to let her use his hovercar, she wondered how he had really felt when she rather abruptly left him at the table at the pub. She hadn't been ditching him, exactly, and she had no doubt she'd made the right choice. After all, if she hadn't left Dizzy Blues, her friends wouldn't be alive right now.

But the real question was, would Moriarty understand? Did he feel like her friends were more important to her than he was? Was he so offended he wouldn't ask her out a second time, for fear she'd have to go running off again? Because Jaymie couldn't promise that she wouldn't. She felt a duty to Lestrade and Holmes, and their friendship was something she couldn't bear to lose.

But as she stood next to the car, staring off into the misty fog rolling slowly down the streets of Loudron, she realized she didn't really want to lose Moriarty either. Why did things have to be so blasted complicated all the—

"Jaymie!"

She suddenly heard someone calling her name, and she turned and saw a tall young man jumping out of a hovercab, dressed in a finely tailored suit that was now slightly disheveled.

"James?" she asked in surprise, blinking and wondering if maybe she was imagining things.

He dashed over towards her, a look of deep concern in his eyes. "Are you all right?" he asked, glancing around at the cluster of patrol hovercars, their sirens still blaring and their lights still flashing in the darkness. "It looks like a full-blown crime scene here!"

"I'm...I'm fine," Jaymie said, still shocked to find him here, and trying to process what that might mean. "You didn't have to come. I would have returned your hovercar to—"

Moriarty, however, was already shaking his head. "I don't care about the car. I was just...just worried about you." He looked down at the blaster in her hands, and his eyes widened. "You didn't have to..."

Jaymie started to glance away, but she stopped and wouldn't let herself. She had nothing to be ashamed of. "Some crime lord sent a hit man after Holmes and Lestrade. I got there just as he was going to shoot them, so I had to shoot him instead. I can't believe I did it, really. I just couldn't..." She let her voice trail off, not sure how to finish.

She felt a splash of water on her forehead, and she looked up and saw that the mist was now turning into rain. She shivered slightly, and before she knew it, Moriarty's trench coat was off and around her shoulders, despite her protests that she was fine. His eyes had never once left her, and she saw a mixture of relief and worry trapped in his gaze.

"Jaymie Watson, I don't know what to make of you," he said softly. "The medical student who moonlights as a private investigator, claiming she's just an assistant and then turning around and beating Civic Security to the scene of a crime to take out a hit man. You're…you're a beautiful conundrum. I think I could spend a lifetime getting to know you, and you'd still amaze me."

She glanced up and was surprised to find a sudden flicker of sadness in his eyes as he said it, though it was there for only a second and then was gone. She didn't know where that sadness had come from, and she found it strange. She wanted to ask him about it but once again found herself unable to form the words.

"Would you like me to drive you home?" he finally asked, breaking the silence, but she shook her head.

"I'll probably just catch a ride with Holmes and Lestrade. Thank you for dinner, though—I'm sorry I didn't get to finish it."

Moriarty smiled and laughed quietly. "Oh, don't worry about that. I'll just have to take you there again sometime."

Jaymie's heart leapt, and she couldn't keep the excitement out of her voice. "Really? I thought maybe you'd never want to see me again after this mess." She paused, feeling hesitant again. "I wish I could promise it's not always like this, but with Holmes, it's, well…"

"You don't have to explain—I understand," Moriarty told her. "But believe me, I'm willing to take the risk."

He flashed her another smile, and Jaymie watched as he climbed into his hovercar, oblivious to the fact the sprinkling rain had now become a downpour and her fancy dress was getting soaked. She kept watching him for a long time, even as the crowd that had gathered around the crime scene scrambled for cover.

It wasn't until long after he had gone that she realized she was still wearing his coat.

#

Although Jaymie went straight to bed as soon as they arrived at the flat, neither Holmes nor Lestrade slept that night.

Once they made it back to the flat, Holmes immediately grabbed a pen and paper and started scribbling down notes (he never liked to use a techpad while he was doing "intensive brainstorming," as he called it), and Lestrade went to work on Rozine's techpad, which Holmes had been smart enough to hide in the library so it wouldn't be discovered by Jinxx. Though he charged it for an hour and was certain it had full power, for some reason, he still couldn't get it to turn on. That only served to further convince him there was something of great importance on the device, some information Jane Rozine had gone to great lengths to safeguard.

Though he and Holmes both sat in the drawing room to work, neither one of them spoke. At this point, words would have been a waste of time. They just needed to solve this, and they needed to solve it *now*. The appearance of the hit man hadn't turned out to be a game ender for them, but it very well could have been, and it was clear their mysterious crime lord opponent, whoever he was, was now playing for blood. And they didn't have any idea how much time they had—days, hours, or minutes—until the crime lord struck again.

It wasn't until the first tinges of pink appeared on the horizon, signaling the sunrise, that Lestrade finally found the right combination of buttons on the techpad and switched the device on. He glanced at the screen, and then his expression grew grim.

"Holmes, I think you should see this."

His friend grabbed the device and quickly skimmed the message from Jane Rozine that had appeared on the screen: "If you're a member of Apex and you're reading this, know that you won't get anything else from me. You've already taken everything from me you possibly can, and this information is only what you already know. If you're not Apex, then God rest your soul. Because if you aren't with Apex, and you're holding this device, you're as good as dead."

Case No. 6: Double Blind

Chapter 1: The Conundrum

Sherlock Holmes didn't believe in unsolvable puzzles.

He had never once given up on solving a case, and had never, ever admitted defeat. He had stuck with many cases long after Civic Security had thrown in the proverbial towel. Of course, that was often because they had missed some perfectly obvious clue that any thinking being would have noticed, but well, that was just the way it was with Civic Security. Once Holmes started a case, he was determined to see it through and solve it, whatever it took.

Yet no case had ever confounded him as much as this one. He wasn't about to admit it to Watson or Lestrade, but he had no bloody idea how any of the pieces fit together. Well, that wasn't quite true. Hazy threads of connection *were* beginning to weave together in his mind, but they were still very vague. This mysterious crime lord—whoever he was—had been working with Jane Rozine, who later committed corporate fraud in an unsuccessful attempt to outsmart the law and get ahead in whatever game she was playing. The crime lord must also have been working with the drug runner and smuggler Jok Urdi, probably getting wealthy off this partnership, and then offing Urdi when his continued existence became inconvenient. The crime lord had then employed Adler, who had *almost* pulled off that bank heist. But while Holmes had been able to connect the crime lord to each of these cases individually, he didn't see how the crime lord and all three of the cases fit together as a whole. What connected Rozine, Urdi, and Adler?

He just couldn't see how those cases were related to each other, and he wouldn't have ever put them together, if Adler hadn't told him that to save his life, he had to.

A teleporter, drug running money, and a vortex diamond—they were all pieces of a larger puzzle, and it seemed to be a puzzle he couldn't solve. It was maddening. In an attempt to make some sense of this mess, he had turned one of the walls in his bedroom into what he called an "association map"—he had taken pictures, words, thoughts jotted down on slips of paper, and everything else he had gathered during his quest to solve this case and then pasted them onto the wall so he could look at them all together. Usually standing back and looking at a cluster of information like this made his mind run wild, and it wasn't long before his brain would begin playing a mental game of "connect the dots," and he would have the case solved within minutes. But this particular association map was doing nothing for him, and for the first time in his life, he realized his brain was devoid of a single thought. He had nothing—absolutely nothing. And the worst part was, he knew what was causing him to hit a dead end, and there wasn't anything he could do about it.

He took a dart from a dart board Lestrade had given him as a yuletide gift years ago and tossed it at the center of the association map, nailing a blank piece of paper. That was the piece of paper symbolizing the identity of the crime lord, and it was a bit of knowledge Holmes would give just about anything to learn. He knew the crime lord was male (judging by Jinxx's use of the masculine pronoun in reference to the crime lord, while he was so inconsiderately trying to kill them yesterday), but precious little else. Was he young? Old? A prominent member of society leading a double life, or a recluse orchestrating everything behind the scenes?

In spite of himself, Holmes felt a slight chill as he recalled the rather ambiguous clues Jinxx had let slip. Supposedly this master criminal was both a twisted man of science and a mafia lord. And what did that add up to? Possibly the greatest challenge Holmes had ever faced. Holmes didn't approve of such maudlin terms as "archenemy," but if he had to apply it to someone, this would be it. He'd tried researching the term "Apex," wondering if it would shed some light on the crime lord's identity, but that had proven to be another dead end. The term brought up too many hits on the digital information network: it was the name of an archaic Yopilian form of meditation; a now inactive crime ring on Itred; the prototype for a super-efficient hyperspace engine; and countless more. Holmes doubted he'd stumble upon the right association by chance, and he hated aimless speculation.

He supposed he should be afraid this crime lord would eventually kill him, but he honestly didn't fear death. What he feared was dying without knowing why he had died, or who had been clever enough to finally kill him.

His comlink beeped, and he picked it up, irritated by the untimely interruption.

"What is it?" he snapped, not bothering to ask who it was, assuming it was either Lestrade or Civic Security, who would likely be used to his rudeness anyway.

But the voice he heard next didn't belong to either of those, and it filled him with a sudden, icy dread.

"Ah, Sherlock Holmes. So good to finally speak to you."

The voice was somewhat distorted, probably by some electronic device designed to keep the speaker's identity a secret. But special device or no, Holmes had a feeling he knew exactly who this was.

"You know, you're not very good at killing me," Holmes said, and the man on the other end of the comlink laughed.

"I suppose I do deserve that particular insult, don't I? I really thought Jinxx was more than capable of doing the job, but apparently I hadn't counted on your secret weapon—a certain Miss Jaymie Watson."

For the briefest fraction of a second, Holmes felt his heart stop. When he finally spoke, his voice was low and very, very cold. "Whoever you are, I want you to listen, and listen closely. Your business is with me—and me only. Not any of my friends. If what you really want is to meet and settle this in person, then fine. But if you hurt my friends, I will spend the rest of my life hunting you down, and making sure you pay."

The other end of the link was silent for a moment, though without seeing the other man's face, Holmes had no way of knowing whether he was simply thinking or truly intimidated.

"You think I'm some sort of monster," the man finally said. "And I think some part of you even fears me, though I'd be hard pressed to get you to confess that. You're a worthy opponent, Holmes, far more my equal than pathetic yes-men like Urdi and even Adler. So many of the beings I'm forced to use to carry out my work lack the ability to think creatively, and it drives me mad. But not you. I just wish we weren't on opposing sides."

"Why don't you join mine, then?" Holmes was already beyond frustrated with this call; he was sure the crime lord hadn't called to give away clues—he was just gloating, and Holmes hated criminals who gloated. But Holmes was determined to keep leading him on, to keep him talking, because at the same time he was trying to hook his comlink up to his techpad, patching it into software that could hopefully trace the call. If he was lucky, he could pinpoint exactly where the crime lord was standing.

The software was supposed to be undetectable, so Holmes was stunned by the crime lord's next words.

"Come, Holmes, now you're just being amateurish. Trying to trace my comlink? That's very Civic Security of you. Go ahead if you must, but you won't find me. This comlink is protected, and by the time you crack it—*if* you can crack it—our conversation will be long over."

"Then why *did* you call me?" Holmes said. "Because this conversation has become little more than a waste of my time—and it became that a long time ago."

The crime lord laughed again, and Holmes' inability to faze him was exasperating, especially since Holmes was apparently the only one who was becoming irritated.

"Just a friendly warning, though I know you won't listen to it. Drop the case now, and I might reconsider my decision to get rid of you. I also wouldn't mind taking a look at the techpad you recovered from Rozine's mansion; that might put me in a more benevolent state of mind while I'm pondering your fate."

"There's nothing on that techpad—at least nothing I've been able to access," Holmes said, and that was the truth. The device had been very skillfully encrypted, and though he continued to work on it, he hadn't cracked it yet.

"Ah, too bad. Just keep trying, because I have faith you'll get through eventually. You always do, don't you, Holmes? Well, I shouldn't keep you. You have some things you need to think over, and I have a feeling you'll be getting another call very soon—and it's one you won't like."

"What?" Holmes asked, but all he heard was a quiet beep, meaning the crime lord had just switched off his comlink.

"Who the bloody devil are you?" Holmes shouted into the comlink, knowing no one could hear him but too frustrated to care. He hated feeling so powerless, as if now he was just another one of the helpless pawns in this crime lord's game...

Beep! Beep!

Holmes' comlink went off again, and he answered it almost before the second beep.

"Holmes, this is Athelney." He could hear the weariness in her voice and wondered if she was pulling a double shift. "I need you down at my station—now."

"What's happened?" Holmes asked. Normally he would have given Athelney grief for asking for his help—which was a rather rare and therefore monumental occasion—but he was in no mood for banter now. This was the call the crime lord had predicted, and it couldn't be good.

"I don't have a blasted idea," Athelney said curtly. "But it's very, very bad."

Chapter 2: The Cover-Up

An hour later, Holmes and Athelney stood in a lab inside the Loudron Regional Medical Center in Quadrant A, watching as some of Athelney's inspectors slid the body of a murdered lab tech into a bag and carried it away from the scene. Athelney had marched into the room with her trademark air of stubbornness and determination, though her face was gaunter than it used to be. She was still recovering from the nearly fatal injuries she had received during the prison block explosion, and she had only very recently returned to work.

Inspectors had already started collecting evidence before Holmes and Athelney arrived, an action that had frustrated Holmes to no end. Yet even though some key clues were now probably missing, he could easily deduce what had happened. The lab tech had been working at the counter along the far wall when an attacker had come in, stabbing the tech from behind with a lethally high dose of vraxil, a sedative normally kept in a password-secured, refrigerated safe. The lab tech had struggled, as evidenced by the tools and medical supplies that had been knocked off the counter and were now lying scattered across the floor. The tech had died less than one minute after being injected with the chemical, and hadn't even had time to press the emergency alarm. His body had been found by a University of Medical Arts intern who now sat huddled in a corner with her head in her hands, too traumatized by the experience to talk to Civic Security. It was the first-ever recorded murder in the hospital, and it was a crime that should have been impossible. The only two people with approved access to vraxil were the lab tech and the lab supervisor—who had been found slumped over her desk, dead from a shot of the same sedative.

"So, any ideas at all about what the devil just happened?" Athelney asked the hospital CEO, who was standing next to them and staring blankly at the lab where the tech had been murdered. She had a hollow, distant look in her eyes, as if she was still in shock and unable to process what had occurred.

Holmes already knew this woman wasn't a suspect. There was a certain level of shock you just couldn't fake, and this far surpassed that. The CEO was feeling every bit of this trauma, and she was just as clueless as everyone else in the room (except, perhaps, for Holmes, who had never been completely clueless in his life. Well, *almost* never).

"Vraxil was a new drug, just recently developed by a professor named Dr. Gavyn Hortz, who works at a university on Itred," the CEO, Jyessa Smythe, said slowly. "Braxton, the tech, and Vbria, his supervisor, picked up the delivery yesterday and began performing tests on it this morning. It hadn't been cleared for testing on sentients, and I wasn't aware that anyone other than Braxton, Vbria, me, and the professor who developed it even knew it existed. Well, and that poor intern, who—God help her—may never want to work here again, and I wouldn't blame her. I never should have cleared that drug for testing. The medical centers on Itred wouldn't take it—said it was too dangerous. I didn't like it either, but Vbria was convinced they could lessen its harmful side effects."

"So I assume the drug's been stolen, and we could have some kind of bio-terror threat on our hands," Athelney said, but Smythe shook her head.

"That's what's even stranger. The refrigerated safe was broken into, and only one bottle was stolen. When we did a bio-scan of Braxton and Vbria before the bodies were...taken away, we found the chemicals they had absorbed were exactly the same amount that would have been contained in that stolen bottle. The drug was used to kill them, then the bottle was discarded in the hallway with no fingerprint residue."

"That's too much trouble to go through for a random murder," Athelney said. "Whoever broke in must have wanted something to do with the drug."

"I'm not so sure about that."

Holmes knelt on the floor, examining the array of tools and vials that had fallen on the ground during the tech's struggle with the unidentified attacker. "Don't get too hung up on the drug as the motive for the crime, Athelney. I know you always have a tendency to gravitate towards the obvious, but please, try to resist. Perhaps it was just used as the murder weapon, and the criminal was after something else."

Athelney frowned, crossing her arms over her chest in a manner Holmes would have best described as a "huff." "Well, please—enlighten me."

Holmes glanced around the room. He actually didn't have anything—yet—but of course Athelney didn't need to know that. It simply frustrated him when people jumped to conclusions too quickly, often causing them to miss an all-important clue. The correct solution wasn't always immediately visible, especially if you were dealing with a particularly clever criminal, and Holmes already knew that he was. Still, there was no such thing as a perfect crime, and all criminals, no matter how good, always left traces somewhere. You just had to know where to look.

His eyes drifted over the scene, taking in all the details and looking for anything Civic Security may have missed (and knowing Civic Security, they had undoubtedly missed *something*). He mentally sorted out all the tools on the floor: a pair of forceps, scissors, six plasti-glass vials and a tray to hold them, a shiny silver...

And just like that, he had it.

"Don't move!" Holmes ordered an inspector who was just bending down to collect the tools and bag them up as evidence. Holmes snatched a pair of protective gloves away from a different (and rather stunned) inspector, hurriedly snapped them on, and began picking up the vials and setting them in the tray. Sure enough, there were two empty slots. He searched all around the room, but the extra two vials were nowhere to be found.

"This is exactly the sort of very telling clue that Civic Security always ignores," Holmes said, holding up the tray and chastising the two inspectors who would have picked it up without ever realizing its significance. "Two of the vials on this tray are inexplicably missing—snatched, no doubt, by whoever killed the lab tech and supervisor."

Athelney took one of the vials from the tray, and as she examined it, he watched her irritation at his dressing down of her staff turn to grudging admiration as she realized he was right. "Good eye, Holmes," she said curtly, quite possibly the first compliment she had ever paid him. She handed the vial to Smythe. "So what exactly is in these, and why might it be significant to this case?"

Smythe took the vial and studied the label, then her eyes widened in shock. "Embryonic cell samples!" she exclaimed, as if not quite able to believe what she'd just read. These types of cell samples were sometimes taken from unborn beings still in the womb to use for testing purposes, although the sample-taking didn't harm the mother or her child. "But what are these doing here? These are supposed to be in a refrigerated storage unit in another lab—Braxton hadn't been cleared to use these in his testing."

"Ah, now we're getting somewhere," Holmes said with a smile, setting down the tray and pacing through the lab. "This is magnificent."

Smythe looked over at him, her expression a mixture of disbelief and distaste. "I'm sorry, Mr. Holmes, but I fail to see how this is 'magnificent.' Two of my employees were just murdered, and now I've discovered they may have been doing something illegal."

"Yes—that's why it's magnificent," Holmes said, then let out a sigh. Why could these people never seem to keep up with his intellect? "I found it highly unlikely someone would kill two hospital employees over a new type of sedative, and the discovery of those embryonic cells means something else was going on here."

"I don't see why embryonic cells would be needed to test a sedative," Athelney said, and it took all of Holmes' admittedly meager supply of patience not to show his exasperation.

"They weren't needed to test the sedative—they must be part of some other project. The sedative likely means nothing, and that project could have simply been a cover-up for what the employees were really studying. Yet something must have gone wrong with the real project involving the embryonic cells, which was why Braxton and Vbria were killed. And I think I know who killed them."

Athelney frowned. "Come now, Holmes, you can't assume every crime from now on is staged by your mysterious crime lord. Now aren't you the one who's jumping to conclusions?"

Holmes shook his head. "No—the crime lord called me right before I came over here and told me this case was related to whatever overarching, diabolical scheme he is plotting."

That immediately wiped the smirk off Athelney's face. "Oh."

Holmes walked over to the lab's lone window, staring out across the Quadrant A cityscape, which looked somewhat gray and dreary under an overcast sky. He knew everyone was staring at him, waiting for him to say something brilliant that would reveal how this new clue related to the crime lord's overall scheme, but honestly, he was still just as puzzled as before. His excitement regarding the discovery of the embryonic cells had already begun to diminish, as he realized it was just another maddening, seemingly random clue to add to the sludge of data. This was the only case Holmes had ever worked on where each additional clue caused the case to make *less* sense. It was getting utterly ridiculous. He had the suspicion that was why the crime lord had called him; he'd only given him another clue because he was certain Holmes wouldn't be able to make sense of it, and it would only frustrate him further. *The blasted vodog.*

"Listen, I need you to get me as much information as possible on the professor who developed vraxil," Holmes said.

"But I thought you said the vraxil had nothing to do with the case," Smythe said, looking slightly confused.

"But that doesn't mean the professor himself has nothing to do with this case," Holmes corrected her. "I'm going to run every lead we have into the ground—and we *are* going to solve this."

Athelney nodded brusquely. "Then let's finish this, Holmes."

I will—even if it's the last thing I do, he thought as Athelney exited the room and began barking orders to her team of inspectors. And for all he knew, it very well could be.

#

Jaymie laced her arm through Professor Moriarty's as they strolled down a walkway along the Trymes River in Loudron, enjoying the cool evening breeze. They hadn't spoken in a few minutes, but the silence wasn't awkward; they were simply admiring the scenery, observing the tiny white blossoms blooming on the fghon trees and watching the way the glowlamps reflected off the water.

She'd gone on several dates now with Moriarty, and as she'd gotten to know him better, she was more and more impressed. Besides being a brilliant medical scientist, he was also an artist, and he had given her one of his impressionistic paintings, which she'd proudly hung on her wall at home. It was a painting of a city at nighttime, with a touch of the surreal; instead of white specks, the stars were depicted as orbs of a dozen different colors: blue, purple, orange, red, green, and more. The painting was called "A Rainbow of Stars," and he said he'd painted it especially for her, though when she asked why he thought it represented her, all she got was a teasing smile and a promise that he'd tell her someday.

Someday—the only problem with "someday" was that it had the tendency to always be out there drifting somewhere in the vague future, and sometimes it never did end up becoming "today."

Jaymie was certain now Moriarty liked her, and she liked him a lot, as well. Except, she wasn't sure she was in love with him, at least not yet. She didn't know what was holding her back; so many of the women at the university were very jealous of her, and Moriarty seemingly had all the perfect traits: he was handsome, smart, cultured, and well-mannered, and he was very attentive to her needs and concerns. It was just...well, Jaymie wasn't sure what it was. She wanted to love him back, but maybe she was simply afraid to. Perhaps she still just couldn't come to understand why it was he seemed to like *her*. Though her family was wealthy, he came from a rich family as well and didn't need a relationship with her to improve his social status. She truly believed he cared for her, but maybe she was too in awe of him to think of him as being attainable. Still, she supposed she might grow more comfortable with time, and she was more than willing to wait. She had a feeling those deep green eyes held secrets she had yet to discover, and he very much intrigued her.

"Beautiful, isn't it?" Moriarty finally said, breaking the silence, and Jaymie nodded.

"It reminds me of the fghon forest on Scoztan, although there you don't have any skyscrapers poking up above the trees."

"Do you ever want to move back to Scoztan?" he asked, and she shrugged.

"I love Scoztan, but do I want to be closer to my mother? That's the real question."

Moriarty laughed, a teasing smile tugging at his lips. "I see then. You're not close to her, I take it?"

Jaymie shook her head, stopping beneath one of the fghon trees and staring out across the river. "We just never connected, though I can't really say why. We're such opposites, I guess, and she wanted something different for my life than what I wanted. She didn't like the idea of me studying medicine, and she didn't want me to come to the university here. She'd rather I be a 'high society lady,' I think."

"But that wouldn't make you happy," Moriarty said softly, nodding in understanding. "Sometimes it takes a while to discover your destiny, and it can be difficult when others don't have the same vision you do."

He gestured to one of the metal benches next to the river, and Jaymie took a seat, feeling a little puzzled. She wasn't sure what he was doing, unless he had something more serious to tell her and wanted her to be sitting down. Her stomach twisted slightly, and she wondered if maybe he was going to tell her that while he'd enjoyed their dates, he didn't feel there was a future for their relationship. If only she'd been more encouraging or less awkward or... *Less like Jaymie Watson*, she thought gloomily.

"I don't quite know how to say this," Moriarty began, and Jaymie's heart sank. That wasn't a good start.

"I suppose I'll just be blunt—you know how I am. I really like you, Jaymie, as a person and for your work. You're a brilliant student, and I think you have an incredible future ahead of you. Call me selfish, but I'm not willing to let you slip away and have someone else take advantage of those skills. How would you like to come work for me and join my research team?"

Jaymie was so surprised by his question (especially since it was completely different from what she'd been expecting) that she started laughing, thinking he must be joking. It wasn't until she turned to face him, and saw the look in his eyes, that she realized he was being absolutely serious.

"Oh—I...I don't know what to say," she stammered, caught off guard. "I'm not sure I understand what you mean."

"As I'm sure you're already aware, I'm starting a new research project, an offshoot of that synthetic nerve study I was telling you about the day we first met," he explained. "I'm still not at liberty to give away many details, but I'd like to invite you to a gala where I'll be announcing the project in front of a group of scientists and investors. You can give me your answer then."

"You want me to join the project?" Jaymie asked, still struggling to process what he was asking her. She couldn't believe it—as a graduate student, she was being asked to join a research team with one of the best professors at what was arguably the most prestigious university in this galactic sector. This was exactly the sort of work she had always dreamed of doing, and she'd be working on research that was probably on the cutting edge of medical science. How could she refuse?

"Of course I accept," she said, and Moriarty laughed.

"I'm glad you're so excited, but please, do take some time considering it," he said. "It will be a major commitment, though it shouldn't take too much time away from your studies. However, it may interfere with some of your other...extracurricular activities."

He means investigating with Holmes. It didn't take much effort to read between the lines. At first, she was almost irritated, wondering if this was a direct ploy by Moriarty to distract her from spending too much time with Holmes, but then she realized it was only fair. She really wouldn't have time to do both—and she would have to choose between them. And Moriarty was being kind enough to give her time to decide.

"Thank you very much for the offer," Jaymie said, and she meant it. "I'll think over it very carefully."

"Good." Moriarty took her hand and squeezed it slightly, her words bringing a warm smile to his face. "And I want you to know, no matter what you choose, it won't have a negative impact on how I feel about you. It's your choice—make the one that's right for you."

Chapter 3: Loose Ends

Holmes wasn't really expecting Dr. Gavyn Hortz to be cooperative, so he wasn't shocked when the man didn't return any of Athelney's calls. If the professor was in any way involved in something suspicious, he'd more than likely already taken care to vanish from the public spotlight. And sure enough, when Athelney finally did manage to reach the man's secretary, he claimed his boss was "on holiday." He said he didn't know where Hortz had gone or what time he would be returning. *And Hortz had probably thought that wouldn't sound at all suspicious— the clear mark of an amateur.*

Holmes had taken the liberty of looking up Hortz on the public digital information network, and had made two very curious discoveries. First, that Hortz apparently had a reputation for being difficult to work with, and second, that he had recently completed a genuinely groundbreaking study: the famous "Pulsator Project," a study on artificial nerve creation. And this was where things had begun to look truly interesting.

Tracking down Dr. Hortz wasn't going to be easy, but it wouldn't be impossible, because no one could completely disappear off the radar. It was exactly like diving into a body of water: you could disappear beneath the surface, but the jump itself always left ripples that revealed where you'd gone. And following those ripples was how Holmes eventually found himself sitting across from Dr. Hortz at the Drunk Gypsy.

It was past 2 a.m., and most every other being in the pub had gone home, except for a few Gerfrians gathered around a table and one man in a dingy coat (obviously Dr. Hortz) sitting on the very last stool at the bar, his back to the door. (It was another sign of an inexperienced criminal, because masters *never* placed themselves in a spot where they couldn't easily keep an eye on a building's entrance.) Holmes set his glass of ale down on the bar right next to the professor, attempting to make the sound as loud and obnoxious as possible.

Hortz flinched, but he didn't overreact or jump too suspiciously, which Holmes had to give him credit for.

"Mind if I join you?" Holmes asked, and the man snorted.

"I'd prefer that you didn't," Hortz replied in a clipped accent far too refined to belong to your ordinary Quadrant B scumbag.

"Oh, I think you'll be very interested in what I have to say," Holmes said, taking a seat next to him. "I highly doubt this is where most professors 'on holiday' would choose to visit, though I do have to compliment you on trying to blend in with the locals. Of course, you did a rather poor job, but at least you tried."

The professor spun around, a mixture of panic and anger in his eyes as he reached inside his coat.

"There's no need to pull a blaster on me," Holmes said, holding up his hands. "You've already lost this hand, I'm afraid, but if you can help me, perhaps I can save you from the crime lord who will be coming after you, and I think we both know he's the one you should really be worried about."

The professor slowly took his empty hand back out of his coat, shaking his head at Holmes. "How did you find me?" he asked.

"It wasn't as easy as I'd hoped, but ultimately not really a challenge," Holmes said, casually taking a sip from his mug of ale. "You didn't get far after you committed the murder, did you?"

Hortz glared. "You can't prove that."

"No, but it makes sense," Holmes said. "Especially since you seem to know exactly what I'm talking about. Only a limited number of beings knew about the sedative, and only three are left alive—you and Smythe and some poor intern. And since Smythe and the intern are obviously not guilty, that leaves you. Being its creator, you would have known exactly how much of the vraxil to administer in order to make the dose lethal, and the fact you even considered developing a drug the University of Itred believed was highly dangerous calls your medical ethics into question."

Hortz's face grew increasingly paler as Holmes went on with his story.

"Now, as for how I found you here... Once I deduced you'd committed the murder, I figured you'd go into hiding. I had a friend of mine in Civic Security check the passport records to see if any travel authorization cards from Itred had recently been swiped. Sure enough, your card had been scanned as you entered Eglon a day before the murder, but you had never been scanned back out—hence, I presumed you were still here. Now, you didn't want to stay anywhere near Quadrant A, where you committed the murder, and you'd heard Quadrant B is the place beings with less than stellar pasts go to disappear.

"While that statement is correct, you're a little too 'high class' to completely fit in with the dregs of society skulking about this quadrant. I did some asking around, and it didn't take long to trace you here. I was almost prepared to waltz into the pub and accuse *you* of being the crime lord behind all this, but you've made too many mistakes to be a true criminal mastermind, and I can see by the fear in your eyes you're just another puppet. And you're afraid you're going to meet the same fate as Adler."

Dr. Hortz stared dumbly at Holmes, an indication he'd nailed all the facts correctly. Holmes took another sip of his ale and waited, deciding it would only be charitable to give the professor a moment to figure out his next move. Hortz had to know by now he was doomed, and it was too late to try bolting; all that remained was for him to decide whether or not it was worth it to start talking.

"I'm not going to help you," the professor finally said, his eyes glowering darkly as he pushed away his half-finished glass of ale. "I may pay for my failure with my life, but I see no reason to help you, Sherlock Holmes."

"Ah, so you know who I am," Holmes replied. "Very good. And do you know exactly who it is you work for?"

The man's lips curled into a sneer, although Holmes had a feeling the venom behind that smile wasn't entirely meant for him. "'Who I work for?' I'm not working for anyone. I'm being manipulated against my will and forced to play a part not of my choosing in this blasted scheme. I crossed the wrong man, Mr. Holmes, and now he's turned me into a mindless puppet that's compelled to follow his every command. Since I've given him the cell samples, he'll see no more need for me. I'll be dead within a week, and none of you fools will care."

"I can offer you protection, but you're going to have to cooperate," Holmes said. "I assume people's lives are in danger, and I want to know how these embryonic cells fit into the crime lord's master plan, and whether that master plan has anything to do with the Pulsator Project. Tell me: who else was involved in that research?"

"No one of significance—it was *my* project," the professor said bitterly. "Except now, it's being adulterated by that criminal madman. He thinks he's playing God, and now God may indeed be the only one who can stop him. As I said, Mr. Holmes, I was a fool to underestimate him, and you'd be a fool to do the same."

He suddenly jumped to his feet and whipped out his gun, and Holmes froze, knowing he needed to choose his next words very carefully. Apparently, Hortz was more desperate than he thought, and now Holmes wouldn't put it past him to try something crazy.

However, Holmes' bartending friend Padric O'Vax also saw the flash of metal, and his hand darted beneath his apron, and he pulled out a blaster of his own.

"Watch it," he ordered the professor. "No pulling blasters on other customers—this isn't that type of pub."

The professor's eyes flitted around the room, and his eyes widened as he saw several of the Gerfrians pulling out their weapons and pointing them at him. The Gerfrians might not actually care about what happened to Holmes, but the pub's regulars all took Padric's "no shootouts" rule very seriously and wouldn't hesitate to help him enforce it.

Dr. Hortz cursed and grabbed his satchel, shoving his way out of the pub. As soon as he'd cleared the door, Holmes darted out after him, but the sneaking scum had disappeared faster than he thought the professor could. He couldn't pick up the trail again, and the next morning when he woke up, one of the headlines on his most frequently consulted news site stated a well-known Itredian professor had died in a late-night boating "accident" at a resort in Quadrant A.

Another loose end so neatly tied up, Holmes thought, slamming his techpad down on the kitchen counter in frustration. He was tired of waiting for the crime lord to make a mistake. If he didn't make one soon, Holmes knew his own body might be the next one found floating lifelessly down a river in Eglon.

#

When Jaymie got home from her classes that Friday, she found Holmes sitting on the couch and staring blankly at the wall. This was often a normal behavior for him, so at first she wasn't worried. Yet as she watched him more closely, she noticed the dull look in his eyes, as if he really was in a mindless daze instead of just thinking. She also saw he was sitting on the burnt side of the couch, something he usually avoided, and she wondered if he'd even noticed where he was.

"Holmes, are you OK?" she asked, and a full ten seconds passed before he actually seemed to register her presence, and he snapped out of his mental stupor.

"Hmm? Oh yes. Just…pondering some things."

She saw Jane Rozine's techpad sitting on the table in front of him, but it was switched off. There was also a pile of wadded-up papers sitting on the floor, the causalities of what appeared to have been an unfruitful brainstorming session.

"Maybe you need to take a break—perhaps getting some fresh air might help you think more clearly," she suggested, hanging her coat on the coat rack and then sitting down next to him.

"Yes—for all the bloody good that would do," Holmes said grimly. "It doesn't matter if I'm thinking more clearly—there's nothing left to think about. I'm at a dead end."

"Suit yourself then," Jaymie said, shaking her head. Holmes had been cooped up inside for far too long, but she knew there was no use trying to talk sense into him. Besides, she didn't have time to argue with him anyway; she still had to get ready for the gala this evening, and she'd gotten off school later than she'd planned. Not to mention she still had to decide what answer she was going to give Moriarty.

She went back to her room and got ready as quickly as possible, slipping into her sparkling red dress and fixing her hair. She had just finished sliding a diamond hairpin into her elegant topknot when she heard the door buzzer and realized Moriarty had come to pick her up. She'd tried her hardest to avoid having him come here, but he'd insisted at least this once he be allowed to be a gentleman and drive her to the gala. She only hoped Holmes would be civil.

"I'll get it!" she called, grabbing her fancy jacket and rushing out to the living room, only to find Holmes had beaten her to the door and was already pressing the button to open it.

"Hello," Moriarty said, looking somewhat surprised to find Holmes instead of Jaymie standing in front of him. He appeared very dashing dressed all in black, including a black tuxedo and overcoat. "You must be Sherlock Holmes, then?"

"Yes—lucky guess," Holmes said. "Though I could just as easily have been Lestrade, and you might have offended me if you'd guessed incorrectly."

Moriarty smiled, either oblivious to Holmes' moodiness or purposefully ignoring it. "Oh, it wasn't a guess at all. I knew you had to be Holmes, what with the trench coat and the bi-colored eyes—'heterochromia,' I believe the trait is called? Jaymie talks about you often. And my intent certainly wasn't to give offense, though I can't see why Lestrade would have been offended at being mistaken for the great detective Sherlock Holmes anyway. Unless, of course, he was cross at the moment, or mistaking someone for Sherlock Holmes is generally considered to give offense in this quadrant. I'm positive, however, you're universally well-loved?"

"Universally well-needed is perhaps closer to the truth," Holmes said curtly, and Jaymie could tell he was slightly taken aback by Moriarty's quick wit. The two men continued to stare at each other for a moment, and though neither one of them said anything, she could feel the tension slowly mounting. It was obviously the first meeting of two men who, regardless of the fact they had never met, had already decided they thoroughly disliked one another, and even their veneer of artificial politeness couldn't cover up that fact.

Holmes finally glanced away from Moriarty and looked Jaymie over, taking note of her fancy dress. "I didn't realize you were going somewhere this evening, Watson," he said somewhat disapprovingly. "It would have been nice to know this a little ahead of time."

"I don't believe she needs to ask your permission," Moriarty said, and though his tone wasn't unpleasant, she was sure Holmes felt the verbal barb all too well.

"Um, maybe we'd better go ahead and go," Jaymie told Moriarty, slipping on her coat and moving towards the door, hoping he would take the hint. "We don't want to be late for your gala."

"A gala—it sounds quite stimulating," Holmes said in a tone that indicted he believed it would be nothing of the sort. "So these are the types of things Watson is to be expected to start spending all of her time on now?"

"Holmes, please don't be so cross about this," Jaymie said, giving him a reproachful look. "We really do need to go. I can help you later, if you need me to."

"Help?" Holmes asked. "You haven't seemed to be doing much of that, of late. Lestrade and I have been hard at work these past few weeks, trying to save lives and solve this case, while you've been gallivanting about with that professor as if nothing were at stake. I must say, I'm disappointed in you, Jaymie Watson."

And with that, Jaymie finally snapped. She had taken a lot of grief from Holmes in the six months she'd known him, but she'd let most of it slide right off, just telling herself that was how he was. But this time, he had gone too far. She'd just been agonizing over Moriarty's offer, and the only reason she'd *had* to agonize was that in order to accept it, she'd have to give up her adventures with Holmes. She'd been concerned for *him* and how it would make *him* feel, and she'd been seriously considering turning Moriarty down because of it. She suddenly realized how much of herself she'd suppressed over the past six months because of Holmes, and how much she'd given up for him. But no more.

"I'm sorry, I'm going to need just a minute," she told Moriarty, and then she grabbed Holmes by the arm and dragged him forcefully back to his room. They were going to have at it right now, and this time, there would be no holding back.

As the door slid shut behind them, Holmes gaped at her in astonishment, but she didn't give him a chance to speak.

"Disappointed—in me?" she said, whirling around to face him. "I've had it with you, Sherlock Holmes. I'm tired of being treated like this, like I'm just another resource you can pick up and toss away at whim. I'm not like your techpad, though maybe you think I am. I want to solve this case as much as you do, but I can't just pretend like Moriarty means nothing..."

Her voice trailed off as she glanced over at Holmes' "association map," and her eyes widened in shock as she saw none other than Moriarty's picture pasted up on the wall.

"Holmes, what is that? Why is Moriarty on your map of clues about the crime lord case?"

"Because for all we know, he very well could be a part of this scheme," Holmes said stiffly. "Adler told me to suspect everything new that's come up since the Sunset Enterprises fire, and Moriarty *is* a recent development. I think it's best to consider all angles, don't you?"

Jaymie could feel her face reddening—not from embarrassment, but from anger. "Holmes, that's utterly ridiculous! How can you think Moriarty has anything to do with this? You're...you're being obsessive—and petty. I'm going to take that down right now, unless you give me a reason—an actual, legitimate reason—why it should stay."

"I don't like him," Holmes muttered, but Jaymie wasn't about to placate him, not this time.

"You'd never met him until tonight, and then you were terribly rude to him. The only reason you don't like him is because my friendship with him interferes with your life. It's always about *you*, Holmes, isn't it? No one else matters. Lestrade doesn't matter, Chief Bevill doesn't matter—I don't matter. You're the brilliant one, single-handedly saving the galaxy, and the rest of us are just pawns it proves convenient to use once in a while. In fact, you're not so different from this mysterious crime lord, are you? Set aside a few moral qualms, and you're *exactly* the same, moving about the beings in your life as if they were mere pieces in the game you're playing."

"We are not alike!" Holmes fired back. "I use my mental powers for good!"

"Well, that sounds noble, but is that really it, Holmes?" Jaymie said. "You told me once you didn't want to use your telepathic ability because you didn't think it was right. I was impressed then, but I'm not so sure now. Is it really about morality, or is it just because you want to prove that, even without your special abilities, you're still smarter than everyone else? You're such a genius you don't even need your telepathic powers to save the day. You don't need that, or any other being. You don't need *me*."

Holmes stepped back, stunned, her words hitting him like a slap in the face. "Jaymie, I—"

"No, Holmes," she said. "When I said I was done, I meant it. I'm going to get ready for that gala, and I'm going to tell Moriarty I'm accepting his offer to become his assistant. I'm tired of being expendable."

With that, she turned around and stormed back to the living room, her heart pounding so fast she almost felt faint. She couldn't believe she'd just said all that, and her mind was still spinning. She was sure she'd regret some of what she'd said as she recalled it later, but she was too upset now to analyze what had happened. As she walked down the hallway, she glanced at herself in the mirror, and she found her eyes were red from crying. She hadn't even realized she *was* crying, and she angrily wiped away the tears. She would go to the gala, and she would have a good time, because she was convinced she was making the right decision. She would forget about how Holmes had hurt her, even though she felt that sharp, shooting pain with every breath she took. Sherlock Holmes didn't need her—she would just have to train herself not to need *him*.

Chapter 4: The Moment of Truth

Jaymie didn't speak another word to Holmes, refusing to acknowledge him as she exited the flat. Moriarty tipped his hat to Holmes in an infuriating gesture of triumph, and he smiled as the door to the flat slid closed. Holmes stared at the door for a second after they left, and then he took Rozine's techpad and flung it at the wall, shattering the screen and knocking a dent in the wall, as well.

Holmes was clearly livid, but as the device smacked into the wall, he realized he wasn't really angry at Jaymie. He was angry at himself.

His ego had always been ample enough to provide a thick cushion around his soul, preventing anything anyone said to him from impacting him too deeply on an emotional level. If someone was angry with him, he always assumed it was their fault, and they were probably upset with him because he was right and they weren't. Yet this time, Jaymie had somehow managed to cut past all his defenses, and he realized her words had actually hurt him. And he could do nothing but embrace that hurt, because he knew he absolutely deserved it.

She had proved to be invaluable to him, just as he'd known she would the moment she walked through the door of apartment complex 221. Lestrade had told him he'd needed to communicate that better, but he hadn't listened, and now he'd lost his best friend—Jaymie Watson—forever. And it was completely, entirely his fault.

He wasn't sure how long he spent standing helplessly in front of the door, and he was still standing there when Lestrade finally came home from work. Wrapped up in his own thoughts, Lestrade almost ran into Holmes, and he had to quickly dodge to the right in order to avoid bowling over his friend.

"Holmes, is it possible you could pick somewhere else to have a brainstorming session?" Lestrade said in exasperation, picking up a stack of papers he'd dropped. "I realize you can't control when a thought strikes you, but for your own safety, maybe you should..." His voice trailed off as he saw the look of despair in Holmes' eyes, and his expression grew troubled.

"What's wrong?" he asked. "I've never seen you like this. Did something happen in the case?"

"No, nothing like that," Holmes said slowly. "It's worse, really. Jaymie and I had a fight—well, actually it was more just her yelling at me, but...I deserved it. She told me I'd taken her for granted, and that she was done with our partnership. She's going with Professor Moriarty to a gala tonight, and he's asked her to be his research assistant."

Lestrade dropped his briefcase, and he stared at Holmes in shock. "What? And is she going to say yes?"

Holmes nodded, for once hesitant to meet his friend's gaze. "I believe so. And I have reason to suspect my behavior has played a significant role in that decision."

Lestrade walked numbly over to the couch and collapsed into it, tossing his papers haphazardly on the table and not even seeming to care when some of them slid off onto the floor.

"Well played, Holmes," he said bitterly, and Holmes let that insult hit him full-on, knowing he'd earned Lestrade's wrath as well. The inspector wasn't any happier about this than Holmes was, and Holmes didn't need to tell him what the fall-out of Jaymie's decision would be. Holmes' actions had probably caused them both to lose a friend tonight, and if Holmes wasn't careful, he might end up losing Lestrade's friendship too.

"We can't let her do this," Holmes said, and Lestrade shrugged.

"We can't stop her. And if we tried to, we'd only prove once again she was right for calling us selfish."

There was a long, sullen pause, and then Holmes said, "It's not just that. I don't like Moriarty—I don't trust him."

Lestrade let out a long sigh. "Well at the moment, I don't feel very charitable towards the man either, but I think we both know why that is. Not liking him is not enough of a reason to charge after Jaymie and tell her she shouldn't accept his offer."

Holmes shook his head, knowing Lestrade wasn't seeing his point. "That may be true, but that's not what I'm getting at. I just...I have a very bad feeling about him. Even if he had no interest in Jaymie, something would have struck me about him, I think. There was something...off about him, something that didn't feel right. You know those inklings I get—the atmosphere of the room somehow changed when he walked in."

"If you were going to read his mind, the time for that has passed," Lestrade said. "Look, we don't even know where they're going. We're just going to have to wait until Jaymie gets back, and then we'll have to apologize profusely and hope that's enough. I strongly suspect it won't be."

"I'm sorry," Holmes said quietly, and he realized it was the first time those two words had ever escaped his lips. He had the feeling he probably should have uttered them long before now.

He half expected Lestrade to hit him with another bitter retort, but his friend simply nodded, his gaze sad.

"Yeah, I'm sorry too," he said, slowly picking up his briefcase and heading back to his room. He stopped by the broken techpad and picked it up to place it back on the table, but then he hesitated and glanced at it more closely.

"Holmes, look at this," he said, and he motioned for his friend to come over. "Did you notice this?"

"Yes, I had a tantrum," Holmes said shortly. "I didn't mean to—"

"No—shut up and look," Lestrade said, handing him the techpad. Holmes glanced at the broken screen and noticed something strange peeking through one of the cracks. Chipping off the remaining pieces of the screen, he found a data chip cleverly hidden underneath, where it might have remained permanently hidden had he not broken the device in a fit of frustration.

"Clever girl," he exclaimed, suddenly more impressed with Jane Rozine. "What better way to hide data on an electronic device? Anyone looking for information would assume the files would actually be saved somewhere *on* the techpad's hard drive, not hidden on a separate chip inside the device. It's bloody brilliant."

He felt another twinge of regret that Jaymie wasn't here to share in this discovery, but maybe by finally solving this case, he could start righting some of the wrongs he'd committed.

"Fetch me my techpad," he commanded Lestrade, and the inspector dashed into Holmes' room. He heard the sound of Lestrade madly shuffling through stacks of papers, followed by a loud crash.

"Your room is a blooming mess!" Lestrade called. "Where is that ridiculous techpad?" There was another crash, and then Lestrade finally emerged from the room, tossing the device to Holmes. "How do you ever find anything in there?"

Holmes ignored the question. He inserted the data chip into his techpad and immediately began downloading the files stored on the card, praying they included actual documents and not some kind of virus, because he didn't have the time or patience to check before he started. As soon as the files finished downloading, he clicked on the first document that popped up and hurriedly began skimming through it. And what he saw shocked him—it was a compilation of research regarding vortex diamonds.

"Amazing!" he exclaimed, his eyes darting across the screen as his sharp mind rapidly absorbed the information. "Lestrade, do you know anything about what the diamonds actually do?"

"Aren't they just interesting artifacts?" he said, giving Holmes a puzzled look. "You know, just a curiosity or a museum piece?"

"That's what everyone assumes," Holmes said. "But Rozine has gathered research here...this changes everything. Apparently the compound can be used as a power source—don't you get it?"

The blank expression on Lestrade's face indicated he clearly didn't, and Holmes was forced to take a deep breath and prepare to start from the beginning.

Except he never got a chance to go back to the beginning, because all of a sudden the door buzzer sounded loudly. Both Lestrade and Holmes jumped at the unexpected noise, and they looked at each other uneasily. It surely couldn't be Jaymie coming back already, and they never received visitors.

Lestrade slid one hand onto his blaster as he went to answer the door, but his weapon, as it turned out, was entirely unnecessary. It was only Mrs. Gdo, Rozine's former housekeeper, whom Holmes had consulted on a previous investigation.

"Hello, I've come for my payment," she said, looking just as nervous and uncomfortable as she had that day at Rozine's mansion.

"Of course," Holmes said. He'd almost forgotten about promising to pay Mrs. Gdo for her trouble, and though her timing was a little inconvenient, he doubted she'd consent to wait while he digested the rest of Rozine's hidden files or agree to come back another time. "Follow me—I've got it in my room."

Mrs. Gdo stepped hesitantly into the flat, lagging a good distance behind Holmes as he headed back to his room. Unfortunately, he didn't know exactly where the payment was now, because it had previously been underneath one of the stacks of papers Lestrade had so carelessly disturbed. Contrary to Lestrade's accusations, the room was most certainly not a mess, because the word "mess" implied disorder, and Holmes knew exactly where (almost) everything was in that swarm of what others might have called chaos. However, Lestrade had disrupted that organization, and now it was going to take forever to find everything again.

"I'll be just a minute," Holmes said, tossing papers everywhere in his attempt to find the envelope. He finally spotted it under his bed and was just about to reach for it when he heard Mrs. Gdo let out a shriek.

He immediately sat up, though of course his head was still under the bed, causing him to hit it—hard—on the bed frame. He bit back a curse as he slid out and looked up, wondering what the devil Mrs. Gdo was going on about now.

Her face had gone white as a sheet, and she was pointing, terrified, at one of the pictures in Holmes' association map.

"Those eyes," she gasped. "Those are just like the eyes of the ghost I saw at Mrs. Rozine's mansion!"

Holmes glanced at the picture she was pointing at, and his blood instantly ran icy cold. She was pointing at the picture of Moriarty, and with that clue, everything suddenly, terrifyingly made sense.

Holmes rushed out of the room, almost tripping over a pile of clothes. Poor Mrs. Gdo was still standing in his room, overcome by shock, but he no longer had time to deal with her. He grabbed his trench coat and Rozine's smashed techpad, knocking over the coat rack in his haste.

"Holmes, what the devil is going on?" Lestrade demanded. "Have you finally gone barking mad?"

"The crime lord—I know who he is," Holmes said simply, punching the release button on the door. "I only pray to God it's not too late to stop him." *And to save Jaymie*, he added to himself. Because he'd finally realized that was the only thing that really mattered.

Chapter 5: The Gala

Jaymie swirled the Yopilian wine around in her long-stemmed glass, staring blankly at the clear, amber-colored liquid. She was sure it tasted divine, but she hadn't really had the heart to try any of it yet. Her fight with Holmes had put her in an ill humor she just couldn't seem to shake, not even while admiring the splendor around her.

The gala was being hosted at an upscale Quadrant A club called the "Rvarian Rendezvous," and it was so posh it made even the Matrié d'Poll look like the Drunk Gypsy. Moriarty had rented a private ballroom at the back of the club, and it was decorated lavishly in elegant black and white. The walls were covered with a white, burnished metal that had a hint of glitter, and the floors were the finest Tryidian black marble. From the ceiling hung a chandelier so massive the decorative metal chords holding it up were thicker than Jaymie's arm. A classical band from Syfria played nondescript background music, and guests milled about the room, talking and laughing quietly amongst themselves. Jaymie recognized several of her professors from the University of Medical Arts, as well as several leading researchers from Scoztan and Itred. Though everyone was attempting to make small talk, it was obvious everyone's thoughts were primarily on Moriarty's announcement, and what his mysterious research project would be.

No—what our *research project will be,* Jaymie corrected herself. It was hard to get used to the idea she was about to become a part of all this. She would be operating on the cutting edge of science—and maybe even this time, her mother would be proud of her.

"Enjoying yourself, my dear?"

Jaymie turned and saw a diminutive Andronidan standing behind her, also holding a glass of Yopilian wine.

"Oh yes," she said, reaching out her hand to greet him and feeling grateful for the distraction from her morose thoughts. "I'm Jaymie Watson, a friend of—"

"Yes, he's told me all about you," the man said, smiling politely. "He's very complimentary of your work, says you show a great deal of promise. By the way, I'm Dr. Vessik Aoedie. I'm also a friend of Moriarty's. We worked together on that dreadful Pulsator Project, and he's asked me to join in his work here."

"What sort of work have you been doing?" Jaymie asked, desperate to get a hint about Moriarty's project, but Dr. Aoedie only smiled chidingly.

"Ah, Moriarty would have my head if I gave anything away, Miss Watson. But believe me, the secret will be worth the wait. This discovery that we're on the brink of—it's going to change the galaxy."

Jaymie felt an excited shiver run up her spine at his words. That phrase was so often over-used by researchers and the media, but coming from a man who had already witnessed the creation of synthetic nerves, she doubted this time it was an exaggeration.

"Or so he claims, at least," Moriarty interrupted, coming up behind them and clapping Dr. Aoedie on the back. "You aren't giving anything away, are you, Dr. Aoedie?"

"Of course not," Aoedie said with a laugh. "I was just telling her we'd all find out soon enough. In the meantime, it appears as though everyone is enjoying the party."

"Yes indeed." Moriarty glanced down at Jaymie's still unfinished glass of wine, the same glass he'd handed her an hour ago, and his expression turned to one of concern.

"Are you feeling all right, Jaymie?" he said. "If you'd rather have something different to eat or drink, or if there's anything else I can—"

"No, no, I'm fine," Jaymie said, waving him off. "It's just...well, it's nothing. Everything is wonderful." She didn't want to talk about her fight with Holmes again, especially not with Dr. Aoedie standing here with them. She had told Holmes she was moving on, and she couldn't allow herself to keep looking back. "As I said, I'm perfectly fine."

Moriarty gave her a gentle smile, the kind that never failed to twist her stomach and tug at her heart. "I can't tell you how happy your presence here makes me," he said softly. "I hope you'll be impressed with the project. Having you on board was critical; to me, you are the most important piece of this puzzle."

"Of course, there are many important players here tonight, and I'm sure she *will* be impressed," Dr. Aoedie said, and Jaymie glanced at him, for a minute thinking she'd heard something strange in his voice. His pleasant tone had taken on a slight edge, and though neither he nor Moriarty's expressions really changed, some silent communication seemed to pass between them, and Moriarty stiffened. A sudden, unspoken tension had developed between them, but it dissipated quickly, and Moriarty gave Dr. Aoedie a curt nod.

"Of course."

"Well, shall we prepare to make the grand announcement?" Dr. Aoedie asked, gesturing towards the stage. "I believe we've waited long enough."

"I'll join you on stage shortly," Moriarty said, and as soon as the doctor's back was turned, he squeezed Jaymie's hand. "Wish me luck," he whispered with a wink, bending down close to her ear so only she could hear his words. "This is about to change your life forever."

He started to pull away, but as their eyes met, he hesitated, his expression growing suddenly serious. He slowly leaned in again, and before Jaymie even realized what she was doing, she'd shut her eyes and leaned in as well. It was just a quick kiss—anything longer would have drawn too much attention—and none of the other guests seemed to notice. But Jaymie's heart was still pounding even after he let her go, and she realized in that brief moment, she'd never felt more confused, or more wonderful.

And she realized that maybe, finally, she did love Professor James Moriarty.

#

Holmes' plans were typically so well thought-out, he could envision them as a digi-drama playing in his mind, where he could see every detail fall neatly into place, every action occurring just as he predicted. Yet this time, he had absolutely no idea what he was doing. He had spent the entire ride over to the Rvarian Rendezvous (as Lestrade drove madly and broke just about every traffic law in the Eglon book of ordinances) doing frantic research on his techpad and putting together the final pieces of the case. He was now certain he could dethrone Moriarty with the evidence he had, but the consequence of spending all that time doing research was that he hadn't been able to start plotting how to go about breaking into the club itself. He was forced to do the one thing he hated but Lestrade seemed to thrive on: making it up as they went along.

Right now the two of them were crouching behind a trash compactor at the back of the Rvarian Rendezvous, watching the back door and arguing about how to get into the building. They'd figured out the location of the gala from an invitation they'd found in Watson's room; Holmes hadn't wanted to search through her personal effects, figuring he'd treated her badly enough already, without violating her privacy, but Lestrade thought under the circumstances it was unavoidable.

Two stern-faced bouncers were stationed at the back door of the club, presumably to scare away any potential party crashers. They were dressed in fancy black suits, and while they probably didn't run into much trouble at a club as posh as this one, they looked as though they wouldn't have any problems dealing with it if they did. Holmes doubted they would prove to be very cooperative, especially if Moriarty had told them to be on the lookout for him and Lestrade.

"We're wasting time!" Lestrade hissed, gripping his blaster and glaring at Holmes. "I say we just walk up there, wave our guns, and order them to let us in."

"That is a perfectly awful plan!" Holmes whispered back, and Lestrade's glare deepened.

"Yeah, but we're running out of time. Every second we spend out here arguing is another second Jaymie's trapped in there. I think we've waited long enough."

Holmes sighed. "Good point. Follow my lead then; on the count of three: one…two…"

"Forget this," Lestrade interrupted, jumping up from his hidden position and marching towards the door.

Holmes cursed to himself and scrambled after his friend, frustrated Lestrade hadn't waited for his cue yet left with little choice but to follow him now that he'd set the plan in motion.

The bouncers heard their footsteps, and they immediately stood to attention.

"The entrance to the club is around front," one of them said, her eyes narrowing in distaste as she saw their disheveled and dirty clothing (a consequence of hiding behind the trash compactor).

"We're not here to visit the club—we need to get to Professor Moriarty's gala," Lestrade said firmly. "I'd appreciate if you'd step back and let us in."

The bouncer looked them over disapprovingly. "You'd need an invitation, which, judging by your appearance, you probably do not have. What you can do, however, is turn around and leave before I find the need to call…"

The woman's voice trailed off, and her eyes widened as Lestrade pulled out his blaster and pointed it at the two bouncers. With his free hand, he whipped out his Civic Security badge.

"How's this for an invitation?" he asked. "We're getting inside this club one way or another—now, would you like to cooperate or not?"

The other bouncer started reaching for the panic button on his comlink, but before he could press it, Holmes nailed him with a stun bolt. Lestrade fired a stun bolt at the female bouncer as well, and both crumpled to the ground.

"Nicely done," Holmes said with a slight hint of sarcasm. "I think they were quite intimidated."

"Shut up," Lestrade said, dragging the female bouncer behind the trash compactor. "Those stun blasts will keep them unconscious for about ten to twenty minutes, which doesn't buy us a lot of time. We'd better crash that party in a hurry."

They traded their own outfits for the bouncers' uniforms, and since Holmes was more slender than Lestrade, he'd gotten stuck with the female bouncer's outfit. It was still a little small, and the pants weren't quite long enough, but it would have to do under the circumstances. Holmes and Lestrade sneaked into the club, taking a hallway to the ballroom at the back of the building, where Holmes guessed the party was being held. They burst through the doors of the caterer's kitchen, and while the chefs and waiters gave them puzzled looks as the two "bouncers" barged into the room, no one dared to ask them any questions. They weaved their way through the maze of ovens, counters, and stacks of pots and pans, and then stopped in front of a door leading to the main ballroom. They peeked through the tiny glass "porthole" in the door and saw Moriarty making his way to some sort of platform at the head of the room. Holmes noticed Jaymie standing off to the side of the stage, dressed in her sparkling red ball gown, and several other leading scientists and researchers. Moriarty was apparently getting ready to make a speech, and Jaymie appeared to be safe for the moment.

Holmes used the control pad next to the door to open it just a crack, and then he leaned in closer, straining to hear what Moriarty was saying.

"...I know you're all very curious about the project that's going to be revealed here tonight, so I won't drag out the suspense any longer." There was a polite smattering of laughter, and Holmes rolled his eyes. Two groups of people were very good at "dragging out the suspense," and those were academics and politicians. Yet he found, for once, he wasn't entirely eager to get to the point, because he knew how disturbing the revelation of this project was going to be.

Moriarty disappeared for a moment back stage, and when he returned, he was pushing a cart with a gigantic black box sitting on it. The box was at least half a meter taller than the professor, and it appeared to be manufactured from some kind of plasti-alloy. One side had what seemed to be a control panel, with an array of buttons and flashing lights, but there was no writing of any kind on the box itself. A hush fell over the crowd as soon as they saw the mysterious black box, and everyone was obviously dying of curiosity to see what was hidden inside. *If only they knew...*

Holmes looked over at Lestrade, and his friend silently nodded. Holmes wasn't sure what would happen after he played his hand, and at the moment, he didn't really care. Taking down Moriarty and saving Watson was really the only goal right now—let the chips fall where they may.

"Good luck," Lestrade whispered. "It's been a good ride, Holmes. I probably have absolutely no logical reason to say this, but I don't regret all the crazy adventures we've been on. I'm proud we were friends, no matter what happens here today."

"Don't say your last goodbyes yet," Holmes said, pocketing his blaster once again (he didn't think he'd be needing it, and he'd really only brought it along because Lestrade had insisted). "It's bad luck. But for the record, well, I'm proud to call you my friend as well, Inspector. Even if you still insist on working for an organization as ridiculous as Civic Security."

He punched the door's release button, and then the door opened with a whoosh, ushering them on to what would prove to be either Holmes' finest moment, or his last. *Or maybe even both...*

Chapter 6: Calling the Bluff

"And now, I proudly present," Moriarty was saying just as they stepped into the room, "perhaps the greatest scientific achievement of the century..."

"Well done, Professor!" Holmes clapped loudly, the sound echoing through the ballroom, which had fallen into shocked silence at his unexpected entrance. "It's a fair statement, though admittedly not a very humble one."

Moriarty froze, and he scanned the crowd, quickly locating Holmes and Lestrade. To his credit, he didn't gasp or lose his composure; the only indication he'd been caught off guard was in his eyes, which narrowed ever so slightly.

"Excuse me? I don't recall placing the names 'Mr. Sherlock Holmes' and 'Inspector Isin Lestrade' on the guest list."

Jaymie spun around, and as her eyes met and locked with Holmes', the shock on her face turned to anger and disappointment. She mouthed the words, *What are you doing here?*

Holmes wished he could have taken her aside and explained everything quietly before he publicly confronted Professor Moriarty about his crimes. But unfortunately, there wasn't time for that, and she would have to hear the truth at the same time as everyone else in the room—even though it was a terribly cruel way to learn someone you admired, and maybe even loved, was a madman.

"We took the liberty of inviting ourselves," Holmes said, making his way through the crowd and jumping up onstage beside Moriarty. All the guests were so stunned by his sudden arrival that they didn't try to stop him. "Hope you don't mind, though I suspect you do. I don't think I need to ask if you know why I'm here."

"What is the meaning of this?" Dr. Aoedie exclaimed angrily, glaring first at Holmes and then at Moriarty. "I'm going to call security and have them thrown out immediately."

"By all means, go ahead," Lestrade said, then pulled out his Civic Security badge. "But I don't think the club's owners are going to argue with this, unless they want to go down with you."

"This is ridiculous!" Dr. Aoedie spat, his face as flaming red as his temper. "I demand you leave at once. This is a peaceful gathering of scientists, for the purpose of discussing research. I have no idea what you think is going on here, but it certainly isn't anything illegal."

"Maybe you believe that, but I'm guessing you don't," Holmes said. "But let's not waste any more time with small talk. The reason I'm here is this: I'm going to tell you a story, Professor Moriarty. It's a very long and complicated story, so I'd like you to listen very carefully, because at the end I want you to tell me how much of it is true—though I expect most of it will be. More of it's conjecture than I usually prefer, but you're a very clever criminal, and you didn't leave me as much concrete evidence as I would have liked. But I digress again."

"You don't have a right to call me a criminal," Moriarty said coldly, and Holmes shrugged.

"Well, we'll let the audience be the judges of that. Our little story begins three years ago with a young doctor from Itred. He was fresh out of medical school, graduating at a remarkably early age. I wasn't surprised to hear this really, because as much as I hate to admit it, you *are* a genius, Moriarty. You are brilliant—probably more brilliant than anyone in this room realizes. That's why Dr. Gavyn Hortz hired you to join his research team on the 'Pulsator Project.' But you didn't get along very well, due to an inevitable clash of egos. He knew right away that although you were less experienced, you were already far more intelligent than he'd ever be, and he despised you for it. He even went so far as to leave your name off the published roster of his research team. He listed everyone's names *but* yours in the credits, and while he had to include the line 'and other contributors' for legal purposes, that really wasn't fair, because I suspect that 'other contributor'—you—actually came up with most of the research.

"You were beyond livid, and there was no question you were going to have your revenge on Dr. Hortz. But spreading gossip about him or filing a lawsuit seemed so petty, especially when you were already developing grander scientific designs. You decided to pursue those, and let Dr. Hortz become collateral damage in the process."

"You cannot prove that," Moriarty said simply, his voice cold but perfectly under control. Blast, the man was so bloody calm; there was nothing in his expression, his posture, not even a flicker in his eyes to give away the slightest hint of guilt. Moriarty's guests were now all staring at Holmes, a range of furious, shocked and incredulous expressions on their faces. A person with less self-confidence than Holmes might have started doubting his theory at this point, but he wasn't about to back down now that he had started. He was going to call Moriarty's bluff, and besides, he had bigger guns yet to draw.

"No, I can't prove that," Holmes admitted. "But I suspect it's true. You see, your ill-fated assassin Jinxx was good, but a little more talkative than he should have been. An assassin's deadliest weakness is overconfidence, and the blasé ones tend to tease their victims, saying more about their plan than they should because they figure the victims are going to be dead soon anyway, why not taunt them? But you can see by the fact Lestrade and I are still standing here today, he failed, and he gave us an all-important clue: 'Apex.' It could have meant any number of things, but it does happen to be the name of a supposedly long-dead crime ring on Itred. I ignored that lead at first, because it didn't seem relevant—that is, until I connected you to this puzzle. Apparently Apex was run by some prestigious, unidentified Itredian family, and though all its operatives were eventually caught and the ring was shut down, the originators of the crime ring disappeared and their identities were never revealed. Perhaps that could be the Moriarty family? Everyone knows you're a wealthy man, but go back more than two or three generations, and you find no family money at all. You're not politicians, merchants, or anything of the sort. So where did all that money come from? Perhaps a life of crime? Just some food for thought.

    "Your family likely had to shut down Apex due to increasing government suspicions, but you kept those contacts alive, just in case you'd ever need them in the future. Your scheme was going to take a lot of money, even more than you already had at your disposal, so you dug up one of the best criminal scumbags you could find: Jok Urdi. Where you found him, or how you found him, is one of the things I wasn't able to piece together, and as much as I'd like to know, that's really not relevant at this point. What I do know is that you put him in charge of a new crime ring, and your drug smuggling activities starting bringing in a substantial amount of income.

"That' when you made another influential friend—a certain Dr. Aoedi at the University of Medical Arts here in Loudron. He was a consultant on the Pulsator Project, and coincidentally, a consultant for an 'unidentified project' with Sunset Enterprises, though by now we all know what that was. I suspect you started helping Jane Rozine with her teleportation project, doing to her exactly what Dr. Hortz did to you—stealing her research. You began working on a teleporter of your own, and you quickly eclipsed her. She started getting suspicious, however, and withheld the one piece of research you desperately wanted: the Trop diamond. The diamonds actually aren't diamonds at all; although they've been revered as artifacts for centuries, they were originally used as a power source on the ancient planet of Tribic. Their true use was forgotten centuries ago, so it was an incredible stroke of luck when Rozine or one of her scientists uncovered what they truly are. The so-called 'infinity complex' of the diamond is appropriately named, because the compound can produce an eternally self-sustaining supply of energy. You kept returning to Rozine's house to search for her research files, because she was too clever to keep them at her factory. Except, you made the first in a series of very small but ultimately game-ending mistakes, and you let her see you.

"Rozine knew her time was limited, so she panicked and burned down her factory, in an effort to get more money to speed up her research. However, she got caught, and that's when your plan started to unravel. You quickly severed all ties with the teleportation project, afraid the government might trace something back to you. Then you had another problem crop up, this time in the form of Jok Urdi. You see, the former pirate leader didn't like taking orders from you, especially since he was used to making decisions on his own. He got involved with a Quadrant B actress, against your express wishes. Well, she jilted him, and even though you ordered him to just let her go, because you didn't want things to get too 'messy,' he couldn't tolerate that, and so he had her murdered. Without that murder, Lestrade, Watson, and I may never have caught onto the drug smuggling ring, and the downfall of that crime ring crippled your plans again. This was probably when you first realized the three of us could become more than just a minor nuisance.

"You needed a better underling, and also someone more familiar with my methods, and whom you hoped would be a distraction for me—though this ultimately proved unfruitful, I must say. You used your teleporting device to break Irene Adler out of the prison on Traxil, a brilliant move on your part. Of course, now they'll be taking measures to block the use of teleporting devices in that prison, but you have achieved the dubious honor of being the first person in a millennium to successfully break someone out of that prison. You sent Adler after the Gvidi diamond, which she successfully obtained, and it took me a long time to figure out what that had to do with any of this. It served a double-pronged purpose: it got you the power source you needed, and put Adler in a position to assassinate Urdi, who you knew would talk as soon as it proved convenient for him. That assassination also diverted attention from the diamond itself. Your brilliant little trick threw me off for weeks, for which I must commend you. Except, Adler ultimately failed you too, and she wouldn't kill me. So you had to kill her. By this time, things were starting to get *very* messy, and I was catching onto the fact there was some larger force at work.

"You decided now was the time for Hortz's payback. You must have found some way to threaten him into helping you, and you made him break into the hospital to steal those embryonic cells. Another clever move on your part, making it appear as though someone had broken into the hospital to steal the vraxil and distracting us from the cells themselves. You're very good at the bait and switch bit, but it started to become a pattern, and that's where criminals always seem to get hung up, I'm afraid. You create a pattern, you become predictable…and you eventually get caught. Hortz was a loose end you should have tied up a lot more quickly. I met up with him in Quadrant B, and though he didn't give me much information, it was enough.

"And now," Holmes said, stopping his pacing and coming to a halt in front of Moriarty, looking the man directly in the eyes, "we come to your tour de force—the whole point behind your madly brilliant scheme. What do a teleporter, the Gvidi diamond, a hijacked synthetic nerve project and embryonic cells all have to do with each other? A bloody puzzle indeed, but it was Dr. Hortz who gave me the creative spark I ultimately needed to solve this case, though I didn't quite realize it at the time. He said you were mad, that you were playing God. And what does God do? He creates things—and you've created something too, something you were going to reveal here this evening. So sorry to 'steal your thunder,' as they say, but I'm afraid I'm going to have to do that honor instead. I'm sure everyone here is quite eager to see the results of your work."

He stepped towards the box, and Dr. Aoedie darted in front of him, his expression livid.

"You can't do that!" he shouted. "You are trespassing here, and it will not be tolerated!" He reached out to grab Holmes, but Lestrade was quick to lower his blaster, stopping the man in his tracks.

"I'd like to see the end of this, if you don't mind," Lestrade said coldly, and though the doctor's temper obviously was still fuming, he carefully stepped back and stood next to Moriarty. Aoedie didn't like what was happening, but he wasn't foolish enough to argue with the end of a blaster.

Holmes placed his hand on the latch to the box's door, almost certain of what he was going to find inside—and hesitant to open the box for that very reason. But they'd all come too far to stop now, and it was time for the moment of truth. The game ended right here, right now. Taking a deep breath, he flung open the door, and everyone let out a loud gasp of horror and astonishment as they saw what was inside.

Holmes turned to Moriarty. "May I present the first clone—*your* clone."

The man inside the box was an exact copy of Professor Moriarty: his dark brown hair was styled just like the scientist/crime lord's was tonight, and he was wearing an identical suit. Facial features, eye color, everything was a perfect match of Moriarty's, and the effect was more than a little unsettling. Holmes hadn't known the clone would be Moriarty's (he'd just known there would be a clone), but he supposed it made sense. After all, who else would the most brilliant criminal mind of this century find fit to clone, other than himself?

The clone stared out at the crowd with glassy, unblinking eyes, probably an indication he was being kept in stasis and wasn't actually conscious at the moment. Various tubes were hooked up to the clone's body, feeding him nutrients in addition to the chemicals that were trapping him in a coma.

There was a long, agonizing moment of silence as the audience struggled to accept what they were seeing. Then someone let out a quiet expression of "God almighty, save us," and that broke the ice. The room quickly dissolved into chaos, and everyone began talking at once, some marveling at the clone onstage and others cringing in revulsion. Cloning as a theory had always had its supporters and detractors, and both camps appeared to have representatives in the crowd tonight. What everyone seemed to agree on, however, was that this was a completely unexpected revelation that could not help but forever change the way the galaxy looked at science.

Even with all the chaos erupting around him, Moriarty remained eerily calm, like the eye of a storm. He allowed the panic and shock to swirl around him but not buffet him into reacting himself. Holmes didn't trust this calm; the fact Moriarty wasn't panicking meant he probably still had a few tricks up his sleeve (or at least thought he did), and he was determined not to let Holmes' untimely interruption dissolve his plan.

But right now, Moriarty's reaction wasn't important, and neither was the audience's reaction, for that matter. There was only one being Holmes cared about at the moment, but he hadn't worked up the nerve to glance over at her yet, because he knew this revelation would hit her on a deeper level than anyone else in this room.

Jaymie was staring at Moriarty, and though the look of disbelief and horror on her face matched the looks of many others in the room, there was something in her eyes no one else had—an acute sense of betrayal. She looked as though someone had just stabbed her in the heart, and kept twisting the knife around just to drive the biting pain even deeper.

"Moriarty—what the bloody devil is this?" she asked, her voice so aching and accusing, all at the same time, that even Moriarty's hard heart surely had to feel a twinge of pity.

Holmes had thought she might first turn on him, rather than Moriarty, reproaching him for making up a false story about Moriarty out of jealously. But she'd heard Holmes' breakdown of Moriarty's plans, and it didn't seem like she was trying to deny it. She was angry at only one being now, and that was Professor James Moriarty. Holmes had been frightened enough when she unleashed her wrath on him a few hours before, but he had a feeling that would be nothing compared to what she was about to unleash on Moriarty.

"Jaymie, I..." And now, for the first time, Moriarty seemed to falter. His eyes lost their steely coldness, and he turned to Jaymie, a quietly pleading expression on his face. "This is not the way I wanted you to hear this. There's so much more you don't know about—"

"Shut up, you can see he's called our hand," Dr. Aoedie said, and Moriarty's eyes flashed.

"And what do you know? You were nothing but an assistant on the project; the science is mine, the plan was mine, the clone is mine." He glanced at the black box on the stage, studying his creation. In that moment, he looked as though he truly did believe he *was* God, and Dr. Aoedie flinched, feeling all-too-keenly the aura of the professor's power. "Your ideas would still be nothing but vague theories if not for me, Dr. Aoedie, and don't you *ever* forget that."

Slowly, Moriarty turned back around to face Holmes, a murderous fire burning in his eyes. "Well, Holmes, you are right. That's what you've been dying to hear me say, isn't it? Your ridiculous tirade has ruined my party. And you spoiled my surprise—I hate it when people do that."

"I just crashed the party—you're responsible for ruining your own plan," Holmes said. "You should have been more careful when breaking into Rozine's mansion; if Rozine's housekeeper hadn't helped me identify you, I wouldn't be standing here right now. However, you can't go back and undo those mistakes, no matter how much you might want to. What you *can* do is clarify how and when you first decided to try your hand at cloning, because I'm quite curious about that. Perhaps it was during the synthetic nerve project. After all, once you've created artificial nerves, why stop there? It was the logical next step in that research. You used those embryonic cells to complete your first cloning experiment, which we see now before us. Perhaps you altered your vortex diamond-powered teleporter so it took the embryonic cells—and your own DNA—and dematerialized them, but when it put them back together, it created a whole new person. It's beyond cutting-edge science, it's almost magic. Now, whether or not it's ethical is a whole different discussion, which I'm sure you'll be having with Civic Security at some point in the very near future."

"It's a legitimate scientific experiment," Moriarty said. "I'm certain that's the way history will judge it. Perhaps you disagree with the methods I took to reach this point, but it was all in pursuit of progress, and that's what really counts, isn't it? Remember the man who invented the first hyperspace engine allowing for faster than light travel? He's now lauded as a genius, but no one ever mentions he spent twenty years in jail for corporate fraud, cheated on his wife, and gambled away most of the money he earned from that invention. Nobody cares how you do something—it's the end result that matters."

"You're mad," Lestrade said, and Moriarty merely shrugged.

"It's all about your point of view. This technology was inevitable—I just arrived at it first. This cloning process is going to change the galaxy. Think of all the applications: we can create entire armies of soldiers from the DNA of one being, manufacture a whole new workforce for a company in a matter of weeks, even recreate a being who is dying!"

"Yes—or have people creating clones just so their organs can be harvested," Lestrade said darkly. "That's why a lot of beings think creating clones is like opening 'Pandora's Box.'"

"How people apply my technology is not my business," Moriarty said. "I'm simply its creator—let others argue over how it should and shouldn't be used."

Lestrade tensed, and Holmes saw him tighten his finger around the trigger of his blaster. "You miserable vodog—"

Holmes put a firm hand on his friend's shoulder and carefully pulled him back. He wasn't arguing with the insult (he believed it to be quite well-deserved); he just knew killing Moriarty now probably wasn't the best idea. They weren't officially here on the authority of Civic Security, though then again, Holmes had never really played by their rules in the past. They just hadn't gotten to that moment of desperation yet, though if Moriarty tried to pull something, they might have to...

"No, Holmes, don't stop him."

Holmes looked up at the sudden sound of Jaymie's voice, and he glanced back at her in a certain amount of surprise. Moriarty, Lestrade, and Dr. Aoedie turned to glance at her as well, though Moriarty was obviously the one those words cut the deepest. Holmes was suddenly very glad he wasn't in the professor's shoes...

Chapter 7: Frankenstein's Monster

Jaymie couldn't stand silently anymore. She'd listened to Holmes' long and complicated tale, and though she knew it would take her weeks to sort out all the details he'd gone through in rapid-fire succession, she'd caught the underlying message: Moriarty was a crook, and they'd all been had. Jaymie felt like such a fool; she couldn't believe all the lies he'd fed her, and that she'd actually believed he was a gentleman. But even worse than that was the fact part of her still wanted to try to deny all this, even though she knew it was all true. *Because part of her still loved him...*

"You *are* a miserable vodog," Jaymie finally said. She could tell her voice was shaking, but she clenched her fists and fought to keep a stiff upper lip, unwilling to let Moriarty see what a blow he'd dealt her. "What you've done is so wrong, I can't...I can't even begin to process it. I thought I knew who you were, but apparently, I gravely misjudged your character."

"Jaymie, please try to understand," Moriarty said. "I know you might not agree with my methods but—"

"I don't agree with any of it," Jaymie snapped. "I'm such an idiot, and I've never been more ashamed of myself. I can't believe how you used me. You gave me all those speeches about how Holmes didn't appreciate me and took me for granted. But all I was to you was another pawn, wasn't I? You wanted to distract me from helping Holmes, and even recruit me to your little project."

"No, that's not it," Moriarty insisted, and though he wasn't quite begging, he was perilously close to it. "Although it *was* one of my associates who stole your knapsack the same day of the Quadrant A

Bank of Eglon break-in, I was looking for information on Sherlock Holmes' activities, not yours. And when I sent that made-up cyber crime case to Holmes, requesting he help me find the being stealing my research files, I was hoping *he'd* come, so I could size him up and judge just what I was up against. I wasn't expecting you at all. At one time I may have been intending to use you as part of my plan, but that was never all of it, and has no part in it now. Jaymie, I believe all those things I said to you. Please trust me."

    Jaymie stared into those deep green eyes, and she felt her heart wrench. Yes, the despicable thing was, she *did* believe him, at least in part. Perhaps he hadn't meant to just use her and toss her aside, like he had Urdi, Adler, and Hortz, but she also realized it wasn't possible such a narcissistic, amoral madman could really and truly love her—at least not in a way she wanted to be loved.

    "I can't," she said, and she glanced over at Lestrade and Holmes. There was a definite look of relief in their eyes, as if they hadn't been expecting her to accept their story so easily, but there was also a certain sadness in their expressions. They knew how much this was hurting her, and she could tell that pained them as well. She realized these were her real friends, no matter how much they might confound her at times. They were a little rougher around the edges than Moriarty might have been, but they got things right when it counted, and she knew they'd always have her back.

    "I'm calling Civic Security!"

    Dr. Aoedie scanned the crowd, and he saw one of the guests—who'd apparently had enough of this chaos—starting to dial out on her comlink.

"We need to go—now!" he hissed at Moriarty. "We'll find some other world we can peddle your pet project on. I told you that you were a fool for allowing Miss Watson to become a part of this project. Let's try to salvage what we can and get—"

"Oh, you're not going anywhere," Lestrade said, gripping his blaster. "We—"

"Enough!"

Without warning, Moriarty's fist darted out like a viper, swinging at the side of Lestrade's head. The inspector reacted quickly enough to dodge the blow, but he stumbled back into Holmes, almost knocking them both over. Moriarty whipped out his own blaster and fired a warning shot, and Lestrade fired one back, forcing Moriarty and Aoedie to duck behind the clone case.

At the sight of blaster fire, all semblance of order in the room disappeared, and people ran screaming for the exits, scrambling over each other in their haste to avoid being caught in the crossfire. They knocked over tables and chairs, and one of the guests pulled the emergency alarm, causing red lights on the ceiling to start flashing and klaxons to start shrieking, their strident wails filling the ballroom and only adding to the mayhem.

Lestrade slammed into Moriarty, and the two of them crashed into the clone box. The box began to tilt, and with a gasp, Jaymie saw it teeter and start to fall towards the floor. "Catch the box!" she cried, but it was too late, and the box hit the stage with a loud bang. The clone's body fell out of the open box, breaking free of the tubing that had been connected to him, and apparently cutting off his supply of the chemical that had been keeping him in stasis.

For a moment, everyone stopped struggling and stared in horror as the clone lay motionless on the floor of the stage. Though he hadn't twitched or shone any signs of movement, his eyes were now closed.

"Dear God," Holmes said, and they all watched as the clone moved first one finger, then his hand, and then his brilliant green eyes flew open.

"Where am I?" he said in a voice that was a pitch-perfect match of Moriarty's.

No one said anything for a moment. The clone shuddered and then slowly sat up, seeming a little disoriented at first but overall far more lucid than Jaymie would have guessed a creature gaining consciousness for the very first time would be. She'd assumed he'd be somewhat childlike at first, taking a while to become aware of his surroundings, but maybe that wasn't the case.

"Where am I?" he repeated, a little more forcefully, and then he glanced up and locked eyes with Moriarty.

"It's me," he said, his voice as eerily calm as Moriarty's had been earlier. Moriarty stared at his clone, struck dumb by his own creation.

"He's not supposed to be like this, is he?" Jaymie said quietly, and even Dr. Aoedie appeared uneasy.

"I wasn't sure how much cognitive function he would have when we created him," Aoedie said, and the clone's head snapped around.

"You created me?" he said, then shook his head, pointing straight at Moriarty. "No, he did."

The clone stood unsteadily to his feet and took a step towards Moriarty, but Moriarty gripped his blaster and leveled it at his double, his fingers trembling.

"Yes, I created you, and I wasn't ready for you to wake up yet. You need to get back inside that box. This is no longer the time and place to introduce you to the world."

The clone blinked, his emotionless face one of the most unsettling things Jaymie had ever seen. "It's too late for that, isn't it? You think because you created me, you are better than me, don't you? You think you're like God, but you're not. I wasn't created from nothing—I have your features, all your knowledge, your memories. I am you. I *am* Professor James Moriarty."

Moriarty's expression darkened, a mixture of frustration and, finally, a glimmer of real fear. "No, you aren't Professor James Moriarty," he said. "You're my clone—not me. If you have all my memories and knowledge from the past, then you have to know that to be true."

The clone smiled, the sort of haughty, condescending smile one might have expected from Moriarty himself. "I am at least your equal, if not your superior. You should have thought of that before you started messing with powers beyond your control."

"I didn't create you to be lectured by you," Moriarty said harshly. "Now, get back in the box, or I'll blow your head off, and you'll cease to exist as quickly as you came into being."

"I don't think so."

One second the clone was standing perfectly still, and then he darted towards the left, knocking into Lestrade. Moriarty fired at him but missed, and Lestrade hit the stage, knocking his head against the floor and passing out. The clone snatched his gun, but instead of pointing it back at Moriarty, he trained the gun on Jaymie.

Jaymie froze, time suddenly seeming to grind to a screeching halt. Holmes took a step towards her, but the clone brandished the gun.

"Leave her out of this," Moriarty ordered, but the clone laughed.

"Why? Because I'm you, I know she's the best bargaining chip in this room. And because I am also my own creature, I can choose not to be as attached to her as you seemingly are, and I'm not afraid to shoot her if you won't let me walk out of here."

"And what the bloody devil do you plan to do out there, in the real world?" Moriarty asked angrily. "I don't care if you have all my knowledge; you're still a new being, and you're a fool if you think you can survive on your own in my world."

The clone laughed quietly, moving towards Jaymie and bringing the cold end of the blaster's barrel even closer to her forehead. "Oh, I'm not sure about that. See, I know what you've been up to, and I remember what's worked, and what hasn't. We have a brilliant mind, but *you* made too many mistakes—mistakes I don't intend to make this time around."

"The world will not accept two Moriartys," Jaymie said, and the clone's lips curled into a smile.

"I know—there's only room for one of us. And that's me."

He whirled around and shot Moriarty square in the chest, the other man instantly crumpling to the ground. Too stunned to do anything but act on instinct, Jaymie took advantage of his moment of distraction, whipped out her own gun, and shot the clone just as he was turning back around to fire at her.

The clone gasped and clutched at his chest, staring in disbelief at the smoking hole she'd just burned through his sternum. He stepped forward and then faltered, collapsing not far from where the real Moriarty now lay, his body wracked by spasms of pain. "It...should have worked," the clone gasped, and then his eyes closed and he was gone.

Jaymie dropped her gun and sank to her knees, overcome by shock herself. Holmes rushed over towards her, reaching to help her, but she waved him away.

"Get Dr. Aoedie!" she commanded, pointing to the scientist, who was trying to make a quick and cowardly exit through the catering kitchen. Holmes dashed off without questioning her, and she was left alone with the professor, who was now fighting for every breath. She crawled over towards Moriarty's side, and she immediately saw calling an emergency medic would be of no use.

"Killed by my own creation," he gasped, a bitterly ironic smile on his face even now. "I should have seen that coming."

He grasped Jaymie's hand with weak fingers, and he looked up at her sadly. "I'm sorry, Jaymie Watson. I'm sorry for so many things, but most of all, for..." And then he ran out of breath again, and his body shuddered.

When he finally opened his eyes, they looked dull and glassy, and he seemed to have recognized he had only seconds left. "Re...remember that painting I gave you, 'A Rainbow of Stars'?"

Jaymie simply nodded, powerless to speak.

He smiled wistfully. "Please keep it...if you would. I...I know you probably hate me, and..." He paused, overcome by a fit of coughing. "I told you I'd...I'd tell you someday why I painted it especially for you, and it appears that since I won't be having anymore 'somedays,' I'd...I'd better tell you today. I'd like to keep...at least one of my promises."

Jaymie glanced away, both desperate to hear what he had to say and dreading it at the same time. She was still furious over what he'd done to her, but she was also very much filled with pity for this brilliant man who had become so corrupt, so twisted. She could envision a future that was so different from the one he'd chosen, a path that wouldn't have ended here, like this.

"Jaymie, you see the world in a special way," Moriarty said quietly. "'A Rainbow of Stars' is the metaphor I think you embody. You…look beyond the ordinary, and you have the capability to grasp the impossible. Holmes may have shaped you, but he…he didn't create you. You already had that special spark; that's why you so fascinate him. You're just as brilliant as he is, and don't…don't you ever forget that. I wouldn't mind losing to Holmes so much, if it didn't also mean you'd spend your life thinking better of him than you do of me."

His hand slipped out of hers; he no longer had the strength to hold it. "I'm sorry, Jaymie Watson. For all that—"

Jaymie could tell by the look in his eyes there was more he wanted to say to her, but it was destined not to be. He choked, and then he suddenly slipped away, his eyes closing and his body going limp.

Jaymie sat next to him, too numb to stand up or even look away. She realized she hadn't said a single word to him as he was dying, and now she wished she had had a chance to, even though she wasn't sure what she would have told him.

"Well, that's one for the history books," Holmes said quietly, walking up behind her. He'd hit Dr. Aoedie with a stun bolt, and the man was now tied to one of the decorative marble columns in the ballroom, where he'd remain until Civic Security arrived and arrested him. "So in the end, it was 'Moriarty who shot Moriarty.' Terribly ironic." Jaymie almost thought Holmes was mocking his now fallen adversary, but there was no humor or sarcasm in his voice.

Jaymie slowly stood up and turned to face him, and then suddenly, inexplicably, Holmes wrapped his arms around her in a hug, squeezing her so tightly she almost couldn't breathe. She immediately wrapped her arms around him and buried her face in his trench coat, not bothering to think about how unexpected and uncharacteristic this was.

"I'm sorry," Holmes said, and he didn't have to say anything more. Jaymie knew exactly what he meant, and she couldn't be gladder to have her very best friend back.

She wasn't sure how long they stood there, and she didn't open her eyes again until she heard the wail of sirens outside the club, Civic Security finally arriving on the scene. Holmes let her go, and they stood there awkwardly, neither sure what to do or say.

Civic Security came bursting into the room, guided in by the club's owners, and the barrage of questioning began. Holmes recapped the story he had told the gala's shocked guests about Moriarty's plot, and though the officers were staring at him in awe throughout all of it, he didn't seem to be enjoying this chance to demonstrate how he'd once again out-matched Civic Security. Several medics began attending to Lestrade, who had suffered a mild concussion, and the medical examiner slipped the clone into a body bag and then returned for Moriarty.

Jaymie took one last glance at the professor, and imagined those sparkling green eyes she'd never see again. He'd broken her heart, and she was sure the flood of pain and sadness would return after the shock had worn off. Her heart ached for all that could have been, and now never would. He was a villain; he couldn't have done all those things and *not* be a villain. And yet, there had been some light mixed in with the darkness. But that was the trouble with darkness: it had the tendency to overpower the light, and in the end, it had snuffed it out. Moriarty wasn't really so different from Holmes, but the gap between them did make all the difference in the world. Even if Moriarty had lived, there would have been no future between her and him. But oh, what a beautiful lie that was to believe at one time...

Holmes put his arm around her shoulders, and together they walked out of the club, neither one of them looking back. They had made a fresh start here, and though Jaymie knew they'd inevitably run across rough patches in the future, she also knew she wouldn't be doubting Holmes' friendship again. She couldn't change him, at least not completely; he'd always have that massive ego, and she'd probably never be able to free him of that vexing habit of being so self-absorbed. But she thought she understood him a little bit better now, and his actions today proved he valued her friendship as much as she valued his. She no longer had to have any uncertainty about whether or not he truly cared for her—and that was what mattered most.

Chapter 8: A New Start

Lestrade watched Jaymie and Holmes walking out of the club, sighing somewhat wistfully as they slipped out the door. Holmes had promised to bring the hovercar around, arguing that Lestrade, with his concussion, shouldn't be driving yet. Although the medics had assured Lestrade the concussion was only a mild one, he had a splitting headache and longed to collapse into his nice warm bed back in Quadrant B and pray the rest of the week was absolutely and completely boring.

It would take Civic Security weeks to sort out this convoluted case, and with Moriarty dead (well, both Moriartys, actually), there might be some things Civic Security would never know. But true to form, Holmes had pieced enough of the details together at the last second to save the galaxy from the terror that the crime lord(s) could have been.

Yet even more important than that, they had saved Jaymie. Holmes had finally come to grips with what he had probably sensed all along: that Jaymie was an indispensable part of his investigations, and next time, he wouldn't let her slip away so easily.

And where did that leave Lestrade? He didn't know. He knew he was beginning to feel something for Jaymie beyond just friendship, and though he knew Holmes didn't think of her in that way, and probably never would, Lestrade wasn't sure how he'd feel about his other best friend "barging in." For now, he was content to wait, just grateful for the fact Jamie was back. There were some things it was simply best not to rush.

Holmes pulled the hovercar to a stop in front of the back door to the club, and one of the medics helped Lestrade into the vehicle, despite his protests he could manage it on his own.

As the door shut, they sat in silence for a moment, no one really sure what to say.

"Well, that was exciting," Lestrade said finally. "Let's not do something like that again for a long, long time, OK?"

"Of course," Holmes said, quite obviously intending to completely ignore Lestrade's suggestion the minute an intriguing case came along.

"I think we can probably afford to take the next few days off," Jaymie said. "I suspect we've all earned it."

"Very well," Holmes said. He was silent for a second, and then he quickly added, "But don't get too relaxed. I just checked my techpad, and it appears the Eglon Ruling Council may have a new puzzle for us I'd like to attend to as quickly as possible. Apparently, funding supposed to be sent to a relief effort on Yopilia was transferred but never arrived in the Yopilian government's account. Days later it was found in a former ruling councilor's personal account, but here's the catch—the councilor has been dead for two years, and there's no record of where, how, and why the money ended up there."

Lestrade moaned. "Holmes, give it a rest would you? I don't even want to think about another case right now."

"Oh, you don't need to think about it, I've already solved it," Holmes said matter-of-factly. "I'm merely going to give you the name of the being you have to arrest."

Jaymie and Lestrade shared an incredulous look, and Jaymie finally shook her head.

"Holmes, you're impossible. How do you do it?"

Holmes grinned as he pulled away from the nightclub and merged into traffic, taking them back to Quadrant B, apartment complex 221. "Elementary, my dear Watson."

THE END

Printed in Great
Britain
by Amazon